Her Hidden Courage

Mary Wood was born in Maidstone, Kent, and brought up in Claybrooke, Leicestershire. Born one of fifteen children to a middle-class mother and an East End barrow boy, Mary's family were poor but rich in love. This encouraged her to develop a natural empathy with the less fortunate and a fascination with social history. In 1989 Mary was inspired to pen her first novel and she is now a full-time novelist.

Mary welcomes interaction with readers and invites you to subscribe to her website where you can contact her, receive regular newsletters and follow links to meet her on Facebook and Twitter: www.authormarywood.com

BY MARY WOOD

The Breckton series

To Catch a Dream
An Unbreakable Bond
Tomorrow Brings Sorrow
Time Passes Time

The Generation War saga

All I Have to Give
In Their Mother's Footsteps

The Girls Who Went to War series

The Forgotten Daughter
The Abandoned Daughter
The Wronged Daughter
The Brave Daughters

The Jam Factory series

The Jam Factory Girls
Secrets of the Jam Factory Girls
The Jam Factory Girls Fight Back

The Orphanage Girls series

The Orphanage Girls
The Orphanage Girls Reunited
The Orphanage Girls Come Home

The Guernsey Girls series

The Guernsey Girls
The Guernsey Girls Go to War
The Guernsey Girls Find Peace

Stand-alone novels

Proud of You
Brighter Days Ahead
The Street Orphans
A Lasting Promise
Her Hidden Courage

Her Hidden Courage

Mary Wood

PAN BOOKS

First published 2026 by Pan Books
an imprint of Pan Macmillan
The Smithson, 6 Briset Street, London EC1M 5NR
EU representative: Macmillan Publishers Ireland Ltd, 1st Floor,
The Liffey Trust Centre, 117–126 Sheriff Street Upper,
Dublin 1 D01 YC43
Associated companies throughout the world

ISBN 978-1-0350-3681-3

Copyright © Gaskin Hinckley Ltd 2026

The right of Mary Wood to be identified as the
author of this work has been asserted in accordance
with the Copyright, Designs and Patents Act 1988.

All rights reserved. No part of this publication may be reproduced,
stored in a retrieval system, or transmitted, in any form, or by any means
(including, without limitation, electronic, mechanical,
photocopying, recording or otherwise)
without the prior written permission of the publisher.

Pan Macmillan does not have any control over, or any responsibility for,
any author or third-party websites (including, without limitations, URLs,
emails and QR codes) referred to in or on this book.

1 3 5 7 9 8 6 4 2

A CIP catalogue record for this book is available from the British Library.

Typeset by Palimpsest Book Production Ltd, Falkirk, Stirlingshire
Printed and bound in the UK using 100% Renewable Electricity by CPI Group (UK) Ltd

This book is sold subject to the condition that it shall not, by way of
trade or otherwise, be lent, hired out, or otherwise circulated without
the publisher's prior consent in any form of binding or cover other than
that in which it is published and without a similar condition including this
condition being imposed on the subsequent purchaser. The publisher does not
authorize the use or reproduction of any part of this book in any manner
for the purpose of training artificial intelligence technologies or systems.
The publisher expressly reserves this book from the Text and Data Mining
exception in accordance with Article 4(3) of the European Union Digital
Single Market Directive 2019/790.

Visit **www.panmacmillan.com** to read more
about all our books and to buy them.

To my darling sister Felicity (Fliss). It broke my heart to lose you. We played as children, sneaked out to meet boys as teens and became wise women together. You always supported my writing, telling me how proud you were – as I was of you when you published your novel. Will love and miss you for ever. Thank you for enriching my life.

And to Elma Fox, a lady I have honoured in this book by naming a special character after her. Elma was the much-loved mum of Patrick Fox, someone who helped me a great deal when I began self-publishing my books by designing covers for me. Elma's life's work was as a nurse and devoted mum. May you rest in peace, dear lady. Thank you to Joanne McInnes for nominating her and for supporting me throughout my journey as an author.

PART ONE

Making a New Life

Chapter One

Poland, 1937

Tamar clung on to Hannah.

Isaac, Hannah's brother, stood looking on.

'We will follow you, Tamar,' Hannah said as she came out of the hug. 'We will, won't we, Isaac?'

Tamar glanced at Isaac. Doing so lifted her world: his tall, slim frame, his coal-black eyes set in his handsome face, and his jet-black hair with a yarmulke – the traditional Jewish cap – covering his crown.

Tamar's heart – broken by the recent loss of her adored mama and the prospect of having to leave the only world she'd known – was soothed a little as a trickle of joy crept into her. Isaac opened his arms to her.

Going into them completed that joy as he held her to him, pulled back her headscarf and kissed her long fair hair.

In answer to his sister, who looked so like him but for her wire-rimmed round glasses, Isaac said, 'We will, Hannah.' Then his eyes lowered to look down at Tamar again. 'Have faith, Tamar. Papa is looking into arrangements for Hannah and me to join you in England. Mama will not budge, so they are staying here, but she is urging Hannah and me to go.'

Hannah hung her head. 'I wish Mama would change her mind. I don't want to go without her and Papa. I am afraid for them. From what we're hearing of the Nazis' treatment of the Jews and Hitler's plans for our country, our community is afraid. Another family left yesterday – the Goldbergs. So many are gone or preparing to go.'

Isaac extended his arm to Hannah and held them both close. 'I too don't want to leave them. It will break my heart, but Mama begged us to. She wants to think of us safe in London, but Babcia is not well enough to travel, and Mama, as any good daughter would, wants to care for her. She won't leave her. When she passes, Mama and Papa will join us.'

'I don't want Babcia to pass.'

'There are many things in life we don't want, my dear sister, but we must have the courage to face them. Babcia is very weary, she is ready to go to Elohim. She knows He has a place in heaven for her by His side.'

Born and brought up in Mechelinki on the Baltic Sea coast of Poland, Tamar, Hannah and Isaac had always known love, freedom and happiness. Now, trepidation had trickled into the hearts of their fellow countrymen and in particular their Jewish community. Many were fleeing to go to America or Britain.

Turning them around to face the sea, Isaac told them, 'Always remember this, our beautiful coast. Remember the times as children when we built things – castles, and towers – in the sand. And how our bodies tingled with the cold when we swam. Always we laughed. I can hear that sound now . . . Let's do it one more time. Let's swim together.'

'But we don't have our costumes, Isaac.'

'And besides, it will be freezing!'

'Ha! Who needs costumes, Hannah? It is getting dark, no one will come along this way now. And as for the cold, Tamar, my love, we have braved it many times . . . This may be the very last chance we have of ever doing so again.'

With this, Isaac let go of them and stripped off his clothing, leaving only his long underpants on.

Tamar felt her stomach muscles clench as she looked at his strong body. It seemed to spur her on. Dropping her bag, she kicked off her shoes and whipped off her cardigan. Then, without a qualm, she undid the button to her skirt and let it fall, before taking her short-sleeved jumper off over her head, exposing her liberty bodice.

'No! Tamar!'

'Come on, Hannah! It feels wonderful!' With this, Tamar began to roll her stockings down her calves. Bending, she pulled them off before stepping out of the crumpled pile of her clothing.

Laughing, she lifted her head. Isaac was staring at her. There was something in his eyes she hadn't seen before. It further enhanced the strange, tingling sensations gripping her.

'I'm leaving you two to it. You're mad! Don't be late for tea, Isaac, you know how it upsets Mama.'

As Hannah disappeared out of sight, Isaac stepped nearer to her. 'You're beautiful, Tamar . . . I love you.'

This time, being in his arms was different as the most wonderful feeling she'd ever experienced with him crept over her and the tingling sensations deepened. Never before had the bare skin of her body touched his.

Isaac stepped back. 'We mustn't. But . . . Oh, Tamar.'

Taking charge, Tamar held his hand and pulled him towards

the sea. 'Come, let us swim, my darling. Make memories to look back on and to hold dear.'

It wasn't what she wanted to do. She wanted to cling to him, to yield to the desire gripping her, but she had sinned enough by exposing her flesh to him. Though her liberty bodice and pants covered most of her, they didn't cover all her bathing dress would have done.

The water stung as if icy-cold fingers had clutched her. Splashing Isaac, she giggled as he ducked, but then regretted her action as he dived underwater and grabbed her legs, pulling her under. Kicking out at him made him release her. Their laughter hung on the air as they surfaced.

For a moment their eyes held, giving them the promise of their future, and yet, would it happen? So many forces were against them. What if Isaac never made it to London? What if the Nazis did the unthinkable sooner than they thought? But then, maybe none of it would ever happen, and it would remain a rumour, and they could return and once more know that feeling of freedom.

Wanting that sensation now, Tamar crouched down and swam along the coastline, allowing the feel of the water, no longer icy, to take away all bad thoughts and give her peace. Isaac would come to her in London. They would one day marry and return. And they would bring up their children here and surround them with love and protection just as they had been themselves.

As they walked home hand in hand, that dream was shattered as Isaac told her, 'I don't think the Nazis will dare to try to take our country, Tamar. The world wouldn't allow it. We will come back here, you'll see . . . Only, it may be sooner for me. Already our armed forces are building in readiness.

I – I'm sorry, my darling, but I am thinking of joining the Polish army if nothing changes. I would not be able to stay in London while my fellow countrymen fight.'

Tamar clung tightly to his hand. There was nothing she could say.

Isaac stood still and took her into his arms. She felt his body heave. Clinging on to him, she wept with him. Their world had suddenly collapsed. Why were they hated as a people by the Nazis? What had they ever done to them, or to anyone? They were taught peace and love. Theirs was an ancient religion – the first to recognize one God. They did no harm. They worked hard and contributed to the wealth of any land they lived in – the only thing they didn't have was a land of their own since being driven out of their homeland in biblical times. Always they were persecuted, vilified, and yet she had only known them to give out love.

Isaac lifted his head, took a deep breath and smiled down at her through his tear-soaked eyes. 'Everything will be all right. Our children will know the joys of swimming in the Baltic and playing on the sands. I promise.'

Tamar smiled back and nodded, though she couldn't feel the truth of this in her heart.

A few days later they stood on the port side of Gdynia, wanting to hold each other, but knowing that would be frowned upon by Tamar's papa and the other passengers awaiting the arrival of the ferry to take her and Papa to Karlskrona, Sweden, the first port of call on their long journey.

To Tamar, it felt as though she was leaving her world behind – most of all, her mama. It was as if they were abandoning her to that small patch of cold earth that held her body, and yet she told herself, *Mama is happy, she is with*

Elohim in heaven. He will take care of her, and I will be with her again one day.

Memories of her mama that were fading away day by day flickered through Tamar's mind. She looked up at Isaac. Soon his face would fade as the ferry drew away from the portside leaving him there. He would go back to his job as a silversmith until the day he could come to join her. But what of her own life? Papa had told her that he had plans, and she guessed they would be something in the world of jewellery. Papa was an expert jewellery maker working in gold and silver. Always he had dreamed of having his own shop and workshop.

She'd spent many hours with him in his shed when home from school where he had taught her the skills of melting silver and fashioning it into beautiful, delicate chains. Often, she'd been confused over her future, loving making jewellery but also wanting to one day work as a teacher of the languages she loved – mainly English, but she spoke German too, though she now hated the people of the country. And French, a language she'd only recently studied but which she loved more than any as it was less harsh, almost poetic, with the way its everyday words sounded.

Having left college two months ago, a week after her nineteenth birthday, Tamar now felt lost as everything she thought might happen – including going on to be an apprentice teacher in her local school – had been taken away along with all her dreams.

'Ah, the ferry is coming. Say your goodbyes, Tamar.' Turning, Papa shook hands with Isaac. 'Maybe by the time you arrive in London, my boy, I will have employment for you. My plans are to look for a shop and workshop of my own. I have contacts there and I have the money I have saved and from the sale of my house. Keep praying for us.'

'I will, sir, I will.'

Papa hugged Hannah and then turned his back; Tamar knew he was giving her a moment to say her goodbyes.

Her heart broke as she did.

Taking no notice of convention, she clung to Isaac. 'I love you. Make it soon that you come to me.'

'I will, my love. Go now. Don't linger, it is too painful.'

Hugging Hannah to her, Tamar didn't look back at Isaac. She knew he had turned away. She'd seen the slump of his shoulders and felt the heaving of his body.

'Go, Tamar. We will come soon.'

Hannah kissed her cheek, joining their wet faces for a second. With this, Tamar ran to her papa's side and picked up her case. It wasn't heavy, she'd only packed a few clothes and two of her favourite books – *A Christmas Carol* and *Jane Eyre*, both in German. She could buy English versions when she arrived, but these had been given to her by her mama and had been a huge part of her childhood. Tucked into the cover of *Jane Eyre* was a love note written by Isaac when he first realized his childhood love for her had become a true falling in love that would last them a lifetime.

For her, the feeling had come much earlier – she had always known he was her life, not just a playmate.

Loneliness engulfed her, and yet it was broken by a trickle of excitement. Always she'd wanted to see the world – especially the parts of it whose languages she spoke.

Shaking herself mentally, she told herself she would look on this as an adventure. A new phase of her life. Her first steps into adulthood.

Tamar didn't look back from the deck they were seated on. To do so would have hurt. Isaac would have gone out of sight. And dear Hannah, who had always been like a sister to her, would have walked away with him.

But they would come. They would! She would be reunited with them and be held once more by her beloved Isaac. The dreams they had would come true, but in a safe land – a land where they had never heard of Jews being persecuted, where they were allowed to live in peace to carry out their daily lives.

Their choices had been London or the United States, as both were welcoming refugees from the Nazi regime – or people potentially in danger from it. Papa had chosen London as Ruben, a cousin of his, lived there and had long ago established a firm of silversmiths. This meant that Papa would have employment, and Ruben had communicated that he had found them accommodation. He'd said it was a small flat above a shop owned by a kind and jolly lady called Elma. Ruben had joked to Papa in his letter that she was the woman he wanted to marry – a bachelor, Ruben had said that Elma had never married either. *But she isn't Jewish and won't hear of converting, and so she must remain a desire within me*, he'd written.

Papa had chuckled when he'd read this out to Tamar. His head had shaken from side to side. 'Ruben is incorrigible! A man for the ladies. But then, he was never blessed as I was with a good and beautiful woman like my Miriam.'

Tears had flooded his face, and he'd willingly let her hold him as she cried too. But he had soon composed himself and patted her back as he'd said, 'But it is a new life we must look forward to, Tamar, my dearest. A new life.'

They had to follow the much longer sea route to avoid passing through Germany, and most of the rest of the journey would be by sea, but now, as she could see land approaching, Tamar thought, *What will this new life have in store for me? How will I cope with it all?*

Sighing, she tucked her arm into her papa's. She would do her best to settle and make life happy for him. He had done so much for her. Even now, it was her safety he was thinking of in uprooting. As painful as it was for her, it was doubly so for him as he left his precious Miriam behind.

Papa turned then and looked at her, and as if he was trying to convince himself, he patted her arm. 'Everything will be all right. I will make it so.'

Tamar nodded. But in her heart there lay a feeling that not even her beloved papa, who'd always made her world right, could ease the pain of. Nothing but being with Isaac again could do that.

Chapter Two

London

The sensation of standing on land that didn't rock beneath her feet made Tamar's legs wobble. She clutched her papa's sleeve to steady herself. He laughed down at her – a sound drowned out by the hustle and bustle of the dockside of Harwich in England. They'd arrived!

Tired to her bones after sea and train journeys with little sleep, the prospect of yet another three hours to London daunted Tamar.

Papa putting his arm around her gave some comfort, as did looking up at an almost cloudless sky.

'Almost there, Tamar. Already, I feel we are safe. No Nazi will ever penetrate these shores. Britain is a great country. We will settle and be happy, I'm sure.'

It was a bleary-eyed Tamar who finally arrived at Euston station. She'd slept all the way on this last leg of their journey, and now had a feeling of being disorientated. How was it that she was here, and not in their home in Poland?

As realization of their situation came back to her, Tamar's eyes stung with unshed tears. With a heavy heart she lugged her case along the platform. Papa had consulted his instructions from Ruben and guided them towards a sign saying 'Underground' with an arrow pointing downwards.

'This way, Tamar. We will soon be in Spitalfields. Ruben will meet us at a station called Liverpool Street, and take us to Brick Lane where he lives and where we will live too.'

Descending the steps made Tamar feel she was going deep into the bowels of the earth. Both fear and excitement gripped her. People jostled them as they deftly negotiated the steps at a much quicker pace and overtook them, one almost toppling Tamar as he banged into her case, leaving her unbalanced.

But the anxiety of this was quickly taken over by the sound of what she knew was called a tube train – and that's what it looked like. A long snake-like tube with what seemed like hundreds of people trying to get off and to board at the same time. Fear took over at the sight and Tamar hung back.

'Come . . . come, we need to get on, my dear.'

Obeying her papa, Tamar took a deep breath and almost plunged into the gaping hole of the train, then did as others did and grasped a leather strap hanging from the roof.

Papa, looking older than she'd ever seen him, sat heavily on his sturdy case.

Never had Tamar felt so glad as to see the sign announcing their station, though getting off was just as much of a fight as getting on had been as new passengers pushed their way onto the train, barring her way. 'Please, this is my station! Let me pass!'

Without speaking the other passengers moved to give her room to get through. Frantic as to whether Papa had made it, Tamar's head bobbed on her shoulders as she looked this way and that.

At last, as the crowd thinned, she saw him. As he spotted her, he laughed. 'Well, I think we have just been initiated into London life, Tamar – our new home.'

She didn't want it to be. She wanted her own home. Her peaceful, beautiful haven. At this thought, a tear did spill over, but she wiped it away with the back of her hand and made the excuse that the smoky atmosphere was affecting her.

Coming out of the station and seeing London for the first time, Tamar was struck by the hustle and bustle of it, and the sight of flags everywhere – strung between buildings, and hanging out of windows.

Papa commented on it as he came out of Ruben's bear hug. A man of Ruben's size could give no less and Tamar thought her ribs would crack under the pressure of the hug he gave her. He smelled of freshly smoked tobacco, and his moustache tickled her cheek. Handsome despite his fifty-four years, he had a twinkle in his eye. Tamar liked him on sight. His whole countenance gave out a feel of everything being fine and jolly.

'Welcome, my dear, dear cousins,' he said in Yiddish.

'I speak English, Cousin Ruben.'

'You do, Tamar?' Ruben looked towards Papa and, once more in Yiddish, he said, 'You never said in your letters to me that Tamar was such a beautiful and clever girl!'

'I don't like sharing her. Already I have to with the young man she loves.'

'And he is coming over too, I understand. Well, you, my dear, will be an asset to your father, and to our community. Many struggle with the language. But come, I have my car parked outside. I will drive you to your new home.'

As Ruben hadn't answered Papa when he'd mentioned

the flags, Tamar asked, 'Why is everywhere decked in flags, cousin?'

'Ah, tomorrow the new king is crowned, and there will be celebrations in every street. He is the brother of the real king, but that man didn't play by the rules – can you believe that he actually went with women? Ha!' Ruben's head went back, and his laughter bellowed out, attracting disapproving looks from passers-by. Ruben nodded towards them. 'You will find the British are a pompous lot. All such sins of the flesh must be done in the utmost secrecy, and if you are royal, done, dusted and never spoken of. King Edward paraded his woman for all to know about. And to top it all, in his case, the latest lady is a divorcee! Oh, the scandal! It has been funny to watch. But all is settled, Edward has abdicated, and the new King George is a pillar of society and, they say, ruled by his wife who looks like a gentle soul but harbours a rod of iron.'

Tamar couldn't help but laugh. She felt an excitement too at having landed in London for such an occasion.

'Right, let's get you to Elma's. Salt of the earth, Elma. She helps many Jews, and you will find many need it. It is difficult to get work and when they do the pay is poor.'

Ruben said this in a matter-of-fact way, when it was a revelation to Tamar. Always her fellow Jews in her community had wealth.

'Yes, you may well look shocked, but, sadly, it is so. The streets of London are not paved with gold. Many of our community frequent the soup kitchen in Brune Street.'

Ruben helped her into his car, a red Austin 7. He proudly patted the roof as if it was a treasured possession as he told them, 'Elma donates vegetables to the kitchen after they are no longer saleable – but not rotten, you understand, so they make a good basis for a hearty soup. She was brought up by a Jewish family after she escaped an orphanage and so cooks kosher foods. One day, I am hoping—'

'Ruben, it is hard for someone to convert to Judaism,' Papa told him.

'For most, yes, but Elma has been instilled with our values, our traditions and our food, as was her sister, Irene. The Jewish couple who adopted Elma collected Irene from the orphanage after hearing about the plight of the children there. They were childless and gave a happy upbringing to the girls. Sadly, they have passed away. Irene married a Jew and is fully converted. Elma . . . I just don't know. Something ties her to someone she calls "Our lady", the mama of Jesus – the so-called divine prophet. The orphanage was run by Catholic nuns, and they filled the children with all this nonsense. It made a big impact on Elma, but not so Irene.'

Tamar felt uncomfortable at hearing this. She had long questioned the role of Jesus and wasn't as sure as her fellow Jews that He wasn't the prophet, and often felt ashamed of the part the Jews played in persecuting Him. But she didn't say so. To do so would be a dire breach of her faith which she loved dearly and respected.

'Here we are. Brick Lane. Elma's shop is that grocery shop on the corner, and your flat is above it. You will look out on Quaker Street from one window and Brick Lane from the other. A busy, commercial area, but a street of opportunities too.'

Ruben tapped his nose and gave a look of conspiracy towards Papa.

Papa grinned. 'Opportunity is all I need, Ruben.'

'Don't worry, I have contacts who own property around here. Leave it with me . . . You do have start-up capital?'

'I have, though I need to know what it will take. There's equipment to buy.'

'We'll talk. I have much that I can loan you from my own workshop and employment for you to begin with while you sort everything out. But we're here now. Come and meet the lovely Elma.'

The shop doorbell clanged as Ruben opened it.

Tamar found herself looking at a beautiful young woman of around her own age. Her eyes were black and sparkled against the whites. Her ebony skin covered chiselled, high cheekbones. Her teeth were like pearls as she flashed a lovely smile. Her hair bubbled around her face.

She came forward and clasped Tamar's hand. 'So, you're Tamar – an unusual but lovely name. I'm pleased to meet you. I'm Florence, and I work part-time for Elma. You're all welcome.'

The greeting held such warmth that Tamar felt at home for the first time. 'Pleased to meet you, Florence, and thank you. My name's in the Bible – daughter of David. She had a tragic life. Mama chose it, as I am daughter of a David too. Do you live around here?'

'Oh dear, well, I'm sure that won't happen to you, Tamar. And yes, I'm from the next street – you'll be able to wave to me from your window. I'll show you your flat after you've met Elma . . . Ah, here she is.'

From a back room came a middle-aged lady who seemed to be all bosom under her flowered overall. Her hair was a mousy colour, mostly caught into a hair net, but with some curls escaping to flop onto her face. Her cheeks, plump and rosy, swelled as she smiled a huge smile, and her blue eyes shone a welcome. 'You're 'ere! 'Ow lovely. I'm Elma, and I want yer to know I've been looking forward to yer coming. Yer flat's ready for yer.'

'Elma's hoping you'll keep me in check, but no one can do that when I am around the love of my life.'

'Go away with yer, Ruben. Let our guests settle in before yer fill them with your nonsense.' Elma laughed. A lovely sound that filled Tamar with joy. She just knew she was going to love her.

'Shall I show them up now, Elma?'

'Yes, luv. And make them a cuppa . . . That's if yer drink tea, me lovelies . . . Or even if yer can understand a word I'm saying to yer?'

'We do, thank you, Elma. I speak fluent English and Papa has many words he understands too. He's working hard to master conversation, but I will interpret for him until then.'

'My, yer going to be a godsend to yer fellow Jews, luv. A lot of them 'ave to mime what they want, poor things.'

'It depends where they come from, Elma. I speak Polish of course, German and Yiddish, but also have a good knowledge of French.'

'Blimey, girl! You're a marvel. Most Jewish refugees are from Germany, I think. Isn't that so, Ruben?'

'It is . . . Maybe you could give English lessons, Tamar? Though not many would be able to pay you. There are a few who could, and handsomely. You could charge them double the rate, making them pay for those who are poor.'

'Give her a chance, Ruben, luv. She's only this minute come through the door and you 'ave an enterprise lined up for 'er. Besides, yer've never offered yer services and yet you speak Yiddish.'

'I've enough on my plate, Elma. I've my business and spend a lot of time chasing you.'

'Ha, you're bleeding daft!'

The laughter following this broke the last of the tension

that meeting new people can bring. Tamar knew she was going to be very happy here and hoped with all her heart that it wouldn't be long before Isaac and Hannah arrived. She wanted them safe, but above all wanted Isaac by her side as he had always been.

The flat was lovely. It was strange as they'd always had a garden, but here there was no outside space. And the view wasn't of the sea and endless sand, but of other buildings that Tamar felt she could touch if she leaned out of the window, but knew were across the busy street below. Then there was the noise that seemed deafening when Florence opened the window to point out her own flat across the road.

'See, I can wave to you . . . Oh, Tamar, you look afraid. Don't be. It's a strange feeling leaving all you know, but London will soon swallow you up in its excitement and pace.'

Not able to understand how Florence spoke English without an accent, Tamar asked, 'Where are you from, Florence?'

'I'm from here. I'm born and bred an English girl. My ancestors were brought over as slaves from Guinea but that was over a century ago and it is now French Guinea. My family live in the Midlands. I'm in London training to be a nurse but earn extra working a few hours for Elma. My dad's a doctor. He works in a hospital in Leicester. Have you heard of Leicester?'

'Yes. I know it's in the middle of England and has a thriving textile and shoe-making industry. I've studied a lot about this country. But that's wonderful, it must be so rewarding being able to help people get better. I work with my papa – well, I did.' After explaining her work making jewellery, Tamar said, 'But I'm really hoping to train as a teacher one day.'

'Nursing is rewarding and my passion, but it isn't always easy, Tamar. You'll find prejudices here – not condoned, or anything like that, but among the people. I have, and I'm British! But best to deal with it with humour and move on. We can't change the world.'

The more she chatted with Florence, the more Tamar liked her. It was as if she'd known her for ever and was glad when she seemed to feel the same as she said, 'I'll tell you what. Give yourself a couple of days and then I'll take you sightseeing. But before that, there's the coronation tomorrow and I'm planning on going to The Mall – that's the name of the road leading to the palace. I want to see everything I can. Would you like to come too, Tamar?'

'I'd love that, Florence, thanks.'

In Yiddish, Papa said, 'Are we having that cup of tea, Tamar?'

Tamar turned to see how tired her papa looked and felt ashamed that she'd not paid him any attention. He must feel lost with how she'd chatted away and he could only understand the odd word.

'Yes, Papa. I'll get Florence to show me where everything is. You sit down and rest a moment.'

Papa chose the armchair next to the fireplace. In a beige colour that matched the small sofa, it looked very comfortable and fitted well into the bright sunny room that had been decorated with flowered wallpaper in browns and golds and a plain brown rug that covered the square of floor between the sofa and the chair. The rest of the floor was covered in beige linoleum. The curtains were a light cream.

'I see you've had a proper look around the room, Tamar. What do you think?' asked Florence.

'I love it. And can't wait to see the rest of the flat, but Papa is asking for his cup of tea, so maybe the kitchen first?'

The kitchen was even brighter than the living room. Its plastered walls were painted with a light blue gloss paint. There were yellow curtains with a pattern of blue cornflowers, and though not big, it had been carefully fitted out with a cooker, a cupboard with a wooden top that stood at the same height as the cooker, and a small wooden table with two chairs. At the end of the room a door led to a pantry with a cold slab. Inside were tinned food, bread and a slab of butter, jams, milk, eggs and a cooked joint of lamb, besides a basket of potatoes and vegetables.

'Oh, that's so thoughtful of Elma!'

'She's a lovely lady . . . I wish she would take Ruben up on his offer. He loves her and she is lonely. Oh, she won't admit it, but I know she is.'

'I understand that she has never been married?'

'That's right. Her young man was killed in the Great War. And as not many men came back, she never had the chance again . . . That is, until Ruben landed here fifteen years ago. I know she likes him, but I'm not sure she loves him. And in any case, there's the religious barrier. Neither will give way and follow the other's beliefs.'

'That's a shame. Are you a Christian, Florence?'

'Yes, but I make it a rule not to speak of religion, especially as this is a community with many Jewish people. I don't want to offend anyone. Generally, we all live in harmony. We Christians go to our church and have our ceremonies, and your people go to their synagogue.'

'That's how it was in Poland, we all lived and let live.'

Florence sighed. The sound spoke volumes and gave Tamar

the understanding that prejudice was everywhere, not just among the Germans.

As she filled the kettle at the pot sink, Florence said, 'Not everyone thinks that way. You will come up against those who have hatred in their heart for anyone who is different to them.'

This was a concept that Tamar couldn't take in or understand. She wondered how she would deal with it. But she thought that if it happened, it couldn't be as bad as she had heard it was in Germany, where all human rights were being taken away from Jewish people and they were not allowed to walk on the same side of the road as non-Jews.

'Anyway, I don't want to be worrying you, it may never happen to you. You have no outward appearance of being different. Follow me and I'll show you the rest of the flat while the kettle boils.'

This annoyed Tamar. How 'different' should she look? Yes, she had blue eyes and fairish hair, which wasn't how most of her friends were, but that didn't mean she was out of the ordinary. She just took after her mama, who had been born in Germany.

The flat, laid out on one floor, had a homely feel in every room. There were two bedrooms, each furnished with a bed and a mahogany wardrobe and dressing table that shone in the light of the sun coming through the windows. One had plain yellow curtains and a yellow bedspread, and the other blue curtains with daisies printed on them and a matching bedspread. The one with blue curtains faced the same way as the lounge and was nearer to the view of Florence's flat.

'I'll have this room. It's lovely and I can wave to you from my window.'

'Yes, and we could have a pad and write messages to one another and hold them up!'

Tamar laughed out loud at this and Florence joined her. It was as if they were children who'd discovered a secret way of communicating.

'Come on, let me show you the bathroom.'

'There's a bathroom?'

'Yes, aren't you used to having one?'

'No. We had a bath we hung outside and brought in and filled on bath night, and the toilet was outside – it was awful in the winter as it froze and became stinky!'

'Ha, all modern conveniences here, love!'

They giggled again, and Tamar felt as if she had known Florence all her life.

The kettle whistling took them back to the kitchen.

Florence poured the water onto the tea leaves.

'It's so kind of Elma to make sure we had what we need in the cupboards to give us time to stock up.'

'Elma's wonderful . . . She has taken jibes about employing me, but only from strangers. Those who live close enough to say hello to me are all right . . . Anyway, let's get this tea through to the living room and then I'll leave you in peace. I'll call for you early tomorrow, though, as we have to get to The Mall before the masses do. I'll be knocking on your door at about six a.m. Elma is up then and will let me in.'

As she saw Florence to the door, Tamar had a moment of wanting to hug her. In Florence she saw a friend. Someone she could confide in and become close to. Someone who would make this move to a strange country bearable.

It seemed Florence felt the same as she turned back when she went through the door and put her arms out. Tamar went into them. 'You'll be fine, Tamar. We'll look out for one another, eh?'

Tamar, near to tears, could only nod as she came out of the hug.

Suddenly what lay ahead seemed less daunting. Everything about her arrival here had been alien to her, but she would do her best to fit in and to help Papa to settle. And, she thought, all would come right once Isaac arrived.

Chapter Three

Tamar, though feeling damp through to her skin, couldn't take her eyes off the spectacle of the magnificent golden coach that drove the King of England, George VI, towards the beautiful Buckingham Palace.

'Oh, the Queen is so lovely. She waved at us!'

Tamar looked at Florence as she said this and saw the joy lighting up her eyes.

'If only this drizzle would stop, it would be the perfect day. But oh, Tamar, as my mum would say, "Them folk are beautiful."'

Tamar laughed with her. 'I never thought to see such a sight in all my life!'

'Oh, look, there are the princesses, Elizabeth and Margaret. Isn't Margaret lovely to look at?'

Tamar looked at the two young girls and thought how privileged they were. At that moment the smaller of them, who Florence had said was Princess Margaret, looked in her direction and smiled. Tamar's heart warmed. She lifted her hand and waved. Princess Margaret waved back. Not what Florence had called the royal wave, but a proper shaking of her hand and with a big smile on her face.

It was a moment Tamar would cherish for ever.

As the carriages went by, people around them began to jostle.

'Come on, Tamar, we need to get near to Queen Victoria's statue to see the family come out onto the balcony.'

But as Florence grabbed her hand, Tamar's thoughts of what a wonderful day this was turned into horror as Florence's body shot forward and a big man behind her said, 'Move out the way, scum, yer've no right being 'ere!'

Tamar screamed at him, 'Leave her alone! Stop it!'

His tone changed as he asked, 'Where are yer from, anyway? Yer've got an accent I ain't 'eard before.'

Without thinking, Tamar answered, 'Poland.'

'Well, yer ain't welcome 'ere. And Mosley will see yer all off.'

Tamar heard him hawk, then spittle hit her face, bringing bile to her throat. Florence grabbed her arm and ran with her as best they could in the opposite direction to the crowd. Some stepped aside for them, but others hurled insults.

By the time they came to a clearing and were able to leave the hordes of people, Tamar's sobs wracked her body. Florence held her to her. She didn't speak, but gently rubbed her back.

'I can't bear it, Florence. How do you stand having such horrible things said to you and being shoved like you were?'

'I don't. Every time it happens it cuts me in two. And it makes me feel so small. But then, I know I'm not. I'm one of God's children and loved by Him. A man like the one who just shoved me and assaulted you with his vile words belongs to the devil.'

'Doesn't it make you afraid to go out?'

'No. I am as British as they are. I have a right to walk the streets. I just do what I did then and run away from the wickedness of them.'

'Who's Mosley?'

'He's the leader of the fascists. They are Nazis at heart.'

Tamar's blood ran cold. 'I . . . Are there many of them in Britain?'

'Quite a lot. There was a right carry-on in Cable Street last year when the fascists held a march down there and all the members of the Jewish community came out and blocked their way. Others joined them too. Which was good to see. But riots broke out, people were hurt, and hundreds arrested.'

'Jews?'

'Yes. You see, they were stopping a lawful march, but I didn't blame them. They did the right thing in my eyes.'

Fear trickled through Tamar. 'I thought we had escaped to freedom, but it seems there's hatred for us here too.'

'No, love. The fascists are in the minority . . . Look, you've only been here for a day, don't judge it by that rotten bloke. Most are welcoming and don't give us trouble, you'll see.'

Tamar didn't feel reassured, but there was no turning back for her and her papa. Making her mind up not to judge and to hope nothing like the incident just now ever happened again, she took the hand that Florence held out to her.

'It'll be all right, I promise. Folk around where we live are lovely. Good old honest Cockneys.'

'What's a Cockney?'

'Ha, you've a lot to learn. It's what the folk of the East End of London are called. And most Cockneys are jolly and kind and look after one another. You've landed in the best area. There isn't much goes on of what you saw just now. Most get along just fine.'

This brought a small amount of relief to Tamar. But still

parts of her heart were trapped in the fear she'd experienced and the awful feeling of not being worthy – of being a second-class citizen.

It wasn't a comfortable feeling and it had taken the joy out of the day and the wondrous spectacle they'd witnessed. *Will I ever belong here? Poland is my home; I just want to go back!*

The recognizable smell of something delicious cooking met them when they arrived back home. Tamar gave an exaggerated sniff. 'Mmm, cholent!'

'Ha, that's what Elma calls it, but to me it's just a delicious beef stew.'

'It is, but it's special too. Traditionally, it's cooked ready for the Sabbath when no work, not even cooking, can take place. It's made ready and kept warm in the coal oven. But it's only Wednesday! And it's making me hungry.'

'Elma cooks it any time. She always cooks in the Jewish way. It's how she was brought up.'

'Well, I won't be saying no if she offers me some.'

Just as she said this, Elma came through from her kitchen into her shop. 'Ah, there yer are. I've been worried about yer going up west. There's a snobbery up there over anyone being a bit different – posh lot, they are, and think themselves somebody.'

Florence surprised Tamar by saying, 'Oh, there was none of that, Elma. Everyone was in a lovely happy mood for the King. It was wonderful.'

Tamar didn't deny this, picking up that Florence preferred to ignore it. But anger boiled inside her still as she thought of the frightening incident. Never had she been faced with anyone seeing her as a lesser person because of being different. She'd only been faced with the fear of it happening from warnings about the Nazis' intentions.

Still she had a sick feeling in her stomach over the incident. It had made her fears a reality. How could it be allowed? Why should her people have to flee their homes and the businesses they had built up? Why should they be subject to what the man had put her and Florence through?

'You're quiet, luv. Did you enjoy seeing the parades, eh?'

'I did, Elma, thank you. I've never seen anything like it.'

'That's good. Now, I'd like to bet you're both hungry? Well, you're welcome to a bowl of me cholent, and so is your dad. I'll put some by for him as he went out about two hours ago.'

In unison, they answered, 'Yes, please!' then giggled as they looked at each other.

'Well, yer've found a good friendship together by the looks of things. I'm glad for yer both . . . Right, I shut up shop for an hour in five minutes, so make sure you're down for then and it'll be on me table ready for yer.'

When Tamar went upstairs an hour later, she thought of how much easier Florence and Elma had made settling in for her. Already this felt like home, although she'd hardly been here a day and nothing was familiar to her – no ticking grandfather clock, no ornaments she recognized, or furniture she'd lived with all her life. Nothing of her and her father's except clothes. And it was as if Mama hadn't existed as there wasn't a trace of her in this place.

With this last thought, Tamar hurried to her bedroom and pulled out the small case she hadn't yet unpacked. In it were three photos of Mama. All had beautiful silver frames that Papa had made. One was of Mama's and Papa's wedding. Then there was one with the three of them standing against the garden gate with a full view of their lovely house behind them. And a third one with Mama on her own, smiling – a rare thing to see on a photo, as mostly smiling for the camera wasn't encouraged. But they'd been on a picnic on the beach and Papa had been taking photos. He'd said something that made Mama laugh and had clicked his camera, capturing her beauty, and her joy, for ever.

A lump came into Tamar's throat. She swallowed hard. A tear plopped onto her cheek, followed by another, and then a torrent. Her sobs shook her body as she cried for her mama, for the injustices of the world that had taken her from her beloved home and her adored Isaac and Hannah, and of how they thought they had escaped what might be, only to find there was hatred here too – a fascist party who hated anyone with dark skin and her people, the lovely, kind, hardworking Jewish people. *Why? Why are we persecuted and hated so much?*

Getting off her knees, Tamar lay across her bed, clutching her laughing mama who was no more, and let her body weep.

An hour later a sudden noise woke her. A knock on her bedroom door and Papa's voice coming to her brought her hazy mind back to where she was and why.

'Tamar, dear, I'm home and have exciting news . . . Are you all right?'

Him speaking in Yiddish further confused her brain for a moment. It was as if both her worlds were colliding, and she belonged in neither of them.

'Tamar?'

'Sorry, Papa, I was asleep. Come in.'

The door creaked as he opened it, as did his tread on the floorboards before he reached the rug next to her bed.

'Tamar, my dear! You've been crying . . . Oh . . . I see, it's Mama.' His body dropped heavily as he sat on the end of the bed, just missing her feet.

'It's everything, Papa. I – I just felt I couldn't cope . . .'

She told him of the incident in The Mall.

'Tamar, those kinds of people are everywhere in the world – bigots and bullies. But weigh the few of them up with the millions of good people and they pale into insignificance.'

'But they are ruining our lives, Papa. Because of them, we have had to move from our home.'

'Yes. They are rising up, and have gained power in Germany, but they will be beaten. The rest of the world will stop them.'

His voice grew in strength, giving Tamar comfort as she hung on to his every word.

'No one can influence what is happening inside Germany, but the Nazis will be stopped . . . Only, try to remember that they are just a body of people in a country. They are not the German people as a whole. Many don't agree with the ideals of the Nazis, but if they are vocal about not doing so, they are in danger.'

'But why are they against our people?'

'Ruben and I have been discussing this today. Ruben is very knowledgeable on the history of our people and the persecutions we have suffered.'

Tamar sat up, eager to learn the reasons for all that was happening. 'Did we do something bad?'

'In Hitler's eyes, yes. He was a soldier in the German army during the last war. It seems that he and others never got over the defeat of the German Empire. They believed, and spread the word, that the army hadn't lost the war on the battlefield, but they'd been stabbed in the back by the Jews and the communists who'd given their vote to a left-wing government – a government that threw in the towel.'

'So now he wants his revenge?'

'Yes. How far he will go, I don't know, but he wants a supreme German race. The Jewish people are treated like scum. But it isn't just his hatred of us and other races, he also has an ambition to win back the lands that were taken from Germany after the last war.'

Tamar shivered as a sudden premonition fleetingly visited her thoughts – Hitler would try to exterminate the Jewish people from the world!

'We are safe here, my dear, try not to worry. Yes, there are odd pockets of fascist Jew-haters, but the British as a people do not hate us. Remember that. It is only the few. You had the misfortune of meeting one of them today – after only being here for such a short time – but you may never meet another one.'

'But Florence is hated too, for the colour of her skin, and yet she and many of her ancestors were born here!'

'Where you are born doesn't define you, Tamar. You were born in Poland, but you are Jewish first and Polish second. In a way, Florence is lucky. There is a country that she belongs to. Her ancestors were stolen as slaves from Guinea. That is her true nation. We Jewish do not have that.'

With these words, Tamar had the sinking feeling of being an alien wherever she went. Her eyes sought desperately for her father to give her comfort.

'Tamar, it's all right. You are all right. We will make Britain our home and will be safe. We'll work hard and make a new life.'

She didn't want a new life; she wanted her own! And she would fight for that. One day she would return to Poland. She would marry Isaac, and they would raise a family and that wouldn't be in a foreign country, but back in beautiful Mechelinki. Their children would know the freedom that they had known until now. They would play on the sands and laugh with the same childhood joy she and Hannah and Isaac had known.

She would hold on to that dream. She would not just hope it came true but make it do so.

'Come into the sitting room, my dear, I have so much to tell you. And I have a treat. Ruben has given me some mint tea, your favourite.'

Latching on to the optimism Papa was trying to show, Tamar jumped up. 'Mint tea! Oh, my favourite, Papa. Only I will infuse it. You are too impatient and don't allow time for its best flavour to emerge.'

Papa laughed out loud. 'You sound just like Mama . . . Bring the photo of her laughing. We will hang it in the sitting room. She will always be alive to us. We will consult her on our problems and share our new life with her. The one of our wedding . . .' Papa hesitated and swallowed hard. When he spoke again his voice croaked with emotion. 'Let us hang that in the hall between your and my bedrooms, but close to mine. We can say good morning to her and goodnight. And then you can have the last one in here, so she looks after you while you sleep.'

He turned abruptly and went out of the door.

Tamar held the photo up with the three of them and their house in the background – the place that would always be her home in her heart.

Gazing at it, her earlier resolve to make her dream come true strengthened. She'd make this photo the focus of that determination to do whatever it took to one day return to where she truly belonged.

Chapter Four

Four months later, excitement zinged through Tamar as she stood on Euston station. At last Isaac and Hannah were on their way!

So much had changed since she and Papa had arrived here. The good news Papa had for her on the day of the coronation had materialized into them opening a jewellery shop with a workshop at the rear.

It had turned out to be perfect for them and only four doors down from Elma's!

Within weeks it had been fitted out with all they needed for their trade. Most items had been supplied by Ruben, but Tamar had discovered the reason for Papa's case being so heavy on their journey over here was that he'd packed a roll of his own hand tools – various sized pliers: round-nosed ones, snipe-nosed ones and fat-nosed ones. She'd laughed at his joy and excitement as he'd revealed them to her. And then to find he'd also brought all manner of tweezers, binding wire, a centre punch and a steel square! The latter he used to centre a stone.

She'd been flabbergasted that he'd managed to carry it,

but then, he had a love of his tools, and no others would do.

Now, they had everything they needed as besides the machinery that Ruben had lent to them, Papa had bought shears, cutters, clamps and a soldering block second-hand from a dealer Ruben knew.

Another used item they'd found had been installed at the back of the workshop – a huge safe. In this they stored a small number of nuggets of gold and silver and some precious stones, all of which had taken the largest amount of Papa's capital and were just enough for them to work with for now. Then each night, the display of jewellery they had for sale was packed away inside the safe too, giving them a sense of security.

And best of all, Tamar had her own workbench where she fashioned delicate bracelets from the leftover silver and gold Papa didn't use. This had been built into a small space behind the shop door, enabling her to be on hand to deal with any customers. But it was also in full view of the shop window, where a small crowd often gathered outside to watch her work.

Business was growing too. Papa had a list of orders for personalized pieces, mostly from the rich in their Jewish community. But word was spreading of their excellent work and beautiful designs, bringing in other customers too.

That could only get better with Isaac's arrival. He was second to none at annealing the gold and silver – a process that used heat to reduce the hardness and internal stresses of a metal, making it softer, more pliable and easier to work with.

But that wasn't all that would get better by him coming – her heartache would vanish the moment he held her in his arms.

No sooner had this thought left her than the sound of the approaching train rattling along the track almost deafened her and everything around her became misty in a swirl of smoke puffing from its chimney. As the noise stopped and the air cleared, there he was, amid the shouts of the porters, the hurrying of bodies brushing past him, and the rumble of luggage trucks. Her beautiful Isaac.

Unable to move or control her tears, Tamar stared at him as if he was a mirage. Somehow, she felt he might suddenly vanish, and that this wouldn't be real but rather a figment of the dream she'd dreamed so often.

But then the sound of her name on his lips put her world to rights. He was here. Her beloved had at last arrived to be with her.

As if propelled forward, they ran towards each other, all convention forgotten as they collided and clung together. Tears and laughter mingled, showing their joy as the hug went on and on.

'Hey, I've arrived too, Tamar!'

Coming out of the circle of Isaac's arms but not wanting to, Tamar grinned at Hannah. Her dark curls were dishevelled, her glasses were misty from being worn many hours, but her grin made her beautiful.

'Oh, Hannah! Hannah . . . I can't believe it.' The hug they shared brought back to Tamar their wonderful friendship that had, and would, sustain them for ever.

Stepping back, Tamar dried her eyes. 'My cousin Ruben is waiting outside to take us home . . . Oh, Isaac, Hannah, I'm so happy you're here.'

Both had wide grins on their faces. It was Hannah who answered. 'Really! Ha, I wouldn't have known!'

Their grins turned to laughter, and Tamar joined in with

them, feeling as she did the small amount of tension she'd held inside melt away. They were here, they were the same as ever. Nothing had changed except for where they were, but even that was becoming home to Tamar, and she hoped it would for them too.

Ruben greeted them as if he'd known them all his life, a welcome that Tamar could see pleased them both.

Once settled in the car, Tamar sitting in the back with Isaac, holding his hand as if she would never let him go, Hannah turned to look at her from her seat in the front and asked, 'Are we all living together?'

'No. You and Isaac are going to share a flat above Elma's shop. You will love Elma. Did you get my letter?'

It was Isaac who answered. 'No. We have only had one from when you first arrived here and weren't happy. Except for having met two lovely people, Elma and Florence.'

'Oh no. I have sent so many more, trying to keep you up to date with all that was happening here. I had six from you, the last telling of your arrival, and then the telegram you sent from Harwich.'

Tamar went on to tell them of how she and Papa had lived in Elma's flat for the first two months, but hearing they were coming had spurred them on to get the flat above her papa's shop sorted and they had now lived in it for the past two months and made it home.

She could feel the tension in Isaac as he looked out at the traffic and hordes of people. It had taken Tamar time to get used to these surroundings, but they were becoming more normal to her every day.

'There is so much to show you both. Florence has been showing me it all bit by bit – palaces, cathedrals, parks, Trafalgar Square, theatres . . . Oh, I so want to go to the theatre.'

'Then we shall, darling Tamar . . . It's so good to be with you.'

Looking into Isaac's dark eyes smiling down at her, Tamar felt her stomach clench. 'And for me to be with you, Isaac.'

With this, he kissed her nose, but a telling cough from Ruben had them jumping apart and then giggling together. And with this, Isaac's tension released, and she felt his body relax.

'How are things at home?' she asked him.

'The same, but different. News reaches us from relatives of some of our community still in Germany that unnerves us all. They are living in fear and have had their basic rights, businesses and jobs taken from them. Our mama's sister, Aunt Matilda, who lived in Austria, has emigrated. Mama is distraught because she hasn't heard from her as to whether she arrived safely in America.'

'I'm sure she will hear from her soon. It takes a while to sort everything out.' Tamar wanted to shout out, *Why? Why is all of this happening?* but it seemed such a futile question. There was no valid reason, it was just happening and it didn't seem that anyone was doing anything to stop it.

'So, nothing has happened in Poland, has it? Our community is still safe there?'

'No, nothing . . . Well, the fear is mounting. The numbers of refugees trying to get away soars, and there are more calls for volunteers to be trained to fight.'

Tamar held her breath.

'I will go back if things escalate further, Tamar. I must.'

'I know, and would expect no less, but it breaks my heart to think of it . . . Here we are, Bridge Street. This is where we live, and Papa's shop is . . . Look, there!'

Brume's Bespoke Jeweller's stood out from its neighbours

with its black frontage and big shining window showing glittering pieces of jewellery displayed for all to see.

Isaac smiled. 'It looks good. Have you and your father painted the front?'

'No, Ruben had a decorator come . . . Oh, Isaac, Papa is so happy to have his own shop at last. And I love working in it . . . I've sold two of my bracelets so far.'

This last she said with pride.

Isaac squeezed her hand. 'It's good to hear the enthusiasm in your voice, Tamar. It is making me have hope in my heart.'

'There's always hope, Isaac. And here, in London, you latch on to that. The Cockney people approach life in a way that makes everything seem like a minor happening.'

'And they are all right with you and our people?'

'Yes . . . There is a little . . . well, not among the Cockneys. I'll explain another time. But first, prepare yourself, the Cockneys have an English all of their own. What English you know will hardly ever be heard here!'

Isaac looked puzzled, but there was no time to explain as the car came to a halt outside Elma's grocery store. Within minutes they were out of the car and Elma was greeting them – though that was after they had woken Hannah.

'I hadn't noticed that you'd fallen asleep, Hannah. You must be very tired. I know I was when I arrived.'

'I can hardly put one foot in front of the other.'

As she said this, Elma gave her a wide smile. 'Come on in, girl, I'll soon sort yer a cuppa. That puts everyone right!'

Hannah looked shocked and mystified. Tamar laughed. 'I did try to warn you, but you were still snoring. They don't speak the English we were taught, but it is a lovely warm language, and you soon get used to it.'

Once inside, Elma said, 'Keep your eye on the shop, Tamar, I won't be a mo. I'll soon get the kettle boiling.'

'I think we'd be best to get upstairs and I'll make them one, Elma, thanks, love.'

'Don't leave me with 'im!'

Both Hannah and Isaac looked amazed when she and Ruben burst out laughing. Then Ruben said, 'Ha, no one will stop me, Elma. One of these days, you will love me as I love you!'

'You're bleedin' crackers. Don't listen to him, me darlin's . . . 'Ere, busy yerself, Ruben, and 'elp with their luggage, it'll keep yer 'ands out of mischief.'

This time when Tamar laughed, Hannah and Isaac joined in as she said, 'It's a long story of unrequited love . . . Follow me.'

At last Tamar found herself alone with Isaac. The tea had been enjoyed, the tour of the flat had gone well, but now Hannah, completely exhausted, had gone to bed – in the bed Tamar had occupied – and was asleep.

'Oh, Tamar, my darling. It all feels so strange. Even you don't seem like you any more.'

'I am, Isaac. I've had to adapt, that's all. You will too.'

'You seem so settled, so much a part of it all. I – I can hardly imagine you back home in our little village.'

'My heart is there, Isaac. It never left you. I had to settle in. I had to become part of this place, or I would have been miserable and made Papa miserable too. But I'm still your Tamar. I still love you with all my heart. I've missed you every waking hour and cried myself to sleep most nights longing to be with you. I love you, Isaac.'

His arm came around her, pulling him into his body. He

kissed her hair, and then lowered his face and kissed her lips. Gently at first and then deepening to a kiss that told her how much he loved her and wanted her.

Tamar's response was to move nearer to him, to feel his need for her and to hold him with all the love she had for him – to let him know she was his.

When he pulled away from her, it was as if she had left half of her behind in his arms.

'Oh, Tamar, my Tamar. I want never to leave you again . . . but—'

She put her finger on his lips. 'Don't say it. Not today. Don't let there be "buts". We're together. I know your plans, but it may never happen that you are called upon.'

They clung together and cried together – partly through happiness, but partly through dread of what the future held for them.

Chapter Five

With Florence having been on a week of night shifts, today, a week after they had arrived, Tamar was at last able to introduce her to Isaac and Hannah.

In fine form, Florence giggled as she told them, 'It's good to meet you both and to be released from washing bottoms and emptying bedpans!'

'So, you're a Florence Nightingale then?'

Florence laughed at this from Hannah. 'You just don't know how many times that is said to me, Hannah, but it makes me laugh every time. My mum called me Florence after that lady and always had ambitions of me being a nurse as she had been. And it thrills me that my grandmother – who was also a nurse – met the wonderful lady herself!'

'Oh, Florence, you never told me! That is something to be proud of.'

Turning back to Hannah and Isaac, Tamar told them, 'Florence helped me to settle more than anyone. She's been a friend I could turn to from the beginning.'

Florence smiled at her. A smile that held love. 'You were my saviour too, Tamar. I had no one of my own age around here who would become close to me. I was missing my mum and my family. If I hadn't had Elma supporting me, I would have given up. But then you arrived, and everything changed for me. I had found a friend.'

They hugged again. Tamar felt the tears prick her eyes as they'd suffered a few incidents like the one at the coronation. She hadn't said anything to anyone about them, but always, she and Florence had stuck together through them and come out laughing. The tears remained unshed and the lump in her throat disappeared as Isaac said, 'Well now, this being Sunday and we having observed the Sabbath yesterday, we have a day off today, and that's not to be wasted.'

'And that's why I went to early mass, to be free to meet you both and to do something with you all.'

'Are Catholics not bound by any rules other than attending mass on a Sunday, Florence?'

'Not really, Hannah. We live the values of our faith every day as you do. And that leaves time for plenty of fun – Jesus was a one for the wine, remember? He turned water into it so He and his friends could carry on drinking at a wedding, so He doesn't restrict us from having a good time.'

A silence fell, but only for a moment. Tamar broke it. 'Well then, if it was good enough for this Jesus fellow, it's good enough for us. Let's go and explore and see what we find, eh?'

The moment of tension that had highlighted the difference in their religions passed, and the four of them set out for Liverpool Street station – the starting point to take them to anywhere in London. Today, they were going sightseeing. Tamar couldn't wait to show everything she'd seen to Isaac and Hannah, hoping they would love it all as she had.

Hannah linking arms with Florence further enhanced the atmosphere between them all, making them a happy bunch of friends which no differences could spoil.

Tucking her arm into Isaac's, Tamar had a sudden shiver.

'Are you feeling all right, darling? You can't be cold on such a lovely day!'

Tamar turned to see the other two had lagged behind. They looked deep in conversation, which was making them dawdle. Tamar shrugged. 'Yes, I'm fine. I don't know what it was, but a sense of doom just came over . . . Oh no! Isaac . . . what . . . ?'

The words stuck in Tamar's throat and then turned into a scream that joined the terrified ones of Florence and Hannah.

A car coming towards them on the opposite side of the road had suddenly swerved in their direction, missing Tamar and Isaac but ploughing into Florence and Hannah, sending Florence flying in the air. She landed on the car bonnet, her leg hideously twisted.

Hannah lay trapped under the wheel of the car.

The sound of the engine revving had Tamar drawing in the breath that had left her body with the shock. Isaac's gasp of, 'No! No! Please, no!' compounded her sense of despair.

The front wheel of the car reversed back over Hannah as if she was nothing more than a pile of discarded clothes. Florence bounced off the bonnet.

A voice called out from the open window of the car, hurling vile, racist abuse at them and expressing joy at having hit the two girls, before speeding off.

Tamar couldn't move. Her eyes seemed pinned wide open; saliva ran from her mouth. 'No! No! Help us . . . HELP US!'

Isaac ran forwards and fell on his knees. His arms grasped Hannah's lifeless body. His wails of agony filled the space around Tamar.

'Someone 'elp me, this one's alive!' A passer-by had got to the scene before them.

'Don't move her.' This from a young man who came out of the gathering crowd and ran towards the scene.

Still, Tamar stood where she was, just staring.

'I've had some medical training. We need an ambulance! She may have broken bones and injuries can be made worse if she's moved.' The young man bent nearer to Florence. 'What is your name, miss?'

Tamar saw Florence's expression of fear relax a little as she looked up into the face of one of her own countrymen, but she didn't hear her reply. It was Isaac who said, 'She is Florence, and this is my sister . . . Please help them.'

'I'm Herbert.' Looking up at the man first on the scene, Herbert said, 'Hurry! Go to one of the shops and ask them for an ambulance!'

'Righto, mate . . . I saw it all . . . Bleeding Mosley's lot. They had one of them fascist brass badges on their car.'

'Hurry, please.'

With this from Herbert, the man ran into the shop a few yards down the road but was back in minutes.

'They'd already rung, mate. The ambulance is on its way . . . but that other one looks a goner.'

Another wail of agony came from Isaac, propelling Tamar out of her stupor. She dashed towards him and held him as best she could. Hannah's blank, staring, unseeing eyes broke her. 'No! Not Hannah, please, please, not Hannah!'

Herbert's voice cut through her anguish. 'This one's still alive, and if you're her friends, you need to help her.'

Tamar turned and saw Florence's pleading eyes. 'Oh, Florence . . . Florence.'

Gently taking her hand, she told her, 'I'm here, Florence. I'm here, my lovely friend. I'll take care of you.'

A croaked out 'Ha . . . nan?' from Florence showed Tamar the reality of what she knew. Her lips quivered and a sob wracked her body. But some instinct in her told her to concentrate on Florence. 'I – I think she's . . . Oh, Florence, don't leave me.' It was a selfish-sounding plea, but one meant to encourage Florence to fight. 'Don't let them win, Florence. I love you.'

Herbert looked up at her. 'You're one in a million. Not many offer love to us. She'll be all right. Her signs are good.'

'Are you a doctor?'

'I want to be and study all the books I can get my hands on, but I haven't had the education I need.'

'I'm sorry.'

Florence made a sound. Her body heaved.

'She's going to be sick. Help me to roll her, but gently. Please try not to move any of her limbs from the position they are in now.'

They'd hardly moved Florence when she vomited. Blood shot from her mouth.

'Oh, God!'

Herbert's desperate cry proved to Tamar the seriousness of her injuries. Somehow, she felt a growing strength within her. She needed to block out the cries of Isaac and the knowledge that her darling Hannah had gone and concentrate on helping Florence.

'Florence, you're going to be all right. I know you know the seriousness of your condition, but you're strong. I love you, Florence, and I'll be by your side.'

Florence's eyes began to close.

'Stay awake, Florence. Try to talk to us. Don't go to sleep. You cannot fight while you're asleep. Stay alive for us all!'

Herbert's pleas seemed to get through to Florence. She opened her eyes wide. As she did, the sound of clanging bells filled Tamar with the mixed emotions of relief and dread.

As the ambulancemen took over the care of Florence, Tamar turned back to Isaac. She could do no more than put her arms around him.

'I can't bear it, Tamar. I can't.'

She could offer no comfort, only to say, 'I'm here for you, Isaac, my darling. I will help you – we will help each other.' But then the strength she'd found cracked and she leaned heavily on Isaac's shoulder. 'Oh, Hannah, Hannah, how could this have happened?'

Isaac's voice held a bitter note as he answered. 'Because of the Nazis, that's how. They must be beaten, and their hatred of us, of Black people, and any indigenous groups in favour of their precious Aryan race must be crushed.'

Anger tensed his body and came out as a scream that terrified Tamar. 'Isaac, Isaac, please, please, darling, I'm here.'

Turning towards her, he fell on her, almost toppling her over. His body shook with sobs that came from the heart of him. Tamar held on to him, gave him all the support she could, and kept his face looking away as Hannah's lifeless, bloodied body was lifted and taken away from them.

In an instant the bells began to clang once more, and the crowds dispersed. Herbert had stayed.

'Let me help you. Where do you live?'

A voice behind her made Tamar aware that the Cockney, first on the scene, hadn't left. 'I know the young woman. 'Er ol' man has that jeweller's – Brume's.'

'Oh, yes, I know it . . . Come on, let's get you back there.'
'I want to go to Florence.'
'I'll take you there after you've been home. Both girls were going to the same hospital . . . The ambulance crew didn't know if you could pay medical fees or not, so they've taken them to the London.'

Tamar looked at Herbert, unsure what this meant.

The Cockney fellow answered. 'He means the Royal London 'Ospital, luv. We all call it the London round 'ere . . . By the way, me name's Alf. I live atop of Brierly's sweet shop – drives me mad when they're making toffee. I want to go down and eat the bleedin' lot! . . . Oh, beg yer pardon, miss. You ain't wanting to 'ear stuff like that at the moment. But will yer let me know 'ow the injured girl goes on?' He patted Isaac's back. 'Let me 'elp yer up, sir . . . And I'm sorry for yer loss. It's devastating. If I can do anything, I will.'

Isaac managed to thank him. Never had Tamar seen her beloved looking so broken. Her own heart was wrapped around his – his pain was hers. A pain that held fear too, as now she was certain that Isaac would go to do his bit against the Nazis. She didn't want him to, for deep inside she dreaded that she would never see him again if he did.

The hours following passed in a fog of unreality. Isaac had gone into a shell and hardly spoken, only holding her as often as he could, his body trembling but not releasing his tears.

Papa made all the necessary arrangements for Hannah's burial, which was to take place the day after her murder.

The police had drawn a blank in finding the men who'd killed her. No one they'd been able to talk to who had witnessed the tragedy could even remember the colour of the car, let alone the make. To Tamar, it was a moment engraved on her mind, and yet relived in a haze – there was no detail. Just a happening. A vile, terrifying happening that she knew she would never forget and which would mark a change in her life that could never be undone. For now, she knew the stark reality that her people were not accepted by some in society. At best, they were tolerated; at worst, they were hunted down and killed. The future looked grim to her. They were a race without a country. Would they always be seen this way?

It seemed like days but it was only hours later that she sat holding Florence's hand. Miraculously, apart from broken bones in her legs, Florence wasn't hurt as badly as she could have been.

Any movement caused her pain, as her body was badly bruised. But she was alive and would get through this.

'Hannah?' Florence's voice croaked out the name.

Tamar shook her head. It was the only response she had in her. She couldn't utter the words.

'No! Why? We . . . we're people, just like them. Why, because of our skin, or our beliefs, do we have to be treated so awfully?'

Tamar had no words. She lifted her hand and, with her thumb, wiped the tears tracing a path down Florence's cheeks.

'How's Isaac?'

'In a daze. He doesn't speak much, but when he does, he says he must help our country fight off the threat from Germany. I don't want him to go. Our people are under far more threat in Poland. And yet, I have an urge to go myself. To fight back. To help to save the Polish people from tyranny and our own people from the humiliation the Nazis will subject them to.'

Florence's hand tightened on hers. 'No. Please don't go, Tamar. I couldn't get through without you . . . Will you let my family know where I am and what has happened? Their address is in my flat on—'

'It's been done, love. The police have taken it in hand. Your landlord let them into your flat. They needed to know more about you.'

'My mum and dad will come and take me home to look after me as soon as I am well enough to move. I want that, Tamar. I want my mum more than anyone at the moment, but you will write to me, won't you? You won't go back to Poland, promise me you won't. I know it doesn't seem like it, but you're safer here.'

'Oh, Florence, I don't want you to go anywhere, though I know you must. You've helped me to settle more than anyone. We'll always be friends, won't we?'

Once more, Florence squeezed her hand. 'Always.' She closed her eyes then. Her face showed the pain she was in.

Tamar's anger rose again. Why did some people think they had a right to do this to another human being and to take the life of someone as beautiful as Hannah?

The tear that trickled down her face showed her despair but didn't release her pain. How she would get through the next weeks and months she didn't know, but somehow, she must. She must be strong for Isaac.

It seemed unreal to Tamar the next day as she stared at the coffin. How could lovely, vibrant Hannah be lying inside a box with no life in her? The stark reality of death crowded her. She was never to see Hannah again.

Sobs wracked her body. A strong arm came around her. She looked up into the face of her father. He didn't utter any words, just shook his head in disbelief. His face was etched with sorrow and pain.

But then, there were no words for the senseless act that had taken Hannah from them and brought fear back into their hearts.

After the funeral, they were joined by Florence's parents and two men from the synagogue who Papa had made friends with. The conversation was hushed and stilted as they sat in Elma's front room and ate delicious delicacies, prepared and cooked by her: falafel made of a mixture of chickpeas, fresh herbs and spices, formed into small patties and served wrapped in pitta bread with a crisp, zesty salad – with lemon juice squeezed over the usual salad ingredients chopped into small pieces and mixed together. This was followed by Tamar's favourite sweet, chocolatey rugelach – a buttery, flaky, chocolate-filled rolled pastry.

Everyone ate heartily, as if it was a distraction from having to talk. But when they did chat, the conversation between the men dwelt on the aggression Germany increasingly showed and how reports of their treatment of the Jewish people sent terrifying vibes through their community, leaving them wondering what it might lead to for them all.

Tamar didn't want to hear, so she sat with Deirdre and Joshua, as Florence's parents had asked her to call them.

Deirdre – a round lady with the same coal-dark irises set in whiter-than-white whites of her eyes as Florence had – didn't say much, but Joshua wanted to know what exactly had happened. Going over it all gave Tamar a sick feeling in her stomach, but she understood how they felt – they needed to know, and yet they didn't. That strange world of shock a person enters when they lose someone, or someone they love is badly injured, that makes them seek answers.

With Deirdre shaking from head to toe on hearing the details, Tamar asked, 'May I hold your hand?'

Dierdre's plump hand was cold to the touch. Tamar clung on to it. Reliving the nightmare still shook her as rigidly as it had when it happened.

Without thinking, she leaned her head on Deirdre's shoulder. With her other hand, Deirdre stroked her hair. 'Girl, you've been a good friend to my Florence. Thank you for that. She was lonely down here without her family and friends. Though she may not have been any safer, as we have those in Leicester that are of the same mind as them that did this to my daughter and Hannah.'

'They are everywhere, but from what I read, though growing in popularity here, they aren't liked by the majority, and nor are their views shared by all. I've met some lovely people who take us as we are – normal people with a different religion, or in the case of Florence, a different skin colour.'

'Well, let's hope the majority win. There's a lot of dissatisfaction here, especially among the impressionable young and unemployed. They are quick to blame anyone who doesn't conform to their ideal of white supremacy for the position they find themselves in.'

Tamar nodded her agreement. As she did, a shudder went through her. It held a feeling of dread. A feeling that there was such a lot to face in the future, and she didn't want to. She just wanted to live her life, teaching, making jewellery, marrying Isaac and having fun with her friend Florence. And, in her heart, she wanted to be with Hannah, too, but knew that wasn't possible. Lovely Hannah had gone for ever.

With this, a sob broke from her.

Isaac was by her side in seconds and lifting her from her chair. Holding her elbow, he guided her outside into the small yard behind Elma's kitchen.

Then he took her in his arms. Together, they swayed, cried, and spoke of their love which would sustain them.

'Tamar, much is happening in the world, but nothing will ever break our bond. I love you, my darling Tamar.'

'But you're planning to leave me . . . I can't bear it. Hannah is gone, Florence is going back with her parents, and you are talking of returning.'

'I must. But not yet. We have time. I'll only go if the invasion of Poland seems imminent. But the world won't allow that. They won't.'

'Will we marry before you go?'

'I hope so. I want to marry you now. But convention requires a mourning period and won't allow for that. Though I know that if we could ask Hannah, she would say yes. She wanted nothing more than to see us wed and for us to give her nieces and nephews . . . It . . . it's unbearable that she has gone.'

They clung to each other, lighting a flame inside Tamar, which she knew found a kindred longing in Isaac and was difficult to deny. But they had to. If they gave into their yearning for the act of love to become physical between them, they would taint the passing of Hannah by dismissing their grief and taking a sinful path.

Standing back from her so that she could no longer feel his need, Isaac gave her a watery smile. 'One day, my love. One day, I will truly make you mine.'

'I can wait, my darling. Knowing I have your love will help me.'

'Let's go for a walk.'

Holding hands, they walked down Brick Lane towards the marketplace. Never did Tamar feel so bereft of the life she had known – a walk had once meant a pathway trodden by many thousands of feet over the years, along the shoreline of the Baltic Sea, with nothing but beauty surrounding them and fresh air filling their lungs. Now it meant a built-up smoggy environment, with constant noise, people and traffic to negotiate and not a breath of fresh air to breathe.

But she had her Isaac by her side and that meant the world.

'Let's go to the hospital, Isaac. I want to see Florence and it's afternoon visiting time.'

Isaac hesitated, but then said, 'If that's what you really want, I'll go with you but I'll sit outside and wait for you.'

'Oh no, we needn't go . . .'

'It's all right, really. I – I just want to be outside and there I'll be near to a few trees. There's not many places we can do that. I'll have a smoke and be with my thoughts.'

Tamar understood and knew Isaac needed a little time on his own.

Florence's smile didn't light up her face when Tamar walked towards her. Her body was broken, but more worrying than that was that it seemed her spirit was too.

They held hands and Tamar bent to place a gentle kiss on Florence's cheek. 'You're going to be all right, Florence, love. You will get better and be strong again.'

'H – how can I forget the hatred that led to this, Tamar? It never leaves my mind.'

'Oh, Florence. I'm sorry.'

Florence nodded. 'H – how did it go . . . ? Saying goodbye

to Hannah . . . I – I still can't believe it happened, and she's gone.'

Tamar bent and lay her head on Florence's hand. She had no words. If she spoke her feelings, she would cry and never stop.

Florence pulled her arm away and lay it on Tamar's head, softly stroking her hair, making an answer unnecessary, as the gesture spoke a thousand words between them.

After a moment, Tamar raised her head. 'So, you are going to Leicester? I can't bear to lose you, but I know it's for the best.'

'You won't lose me. You're the best friend I've ever had, Tamar. I'll be back when I'm better. I need my family around me. Dad has paid for a private ambulance to take me and there's a bed waiting at the hospital where he works. They have one of the best surgeons in the field of orthopaedics and I'm hoping he can fix me up and make me like new. Dad said there's no doubt about it, but . . .'

'He will. I'm sure, love. You'll come back all mended and get back to your training. But you will write, won't you?'

'I will, and as I get stronger and get home, I'll be able to telephone you.'

'Hopefully Papa will have a telephone installed by then. He is on the waiting list, but if not, we can arrange by letter for me to be in the telephone box at a certain time.'

Talking about this had cheered Florence and, apart from the lines of pain on her face, she was back to her old self in her spirits. For Tamar, this gave her hope – hope that at least part of her life would get back to being all right once more. Though she knew it would never be the same again.

PART TWO

The Blitz Destroys Their World

Chapter Six

1939

Somehow, as time had passed, they'd found life had some normality. Tamar had come to know the excitement of preparing for her and Isaac's wedding. Her heart had been full of joy – but that was now shattered by the words Isaac uttered as they stood on the dockside, a place they often walked to in search of some of the smells and sounds of their yesteryears.

'I must go, Tamar, my darling. I have to. Hitler has already taken the Sudetenland. The next few days may be my last chance of getting back . . . I – I heard from Witold Pilecki; he wrote to me a while back. He told me that he and his friend, Jan Włodarkiewicz, are talking of forming a resistance group if the army fail to hold back Hitler. They are convinced Poland is next in Hitler's plans.'

'This is why you brought me to the docks?'

Oblivious now to the smell of fish and the shouts of the dockers and merchant seamen, Tamar's eyes opened wide, her mouth stretching as the incredulousness of what Isaac had told her hit home.

'But . . . I . . . It's our wedding day in just two weeks!

You can't! Everything is set for our marriage going ahead during the Christian week of Easter, when all the banks and shops close! It is the only chance we had to get everyone together . . . Please, Isaac, please, don't go.'

'I – I . . . Oh, Tamar, the arrangements are in place. I'm leaving now. That Polish ship over there – it brought grain here, and it sails back to Poland tonight. I'm going with it.'

'And you have arranged all of this without saying a word to me! How could you? I – I even talked about how the cake was being iced today by Elma! Why? Why didn't you prepare me for this possibility?'

'I couldn't. It has happened very suddenly. As you know, I have always written to Witold, but today a Polish sailor brought an urgent message to me. Our people are nervous. Our army is preparing. Witold said that it is now or never that I get back to do my duty! I could not refuse this call from my friend. Already I have waited too long.'

Feeling defeated, Tamar could only say, 'But our wedding . . .'

'Please, Tamar . . . I want you as my bride more than anything in the world, but this is something that I have to do . . . Please, please send me off with your blessing and tell me you will be waiting for me.'

Hearing the anguish in his voice and knowing he would never do this lightly, a fear for her beloved Poland entered Tamar. It had been there for a long time, but now it seemed a reality that Hitler would invade it, and her fear for those she loved who were still living there deepened, helping her to understand Isaac's position.

If she could leave on the boat with him, she would. She'd fight to her death to save her country, but Papa needed her.

His eyesight was failing, and she couldn't ask him to return to Poland, she had to stay with him and look after him.

Taking a deep breath, she looked up through misty eyes, blinked away her tears, swallowed her anger and nodded.

'My heart goes with you, my darling Isaac.'

His arms enclosed her. His sobs joined hers. Desperation held them but was beaten by despair, as Isaac turned away from her and walked towards the ship. As he raised his arm in a wave, someone handed him his haversack. Seeing this, Tamar's anger returned. He'd had time to put everything into place, but not to tell her!

Running after him, she exploded in his face. 'You deceived me! You prepared everything, then you were too cowardly to tell me!'

Never before had she known anger towards Isaac, but now she could have torn at his face with her nails.

'Don't do this, Tamar . . . I – I didn't want to give you time to persuade me against going. If you had, I couldn't have lived with myself, or you . . . I would have been a broken man – a true coward. I am not that now, my darling. It is taking everything I have to leave you like this.'

A call in the beloved language of the Polish people came between them. 'All aboard now, please, sir.'

'Tamar, I . . .'

She put her finger on his lips. 'No, it is I who am sorry. My heart goes with you, my darling. Write often. I love you.'

With this, she turned and walked away, not daring to look back.

Arriving half an hour later at the only place she could go to find the solace she needed, Tamar called out to Florence as she mounted the fire escape leading to Florence's flat, begging in desperate silent prayers that she would find Florence at home after her early shift.

When the flat door opened, so did the floodgates to Tamar's heart.

Then she was in Florence's arms being guided by her up the last remaining steps as she sobbed, 'He's gone! Oh, Florence, how am I to bear it?'

'Let's get into mine first, then you can tell me who has gone, eh?'

Collapsing into Florence's armchair, Tamar put her head in her hands and sobbed.

'Is it Isaac? Has he gone back to Poland?'

When Tamar nodded, she heard Florence release a huge sigh, before going on her haunches in front of Tamar.

'Oh no! Why? I mean, why now? The wedding . . . Oh, Tamar, my dear, I am so sorry.'

Easing herself up as if in great pain, Florence put her arm around Tamar's shoulder. 'All I can say is that we knew he would, it was just when, and from the news, it does sound as though there is no more time to wait. Even our British Prime Minister has issued a warning to Hitler over Poland. He wouldn't do that if the threat wasn't real.'

'I – I know . . . It's the shock. Today I was so happy that Elma was going to ice the cake. I was telling Isaac about it. Why couldn't he have stopped me then and told me our wedding wasn't going to happen?'

'Knowing Isaac, he'd be afraid to. How did he tell you?'

After hearing, Florence gasped. 'But that's cruel! I wouldn't have believed Isaac capable of doing such a thing. He gave you no chance . . .'

'That's just it! He said he couldn't. He couldn't give me

a chance to change his mind as he would never be able to live with himself.'

'Yes . . . I can see that. Seeing you broken like this would have changed his plan. And the Isaac we know and love would have been broken if his country was invaded and he hadn't tried to help prevent that. But poor you. You've had a massive shock . . . Look, the best cure for that is a drink of wine, and I happen to have some. And it's kosher! Made from elderberries by our very own Elma.'

Shocked at this, Tamar asked, 'Is that what you give to your patients?'

'Ha, no, but we should do. Nothing like it to settle you down – the first glass helps you to think rationally, the second to accept, and the third turns you into a giggling wreck!'

Despite her pain, Tamar burst out laughing.

'Ah, but did Elma have the supervision of the rabbi?'

'I don't know, I only know that her biggest customers are the Jewish community!'

'That'll do then. If it's good for them, it will be for me.'

'Let's sit out on the step, eh? I often do to escape the confines of the four walls of this place.'

'You speak as if you hate it here, but it's a lovely flat. Especially since you came back from your mum's and she brought that vanload of stuff for you. She's made it homely.'

Tamar looked around the cosy living room. Besides the armchair, there was a small sofa, both a rusty colour and lightened by embroidered cushions with flowers on them, picking out the autumn-themed colours. Daffodil-yellow curtains hung at the one window, further brightening the room, as did the rug – made of rags, it held yellows and rusty shades woven into a brown background. Under the window stood a gateleg drop-leaf table and two dining chairs.

'It's all right, but when you live on your own and you're used to a large family home with people everywhere, it can feel like a prison! Anyway, not too long now, I'm almost there. Only three weeks till my final exam!'

Tamar's heart dropped. 'You mean, you'll leave? Where will you go?' She wanted to beg Florence not to go back to Leicester. She'd missed her dreadfully when she'd gone to convalesce. A pain sliced her heart at the memory of why.

'It depends on the job I get. There's a position in the Royal London, but there's another in the Leicester Royal Infirmary . . . Not that I'm too sure on that as Dad works there and I don't want to be watched over and reported on . . . I tell you, girl, drinking wine is sinful!'

Tamar giggled. She always found it funny when Florence mimicked her mum's speech.

'And they're teetotal and holier-than-thou with it!'

'So, choose the Royal London then!'

'If I do, I can't stay here. I'd have to look for another place and that would mean asking Dad for more funding and that doesn't seem fair after all he's paid out to help me gain my qualification. But I feel stifled here . . . hemmed in. I've had enough of it.'

As she spoke, Florence poured two generous measures of the light red wine.

'You carry yours outside, Tamar. I still need to hang on to the rail.'

'I noticed you were in pain when you rose just now. Is it your leg?'

'Yes. They put it back together as best they could but after a shift at work, it's burning with pain. I think arthritis has set in, but I must ignore it. My career's at stake.'

'Oh, Florence, I'm so sorry.'

'No. Don't mention it. I know your love for me makes you feel upset for me, but you have enough on your plate. Besides, Elma's wine is a good medicine.'

They sat down on the first step, giving them a view of the flats across the road and the noisy street below. But none of that mattered. It was soothing to Tamar to be with Florence and the wine warmed the cold place in her heart.

Suddenly, nothing felt as bad as it had earlier. 'It's not going to be easy to cancel everything, and it'll break my heart, but I am proud of Isaac. He and his friends and the Polish army will stop Hitler and make it safe for us to return one day.'

'And if Hitler tries his tricks, Chamberlain has said he'll have to deal with the might of Britain! And France echoed that, saying they, too, would fight him. So he wouldn't dare chance it.'

'I don't know. Men like him – tyrants – must have everything they desire, no matter what the cost. Gaining back the Sudetenland was a triumph for him, but now he wants more. I really fear for Poland, and especially the Jewish people still living there.'

'It's not just the Jewish people he's persecuting, Tamar. I have a doctor friend at work who is originally from Africa. His family settled in Germany after the First World War. He escaped from Germany because his family disappeared while he was at the hospital in Berlin. A friend brought him the message, and together they left that night. They travelled in the back of an ambulance to the border of Switzerland and then on foot till they got a lift to France. And finally, they arrived in London via the English Channel and Dover.'

'So Black people too? We never heard of that.'

'Yes, and Liam told me it's also gypsies, and those who

aren't of able body – anyone who doesn't conform to what they consider to be the supreme race.'

'Oh, Florence, the world must stop them. It has to!'

They sat in silence for a while, sipping their wine.

It was Florence who said, 'How . . . ?' And then, 'Don't answer that as the prospect is too horrible to talk about.'

'It's what a lot of people are calling for.'

'But war? Please, Jesus, no!'

'And I'll ask Elohim to do the same – stop any possibility of war and protect Isaac.'

'Jesus will do that too. He will protect Isaac.'

Tamar raised her glass. 'To Jesus, who turned water into wine. Thank you for protecting Isaac, along with Elohim.'

She didn't know why, but this made her giggle. Florence joined in. Before long they were hysterical with laughter.

Tamar sobered first. 'We're mad! I'm meant to be crying as my fiancé has gone to fight a war, and you're meant to be sad at the same thing and comforting me!'

'It's Elma's fault. She must have made this one strong for it to have this effect after just one glass!'

'And it's made me hungry.'

'Let's go and see what Elma is cooking, eh? She said to tell you if I saw you that she was making tea for us.'

'No doubt it will be something delicious, and she will have taken Papa some.'

Elma's kitchen smelled of meat cooking and the steamed-up windows told of vegetables simmering. 'We're hungry!'

'Ha, and tiddly too by the looks of yer. Come and sit down. Your papa's in the living room, probably snoring . . . How are yer, Tamar, luv? It's a big disappointment you've had.'

'You know about Isaac going?'

'I do, Tamar, me darling. Isaac told us – me and yer papa. I couldn't tell yer as you were waiting outside to go for a walk, and it wasn't our place. But me 'eart goes out to yer.'

'Oh, Elma! How am I to bear it?'

'Come 'ere, me darlin'.'

In Elma's arms, Tamar found the comfort she would have had from her own mama – the gentle hold, the stroking of her hair, the solid 'everything will be all right now' feeling.

'Dry your eyes, luv, before you go in to see your papa.'

'The cake . . .'

'It'll keep. I didn't ice it. Them fruit cakes of mine last for years. You and Isaac will cut it together one day, I promise.'

Wiping her eyes on the bottom half of Elma's pinny, Tamar felt better with the world. It had dealt her an unfair blow, but she was brave. She'd come through terrible things happening before and she could this. She was to be proud of Isaac and encouraging in her letters to him . . . But, oh, she would miss him, and now, too, she'd miss the feeling she'd been so looking forward to of at last being married to him.

Florence smiled at her. A smile that told of how sorry she was. But then she turned her attention to Elma and asked, 'Can I lay the table, Elma? I want to do something to help.'

Going through to her papa, Tamar heard gentle snores. She smiled as she caught sight of his now bald head just showing above the back of the sofa and had an urge to plant a kiss on it. Putting her arms around him from the back of the sofa, she bent and did just that. Papa snored deeply before his body shuddered and he muttered, 'Who's that?', barely audibly.

'It's me, Papa.' She didn't ask who he thought it was but lay her head on his.

One of his hands came up and gently stroked her arm. 'I'm sorry, love, I tried to persuade him not to go.'

'He had to. I understand how he felt. And it's not just the prospect of invasion. Isaac has needed to be with his parents since Hannah was murdered . . . Oh, Papa, why is it all happening?'

'The simple explanation is that Germany voted a madman in to rule them. A man obsessed with making Germany great again. Not by merit but by brute force, treading on anyone he sees as a deterrent to his cause, or to blame for Germany's downfall.'

'Yes, I remember you explaining this in full to me before, but what I can't understand is why his own people aren't stopping him.'

'Fear. A powerful emotion that makes men act out of character. Hitler rules by instilling fear in the German people's hearts. They conform, rather than face death. You can't blame them. But I have every faith that there are those among them who are against Hitler's values and are working away silently in the background to help the Jews and other persecuted people.'

Tamar straightened and let out a sigh as she went around the sofa and sat down next to her papa, leaning on him and putting her head on his shoulder. He took her hand into his large, bony one. 'We are all called upon to be brave, and we will be. You must be. Isaac is already showing that he is.'

Tamar looked around the room. So different to Florence's uncluttered living room, this one had a piece of furniture covering every bit of floor space. Besides this sofa that faced the fireplace, there was another – a chaise longue under the window. It was beige, like hers and papa's, but there the similarity ended as these sofas had a ruby-red cover that left part of the seat and the arms bare and was tied to the legs to keep it in place. Two ruby-red armchairs stood each side of the chaise longue, and Elma's best mahogany table and chairs were against the back wall. They were matched by glass cabinets each side of the fireplace, and a long sideboard against the wall opposite the window, with a dining chair on each side of it.

The floor was covered with ruby-red patterned rugs. The effect was overwhelming at first, but then welcoming and cosy, like Elma herself.

Papa tapped her hand. 'We'll be all right. We'll get through this and be one happy family again. Poor Abigail and Daniel, they have their son coming home – but only to fight a war, and they have lost their daughter, the lovely Hannah.'

'And Abigail's mother, too. I thought when she died they would have come here. Isaac begged them in his letters, but no, they don't seem to think there's a danger now. Abigail said that if Hitler truly wanted Poland, he'd have taken it by now . . . I fear for them.'

'Maybe they didn't want to leave the place where they had known Hannah to be.'

Tamar could see this point and agreed with it as Hannah's mama and papa wouldn't be able to imagine Hannah here. And memories that placed someone you loved near to you were precious. All hers of Isaac would be of him being in the same place as her – in Poland, growing up, and here in London. Of them working together day in and day out in Papa's shop and of the walks they'd taken together – especially the one that would take her back to the moment on a cold but sunny day in November last year when, wrapped up warm, they'd sat next to the rushing Thames and had become formally engaged and planned their wedding.

It had been a long time coming, but though a period of mourning had passed, neither had recovered enough from the horror they'd witnessed that had torn their hearts in two. And for a long time they hadn't felt inclined to seal their own lives in happiness when Hannah was gone, and Florence was travelling a long journey back to fitness.

Tamar closed her eyes and let her mind relive the moment when Isaac slipped off the bench and knelt in front of her. His eyes glinting as the sun, low in the sky, reflected in his dark brown irises. 'My darling Tamar, I have something for you. I have a ring to place on your finger. I want us to marry soon.'

Her heart had soared with joy as Isaac slipped the platinum band onto her finger and whispered, 'I love you with all my heart. Please say you are ready, as I am, to arrange our wedding day?'

'I am . . . Oh, Isaac, I am.'

He'd stood then and pulled her up to nestle into his body, before lifting her chin and kissing her so deeply she'd lost herself and become part of him.

When finally they'd stood looking into each other's eyes, she'd told him, 'I have something for you too. It's in my bag. I've been keeping it there for this moment.'

Bending, she retrieved the velvet box she'd stored her gift in. 'It's for both of us – one each. I made them.'

When she opened the box, the silver bracelets looked beautiful, as they'd become entwined as if hugging each other.

Isaac gasped. 'They are . . . I just don't have words . . . *us* . . . yes, they are us. I will wear mine every day, then at night we will entwine them as they are now on our bedside table.'

Tamar's heart had filled and brimmed over with love for her beloved Isaac as she'd placed the bracelet – a simple chain with a tiny heart hanging from a ring near to a silver clasp – on his wrist, and then slipped her own on.

The only difference between them was that Isaac's had a thicker chain. She'd spent hours working on them in secret – any odd moment she had – seeking out the right pieces of silver that came to her from the workshop and would fashion easily into links. All in readiness for this moment.

Another memory jerked Tamar back to the present as she saw Isaac again. He'd lifted his arm to wave, and the bracelet had glinted on his wrist – he'd taken it with him.

Seeking her own, she twisted it around her wrist, wanting to connect. Something told her that Isaac was doing the same at this very moment and the thought brought him to her.

It was taken from her mind, though, as Florence opened the living room door. 'Tea's ready, you two!'

Not feeling at all hungry now, and with a slight headache from drinking the wine, Tamar rose. Florence put her head on one side and looked at her. Her arms opened. 'Come here, love.'

Being in Florence's hug soothed Tamar's mind, but nothing could soothe her heart. That would ache painfully until the day the two bracelets were once more entwined.

Chapter Seven

Talk of war seemed to be the only conversation as the months of 1939 rolled on. In Papa's shop the customers spoke of it as they browsed the pads holding jewellery. In the streets, and at bus stops, complete strangers engaged you in how they thought war was on the horizon. Young men were called to undertake six months of military training, leaving girlfriends and mothers bereft and giving everyone a sense that war would become more than talk – and very soon.

This was compounded by seeing sandbags everywhere, placed in an attempt to ward off as much damage as possible if bombs were ever dropped on the city.

But the worst day of all was the third of September. Tamar thought she would never forget the chill that went through her at Chamberlain's words, full of woe, as he told the nation that Germany had invaded Poland and, consequently, Britain was at war with Germany.

Clinging to the edge of her workbench as his words, outlining how he'd given an ultimatum to Germany and they had ignored it by crossing the Polish border, left her cold and shaking . . . *Oh, Isaac, my darling Isaac.*

* * *

Nothing much seemed to happen after that day. Tamar occasionally had a letter from Isaac that put her mind at rest, though the length of time it took to get one to her made her think that things must have moved on since the day he wrote it.

But then came the fateful day when it was announced that the Polish army had surrendered, and Germany now occupied the country except for the eastern counties, which had been annexed by the Soviet Union. No further letters came after that.

Distraught, Tamar tried to carry on, occupying her mind by working hard but leaving it a disrupted, broken mess by tuning into every news broadcast, trying to find a hint of what had happened to the Polish soldiers.

Questions came at her – had Witold Pilecki and Jan Włodarkiewicz escaped capture? Had they set up the resistance group they had been planning to in the event of occupation? Was her Isaac with them? She hoped with all her heart that was so. If not, his fate as a Jew would be that he'd be forced to live in one of the ghettos they'd heard about where Jewish families were hoarded into grossly overcrowded communities, and fenced in like animals. Or, worse still, was he dead? So many had been shot in battle or after the Nazi victory.

Twisting her bracelet around her wrist, her heart bled with the possibilities, but somehow, she kept the faith that he was alive – that he was touching his bracelet right now and thinking of her. But what of Abigail and Daniel, his parents?

'Stop it!'

Tamar hadn't realized that she'd said this aloud until her papa said, 'I know what you mean. It is very difficult not to think the worst has happened. I almost feel like a traitor to my people for not being there with them.'

'Oh, Papa.'

No matter that the shop was open, they hugged one another, saying no further words, just trying to give and receive comfort.

When the bell clanged it was Florence who walked in, bringing a blast of cold air from the icy December day with her. 'Hey, come on now, no doldrums. Think of the good things that might have happened, eh?'

But then she came to them and hugged them both, and Tamar could see she herself was struggling to do what she said they must.

'Look, it's Christmas soon . . . Oh, I know you don't celebrate or believe in it, but Elma and I – your friends – do. So, we are asking that we pool what food we have and have dinner together on that day.'

'Yes. The answer is yes, we will and thank you, dear Florence.'

This from Papa shocked Tamar, but then she thought, why not? People of different faiths should honour those of their friends. Maybe the world would be a better place if they did. She forced a grin onto her face.

'As long as you don't ask me to pluck the cockerel, then yes, I would love that too!'

'Oh, Elma will see that everything is done properly for you – she does as a matter of course whether anyone is joining her or not . . . But, well, this will cheer her up. Not only is she distressed at what may be the fate of her sister's son who has been called up, but her business is suffering from all the shortages, and she is overwhelmed by the constant queues for any produce that she does have delivered – not to mention that there is already a black market that is threatening her livelihood.'

'Ah, well, tell her it will be more than an honour to join her.' Papa smiled as he continued: 'Ruben won't be best pleased about sharing her, thwarted as he is in his love for her, but then, he is an idiot. I would give up my beliefs for the woman I loved.'

'Yes, and Elma would give up hers for the man she loved, only he shows no signs of loving her, so she stays as she is.'

This further shocked Tamar as she immediately knew it was her papa that Florence was speaking of. Papa then took the wind out of her sails by saying, 'One day . . . one day . . .'

'Papa? Are you in love with Elma?'

'I – I . . . well . . . yes, I am, but how can I betray your beautiful mama who is still in my heart?'

Tamar's mouth dropped open. How was it she had missed this? She'd never put two and two together after all the times she'd looked for Papa and found him at Elma's. Or with all the attention Elma paid him and he lapped up.

'Mama would be shocked, like me, that you have never said anything. It is three years since we lost her, Papa, and when she was alive, as I am sure it would be today, she only ever wanted your happiness.'

Hope came into Papa's eyes. His smile held joy. 'You really think so? I mean, really? And . . . Oh, but what about Ruben? He would kill me!'

'Cousin Ruben probably has a dozen women he looks on as he does Elma, and I'd like to wager none of them are Jewish, which leaves him free to play the spurned lover role, which he does with aplomb. He'll just mark Elma off his list!'

'Go along there right now, Mr Blume, and tell Elma how you feel. With how things are we can none of us rest on our laurels. I intend on telling Liam that I love him and asking him to marry me!'

Aghast now, Tamar asked of Florence, 'You mean, your doctor friend at work? You never said!'

'I know. I only realized when war was declared. And though it doesn't feel like we're at war as nothing we feared – bombs dropping and soldiers landing on our shores to capture us all – has happened yet, it may. And Liam is talking about going into the Medical Corps if things do escalate. It was then that I knew I couldn't bear not to be with him.'

'And does he feel the same way about you?'

'I think so, but there is a sort of code of honour where we nurses are concerned, so he may feel he can't express it. But his eyes tell me.'

'Oh, Florence, I am hoping for you. And why have I never been properly introduced to him?'

'You will if he says yes!'

Florence gave her a lovely laugh.

'I will if he says no too as I'll seek him out and tell him he's an idiot!'

'Ha, I'll tell him that!'

A click as the shop door closed made them aware that Papa had left them. This made them giggle. 'We'd better have a cup of tea and wait a while before we go to Elma's. I was about to close the shop anyway.'

'Well, I hope you have something different to that minted tea you drink. It's just not the same as a good cuppa.'

'I have. We keep it in to offer to customers who work on a design with Papa.'

Over their cups of tea, Tamar and Florence giggled some more at different scenarios that they knew were ridiculous, but the ridiculous was all they had to rely on to keep their spirits up – that, and the odd evening of drinking wine on Florence's fire escape.

'What if they marry and Elma is your stepmum?'

'Ha, and Elma and Papa . . . Oh no, I can't think of that!'

'What? The squeaky bed keeping you awake?'

'Oh, don't! No! They wouldn't, would they? Not at their age, surely? . . . Oh, I couldn't live with them. Papa will have to live with Elma, and I'll stay in our flat.'

'You wouldn't want a lodger, would you? I can't find anything better than that pokey hole I live in, and it drives me mad.'

'Yes! Yes, I would! That would be wonderful, Florence. I cannot think of a nicer flatmate than you! It's a done deal – so, all we need to do is marry Elma and Papa off. Shall we go to Elma's now and see how the land lies?'

A blushing Elma opened the back door to her shop to them. Behind the blush, happiness shone from her. She gave a little laugh and said, 'Come in. Your papa and I 'ave something to tell yer.'

'I think I can guess, Elma, and I'm very happy for you both.'

'Really? You don't mind, luv?'

Papa came through from the living room into the porch then, looking very sheepish but smiling too.

Not giving him a chance to speak, Tamar went to him and hugged him. 'I'm so pleased for you both, Papa.' Her face knocked his wire-rimmed glasses to one side. She giggled and straightened them for him.

'Let's get yer both inside and we can tell yer all about it.'

They followed Elma into the kitchen. Familiar, delicious

aromas of sautéed onions and vegetables met them. It was Papa who spoke for the first time. 'Elma and I love one another and are going to marry.' Tamar waited, afraid that Papa was going to say that he'd abandon Judaism – she didn't want that.

'And I'm converting to David's faith – it is mine really anyway. I were brought up in it and keep its traditions, and being a pretend Catholic just kept me safe from discrimination and the likes of Ruben.'

They all laughed, and it seemed to Tamar that the room filled with joy. And yet, though she felt this with them, her heart was heavy.

The Christmas Day they'd planned passed with them enjoying a pan of vegetable and chicken stew with dumplings – delicious, but not what Florence had been looking forward to. She was all right about it, though, as on Boxing Day she left to go to her family for a couple of days and knew she was in for more of the Christian celebrations than they had offered her – though they had all pulled a cracker and worn the funny hats while they ate.

It was when Florence returned on New Year's Eve that Tamar had the news for her that Papa and Elma were going to marry in the spring – almost a year after the day her own wedding had been planned to take place.

Deciding to celebrate the arrival of the new year, they wrapped up warm and took cushions out onto the step. They'd only just sat down, in the blackened night with all light from surrounding windows hidden, when a voice called up to them, 'Florence . . . Florence.'

Florence shot up to a standing position. 'Liam?'

'Yes, where are you? I heard your voice as I walked along looking for your flat.'

'Can you see the fire escape? We're up at the top. It leads to my flat.'

Footsteps approaching told them he could. Tamar felt Florence's hand grab hers and squeeze it. In a low whisper she asked her, 'Did you tell him how you felt, Florence?'

'No. The moment didn't arise.'

'Well, I'd better go and leave you to it.'

'No, please don't. I – I don't know how to handle it.'

'Just be yourself. He's come looking for you. That must mean something.'

Liam interrupted then. 'It does. It means that I cannot wait any longer for the right moment, so I'm making it happen.'

Tamar stood. 'I'll go and see you tomorrow . . .'

'No, don't do that . . . Tamar, isn't it? The saviour of my Florence.'

He'd called Florence his! A nice feeling filled Tamar. Florence was loved by the man she loved. But still she hadn't reacted to Liam.

'Yes, I'm Tamar, pleased to be properly introduced to you – Florence has told me so much about you. Not sure that I am her saviour, though. She is more like mine.'

'Yes, friendship does that, and Florence has told me how much she values yours, that she was on the brink of going home when you arrived and she at last had someone who cared about her. That you were there and suffered along with her when that terrible atrocity happened that injured her so badly.'

Florence interrupted. 'We don't talk about that, Liam, it's too painful.'

'I can imagine. But you should . . . Oh, dear, I didn't come here to play doctor, or psychiatrist, but to tell you, Florence, that I love you.'

'What?'

'Oh, God! Am I wrong? I thought . . .'

Florence reached out to him. 'No, you're not wrong. I love you too and have done for a long time.'

Putting her hand behind her, Tamar opened the door to the darkened living room and stepped inside. After a moment they came in too. 'You haven't gone, have you, Tamar?'

'No, I'm here. Come in and close the door. Once the blackout is in place, I'll put the lamp on.'

Everything seemed surreal. Had she really just witnessed a first admission of love between Florence and Liam? Her cheeks felt hot. How was she to handle things now? *Oh, I wish I'd left!*

She wished this even more when Liam followed Florence inside.

Once the light was on, she saw how handsome he was, how his dark skin shone and his eyes twinkled with his huge smile that showed whiter-than-white teeth.

'I'm pleased to be properly introduced to you too, Tamar.'

Feeling at once as if she'd known him for ever, Tamar took the hand he offered. 'I've been dealing with a lovesick friend for long enough. It only took a visit from a doctor to make that all right!'

They all laughed, and the tension eased.

'Look, I'm so very happy for you both, but you need time to talk now. I'll pop along to Elma's and see the new year in with them.'

Florence saying, 'You don't have to,' without any conviction, and with no real protest from Liam, let Tamar know that this was what they wanted, and she didn't blame them. Kissing and hugging them both, and giving them her congratulations, Tamar wished them a happy new year, and began to negotiate the steps in the dark – something she hadn't planned on doing as they'd arranged that she would stay on Florence's sofa.

There was a surprising number of people milling about and this gave Tamar some comfort as the streets seemed eerie and unwelcoming in the darkness. But despite this, Tamar had never felt so alone. Tears stung her cold cheeks as she hurried to her own home, with no intention of gatecrashing the evening that Elma and Papa had planned.

Once inside, that loneliness was compounded, leaving her feeling like she was the only person in the world. A world she was unsure still contained her Isaac.

The tears became a torrent as she hugged herself against the force of them.

When she calmed down, she was on her knees in the dark rocking backwards and forwards. But she'd made a decision that helped her and gave her hope. As soon as the bank holiday was over, she would go to Portland Place and talk to someone at the Polish embassy. Maybe they would have news of what had happened to individual soldiers. She had to know . . .

Facing Florence's happiness the next day eased some of the pain Tamar felt. They hugged, Florence chatted on about how wonderful her world was, and how at last she was complete.

'I hope you mean almost complete, love!'

'No, I mean fully and truly complete! Oh, I know it's a sin, but it's a lovely sin. It's God's own fault if he sends us something so irresistibly beautiful and we take it.'

'Well, I think that's passing the buck! . . . But I'm happy for you, Florence. Only . . . well, what if you are pregnant?'

Florence laughed out loud. 'We don't have to be these days. There are ways and means.'

'And Liam came prepared for that?'

Tamar began to feel suspicious of Liam's motives and she didn't like the feeling.

'No, you idiot! I'd have slapped him to kingdom come if he had. It would have been like he was saying he knew he could strike lucky. No, what happened, happened out of our love for one another. Liam was careful, that's all . . . Oh, Tamar, it was all so natural, as if it was meant to be, and it sealed our love . . . We're getting married as soon as we can.'

Tamar's pain dug deeper into her heart. Why hadn't she and Isaac given the ultimate love to each other? Why had they held back for a day that never came?

'Tamar? Oh, Tamar, I'm sorry . . . I – I . . . That was thoughtless of me, I shouldn't have told you. I almost ran round here, unable to contain myself, wanting to share my happiness with the person I love so much, but I've only succeeded in causing you pain.'

Going into her arms, Tamar suddenly felt selfish in her reaction. It wasn't Florence's fault that her own happiness had been snatched away. It wasn't anyone's except for a wicked, greedy man called Hitler.

'No, no, I'm happy for you. At least, I am now I know you aren't in danger of having your belly up, as the Cockneys call it!'

Florence burst out laughing. 'Oh, I do love you, Tamar. You're the best thing to have happened to me . . . Well, you were!'

Tamar found that she could laugh at this as she latched on to Florence's happiness. Doing so helped her to cope once more. But also made her more determined to try to find out if anyone knew anything about Isaac, and if he was safe.

Putting her own concerns aside for a while, she said, 'Happy New Year, Florence.'

'And to you, and to the world. May Hitler fall down a deep hole and not be saved and may we all once again know the life we used to have that he has taken from us.'

'Hear, hear!'

'Anyway . . . There is bad news too . . . Liam is determined to go to help the medical aid workers with the wounded, but I wonder if he will be accepted – being black, I mean. And I find the thought of him going unbearable.'

'We'll get through it together, love . . . Surely, though, he would be accepted on merit?'

'For him, I hope so, but for me . . . Anyway, the prospect that he will be is why we are getting married as soon as we can. We're not getting a special licence, but we're posting the banns on Sunday – Liam attends the same church as I do . . . I didn't tell you that, did I?'

'Ah, so that's why you've become so devout lately, eh? Suddenly not wanting to miss mass and it having to be a certain one? Ha, you have got it bad, girl, and the sooner we get you wed, the better!'

They hugged again and this time, Tamar put her heart and soul into holding her dear friend, not letting any pain she felt interfere with giving love and underpinning Florence's happiness.

Chapter Eight
1940

A week later, with 1940 just seven days old, Florence wasn't so happy.

She entered the shop looking sadder than Tamar had ever seen her.

'Have you got a moment, Tamar? Can we go into the yard?'

'Yes. Why? What has happened?'

Florence sighed heavily. 'Mum has contacted me. She wants a proper wedding – all the trimmings – and she wants it in her church up in Leicester.'

'Well, that will be all right, won't it? I mean, a wedding with family is tradition and will be wonderful.'

'I know, but it can't happen until the spring. And it'll be a nightmare to get it sorted. You see, I am meant to reside there for three weeks before the banns can even be posted! I'm going up there very soon, but oh, I'm going to miss being with Liam and you.'

They hugged then. Tamar had a sinking feeling as she clung to Florence. How was she going to manage? Florence was her rock.

'I've to arrange things at work too. Hopefully I'll get leave, but I'll volunteer at Leicester Royal Infirmary to keep my hand in.'

'I can't bear the separation either, but if it has to be, then we'll cope with it. Maybe Liam will be able to visit – your parents will want to meet him.'

'Father wants him to ask for his permission for my hand . . . Oh, I know they have dreamed of this moment, and they are so very happy for me, but, well, I just want to be married!'

'I know . . . I know more than anyone, love. But you will be. That's a certainty for you.'

'Oh, I'm being thoughtless . . . Poor Tamar, your wedding didn't happen and here I am moaning that mine is delayed. I'm sorry.'

'Don't be. It isn't your fault and without you I would never have got through it all. I – I'm not coping well . . . I just want to know something, anything to stop this incessant wondering. Hoping one minute and despairing the next.'

'You have to do what you said and go to the embassy.'

'I will. When do you think you will go to your parents?'

'In the next few days – as soon as I can. Once I do it, it will soon be over.'

'That's the way to look at it, love.'

Brave words, but they were not felt in her heart. Tamar sighed. Somehow she'd get through it. Life might be like this from now on, saying goodbye to loved ones – that's what wars were usually like, and they couldn't expect this calm to last for ever.

Tamar stood outside the imposing and majestic building of the Polish embassy just six days later. She'd seen Florence off on her train, as Liam was working, and had then decided to come here to try to find out what she could.

She looked up and admired the white stonework and felt a pride at this place being a small part of her – a piece of Britain where she and her fellow Polish had their own to look after them. A least, she hoped it would work out like that.

Once in the foyer, Tamar's nerves kicked in but before she could think about the importance of the embassy, a voice said in Polish, 'Are you here to apply for British nationality, madam?'

The smartly dressed gentleman who'd asked this settled her nerves as his smile welcomed her.

'No. I need to find out if anything is known about my fiancé. He came to Britain to escape the fear we Polish Jews had of an invasion, but then went back to fight for our country the moment the invasion seemed imminent. He left on a cargo ship.'

'This way.'

She followed him through grand halls and they came to a room which stated it was the Polish War Office. A command to enter came in reply to him knocking on the door.

'This is Miss . . . ?'

'Blume. Tamar Blume.'

'Miss Blume wishes to enquire about one of our brave soldiers, sir.'

'Come in. I'm Mr Kaminski, and part of my job is to help in such enquiries, though we haven't a lot of information as yet. But if I cannot find him on one of our lists, I can take your name and address and inform you if any information does come in . . . Now, firstly, what is the name of the soldier you are enquiring after and your relationship to him?'

Tamar gave Isaac's details.

'Very well. Please wait outside, I need to go to another office.'

After half an hour had ticked away loudly on the clock on the wall, Mr Kaminski returned. He shook his head. 'I'm sorry, we have no information. However, that isn't necessarily a cause for anxiety, as at least your fiancé isn't on the known "Killed in Action" list. Though that isn't complete. But not being on it at present does give hope . . . Brume, you say? Are you anything to do with the jewellery shop on Brick Lane?'

'Yes, my father owns it. I work for him.' Why she said the next bit, Tamar didn't know, but she told him, 'Although I love the work, it isn't what I really want to do – it's more of a hobby. But I don't have papers yet to allow me to follow my real vocation.'

'And that is?'

'To teach languages. I speak English, Yiddish, German, and have recently become proficient in French.'

'Really?' His eyes shot up. 'And what have you done about getting papers?'

Tamar blushed. 'Nothing . . . You see, I always thought – hoped – that we would return to Poland, that everything would be all right and Germany wouldn't invade us, and neither did I dream that Russia would annex part of our country . . . It was just that, being Jewish, we had to flee, just in case.'

'Yes, you did the right thing. The news that has been passed to us isn't good for your people. But having such talents, you could be of use in helping your fellow countrymen, and the Jewish community.'

'How?'

'I cannot speak of it yet. I need to let certain people know about you and the talents you have. I have your address; do you have a telephone number and that of another contact?'

'Yes.' Tamar wrote their number on the pad he offered and added Elma's too.

'You may hear sometime in the future from the War Office. But then you may not. That's all I can say at the moment.'

Shocked, Tamar blurted out, 'If there is ever anything I can do, I will.'

'That's good to hear. Plans are in their infancy so don't wait by the telephone, just forget it for now. I just wanted you to know that I am putting your name forward. And I will contact you if any news comes in about your fiancé. Good day, Miss Blume.'

This sounded like a dismissal, but it was said with a smile and a nod, which took the edge off of it being a final command to leave and to ask no more questions.

Outside, the sun shone but held no heat. The sky looked full of snow in the distance and the clouds, white and heavy, were creeping towards her. Tamar pulled the astrakhan collar of her long black coat around her neck as she shivered against the icy wind, and the renewed pain inside her. Nothing was known of her beloved Isaac's fate.

Was that good news? Could anything be? The newspaper boards told of British troops training in the bitter weather in France. It would be even colder in Poland now, Tamar thought. She hoped Isaac was in a warm place.

Not ready to go home, she bought a paper and made for a cafe across the road.

The clatter of cutlery and the voices of the customers took her aback for a moment, but then, finding a table, she relaxed into it as she ordered a mint tea.

Her eyes feasted on a cream scone, but knowing it wouldn't be kosher, she resisted.

Laying her paper out and turning the pages, wanting to read updates of the war but simultaneously not wanting to, Tamar's eye caught the headline *What is it like for them now?*

Tamar recognized Danzig immediately, the city close to her home known as a free city. But she'd never seen what she now saw in front of her, as the photo was of Jewish shops with the word '*Jude*' painted across their windows in red paint.

As the story unfolded, she realized that this was before the invasion. She'd always known there was a large German population in Danzig but there hadn't been any trouble that she remembered. But now, she read that it had been dominated by the local Nazis for a while.

The article went on to say that the Nazi Brownshirts marched up and down the streets in formation, as did the Hitler Youth, with little daggers in their socks.

This news acted as a wake-up call to her. Her body shook – to Tamar, this screamed that things were much, much worse for her people now. Her eyes stung with unshed tears, as she asked herself the same question she'd asked herself a million times: *Why?*

Walking down the street towards Portland Street station, she thought about what Mr Kaminski had said about the possibility of her being of help to the War Office. She couldn't imagine how, unless it was as an interpreter, but whatever they asked of her she would be ready and would do anything she could to help Poland, and especially the Jewish people who had made it their home for centuries.

On the train going back to Spitalfields, Tamar felt lonelier than she ever had as she thought of Florence, soon to marry her Liam, and Papa, soon to marry Elma. But then, if Liam was accepted into the Medical Corps, Florence would be on her own too, and all wouldn't be so bad as they would have each other.

Pulling herself up, she chastised herself for this selfish thought. Poor Florence would then feel as wretched as she did and that was something she shouldn't wish for. Not this empty gulf inside her. No, she wouldn't want lovely Florence to suffer this.

'Are yer all right, luv? Only I thought I saw yer shed a tear. Just seen your young man off, eh?'

Tamar's cheeks reddened and she brushed away the tear she hadn't felt fall as she told this kindly stranger, 'He went at the beginning of the war – well, just before it – and . . . and I don't know if he's alive, or dead. He's just missing.'

'Ah, poor lad, and poor you,' the woman said. 'It ain't easy for them and it ain't easy for us. I've got three lads in France freezing their socks off, bless 'em. They're a pain in the backside when home, but I bleedin' miss 'em now. Me life seems empty.'

'Oh, I'm sorry.' Tamar smiled to herself. She should have added Cockney to her list of languages, as it was one on its own.

'What yer want to do, luv, is get into voluntary work. It gets yer to see 'ow others are suffering as much, if not more than you. And 'elping them 'elps you!'

'I've thought about it. We have a Jewish soup kitchen—'
'You're a Jew!'

Tamar's stomach muscles clenched as if ready to face danger.

'Ha! I wouldn't 'ave known. Not with them blue eyes and what we call mousy hair . . . and your delicate features . . .

Well, I mean, I ain't saying we Jews 'ave different features . . . well, some do. But you're dainty. Yes, you've got dainty chiselled features . . . Ha, I'm digging meself into an 'ole 'ere. It's like I'm saying we Jews usually 'ave big features . . . It's just that . . . you have the look of . . . Oh, I'm being daft, take no notice of me.'

'I know what you're referring to. My mama was German. She converted to Judaism to marry my papa, and I was always considered to look like her, though I do have Papa's nose.'

'It might turn out to be lucky for yer, luv – not being easily recognized, I mean. Might one day be a means of saving yer life.'

'You mean that I could deny my faith? I'd never do that. I'd rather die with my fellow Jews if that was to be my fate.'

'Brave words, but no one can make a difference if they're dead! You should live, even if it does mean denying who yer really are. If atrocities ever 'appen 'ere, you should do all yer can to stay alive, if only to bear witness to it.'

Tamar could see this logic, and it persuaded her. 'Let's hope it never happens; nothing has so far. But you're right, I should help where I can. I had thought of helping at the Jewish soup kitchen . . . Elma – that's my soon-to-be stepmother – donates vegetables from her shop and—'

'Elma Cohen? Soon to be Elma Brume? You must be David's daughter, Tamar! Well, I'm pleased to meet yer. Me and Elma 'ave been mates since we were nippers, and her sister Irene too. Ever since they came into our community when the Cohens adopted them – lovely couple. Couldn't 'ave kids, so gave a home to two from the orphanage. Never imposed their beliefs on them, though. Never forced them to convert – though always hoped they would. Irene did and now Elma is. Pity the Cohens didn't live to see it.'

This took Tamar aback. To learn so much from a stranger! But then, no Cockney was ever that, and this lady was travelling in the same direction and so would know people from Brick Lane.

'I'll see yer at the kitchen then, eh? I'm one of the cooks, but we need 'elp with preparing the food, serving it and cleaning up afterwards. You'd be very welcome, girl.'

'I could come after work, and on half-day closing on a Wednesday.'

'That's good. 'Ave yer made any friends other than Florence? Elma told me David's daughter had a good friend in Florence. She's a nice girl. Strong too. She don't let any of this nonsense about black people hurt her, she just ignores it. And look 'ow she fought back from almost being killed . . . Oh, I'm sorry . . . That were a bad time for you, I 'eard. Tragic. Them Mosley's lot want putting against a wall and shooting.'

Tamar thought that no one deserved that for their beliefs, even if you didn't agree with them. And that the world would be a better place if people were more tolerant. But she didn't say so as this lady didn't mean it, she would never carry out such an act – though the world was peopled by those who would – the hated Nazis.

'I ain't told yer me name yet, luv. I'm Rosie, Rosie Masters. I know, it ain't a Jewish name, but I'm like you, only it were me dad that converted to marry me ma.'

She giggled then. 'I suppose yer know about Ruben chasing Elma? She foiled him for years by refusing to convert – he must be livid that she agreed to the minute David came on the scene.'

Tamar didn't know why, but this made her giggle too, when she should feel sorry for Ruben, who was playing the spurned lover role to a tee.

'I don't feel a bit sorry for him. He's after anything in a skirt, and especially if they ain't likely to convert to Judaism. He only does it to cover for the fact that he really fancies them in trousers!'

Tamar's mouth dropped open.

'Don't look like that, luv. It goes on, though has to be done in secret and covered up or those who are like it could end up in prison, poor bleeders!'

Further shocked, Tamar thought about her cousin Ruben. She'd seen nothing that hinted at what Rosie was saying, and yet, if it meant he would go to prison if found out, she was glad she hadn't. But if Rosie knew, then how many others did?

And how come she was tolerant of something considered a terrible sin? But then, she was no different herself, as she would never condemn anyone for being who they wanted to be . . . But Cousin Ruben! *How didn't I know? And does Papa know? No, he can't as he was afraid of upsetting Ruben by declaring his love for Elma. But then, maybe that was for my benefit. Papa has always shielded me as best he can from anything he thinks I'm better not knowing about.*

'You've gone quiet. I'm sorry if I've shocked yer. I shouldn't 'ave said anything, Elma will kill me!'

'No, it's all right. I won't let on that I know. Anyway, what do I do to apply to help at the soup kitchen?'

'Just turn up, luv, and pitch in. Some poor souls ain't got two pennies to rub together. They spent all they had on getting here, and you'll be an 'elp with your languages too, as not all speak Yiddish, and their native tongue ain't English.'

This pleased Tamar. Ruben and Elma had mentioned it, but it hadn't got further than that. And yet, it was what she most wanted to do – teach English. Well, all the languages she knew.

Her dream had been to give this knowledge to children, but doing so for adults who were struggling to settle into their new life would more than make up for not having the chance to realize her dream of being a teacher.

The weeks seemed to sail by after this first encounter with Rosie. Tamar loved the work at the soup kitchen. Always there was a cheery atmosphere to combat the sadness of those suffering hardship. Many said to her that without this place they would starve and give up altogether.

Gradually, she found that she had two small classes going – one to teach English to French Jews and the other to German Jews. All were grateful and lovely moments came when they told her that because they would soon be able to communicate the skills they had to factory or shop owners, they would be able to find employment.

This warmed Tamar's heart. And on top of this, she so loved Rosie. It felt like she had lost one mama and gained two! Elma and Rosie. And with having two weddings to look forward to – Papa's and Florence's – a lot of her sadness and angst over Isaac became manageable. Except during the night. This was when she wet her pillow with tears, not knowing if she was crying for a never-to-be-seen-again Isaac or not. And she prayed too. Prayed that he was all right and would one day come home to her.

Papa's wedding was first. It had taken time for Elma to complete her conversion. Often she'd say, 'I wouldn't do this for anyone else, David. I ain't no young one to learn new things!'

But she coped well, having been brought up with the traditions and teachings. One thing she wouldn't give up – though it was kept a secret from everyone but Papa and

Tamar – was that she would always love her blessed Mary and continue to pray to her.

With the ceremony over Papa turned to Tamar and told her, 'May is our healing month and today completes my healing. Mama has a special place in my heart. She has healed that place now, and Elma has healed the rest of me.'

Tamar kissed his cheek. 'Be happy, Papa, and make Elma as happy as you made Mama.'

Patting her hand, he told her, 'One day you too will find happiness, my lovely Tamar. One day.'

The feeling of being bereft at him not coming back to the flat as usual was helped by this being the first night Florence would stay. All her things had been moved in earlier that morning and Papa's moved out.

Sadly, for Florence, this wasn't to be the temporary measure she'd thought it would be as what they'd come to look on as a non-war had escalated. Germany had crossed into France and British troops were being pushed back. Casualty figures were alarming, and hospital ships needed more manpower. This had led to Liam being accepted into the Medical Corps. He was to leave a few days after their wedding. They would spend these days honeymooning in a little cottage in Brighton that one of Liam's colleagues owned.

Florence and Tamar linked arms as they walked from Elma's home where the reception had taken place. Neither of them spoke until they got into the flat, then as they both flopped onto the sofa, Florence said, 'Well, I don't know about you, Tamar, but I'm whacked out!'

'Ha! You've no stamina!'

'What's all this dancing in circles about, and where do the older ones get their energy?'

'You mean the Hora? It's a traditional dance. I love it.'

'I did the first few times, but I flagged then . . . It was lovely, though, wasn't it – the whole thing, and the happiness that surrounded it all? But I could do with a cuppa now.'

'Let's sit out in the yard, eh? I love sitting on the bench Papa had installed out there and it's a lovely evening.'

'Sounds good, as long as I can find enough energy to get down there. But can we take a cuppa with us?'

'I can make us one in the little kitchen behind the shop . . . And then we can talk weddings.'

'Oh no. I've had it up to here with weddings.'

'What? Your own's only days away.'

'That's why! I've lived and breathed guest lists and so on. In letters, in telephone calls. The thirty-first of May is a day I am almost dreading! It's been turned into a fiasco!'

'Well, you have a week to get used to it.'

Crossing the room to the wireless, Tamar stopped in her tracks as a voice interrupted the music that had been playing.

'*France has fallen. British troops are stranded on the beach of Dunkirk. An operation to rescue them is being planned.*'

Neither of them spoke for a moment as the awful realization that with France now in the hands of the Germans, it wouldn't be too long before they crossed the Channel and tried to take Britain.

Scenarios of all kinds dominated their conversation as they made tea and took it out into the yard, but in the end, they concluded that there was nothing they could do but to carry on with their lives, and pray to their own versions of God to help all the servicemen and the rescuers.

It was late when they went to bed. To Tamar, it felt that this day had been spoiled by the news that had put a dampener on everything. And yet, she dug deep and managed to smile as she said goodnight to Florence, giving her a hug. 'I'm only in the room next door if you need me, love.'

Seeing Florence to bed like this hadn't been how it had been planned. She'd thought they'd go to their rooms laughing and hopeful for the future. But now, once more, as she closed her own bedroom door and leaned heavily on it, Tamar felt consumed by sadness and a feeling of utter despair that threatened to take her in its grip at not having Isaac by her side and thinking him dead. But she had to keep her mind focused on Isaac being alive or she would be lost.

How had their lives changed so drastically in the past three years? Even now, she often had a feeling of being disorientated – not living where she should, not being with Isaac and Hannah, studying, chatting, walking along the beach path, swimming in the sea, laughing and carefree. Now, the dream she had could never be fulfilled. There was no going back.

A few days later as Tamar stood just behind Liam and Florence, watching them take their vows, with Florence's father looking on proudly and her mum sniffling in the background, she knew all hope wasn't gone for the concept of different races and faiths coming together in harmony.

The church was full of African, Caribbean and British, all a mixture of Christians and, like herself, Jewish. They prayed together, they sang together – joyous songs accompanied by swaying, with their hands in the air. It was a happiness that lifted Tamar and she found herself joining in just as heartily, though not singing the praises of Jesus, just humming to the tunes. It felt like the most wonderful ceremony she'd ever been to.

Once the loving and happy couple had said 'I do' this all escalated as everyone clapped and cheered, then hushed as Liam held Florence's hands and looked into her eyes. His voice – a beautiful tenor – filled the air as he sang 'Love is the Sweetest Thing':

Love is the sweetest thing
What else on earth could ever bring
Such happiness to ev'rything
As Love's old story

Love is the strangest thing
No song of birds upon the wing
Shall in our hearts more sweetly sing
Than Love's old story

The congregation just swayed in silence as Liam's voice soared and his eyes never left Florence's.

Tears streamed down Tamar's face, but though hers were tearing at her heart, they weren't noticed as tears of sorrow as there wasn't a dry eye in the church.

Chapter Nine

They didn't have far to go for the reception, only into the church hall, which took Tamar's breath away as instead of the typical painted brick walls, every inch of wall and ceiling space had been hung with decorations. It looked like a fairyland. And to add to the magic, Florence and Liam hugged her to them as she entered.

When they released her, Tamar said a heartfelt, 'You look beautiful, Florence.'

Florence had chosen a long white gown in satin, with an embroidered, fitted bodice and a flowing skirt. Tiny daisies mounted on a coronet held her long veil in place. Her lovely skin shone, and her dark eyes sparkled with happiness.

'And so do you, my lovely. Lemon really suits you . . . Oh, Tamar, thank you for being my bridesmaid. I know it was against all you believe today, but having you there just made it extra special for me.'

Liam thanked her too, and as he hugged her, he whispered, 'Look after my Florence for me.'

'I will.'

His hug became tighter as his body heaved, but he swallowed

hard and pulled back, giving her a lovely, if teary, smile. She understood. Beneath the surface of all their smiles lay a heartache that would catch them unaware and could be triggered by a simple act, such as asking a friend to look after their new wife.

A lady who hadn't been at the service came in then carrying a casserole dish. Florence's mum greeted her with a hug and a kiss. Florence leaned forward. 'Here's your meal. That's the local rabbi's wife. She and Mum are great friends. She's cooked you your favourite, lamb supreme cholent.'

'That's so kind of her, and of your mum for thinking about me, thank you.'

'Mum's beckoning you.'

A feeling of acute embarrassment blushed over Tamar. Would the rabbi's wife be cross that she'd taken part in the wedding mass?

But the opposite happened. She hugged Tamar. 'My dear, I hear you have been, and still are, going through an ordeal because of our faith. The rabbi wanted me to pass his blessing on to you and to tell you he will be thinking of you.'

'Thank you.'

Tamar didn't trust herself to say any more. The rabbi's wife seemed to understand. 'Enjoy your cholent. I am known for cooking the best one ever!'

Although she smiled and nodded, Tamar thought that she'd better not repeat that to Elma!

There were tears as many came to the station to wave the happy couple off. Tamar took a deep breath as she witnessed Florence clinging to her mum – both crying. There were moments when she longed to do that with her own mama.

But then, without warning, a crowd of young men came

towards them. Fear tightened Tamar's throat as the leader shouted, 'No blacks in Britain!'

Within seconds of him yelling this, and with the men standing with him mimicking him, he suddenly clutched at his chest. His knees buckled.

As Liam, Florence and Florence's father rushed towards him, three of the huge, muscly men barred their way.

'We're doctors, and my wife is a nurse. Your friend needs help.'

'Doctors? Ha, you're nothing but scum!'

Liam remained calm. 'Look, you can beat us up and kick us to death if you want to but do it after we have saved your friend. He could die. He looks like he is having a heart attack!'

Another member of the crowd pushed the two men aside. 'Let them help my brother.'

One of the men still protested, 'But you can't let this scum touch him, Ben!'

'We have no choice! Get out of my way!'

As the men obeyed Ben's command, he turned away from them and bent over the prostrate man. 'Don't die! Alan . . . Please, don't die!'

Florence took him gently by his arm. 'Just move aside a moment, Ben, and let the doctors do what they can. You run to the stationmaster's office and get him to ring for an ambulance.' She turned then and faced the crowd of men. 'Stand back and give your brother air and allow the doctors to help him. As my husband says, you can beat us all up afterwards, but everyone's life is precious to us in the medical profession, and your brother will be cared for.'

All hung their heads. Florence had used the term 'brother' in the way her own community did. But the ruffians had responded. Their faces held shame.

When Ben returned, Tamar stepped forward. 'Are you all right? Did you get an ambulance on the way?'

He looked away. When he looked back at her, his face was awash with tears. She put her arms out to him, and he came into them. 'Me brother has a weak heart. I told him not to come – we were on our way to a rally when we saw all these blacks from the bridge.'

Ignoring this, Tamar said, 'Liam and his father-in-law are excellent doctors, and Florence is a wonderful nurse. They will do all they can.'

'You were with them?' This was said with disgust.

'I love all people, but being a Jew, I feel more hate directed at me than love. These are my friends. Today was Liam and Florence's wedding day. They only have a few days together then Liam leaves to join the Medical Corps on a hospital ship.'

'What? He's going to war?'

'Yes. Aren't you, Ben?'

'I – I failed the medical . . . So, you're a Jew? You don't look like one, nor do you sound British.'

'I'm Polish. I . . . Me and my fiancé escaped before the invasion. My fiancé went back to fight for his country.'

'They lost, though, didn't they, just as we're losing.'

'Oh, I thought you were a Nazi? I thought you'd rejoice in Hitler's victory over France? You're following his doctrine of persecuting anyone who isn't a white, Christian man.'

'No . . . I mean . . . Oh, I don't know. I just became convinced by what Mosley was saying that a lot of our problems were caused by the Jews and the blacks coming here and living off us.'

'Florence didn't come here; she was born here. Her ancestors were forcibly brought here centuries ago as slaves.'

Ben looked shocked.

'She's probably more British than you are, as by your appearance, blond hair and blue eyes, I would say your ancestors were Vikings! They came from the Nordic countries – Norway and Sweden – and stole land, killed the British men and raped the women. That probably happened to one of your great-great-grandmothers, and she was left carrying a baby.'

'I don't know what you're talking about.'

'It's all history . . . Ah, look, your brother is coming round. His life has been saved by those whose lives you want to take. I hope he continues to do well.'

Clanging bells interrupted them.

Florence came over. 'We're going to the hospital with him. Liam needs to hand over to the hospital staff – tell them what he has done so far, and how the sick man is responding.'

'But you will miss the train and then the connecting one to take you on your honeymoon!'

'That doesn't matter. It is more important that we save the life of this man. We know people at the Royal where he is to be taken; it's where I volunteered when I stayed with Mum and Dad. If we go with him, I can get him the right help more quickly than if he has to be assessed again.'

'Will he be all right, miss?'

'He will . . . You're his brother, aren't you? There's room in the ambulance and it will be good if you can come too. Your brother showed signs of fear when he opened his eyes and saw us. You can reassure him.'

Ben turned to Tamar. 'Will you come too? What's your name?'

'Tamar. Yes. But first tell your Nazi friends to leave my friends alone. Let them go home in peace. They've had a big day, a happy day. Don't let that end in tears for them or for them to be hurt.'

Ben shouted to the others in the menacing gang. 'Leave this lot alone and go on your way. One of them has saved Alan's life. It's the least we can do.'

As if it had been a command, the men turned and left.

'Did they all fail the medical?'

'They're farmers.'

Tamar wanted to say, *So they aren't fighting for their country, but feeding it, while creating an internal war in Britain!* But she felt she'd made a difference in some small way with Ben and one man changing his views might lead to others changing theirs.

Inside, the ambulance had been kitted out to carry many wounded, something Tamar hoped it would never be needed for but somehow feared it would.

She sat on the edge of one of the lower bunks next to Ben. He leaned forward and told his brother, 'You'll be all right now, Alan. These people have saved you. Them two are doctors and the lady is a nurse.'

Just out of shear cussedness, Tamar announced, 'And I'm a Jew!'

Alan's eyes opened wide in shock. He glared at his brother.

It was Florence's turn to have a dig. 'We could have just let you die!'

Liam calmed things. 'Sir, you are still in danger.' He turned and gave a cross look at her and Florence; both hung their heads in disgrace.

Liam spoke to Alan, 'Don't worry about what you perceive us to be. At the moment, we are your doctors, and my wife here is your nurse, and we will care for you.'

'Don't let me die, please, don't let me die.'

The desperate plea gave Tamar a feeling of shame. This wasn't the time to taunt a man for his beliefs. She whispered to Ben, 'I'm sorry. I shouldn't have spoken how I did.'

'Maybe you should. You've opened my eyes today to the bigotry we have been fed. I'll not be a Mosley follower from this moment on . . . I . . . well, me and my brother run a farm just outside of the city. We've neglected it of late – the work's too much for me and Alan can't help for long periods at a time. Most of our farmhands left us to go to war.'

'You should apply for Land Girls to help you. Everyone is singing their praises.'

Ben hung his head. 'We don't believe in women working . . . except for nurses, of course.'

'I'm glad I don't live in your world.' Tamar sighed.

'What do you do then?'

She told him how she worked with her father and taught languages – she didn't say this last was to Jewish men, thinking he'd had to accept a lot today that was alien to him.

When they reached the hospital, he asked, 'Where do you live?'

'I'm not telling you that, Ben. My people have had enough to contend with.'

'I – I didn't mean for that reason . . . It's just that you have a different way of looking at things. I live just outside Melton Mowbray – the farm's called Brackensfields. Me name's Bracken – Ben Bracken. If ever you're in Leicestershire again, drop in to visit. I've liked talking to you.'

'Thank you, Ben, that means a lot to me. I'll come in with you as you'll probably be sitting on your own for a while.'

For the next hour, they talked as if they would never stop as they sat on a hard-backed bench outside the emergency room, waiting for news.

They moved from subject to subject. Tamar told him of her life in Poland, and how they had escaped. She opened up about her pain of being separated from Isaac, and about him and how he lost his sister Hannah, and she ended up telling him where she lived as she came to trust him. Something she thought would never happen with a man who had held such views, but she believed him when he said he'd changed them and rejoiced in him saying, 'I can't apologize enough for how I've been and the harm I've caused. I don't know how me and me brother got involved and believed all Mosley said! And I promise you, I'll do all I can to persuade the others against his doctrine. We all belong to the Young Farmers Club. I can talk to them there.'

She told him how grateful she was and how small steps could make a difference, and he went on to tell her that he hadn't had a lot of schooling as he'd been put to work on the farm from a young age. But now, he was restless and wanted to go to war to fight for his country. However, it had been found that he had the same condition as his brother. 'It's something to do with the rhythm of our hearts. It misses a beat but can sometimes miss more and cause us to collapse. Me brother has regular blackouts. That hasn't happened to me yet and it scares me that it may, but we carry on as if it's not there.'

The sun came through the window high up on the corridor wall and caught a light in Ben's hair. It glinted in his eyes as he turned to her. 'I've never met anyone like you, Tamar. I'm sorry about your fiancé, I hope he just turns up out of the blue . . . Things aren't good for Jews in Poland. Does he look like a Jew?'

There it was again, an inference that her race looked a certain way.

'Only, you don't at all. I didn't guess.'

'Isaac looks like himself. His face reflects his gentle nature and his kindness. But yes. He will be recognized . . . I fear so much for him.'

Ben reached out and took her hand. 'He's a very lucky man. Just knowing you're waiting for him will bring him home.'

Tamar took her hand away. 'Thank you. Your friends can comfort you but when your enemy does, then it means such a lot.'

'I'm not your enemy, Tamar. Not any more – nor of that nurse, or the doctors and their family. I've seen how the hatred in me has caused harm. I'm ashamed, but I can change. Alan can too. I'll work on him.'

Tamar sat back. What a strange day this had been – being present at a Catholic nuptial mass, making friends with a Mosley follower. But stranger than all of that, and a minor miracle, making him see that people were just people.

When they called Ben in to his brother, Tamar felt strangely bereft of his company. She got up and walked along the long corridor. Once outside in the evening sunlight, she thought that maybe she would never see him again, but she wouldn't ever forget him.

During the next few months, life carried on. She and Florence saved each other from drowning in their sorrow, mostly through hard work, but by having fun too. Harmless fun – taking walks, sitting in the yard with Elma's homemade wine, chatting and giggling, and sometimes visiting the cinema, and for Tamar, helping at the Jewish soup kitchen.

Shortages became worse, leaving Elma struggling to get stock and to cope with the queues.

Business for the jewellery shop changed and didn't warrant them opening to street trade customers for more than a couple of hours a day. Papa, though, worked hard and long hours, making jewellery to order in his work room. The rich seemed to want to turn their wealth into necklaces, bracelets and brooches – though not the simple bracelets Tamar made, but those with precious jewels encrusted into them. They loved that they could make an appointment and design their own jewellery with Papa.

And so Tamar found herself helping Elma most days, as she was today.

''Ere, luv, weigh out them spuds, will yer? There's a sack of them in the back. Portion them into them brown bags – two pounds in weight in each.'

'But they're not rationed, are they?'

'No, but I ain't had a delivery and I 'ave to ration them a bit meself so that everyone gets a chance of some.'

Handling dirty potatoes was Tamar's second least favourite job in the shop, the least favourite being slicing the ham. She wasn't allowed to eat it and hated handling it, and the smell of it cooking, as Elma did that process herself – though she kept special saucepans for this purpose so as not to cook their kosher food in the same ones.

'Right, we're all done. Now to open the door before they all break in!'

Tamar grinned at the many faces pressed against the window. No one dare bang on it. Elma was a formidable being with her rolling pin in hand. She'd never hit anyone, but it served as a deterrent and kept the crowd in order.

'Two at a time! We can't serve more than that and there ain't room for more!'

A voice from the back shouted, 'Keep me some tea, Elma,

I ain't got any and I'm dying for a cuppa. Me ol' man will box me ears if I ain't got some tonight.'

The others all laughed.

Tamar was glad to hear they were all in good humour. But then, a small boy suddenly shot through the door and all hell let loose.

''Ere, you little devil, wait your turn.' Vera, a big buxom woman, grabbed him by the collar. 'I know you, yer Elsie Thomas's lad. What yer after, eh? A good tanning on your backside?'

'I'm sorry, Mrs Green, 'onest. But me mum's started her pains. I've to get her some Epsom salts as she don't want to be kept 'anging around. She's boiling the pan for a bath – yer don't want to get on the wrong side of 'er when she starts 'er pains, so I 'ave to be quick.'

'Well, go on then, lad, an Epsom salt bath does 'elp. But if she's got money for that, then she's got money for me services. Tell 'er I'll be round later.'

The lad asked for Epsom salts, but then asked for a pack of five fags as well.

Vera stepped nearer and snapped them up off the counter.

'She can't afford them as well. She needs me, and she needs to pay me. She never did for the last one!'

Tamar whipped the packet from Vera's grasp. Vera's mouth dropped open, but before she could say anything, Tamar spoke firmly. 'Please leave the boy alone. Here, take them. Your mum probably needs them more than the Epsom salts.'

Her thoughts were that the boy's mother would be desperate for them if this woman delivered her baby!

The crowd began to shift and complain. Tamar stiffened. Suddenly there was a surge forward. Vera nearly lost her balance. She turned and began to clobber anyone she could reach.

Elma skirted around the counter, rolling pin held high. 'Out! Out, the lot of yer! And especially you, Vera Green. You're a troublemaker!'

Vera stepped back.

'Now, listen to me, the lot of yer. If yer come inside two at a time, you'll all get served. Yer know me policy – a little of everything I've got to each of yer while there's shortages.'

'And it's a fair way of doing it.' Ivy, a little woman, stepped forward. Undeterred by the hugeness of Vera, she said in a firm voice, 'You go first, Vera. With you gone there'll be some order about all of this.'

Vera hmphed but gave her order and left with what she'd been allowed to buy. No one noticed the boy slip away with his purchases. But Tamar was glad to see him running past the window and on his way without any more harassment from Vera.

When the queue finally ended, a peace settled over the shop. Elma grinned. 'Well, that went well!'

'It did. Your rolling pin works wonders!'

They both laughed, then Elma suddenly put her arms out to Tamar. 'Let me give yer a hug, luv.'

In Elma's arms, and feeling the love that she had for her, Tamar had to swallow hard to rid her throat of the lump that threatened to bring the tears once more. They were for the night hours, when alone, not to dampen everyone's lives around her.

'You're going through a lot, luv, but we're all 'ere for yer, you know.'

'I do know, thanks, Elma.'

'I love yer, Tamar. You're the daughter I never had.'

'And you're the best stand-in I could have for my mama. She would have loved you.'

A tear plopped onto Tamar's hair. 'Ta, luv, that warms me heart.'

They were quiet for a moment, just holding each other and giving love. But then Elma came back to herself. 'Well, this won't get anything done, luv. We've to get the deliveries ready. Joe'll be here soon with his bike ready to take them out.'

'Are there many? Only, I'd like to pop along to see if Papa's all right. He forgets to even make himself a drink!'

'No, I'll manage. You go and see to him and tell him I send him a kiss.'

'Ha, you lovebirds!'

Elma giggled like a young girl, which made Tamar blush more than her remark had. Elma had brightened their lives and made settling into a strange country easier than it could have been.

But as she went to leave, the sound of the warning siren made them giggle more and lift up their eyebrows in exasperation.

'They keep testing that blooming thing – it gets on your nerves. See you for your dinner later, luv.'

With this, Elma disappeared inside, but what she'd said about loving her like a daughter came back to Tamar. It lifted her heart and made her do a little skip.

But then her body stiffened as the sound of approaching aircraft filled the air, taking her thoughts from her as fear consumed her.

The sky darkened as the huge, low planes blocked out the late evening sun then plunged her into a zinging world as huge explosions deafened her. A force thrust her off her feet. Her body flew through the air and landed heavily in the middle of the road. Bricks rained down around her; some hitting her legs, bruising and cutting her skin. But still, amid the screams, the choking dust and smoke, more blasts took the world she'd known and turned it into a heap of black dust, raging fires, and cries for help.

Getting up, Tamar wobbled on her legs. She looked around her and tried to swallow but had no spittle as dust coated her mouth. The sound of a car horn, as if a long way away, penetrated the deadly rumble of aircraft.

Turning, Tamar saw a car had swerved into the window of the baker's shop.

Strewn around her, unmoving bodies lay twisted and broken, some without limbs.

But the near-silent world she'd been plunged into disorientated her and made her accept the horror of it all without reacting.

Groping, she got to the broken walls of the buildings and clung on to what was left as she slowly made her way to her papa's shop – only to find a heap of smouldering rubble, hideously tangled with twisted machinery, sparkling diamonds and gold. *But . . . my papa! Papa, where are you?*

This anguished thought became a holler of pain. 'Papa . . . Papa!'

Chapter Ten

Exhausted from the incessant bombing that didn't cease till 4 a.m., Tamar stared down at her papa's body the next day. Mangled and broken, he lay on the slab of the mortuary amid what looked like hundreds of other burned, charred and limbless dead people.

The rabbi's voice chanted prayers over Papa as the undertakers lifted him and placed him in a coffin.

The beloved face that had been part of her whole life looked the same, except for the expression of shock.

Tamar stepped forward, bent over the coffin and kissed him. 'Oh, Papa.'

The arms of the three people she knew she had left in the world came around her. Both Elma and Florence were sobbing. Ruben looked broken.

The rabbi's gentle voice told her, 'My child, your papa is with Elohim now.'

Florence turned her away while Elma stepped forward. Her sobs were audible as she said goodbye and thanked Papa for the happiness that he'd brought her. Then Ruben took hold of the three of them and they huddled into him.

'I'll take care of you all.'

Once the burial was over, Tamar allowed Ruben to steer her away from the graveside and made no protest as he hailed a taxi. 'Go to the soup kitchen and get something warm to eat. I'm going to see to a few things, I'll come for you later.'

The sound of the taxi door slamming shut gave a finality to it all for Tamar. She was leaving Papa behind for ever.

'How am I to bear it?'

'We will 'elp yer, Tamar, luv, and we'll all 'elp each other. Let's see what Ruben says he will do for us, eh?'

Tamar nodded towards Elma, and knew she was trying to be brave but was probably feeling as frightened and lost as she did – and just as sad.

Trying to relax back in her seat, this thought brought home to her what she hadn't considered since the awful air raid that had changed her life the evening before. Shifting a little to ease the aching of her bones from having spent the rest of the night in the crypt of Christ Church, sheltering from the barrage of bombs, Tamar asked, 'Has your shop gone, Elma?'

'Not gone, but damaged badly. And folk who came into the crypt later than us said that looters were 'aving a field day, so no doubt there'll be nothing left.'

'Oh, Elma, what will you do?'

'I'll sort things. Them looters wouldn't 'ave got all me takings. I grabbed the bag with the notes in and it's in the lining of me coat. I shoved it there through an 'ole in me pocket. I only left the copper and silver change in me till. And I've always banked regularly, so I can start again, we'll just 'ave to see.'

Tamar marvelled at this. How could anyone think of starting again after their life had been torn to shreds? She would never make another piece of jewellery as long as she lived!

'You're a proper East Ender, Elma. Nothing can keep you down for long,' Tamar told her.

'I don't know, luv. It'll take something to 'elp me get over losing David. He were the love of me life.'

Still, none of them cried, they just stared out of the window.

As soon as they walked into the soup kitchen, bedlam hit them as it seemed that hundreds of people – most bandaged, bruised and bleeding from open wounds – had made their way there. Above it all a voice could be heard: 'Elma! Tamar! Oh, thank goodness.'

Rosie came towards them with her arms in the air, one of them brandishing a dripping soup ladle.

Then they were in a huddle, and at last, Tamar felt the relief of tears streaming down her face.

Rosie let go of the others and held her close. 'I 'eard, luv. I'm sorry . . . And oh, Elma, your lovely 'ubby.'

'Don't give me sympathy, Rosie, luv. I need to keep strong for Tamar.'

'Right, well, there's hot soup on the go. Let's get yer fed, eh? And it's lovely to see you safe as well, Florence, luv. And yer very welcome.'

Eating was the last thing on Tamar's mind, but she followed Rosie through the crowd.

'Shift up, Raphael, make room for others.'

The gentleman Rosie had spoken to slid along the bench leaving enough space for the three of them to just fit on, with Elma's bulk leaving them a little squashed. But Tamar didn't mind. She needed to be close to Elma and to Florence. They were like the beams of a ceiling, holding her up.

Ruben came for them two hours later. Tamar had never been so pleased to see him. She flung herself at him. He was a family link to her papa. Someone who had known him all his life – as a boy, growing up, meeting and marrying Mama, and then welcoming him to Britain as a little bit of home for him to come to in a strange land.

Ruben's face showed the signs of his tears. Tamar wanted to reach out to him as she sensed a vulnerable man – one who had maybe used bravado to cover his real self.

Thinking this possible, she told him, 'We'll get each other through this, Ruben.'

'You're all I have, Tamar. I will take care of you and look after your affairs. I am an executor of your papa's will; you won't be alone and have plenty of money to see you through. I'll make sure your allowance from your papa's estate is very generous.'

This grated on Tamar.

'That's not what's important, Ruben. Taking care of someone as a person is. I've seen how low in their standing and in their spirit the regulars here in the soup kitchen become because they lack wealth, which they think is so important to our community. You have that wealth and you should give more to the poor – jobs, your cast-off clothes, decent housing, instead of those hovels you rent to them . . . I'm sorry . . . now isn't the time.'

'Maybe it is, my dear. Losing David has made me look at myself. What I have in wealth is quadruple and more to what he had, and yet what he had in life makes me a lonely man and riches cannot compensate for that. I should have a wife and children, but I chased many women and gave my love but denied it, as I craved money. I craved riches more than family life and happiness. You will be my centre of devotion. For you, I will do all the things you ask. I'll do up the hovels into decent living accommodation. I'll find employment for my fellow Jews – invest in the talents they have so they can open businesses. I'll donate to this place. And I'll ask the woman that I truly love to marry me. And together, we will take you as our daughter.'

'That all sounds wonderful, Ruben, and to have you look out for me would be too, but I cannot look on who you marry as a mama to me as I am Elma's stepdaughter, and she is already a mama to me. I like you as my cousin, it is how things have always been.'

He hugged her to him once more. This was a different Ruben, a humble Ruben, and though her heart was broken, Tamar could see that some good would come out of her father's passing. Many would find they had better housing and could earn money so they could look after their families. But a part of her felt sad as she remembered what Rosie had hinted at about Ruben's true self and hoped he would find happiness with the woman he talked of.

Ruben took them to an apartment on Mile End Road, telling them they could stay there rent-free for as long as they needed to. Though sparsely furnished, with one sofa, a rug, a sideboard and a small table with only two chairs at one end, and a sink, cooker and pantry at the other, it was clean and warm.

Besides this, there were two bedrooms and a bathroom.

'It's just temporary. I'll check your place out tomorrow, Elma, and see what needs doing. And by the way, the nearest shelter is the tube station, but there's a cellar here. It's through the door behind the entrance.'

'Well, we'll be sleeping down there no doubt. And, Ruben, ta. This is good of yer. But will yer pick me up tomorrow and take me to me shop? I need to see it for meself.'

'I will, Elma . . . May I hug you? I can see the pain on your face and in your brave heart.'

Elma surprised Tamar by almost collapsing onto Ruben. He held her firmly and yet in a gentle manner. 'I'm here for you, Elma. Can you forget all that nonsense I put you through?'

'Of course I can, yer daft sod! I knew if I ever said yes, you'd run a mile. I came close to doing it, just to get rid of yer, but I'm glad I didn't.'

They both laughed, and Tamar thought it was funny how you could do so even though your heart was broken.

Florence, who hadn't spoken much, asked, 'Would you help me to get to the hospital, please, Ruben? I want to go into work; they'll be inundated and need all hands to turn in to help.'

'I'll take you straight away, Florence, and I'll come back for you and Tamar in the morning, Elma.'

Florence turned to Tamar. 'I've been worrying that I might be needed. I know I'm on a three-day break, but those massive raids will mean the casualties could be in their thousands. Will you be all right, love?'

'I will, Florence. You get going. Take a spare key – there's two on the bunch – and then if you're late back, you can let yourself in. Just in case we're in the cellar.'

Florence hugged her. 'Be safe, Tamar, and look after Elma. No heroics. I may not come back tonight, so stay in that cellar till morning, eh?'

'I promise . . . Well, if the siren goes off, that's where I'll go like a shot!'

After hugging Elma, Florence left with Ruben.

Tamar looked over at Elma. She saw her lean heavily on the back of the sofa and knew she'd been keeping strong for everyone, but now with it being just the two of them, that strength was ebbing from her.

Rushing to her side, Tamar held her. They clung together and cried, till their hearts were empty of tears.

By midnight, it felt as though they'd been transported to hell. The cellar walls didn't blank out the sounds of crashing bombs, collapsing buildings and ducking and diving aeroplanes – every minute seemed like it would be their last.

'I have to go and see if I can help.'

'No, Tamar, luv, you'll only be another worry for those assigned to carry out rescues. Besides, I'd be scared stiff for yer.'

Tamar felt more than glad to agree as it had been a gesture and nothing more. She was terrified of going outside ever again!

Later the following morning, after a breakfast of porridge which had been among the few foods Ruben had dropped off earlier from his own pantry, promising to come back in an hour, Elma admitted, 'Part of me don't want to go back, but the other part can't wait to see the damage and what's left of me business.'

'I know. I feel the same. Seeing Papa's shop and mine and Florence's homes in ruins – probably still burning, or a burned-out pile of rubble – will be painful, but if we don't do it, we'll never be able to face anything that may be in store.'

'Yes. And I 'ave a feeling that's a lot!'

On the journey to Brick Lane, Tamar's stomach muscles gripped her, giving her the urge to scream out that she didn't want to go, but she forced herself – she had to do this.

As the rubble that was the shop came into sight, a figure could be seen standing with his foot against the wall of the shop next door, which had suffered some damage, but miraculously not complete destruction.

When Ruben's car pulled up, Tamar gasped. 'Ben! What on earth . . . ?'

'Who's Ben when he's at home, luv?'

Thinking this a funny saying, but getting the gist of it, Tamar said, 'He was one of the mob that were going to attack us on the station in Leicester. Ben's the one whose brother collapsed.'

'Oh, he is, is he? Well, he needn't bleedin' well come around 'ere starting his games. I wished I 'ad me rolling pin, I'd soon get him running down the road as fast as his legs will take 'im.'

'It's all right, Elma. Ben realized the error of his ways and decided he would leave Mosley's lot and persuade his friends to as well. Give him a chance, love.'

'But what's he doing 'ere then?'

'We'll ask him, eh?'

As they got out of the car, Ben rushed at her. 'Tamar! Oh, Tamar, you're safe!'

'Safe, but very afraid and . . . I – I lost my papa . . . and – and my mama too . . . I – I mean, all I had of her . . . her photos . . .'

With saying the words, her voice broke and her tears once more spilled over. Ben took hold of her and held her to him.

It was a strange, and yet welcome feeling, being in his arms. She didn't resist.

It was a meaningful cough from Ruben that parted them. 'I'm Tamar's cousin and her guardian now, young man, and you are?'

'Benjamin, known as Ben, sir. I'm a farmer from Leicestershire. Tamar and I met on the station. I – I was very misguided then, but I've changed. I heard about the bombing of this street and came at once to see if Tamar was all right.'

'That's good of you to travel all this way. I take it that truck is yours?'

'Yes. I had petrol stored in a barn, so brought a couple of cans and had enough to get here and to get me back.'

'I wouldn't mind a bit of it if you can spare it.'

Tamar had to smile. Ruben never missed a trick.

'Well, yer can sort that among yerselves. I'm going to me shop,' Elma told them, her voice steady and determined, but as soon as she was in full view of it, an anguished cry came from her. They all ran to her side. The reason for her distress was clear to see. The windows were blown out, and the shop was empty – not a morsel left on the shelves. And nothing in the back room, which they had full view of as the inner wall had collapsed.

'Oh, Elma, I'm sorry.'

'The bleedin' thieving lot! I didn't think it would be as bad as this!'

'It won't have been your regulars, Elma,' Ruben told her. 'I came down here after I left you and there were gangs of looters going from street to street. The police kept trying to chase them off, but they threw bricks at them. It was chaos. I didn't stay long . . . I should have told you – warned you as to the extent of it all . . . I'm sorry.'

Elma sighed. 'Me life's work!'

Tamar didn't feel strong enough to go to her so was glad when Ben did.

'I'll help you clear up, missus. I can spare a couple of days before we start to harvest the spuds – it's our only crop this year as things 'ave been bad for us.'

He turned to Tamar. 'I took your advice, though, and applied for Land Girls. We should get a couple soon, so then we can start to pull our weight and produce more to help with the shortages.'

'That's good. How's your brother? Did he recover?'

'He did, but he's weaker than ever. So, it's vital I get those girls.'

Tamar felt strangely shy of him, which contradicted how they'd bonded at the hospital, but it was such a weird experience having him here and his visit being prompted by his concern for her.

She was grateful when Elma said, 'Well, I'm going in. I want to see how much of me flat's intact.'

None of the back of the building, or the flat, were damaged. It all seemed to be confined to the front, with the window blowing out and the looters making off with all Elma had – even the slicing machine for her cooked meats and her cooker from the back kitchen.

'Look, Elma, you can't come back here. Stay in the flat on Mile End till I can sort something out that's better for you.'

'No. This is me 'ome, Ruben. And folk around 'ere are me folk. I'm coming back.'

It was Ruben's turn to sigh. 'Well, in that case, I'll get someone around to fix that window and get the inside of the shop sorted out with new shelves and a lick of whitewash.

And I know where I can get a cooker and get it fitted for you. But I wish you'd listen to reason!'

'Ta, Ruben, mate. I can pay yer. It'll just be a matter of getting stock, and that ain't going to be easy. But I'll be up and running soon, you'll see.'

With the grin she had on her face, Tamar thought that the East Ender spirit she'd heard about and seen so much of was personified in Elma. Nothing could ever daunt her.

Ben moved closer to her, and Tamar found it surprisingly comforting to have him by her side. She looked up at him and smiled. 'Thank you for coming. It means so much after the way we met. You'll need digs if you're staying a few days. I'll ask Ruben . . .'

'No need for that!' Elma put in. 'He can stay 'ere, as I'm moving back in, and I'm 'oping you and Florence'll stay with me too.'

Ben nodded. 'If that's all right with you all, I'd be glad to stay.'

'Well, I suppose I'd better get something sorted as quickly as I can then.' Ruben looked resigned, but not happy. 'I'll get one of my men here to do the repairs first. It won't be a window, though. They'll have to board the gap up for you, but they could get it shipshape in a couple of days.'

'Will you come back for me later, Ruben?' asked Tamar. 'I'll go with you to tell Florence and to bring her back here.'

Ruben shook his head. 'I will, but I'm not happy, my dear.' With this he waved to them all, got back into his car and drove off.

Shyness washed back over Tamar as she and Elma were left with Ben. But he just grinned and said, 'Well, let's make a start. Get me a bucket and I'll pick up what rubble I can.

There's some blokes with trucks, and everyone's throwing their rubbish onto them, so we may as well do that.'

Before long, being with Ben seemed natural again as they worked together to clear the rubble, while others in the street did the same to their own properties, calling out to one another and keeping a sense of humour going.

Suddenly, nothing seemed daunting as these strong and funny people of the East End lifted her spirits and Tamar thought she could cope with anything.

he'd thought, but he could be a different person in the future.

With this thought, she felt herself warming to him again and grinned back.

Within minutes of Ben blocking out the window, the sound of an explosion and the building shuddering filled her with terror. She looked from Ben to Elma. Seeing Elma frozen to the spot spurred Tamar forward. She and Elma clung on to one another.

'Hey, come on now, you two, we're safe down here,' Ben told them. 'We just need something to block out the noise. Have you got a wireless, Elma?'

'Only upstairs. I don't think we'd get a signal down 'ere, Ben.'

Ben looked around. There was something in the corner near to the stairs that caught his eye. 'Is that a piano under that sheet?'

'It is. It belonged to me ol' mum – well, she were me adopted mum, but me and me sister couldn't 'ave loved her more if she'd given birth to us. She taught me 'ow to play, but I ain't done so for a long time.'

Ben surprised them then. 'I can play – mostly classical stuff. Me dad, though a farmer, was a very talented musician. He saw to it that me and me brother had lessons. I took to it, but me brother didn't, though he loves to listen to me playing in the evenings. It calms him.'

This last sentence, and what she'd experienced at the hospital with how concerned Ben was for his brother, showed her that the two men were very close.

'I'll take a look at it. It'll want tuning, no doubt, and for that I'll need some kind of thin rod as I doubt you'll have a tuning fork, but I can do it by ear if need be.'

'Well, I don't think I 'ave anything like a tuning fork, so you may 'ave to do it by ear. But while yer do, me and Tamar'll make a cuppa and prepare dinner.'

Preparing dinner was something Tamar didn't have a clue how they were going to do!

But she soon learned that in a cupboard that stood against the wall under the window was an array of jars holding preserves, from green beans to peas and carrots and fruits – rhubarb, plums and pears. Getting dinner suddenly seemed like something they could do, and half an hour later they sat down, she and Elma on the armchairs and Ben on the piano stool, with plates on their knees filled with fried corned beef, handmade by Elma to make sure it was kosher, and put down here a couple of days ago, just in case, accompanied by peas and carrots and rounded off with a bowl of delicious pears. All to the terrifying backdrop of bombs, shouts, screams and the shaking of the building above them.

Trying to ignore it all was difficult, but somehow they did and chatted along as if everything was normal.

'Now, ladies, I'm ready, so I'll play for you.'

To Tamar, everything seemed surreal as Ben – a farmer with work-worn hands and a ruddy, outdoor complexion – suddenly turned into Ben the musician, producing beautiful music that soothed their nerves and made the world seem right.

'Do you sing, Tamar?'

Tamar laughed nervously, but then thought, *Why not?*

'Do you know a song called "The Three Letters"?' she asked.

'I think so . . .' Ben played a few bars. The music relaxed her and took her to a time that she and Hannah had sung this song. She wanted to sing it just as they did in Polish where it was called '*Trzy Listy*'.

There was a silence when she finished and then both Ben and Elma burst into loud clapping. Blushing, Tamar laughed as Elma said, 'I didn't understand a bloomin' word, but it was beautiful, me little darlin'.'

'Oh, it's about a man who has double-crossed his lady friend. She is singing about the letters she sent to him.'

'Well, he wouldn't get any bleedin' letters from me! But that apart, it was lovely to 'ear the language my dear David often used . . . Oh, I'm sorry . . .'

'Don't be. Papa wouldn't want us not to talk of him, or remember the things he did or said. He always kept Mama alive for me, and he would want the same for himself. He told me recently that you had given him back the life that left him when Mama died, and that he loved you very much.'

Elma dabbed her eyes. 'We had each other for such a short time, but it was the best time of me life.'

Tamar went to hug her, but Ben said, 'Now, now, let me play something lively, and let us celebrate a man who sounds like he was a wonderful person.' With this, he played 'Puttin' on the Ritz'.

The music lifted them all once more. Tamar surprised herself by wanting to dance. She got hold of Elma's hands and did a little jig with her. They ended up howling with laughter.

As the evening progressed, the thought of sleeping down here with Ben being in the same room made Tamar cringe with embarrassment, as did the thought of using the bucket that Elma had put behind a screen in the other half of the cellar, divided off by the stairs coming down in the centre of the room.

When eventually she had to steel herself to go, Tamar found one of her dressing gowns hanging on a hook behind the same screen, with one of Florence's and one of her papa's beside one she knew would be Elma's.

Taking the opportunity, she took off her day clothes and slipped the gown on – better that she did this first, then Ben wouldn't feel so awkward when she told him he could use Papa's.

Once they were ready for bed, wrapped up in the cosy dressing gowns, which Tamar knew only covered Ben's vest and long johns as she could see a peek of both, and Elma had discarded her corset, as her breasts now hung on her waist, they set about making the beds.

Tamar was glad when Elma said, 'Ben, you take yours to the other side of the chairs. Then that gives yer a bit of privacy, and us too.'

She hadn't wanted his mattress next to hers.

When finally all was quiet, Tamar thought of her Isaac. As always, she wondered where he was – was he still alive? Was he a prisoner? Or was he maybe helping the resistance if his friends had managed to get a group established? And, as always, her heart ached with the pain of missing him. She drifted off to sleep with Elma's gentle snores in her ears, and Isaac's smiling face in her heart.

The next day brought relief as they ascended the stairs and opened the shop door and found that there had been no further damage in their street, but passers-by told of how heavily the docks had been hit and the surrounding houses.

It was as they ate their breakfast of hot porridge in Elma's kitchen that the door opened and Florence came through it.

Tamar jumped up and ran to her. 'Oh, Florence, you look exhausted.'

Florence burst into tears.

Elma was by their side in a flash, and all three hugged till Florence calmed down.

'It's dreadful! The injuries, the deaths, the destruction . . .'

'Oh, Florence, love. You need to rest. You've been through so much.'

'Yes, luv, Tamar is right. We'll put the pots on the stove and heat water for you as the boiler ain't lit yet. Then yer can 'ave a nice bath and soak a while.'

'Ta, Elma, that would be lovely. I've been told I'm not to go in today at all and to have a night's sleep, so I'll just rest a while, then I'll help out here. I see you've achieved a lot already!'

'We have. We're shelf stacking today as me orders come in, then business as usual tomorrow.'

'And where the hell did you come from, Ben? Nice to see you again.'

'Thanks for saying that, Florence. I thought you would hate me. I came when I heard about the bombing. I've to go home today, though. Me brother'll be missing me.'

'Well, I'll say "hello and goodbye" now, as I just need to get upstairs to the flat . . . I take it that's where me and you are going to be living, Tamar?'

'Yes, partly. I mean, if the raids continue, then we'll spend most nights in the cellar as we did last night . . . Ha, your face says what I thought! But you'll be pleasantly surprised. We have all the home comforts down there and it's cosy and warm once the stove gets going.'

It was evening as Tamar stood on the pavement ready to wave Ben goodbye, with Florence asleep upstairs and Elma, having said her goodbyes, busy sweeping up rubble from the shop floor.

Ben shocked her when he said, 'May I hug you, Tamar?

I – I want you to know that I am your friend. I'll always be there for you. You have my telephone number; you can ring whenever you need to – or just to say hello. Will you mind if I check up on you from time to time by phoning you?'

'That will be fine. I'd like to know if you and your brother are all right.'

'And the hug?'

His grin made the request harmless. She went into his open arms. When he whispered, 'How I wish you weren't spoken for,' it shocked her, but then he turned abruptly from her, opened his truck door and got inside. With the engine rumbling into life, he wound down his window. 'I'll write and phone occasionally.' And then he lifted his hand in a wave and was gone.

Tamar stared at the empty space his truck had occupied and felt relief that he was gone. His presence unsettled her. She didn't know why, but now his memory would too, as what he had said suggested that he was in love with her. She didn't want that.

But as soon as she stepped back into the shop the feeling he'd left her with vanished as Elma called, 'There's been a Mr Kaminski on the phone. He says he needs yer to phone back, luv. Only, I didn't want to disturb you and Ben.'

Tamar blushed, but then as she took in who Elma had said had phoned, her heart skipped a beat. She stared at Elma.

'Are yer all right, luv?'

'I – I don't know . . . He's from the embassy – the Polish embassy . . . Oh, Elma, what if it's about Isaac?'

'Well, you won't know till you ring, me darlin'. And don't always think the worst. They may 'ave good news for yer. This might be the day both you and Florence receive good news as there's a letter come for her from Liam. She took it into the yard out the back.'

Tamar could only nod. A feeling of foreboding had settled in her. She just needed to make the call. She didn't want Elma to cheer her or make light of everything. Not at this moment. Her head was a swirl of what might be.

With trembling hands, she lifted the receiver and dialled the number Elma had handed to her on a piece of paper.

'Good evening, Kaminski here.'

Tamar swallowed hard. 'Good evening, it's Tamar Brume . . . I'm returning your call.'

'Ah, thank you for ringing back. I need you to come in as soon as possible to see me.'

'Is – is it Isaac?'

'Isaac? Oh, yes, your fiancé . . . I believe there is news of him. Hold on a moment.'

The moment seemed eternal.

'Ah, yes . . . Look, I must see you as a matter of urgency. I will update you on your fiancé when you come in. I want you to report first thing tomorrow, nine a.m. on the dot. Ask for me. You will be shown into my office immediately. Don't tell anyone where you are going. Make something up.'

'But Elma – the lady who took the call – will ask me . . . I – I've already told her you're from the Polish embassy!'

'Tell her you were mistaken. That you misheard the name, and it was your dentist or something. Anything, but keep it top secret that you're visiting me. I'll say goodbye now.'

With this the phone went dead.

Elma came back into the shop where her telephone stood on the counter.

'Is everything all right, me darlin'?'

Tamar turned, forced a smile on her face and sighed with pretend relief. Her hand went to her breast. 'Yes! Silly me, I mixed up the names. That was my dentist. He has an appointment free and realized he hadn't seen me for ages, and I have that dodgy tooth . . . You know, the one that makes me screw my face up if anything hot or cold hits it.' She gave a little laugh. 'Not that I'll let him take it out, even if that's the only cure! I don't want to be left with a gap!'

'Phew, yer 'ad me worried there.'

'And me. Their names are very similar and the only reason the man from the embassy would call is to give me information about Isaac. I'm not sure I want that. I'd rather be as I am, as no news is good news.'

'Yes, that's true. Yer know, yer'd never know you weren't British, with 'ow yer use all our sayings. Even your accent is changing, and you sound more like a posh-bod than a foreigner.'

This pleased Tamar. She made herself grin at Elma. It was good to hear as she'd been working hard on losing her accent. It always marked her as different and threw up a lot of questions that she didn't always want to address.

'Anyway, luv, dinner won't be long . . . Oh, and I forgot, Rosie called earlier while you were out the back. She couldn't stay but she dropped off a bag full of clothes for you and Florence to look through. They might 'elp until yer can get to the shops. I took them upstairs for yer.'

'Oh, that's very kind, and much needed! I feel as though I must stink. I've been in the same things, just washing my undergarments overnight, since . . . Anyway, I don't care what they're like, or where they came from, I'm wearing them, even if they don't fit!'

'That's the spirit – needs must, eh?'

'I – I want you to know that I am your friend. I'll always be there for you. You have my telephone number; you can ring whenever you need to – or just to say hello. Will you mind if I check up on you from time to time by phoning you?'

'That will be fine. I'd like to know if you and your brother are all right.'

'And the hug?'

His grin made the request harmless. She went into his open arms. When he whispered, 'How I wish you weren't spoken for,' it shocked her, but then he turned abruptly from her, opened his truck door and got inside. With the engine rumbling into life, he wound down his window. 'I'll write and phone occasionally.' And then he lifted his hand in a wave and was gone.

Tamar stared at the empty space his truck had occupied and felt relief that he was gone. His presence unsettled her. She didn't know why, but now his memory would too, as what he had said suggested that he was in love with her. She didn't want that.

But as soon as she stepped back into the shop the feeling he'd left her with vanished as Elma called, 'There's been a Mr Kaminski on the phone. He says he needs yer to phone back, luv. Only, I didn't want to disturb you and Ben.'

Tamar blushed, but then as she took in who Elma had said had phoned, her heart skipped a beat. She stared at Elma.

'Are yer all right, luv?'

'I – I don't know . . . He's from the embassy – the Polish embassy . . . Oh, Elma, what if it's about Isaac?'

'Well, you won't know till you ring, me darlin'. And don't always think the worst. They may 'ave good news for yer. This might be the day both you and Florence receive good

Elma was by their side in a flash, and all three hugged till Florence calmed down.

'It's dreadful! The injuries, the deaths, the destruction . . .'

'Oh, Florence, love. You need to rest. You've been through so much.'

'Yes, luv, Tamar is right. We'll put the pots on the stove and heat water for you as the boiler ain't lit yet. Then yer can 'ave a nice bath and soak a while.'

'Ta, Elma, that would be lovely. I've been told I'm not to go in today at all and to have a night's sleep, so I'll just rest a while, then I'll help out here. I see you've achieved a lot already!'

'We have. We're shelf stacking today as me orders come in, then business as usual tomorrow.'

'And where the hell did you come from, Ben? Nice to see you again.'

'Thanks for saying that, Florence. I thought you would hate me. I came when I heard about the bombing. I've to go home today, though. Me brother'll be missing me.'

'Well, I'll say "hello and goodbye" now, as I just need to get upstairs to the flat . . . I take it that's where me and you are going to be living, Tamar?'

'Yes, partly. I mean, if the raids continue, then we'll spend most nights in the cellar as we did last night . . . Ha, your face says what I thought! But you'll be pleasantly surprised. We have all the home comforts down there and it's cosy and warm once the stove gets going.'

It was evening as Tamar stood on the pavement ready to wave Ben goodbye, with Florence asleep upstairs and Elma, having said her goodbyes, busy sweeping up rubble from the shop floor.

Ben shocked her when he said, 'May I hug you, Tamar?

the same screen, with one of Florence's and one of her papa's beside one she knew would be Elma's.

Taking the opportunity, she took off her day clothes and slipped the gown on – better that she did this first, then Ben wouldn't feel so awkward when she told him he could use Papa's.

Once they were ready for bed, wrapped up in the cosy dressing gowns, which Tamar knew only covered Ben's vest and long johns as she could see a peek of both, and Elma had discarded her corset, as her breasts now hung on her waist, they set about making the beds.

Tamar was glad when Elma said, 'Ben, you take yours to the other side of the chairs. Then that gives yer a bit of privacy, and us too.'

She hadn't wanted his mattress next to hers.

When finally all was quiet, Tamar thought of her Isaac. As always, she wondered where he was – was he still alive? Was he a prisoner? Or was he maybe helping the resistance if his friends had managed to get a group established? And, as always, her heart ached with the pain of missing him. She drifted off to sleep with Elma's gentle snores in her ears, and Isaac's smiling face in her heart.

The next day brought relief as they ascended the stairs and opened the shop door and found that there had been no further damage in their street, but passers-by told of how heavily the docks had been hit and the surrounding houses.

It was as they ate their breakfast of hot porridge in Elma's kitchen that the door opened and Florence came through it.

Tamar jumped up and ran to her. 'Oh, Florence, you look exhausted.'

Florence burst into tears.

There was a silence when she finished and then both Ben and Elma burst into loud clapping. Blushing, Tamar laughed as Elma said, 'I didn't understand a bloomin' word, but it was beautiful, me little darlin'.'

'Oh, it's about a man who has double-crossed his lady friend. She is singing about the letters she sent to him.'

'Well, he wouldn't get any bleedin' letters from me! But that apart, it was lovely to 'ear the language my dear David often used . . . Oh, I'm sorry . . .'

'Don't be. Papa wouldn't want us not to talk of him, or remember the things he did or said. He always kept Mama alive for me, and he would want the same for himself. He told me recently that you had given him back the life that left him when Mama died, and that he loved you very much.'

Elma dabbed her eyes. 'We had each other for such a short time, but it was the best time of me life.'

Tamar went to hug her, but Ben said, 'Now, now, let me play something lively, and let us celebrate a man who sounds like he was a wonderful person.' With this, he played 'Puttin' on the Ritz'.

The music lifted them all once more. Tamar surprised herself by wanting to dance. She got hold of Elma's hands and did a little jig with her. They ended up howling with laughter.

As the evening progressed, the thought of sleeping down here with Ben being in the same room made Tamar cringe with embarrassment, as did the thought of using the bucket that Elma had put behind a screen in the other half of the cellar, divided off by the stairs coming down in the centre of the room.

When eventually she had to steel herself to go, Tamar found one of her dressing gowns hanging on a hook behind

'Well, I don't think I 'ave anything like a tuning fork, so you may 'ave to do it by ear. But while yer do, me and Tamar'll make a cuppa and prepare dinner.'

Preparing dinner was something Tamar didn't have a clue how they were going to do!

But she soon learned that in a cupboard that stood against the wall under the window was an array of jars holding preserves, from green beans to peas and carrots and fruits – rhubarb, plums and pears. Getting dinner suddenly seemed like something they could do, and half an hour later they sat down, she and Elma on the armchairs and Ben on the piano stool, with plates on their knees filled with fried corned beef, handmade by Elma to make sure it was kosher, and put down here a couple of days ago, just in case, accompanied by peas and carrots and rounded off with a bowl of delicious pears. All to the terrifying backdrop of bombs, shouts, screams and the shaking of the building above them.

Trying to ignore it all was difficult, but somehow they did and chatted along as if everything was normal.

'Now, ladies, I'm ready, so I'll play for you.'

To Tamar, everything seemed surreal as Ben – a farmer with work-worn hands and a ruddy, outdoor complexion – suddenly turned into Ben the musician, producing beautiful music that soothed their nerves and made the world seem right.

'Do you sing, Tamar?'

Tamar laughed nervously, but then thought, *Why not?*

'Do you know a song called "The Three Letters"?' she asked.

'I think so . . .' Ben played a few bars. The music relaxed her and took her to a time that she and Hannah had sung this song. She wanted to sing it just as they did in Polish where it was called '*Trzy Listy*'.

he'd thought, but he could be a different person in the future.

With this thought, she felt herself warming to him again and grinned back.

Within minutes of Ben blocking out the window, the sound of an explosion and the building shuddering filled her with terror. She looked from Ben to Elma. Seeing Elma frozen to the spot spurred Tamar forward. She and Elma clung on to one another.

'Hey, come on now, you two, we're safe down here,' Ben told them. 'We just need something to block out the noise. Have you got a wireless, Elma?'

'Only upstairs. I don't think we'd get a signal down 'ere, Ben.'

Ben looked around. There was something in the corner near to the stairs that caught his eye. 'Is that a piano under that sheet?'

'It is. It belonged to me ol' mum – well, she were me adopted mum, but me and me sister couldn't 'ave loved her more if she'd given birth to us. She taught me 'ow to play, but I ain't done so for a long time.'

Ben surprised them then. 'I can play – mostly classical stuff. Me dad, though a farmer, was a very talented musician. He saw to it that me and me brother had lessons. I took to it, but me brother didn't, though he loves to listen to me playing in the evenings. It calms him.'

This last sentence, and what she'd experienced at the hospital with how concerned Ben was for his brother, showed her that the two men were very close.

'I'll take a look at it. It'll want tuning, no doubt, and for that I'll need some kind of thin rod as I doubt you'll have a tuning fork, but I can do it by ear if need be.'

Elma shivered then. 'Ooh, though it still strikes cold down 'ere. Light that stove, Ben, there's matches next to it.'

Besides matches, on the trolley next to the stove there was a kettle, cups, powdered milk and some canned food.

On the floor there were four mattresses with a pile of blankets on one. 'I figured there might be the four of us down 'ere.'

Putting her arm around Elma, Tamar found her own tears weren't far away. For some reason, the feeling she'd had a few minutes ago about Ben and his former beliefs had stuck with her. She didn't want him here, disturbing her, making her like him. She wanted to hate him as she did all he'd stood for. Wasn't it men like him who had caused her and her papa to flee from the country they loved? Made them live in fear by persecuting the Jewish people? And now they had Poland in their grip. *Oh, Isaac, my Isaac, where are you? Please be safe. Please . . .*

As this thought came to an end, Tamar was shocked to see the expression on Ben's face. He'd turned to say something and must have seen the hatred in her eyes.

Looking down at the floor, she said, 'Let me and you sit down, Elma, while Ben sees to the stove.' Then she made herself lighten her voice as she said, 'How on earth did you get those two armchairs down here?'

'Oh, they were 'ere as well. Never chuck much out when I can store it. There might come a day, and there 'as!'

Tamar looked around her. She found it strange to see running feet go past the barred, small window at pavement height, and marvelled at how the glow of the stove cheered her. She managed a smile at Ben and saw his pensive expression melt away into a grin. He was right, he could only say he was sorry. He couldn't change how he'd been and how told you I've been preparing me cellar for a few weeks now. I 'ad a mind we'd be hit badly with London being the hub of the country.'

Though worried about Florence, Tamar knew she had to do as Elma said, as now the drone of aircraft could be heard in the distance.

Fear held her still for a moment. She looked over at Ben. His face had turned ashen and his whole body had tensed. But he raised his eyebrows and grinned. 'Let's do as Elma says, eh? We just have to hope Florence finds shelter and is all right. Though from what I know of her, it'll be as Elma says and she'll just want to be at the hospital. Look how she faced up to me and my lot to save me brother!'

This reminder of what Ben used to stand for wasn't comfortable and for a fleeting second Tamar wanted to attack him for the misery he had helped to bring down on her and Florence's people.

This must have shown in her expression as Ben lowered his head.

'I've said I'm sorry, Tamar . . . I lost me way for a bit . . .'

All she could do was nod.

The cellar transformation amazed her as they walked down the stone steps. Though chilly, there was also a homely welcome, nothing like the dingy, cold place they'd spent the night in before.

It surprised Tamar what Elma had managed to do with the cellar, even though she knew that every evening after shutting the shop Elma had busied herself sorting it out.

There was a large rug on the floor, which they heard had been rolled up down there for a long time. 'Still smells a bit musty, but it gives comfort – better than the cold stone floor.'

repaired the wall.' Elma sighed. 'It will be all right, won't it?'

'It will. Oh, Elma, let's have a hug, love.'

The hug was more Elma bear-hugging Tamar, who felt small in the arms of this woman she loved, and yet somehow safe too.

That feeling left dead on four o'clock as the whine of the sirens screeched, filling every space around them.

'Right, down the cellar, everyone!'

'We'll get off, ta, missus. We'll take our chances and get 'ome to our families.'

The foremen of the gang of workers added, 'We've finished here anyway. Just a bit of tidying up.'

'Leave it, we'll clear up after yer, lad. You've done a good job. Yer money's in that envelope on the windowsill. Now get going and be safe.' She turned then to Tamar and Ben. 'Come on, I've everything in the cellar. We can make a cuppa, as I've one of them paraffin stoves, a kettle, and all we need.'

Tamar had been told many times by Elma that if air raids did start to happen, she and Florence were to make their way to the shop and down the cellar. 'Me and your papa will be there waiting for yer, luv,' she'd said. But none of them had ever thought there would seriously come a day they would need it. If only they'd had time to follow this instruction two days ago.

Not able to follow her thoughts through as the pain was so raw, Tamar asked, 'But what about Florence?'

'Well, with this lot that's threatened, she'll more than likely want Ruben to take her back to the hospital – that's if she ever left it . . . Look, love, we can't do anything, we just 'ave to make ourselves as safe as possible, and we will be. I

Chapter Eleven

By that afternoon the window had been boarded up, and Ben had painted the words, *Open for Business as Usual* across it in a way that looked as if a professional had done it. Elma was thrilled with it. Though she did say, 'Huh, it needs another sentence – "No thanks to me so-called loyal customers!"'

'Oh, Elma, love, there would have been nothing they could do, no doubt. These were gangs of outsiders who will have sold your stock on the black market by now.'

Elma hmphed.

Tamar understood. Elma was dealing with trying to piece together the ruins of her lifetime's work. And though putting on a brave face and getting on with things, she was broken inside with this and the loss of Papa. She needed to be angry at somebody.

'Let's have a break, Elma, love. All this banging and clanging of workmen and us trying to clean around them, not to mention deliveries arriving, is giving me a headache!'

'Yer right, luv. Me 'ead's banging as loud as that 'ammer that the bloke's using to put me shelves up, now they've

'Ha, that's a new saying for me, and a good one . . . See you in a mo, Elma. I'll go up and rummage through that bag before Florence wakes up and takes the best!' This she said on a forced laugh.

Glad to be on her own, Tamar ran up the stairs. Her heart pounded in her chest. Somehow, she must calm herself so as not to raise suspicions; she had a whole evening and a night to get through. The thought came to her, *Please don't let that turn into a lifetime of having to get through without Isaac!*

Chapter Twelve

There were some surprisingly good clothes in the bag. A couple of fashionable dresses with fitted shirt-type tops, belted at the waist, as well as skirts with pencil pleats, which fell to calf length. Tamar liked the green one best and thought it pretty and cheerful, patterned as it was with tiny yellow daisies.

The bright blue one, she thought, would suit Florence. Fresh-looking with a pattern of large red flowers, it was just the style Florence loved.

Then there were two jumpers with puffed sleeves and two slim-fitting skirts.

Tamar chose the brown jumper and the beige skirt – the perfect outfit for wearing to the Polish embassy in the morning. Luckily, she still had her coat with the astrakhan collar. Her shoes were scuffed, but hopefully Elma had some polish for those, and the bruises to her face weren't as bad as those on the rest of her body, so they could easily be covered with make-up.

But what about stockings? I have to have those, mine were torn to shreds! Thinking this brought the pain of her bruises on her legs to mind and she felt the sting of them as if to remind her of the awful moment her world had changed.

Will it be changing again? Will what Mr Kaminski have to say completely kill the last strands of my world off? No, please! I couldn't bear it! Please don't let anything have happened to my Isaac!

'Hey!'

The door had burst open. Florence stood there, open letter in her hand. 'Why so glum? Everything in the world is wonderful!'

'Oh, I thought you were still asleep! You haven't had long. Anyway, it may be all wonderful for you . . . but . . .' Tamar just stopped herself from blurting out about her fears and how she would know tomorrow. 'I – I've got blooming toothache!'

'Ah, sorry to hear that, love. Elma told me your dentist rang. But toothache or not, I just have to share my news – I have a letter from Liam! He's going to be in Southampton for a week. He wants me to go down to stay with him! Oh, Tamar . . . my prayers have been answered!'

Tamar made herself jump up and hug Florence – the last thing she felt like was celebrating, but she couldn't dampen Florence's happiness.

Florence made her giggle then as she clasped her hands and did a little jig.

After they hugged again, Florence caught sight of the bright blue frock. 'Oh, my, that's beautiful!'

'It's yours, love. That green one is mine. I hope I've chosen well for you.'

'You have. Where did they come from? And underwear too!'

'I know. Rosie brought them for us . . . And I had an idea – I thought we'd treat ourselves to a bath. Elma got

Ben to lift the tin bath down the cellar while he was here, so if we fill that, then if the siren goes off, it won't matter if we're still soaking as we'll already be down there.'

'Ooh, please don't let it, I'm dead beat. I want to sleep in a bed tonight!'

'You will. I told you, Elma has put four beds down there, and blankets, everything we could need. Come on, let's get our new underclothes down there, and Elma's even taken down dressing gowns ready for us. We'll light the stove, then come up and have our supper, then we can fill the bath and enjoy – bombing raid or no bombing raid.'

'Sounds great, but very ambitious. We can only carry a kettleful at a time. It'll take ages to fill.'

'Elma has two kettles, love. It won't take that long, then we can take a bucket of cold water down to cool it and top it up . . . Let's do it . . . I so need to do something!'

Florence looked at her with a quizzical gaze. 'Something has happened, hasn't it, Tamar?'

Tamar sunk down onto her bed. 'I – I feel that all isn't well with Isaac. I – I don't know why, it's just a gut feeling. I'm going to the embassy tomorrow, on my way to the dentist . . .' Tamar hated lying to Florence. Then found she couldn't. That she had to have someone to confide in and if that broke any rules, then so be it!

'Oh, Florence, please don't say anything to Elma. I – I don't want her worrying. I told her it was my dentist calling me, and was going to let you think the same, but it wasn't, it was the embassy. They have news on Isaac.'

Florence sat down beside her. 'Oh, Tamar. Didn't they say anything – not give a hint even as to whether it was good or bad news?'

'No. They just said there was news, and I have to go in

to see Mr Kaminski. He's the man responsible for collating what has happened to people in Poland.'

'Well, surely if it was bad news, they would have sent somebody round? Let's stay positive, eh?'

'You're right, we have to put on a happy face!'

'We can start with happy feet. You remember that "B" film we saw a while back? A great hit in the early thirties – *The King of Jazz* – and that song Michael Whiteman sang?'

Florence began to dance again as she sang:

'*Happy feet! I've got those hap-hap-happy feet!* Come on, join in!'

'*Happy feet! I've got those hap-hap-happy feet*
Give them a low-down beat
And they begin dancing!
I've got those ten little tip-tap-tapping toes,
When they hear a tune
I can't control the dancing, dear
To save my soul!'

They jigged around, singing loudly before collapsing into a heap of giggles.

A shout of, 'Dinner's ready!' coming up the stairs had them sobering up and running to the bedroom door.

'Good to 'ear the pair of yer having a laff! I've a nice lamb stew on the go. Are yer coming down?'

Feeling as though she could cope now, Tamar took the hand Florence offered and together they went downstairs.

They were met by the heat of the kitchen and steamed-up windows, as well as the delicious aroma of stew. 'Right, the table's laid. Let's sit down and have it, eh?'

'We need to put the big iron kettle on first, Elma, and nip down the cellar to light the stove.' Elma's surprised look turned to a nod of her head as they explained.

Never one to dampen anyone's spirits, Elma said, 'Good idea. It's better to be down there ready to meet what might hit yer than to be taken by surprise. All right, but be quick about it, I don't want me stew ruined.'

With their first kettle simmering away, they sat at the table; each bowed their heads to say their own private prayer of thanksgiving, before tucking in.

'Now, what yer so excited about, Florence? I take it it's something to do with your letter from Liam. Is he all right?'

'He is . . .' Florence explained how she planned to go to Southampton for a few days. 'The letter says they should dock in two days' time.'

'That's lovely news. Will yer get the time off work?'

'I will, as I have leave due to me. I've done a lot of extra hours this last two days – on that first day I worked for fifteen hours! And they were meant to be leave days too! And as it happens, the sister came to me today and told me I must take some days off as soon as I can. She said she didn't want me getting exhausted as I'd be no good to anyone then.'

'Well, that all fits in nicely, luv, I'm pleased for yer. Give our love to Liam, bless him, and tell him we're very proud of him.'

'I will . . . if I can raise my head long enough from kissing him, that is.'

They all giggled at this, and Tamar had the feeling that she could cope. She wouldn't give up hope. The news about Isaac could just as well be good news as bad. She would keep thinking it was good.

By the time they had the bath ready, the siren's blast filled the building, setting Tamar's teeth on edge and filling her with dread. More bombs . . . Hadn't they dropped enough?

Grabbing the towel that Elma had put to warm on the rail of her oven, they all dashed downstairs, just as the first whirring of the Luftwaffe planes could be heard. A sick sound on a sick mission – to kill and maim innocent men, women and children. And to cause needless damage.

'They think they can bring us to our knees . . . Well, they've another think coming.' Elma shook her fist at the ceiling. 'Bugger off, yer slimy geezers!'

Her body shook with fury – a rage that ended in tears.

Both Tamar and Florence were by her side in seconds. It was Florence with her lovely bedside manner who soothed her.

'It's all right, Elma, love. Come on, let's close the cellar door. It's lovely and cosy down here. And we can't make a difference by getting angry.'

'It makes me feel a bit better, though. But then it passes, and I think of what them bleeders have taken from me – the 'appiness I'd only just found. The loveliest man in the world. The love of me life. Oh, I know it weren't for long, but he meant so much to me.'

'Look, I'll put the kettle on, eh?'

'Ta, Florence . . . I'm sorry, girls . . . It just gets to me.'

Tamar, who was swallowing her own tears, put her arm around Elma and guided her to one of the armchairs. 'It's bound to, and you can cry whenever you feel you need to, love.'

'Huh, now you've said that, me tears 'ave dried up! Me 'eart's 'eavy, but that won't lighten for a long time. I'll be all right. I promise.'

'Good. We'll get our bath now. You sit and rest, eh?'

Before they'd cooled the water they'd been bringing down throughout the meal, Elma was snoring away.

'Bless her, I'm going to hate leaving you both.'

'We'll be fine, Florence, love. You go and have the most wonderful week ever. Stolen moments are always the best.'

'I can't wait. I'll go into work tomorrow and tell them, and then I'll go to the station and book my ticket. Ooh, Tamar, I'm so excited!'

Tamar made herself be strong. She mustn't do anything to spoil this wonderful moment for Florence. No one deserved it more. She'd done her bit the moment she was needed. Now at last she had happy moments in store.

Inwardly sighing, she wondered what kind of moments were in store for herself. Why was it so urgent for her to go into the embassy? What did they want of her? But most of all, she prayed she wasn't to hear news she wouldn't be able to cope with.

Splashes of water brought her out of her thoughts. She looked up to see Florence was naked and had a toe in the water. 'Hey, I'm not going to offer you a penny for your thoughts, girl! Just get them stinking clothes off and get in here with me. There's plenty of room. Let's have that soak we promised ourselves . . . a-n-d a glass of wine!'

With this, Florence bent over the other side of the bath and came up with a glass of wine in her hand. 'Cheers. Yours is right next to the side of the bath when you get in, love.'

This was followed by an exclamation of horror. 'Oh, Tamar! You're bruised all over!'

'I'm all right.'

'But why didn't you say? You must be in agony. Oh, Tamar . . .'

'Honestly, I'm all right, love.' The words didn't match

the gasp that the stinging of the water caused. But once most of her body submerged, Tamar felt the soothing effect.

And even more so after a couple of sips of the wine.

Neither spoke for a while, just lay back and let their minds come to a calm place.

The bombing had begun and sounded close. Tamar had a fleeting feeling of fear as the thought occurred to her that they might be safe, but what if the shop took a direct hit? They'd be trapped down here with two storeys of bricks and rubble on top of them!

'I will say a penny for them this time as visible fright just crossed your face.'

'Oh, just thoughts that you probably have about the bombing too.'

Florence nodded. 'From the first day. And it's worse with seeing the casualties.'

'I don't know how you do what you do, Florence. I'm so happy that you're going to be with Liam for a while.'

'I've been thinking about that. Yes, I'm doing my bit – war work, as it's now termed – but I could do more. I could join the Medical Corps too.'

This shook Tamar. She hadn't expected it as she had thought Florence felt fulfilled in what she was already doing. 'You would really consider it? But you'd be in so much danger, and you don't know where they would send you.'

Florence put her head back and laughed. 'And I'm not now?'

The words were hardly out when a nearby explosion shook the fabric of the building. The glass in the small window shattered, and debris scattered around them. They stared at each other.

Florence had dropped her glass with the shock of it and

was now pushing on the sides of the bath to stand up. 'Oh, God! Tamar, that was close.'

Tamar hardly heard her above the screams and cries of distress.

Jumping out of the bath, Florence grabbed a towel. 'I'm going out to help.'

'Me too . . .'

Florence vigorously dried herself. 'No! Stay here, have your soak, you're already hurt badly and should be resting.'

'I can't. I'm all right, honestly. I'd go mad in here knowing you're out there.'

Though she couldn't do it in one movement as Florence had, because of the stiffness of her limbs, Tamar managed to get out of the bath and dry herself.

Seeing there was no stopping her, Florence didn't protest again as she donned her clean underwear and then the uniform she'd just taken off instead of the intended dressing gown.

'All right, if you insist. Let's see what we're dealing with upstairs. If it's safe and intact, I'll need boiled water, and plenty of rags, so rip up a clean sheet, and gather any soothing ointments you can put your hands on.'

Once dressed, Tamar remembered Elma. She ran round the other side of the stairs and couldn't believe her eyes. Elma was snoring away in the chair. The sight made her realize just how exhausted poor Elma was.

'Put a blanket over her, Tamar, and let her rest. Bless her, she's worked her socks off to get her shop shipshape. Let's hope it wasn't all for nothing!'

Upstairs the kitchen glowed with the light of the flickering flames of the building behind them. 'It looks like it's hit my old street but there's nothing damaged here, from what I can see, so get the water boiling, Tamar. Use the kettle and saucepans.'

Tamar struggled to hear Florence over the screams, the cries of agony, and the clanging bells of fire engines, and hopefully ambulances too.

Doing as she was bid, though her body shook from head to toe with the aftershock of it all, Tamar soon had water steaming and had gathered a pile of rags from tearing a sheet she'd grabbed from the airing cupboard that housed the huge boiler.

She'd just assembled ointments and aspirin from Elma's medical cupboard when Florence burst in through the back door.

'It's bad . . . Oh, Tamar, the block of flats I lived in has gone! And the shops next to it are almost flattened!'

Tamar closed her eyes against the memory of herself blown into the street, and of her papa's shop being just a pile of rubble. Her heart went out to the victims of this latest bombing.

'Hold on, Tamar, keep strong! I need you . . . Bring that saucepan of water, I'll grab the rest. And be careful, there's rubble everywhere.'

The living, beating heart of hell met them as Tamar followed Florence through the back gate.

Lying next to their miraculously untouched wall, a small boy whimpered. Tamar bent down to him. 'You're all right, we're going to help you.'

'Mum . . . I want me mum.'

'I know . . .'

'Tamar, hurry, bring me that hot water!'

'Lie still, little one, I'll come straight back.'

As she neared Florence, the heat of the roaring flames scorched her, dust clogged her throat, and bile stung her throat at the sight of a body with no head.

'Shut it all out, Tamar. You have to, to be of any use to those who need help.'

Above the sound of bells, crackling flames, screams and calls for help, Tamar shouted, 'There's a boy, near to our gate. I'm going to him.'

Florence nodded.

Back with the boy, Tamar crouched beside him. 'Are you hurt badly?'

He shook his head.

'What's your name?'

'Stuart.'

'Where's your home, Stuart, and your family?'

His eyes opened wide. His head shook once more. Cradling him to her, Tamar found that he was skin and bone. She lifted him as if he was a baby. 'Show me where, love.'

'No! It's gone!'

Kicking the gate, Tamar took him through and into the kitchen.

'This is the shop, ain't it? Elma's shop.'

In the light of the kitchen, Tamar recognized him as the Epsom salts lad from that day of the near riot in Elma's shop.

'Would you like a hot drink of cocoa, Stuart?'

He nodded. 'Ta, I would.'

Realizing the kettle and most of the saucepans were either outside with Florence or down in the cellar, Tamar dug out a small milk saucepan and filled it with more water than would be needed for his drink.

'When that boils, I'll cool some of it and bathe your cuts and scrapes.'

Seeing him in the light, she could see his nose had been broken and his eyes were blackening. Many patches of skin were grazed badly, revealing red-raw flesh. Her heart went out to him. 'Do you know if your mum and sisters and brothers are all right, Stuart?'

His head shook from side to side as tears ran down his cheeks. 'They're gone. All gone.'

Shock rendered Tamar unable to speak but she put her arm around him and cried with him.

As the saucepan rattled with fierce bubbles, Tamar rose. 'I'll make your cocoa and then I'll fetch Elma. She'll take care of you while I go back to Florence. And Stuart, don't give up hope. Many have been pulled alive from the rubble these past few days.'

Down in the cellar, Tamar had to smile. Despite the desperate situation a snore louder than any she'd heard came from where Elma was.

Waking her gently, Elma shuddered and stared for a moment. 'What's up, luv?' Her lips smacked together.

Propelled from that sleepy state as soon as she heard what was going on, Elma jumped up. 'Leave young Stuart to me, luv, and go and 'elp Florence. God, that bleedin' 'Itler! If I ever meet him, he'd better watch out, I'll tell yer!'

Tamar pictured Elma waving her rolling pin and going hell for leather into Hitler. The thought cheered her and gave her the feeling that she'd take the rolling pin and smash him with it herself!

When they went back upstairs, Stuart slid off the chair at seeing Elma and dashed to her. 'Me mum, and me bruvvers and sisters . . . they're gone, Elma!'

'Look, lad, it's either Mrs Brume or Aunt Elma to you.'

A miracle happened then. Stuart grinned! Having something just the same as it always was – Elma giving him a ticking-off – seemed to put his world to rights for a moment.

But when Elma gathered him into her arms, his grin turned into a sob.

'Now, now, lad. Me and you'll sort everything out, eh? I was only just saying I needed more 'elp – a lad and a bike, who could deliver to them as can't get to me shop. I think that's just the job for you, and it comes with bed and board!'

'But I want me mum!'

'I know, but as sad as it is, we can't always 'ave everything we want, so we 'ave to turn to 'elping others, and I need 'elp. Do yer think yer up to it? Or shall I put an advert up on me board?'

'No! I want it. Ta, El . . . Aunt Elma.'

Elma put him down and ruffled his hair. 'Right, we'll start by fattening yer up. I should never be able to lift a lad of your age into the air! When did yer last eat, eh?'

Stuart shrugged his shoulders.

'Well, I've some eggs. I'll get the pan on. But first, we've to clean up your wounds so yer don't get infected.'

As she went out of the door, Tamar heard Elma say, 'Now, I want yer to be as brave as the soldiers facing a load of guns.'

She smiled. Stuart had a lot to go through, but Elma would care for him and in the end, everything would turn out well for him. Elma, though having no children of her own, was the perfect mum-type.

Florence's shout came to Tamar as she went out of the gate. 'A lot have gone to hospital now, Tamar, but the walking wounded need shelter and food as most have lost their homes.'

A policeman came over to them. 'There's all of that in the church hall for them, luv, we just need to get them there. If they can walk, send them on their way, but those with minor injuries, there'll be a van 'ere in a mo . . . You've done a wonderful job, Miss . . .'

'Mrs . . . But call me Florence.'

'Ha! You're a proper Florence Nightingale!'

Used to this joke, Florence just laughed with him.

At this he pushed his helmet back and scratched his head. 'What else could you be but a nurse, eh? It shows a mile in the care yer give and yer bravery, and with a name like that, well . . .' He went off laughing to himself.

With all the injured and homeless safely on their way, and Florence hugged a dozen times by those grateful to her, all that was left were the firemen busy getting the fires under control.

As she and Florence turned wearily towards home, Florence muttered, 'Well, I think we've earned that glass of wine now!'

Tamar put her arm around her. 'You have, love. And another hot bath, and that's just what you're going to have!'

An hour later, with Stuart tucked up asleep on the fourth bed in the cellar with his belly fuller than Tamar imagined it had been for an age, and Elma in her bed, the two girls lay once more in a hot bath with the screen between them and the others and the pee bucket moved out of sight.

Sipping her wine, Florence asked, 'Now, where were we?'

Tamar giggled but marvelled at Florence's resilience. The giggle relaxed her, though her heart still thumped in her chest.

'Put it behind you, love, you have to. If we nurses dwelt on everything, we'd be useless. We always have a giggle together after a major incident or death – not disrespectfully, but, well, instead of crying. Crying leaves you drained and unable to carry on; laughing exhilarates you and makes you strong so you can once more take on the world.'

Tamar wondered at this but could see the sense of it. Though whether she could do it herself, she didn't know.

Chapter Thirteen

Tamar twisted the hem of her jumper as her nerves almost got the better of her. She looked down at her fidgety hands as she sat across the desk from Mr Kaminski.

'Thank you for being prompt. I did wonder with the East End suffering another raid by the Luftwaffe last night . . . I'm sorry, it must be hell for you all.'

Tamar lifted her head and nodded.

'Well, now. It seems you have withstood the nightmare of that, and have been brave enough to carry on. That is impressive. Many would have used the air raid as an excuse to cry off from coming here.'

'Carrying on is all we can do, sir – that, and helping those stricken during the raid.'

'You mean, you were out in it helping others?'

'Yes, my friend is a nurse, and I assisted her.'

'Hmm, very courageous. I'm beginning to think you may pass the test to do what we have in mind for you . . . But there's a long way to that stage . . . Firstly, I have to tell you . . .' He leaned forward with his elbows on the desk and put his chin on his fists. His stare deepened.

Tamar wanted to beg him to say what he had to say. Instead, he seemed to be putting her under scrutiny. And why did it matter that she had resilience? And what test did she have to pass?

'The news isn't good on your fiancé. I'm sorry. He was working with the resistance and was caught.'

Tamar didn't react. She couldn't. Her eyes prickled as she stared unblinking at him.

'It is believed that he was taken to a concentration camp. The resistance help people who have escaped from these camps and they have been told by some escapees that someone named Isaac, and a German named Wilhelm, aided their escape. They say that they were put to work outside the camp, and this is when it was made possible for them to get away . . . but they also related that Isaac is working for the Germans.'

Tamar gasped.

Her disbelief was replaced with a sigh of relief as Mr Kaminski continued:

'That won't be his choice. He will be being forced to do the work of the Germans. Apparently, he is a guard of his own people, keeping them in check.'

'No! He wouldn't.'

'Maybe you will understand when I tell you that his father is also in the camp. That his mother was . . . exterminated . . .'

Tamar thought she would faint with this shocking news. Her body broke out in a cold sweat. 'Murdered? By the Germans?'

'Yes. From our intelligence, this is being done systematically.'

Tamar swallowed the gasp of horror she felt. Her heart raced and tears threatened. It was all so much to take in.

Kaminski continued without remarking on her obvious

distress. 'We can assume that, as Isaac was a brave and faithful soldier, and even braver when he went underground to be a resistance worker, he took the position so that he could help the situation. Maybe Wilhelm approached him and with his help, Isaac is getting out as many as he can. The resistance then gets the escapees to safety – to outlying farms and such.'

A calm descended on Tamar as her horror turned to pride. 'What are Isaac's chances of living?'

'We do not know. No one can know, but at the moment he hasn't been caught helping people escape and is seemingly safe.'

There was a pause. Tamar wanted to cry out against the injustice of it all, but that wouldn't help. It was happening and if she had a chance of helping it to stop, she was going to take it, and so, when Mr Kaminski asked, 'How do you feel?' she took a deep breath and with it a strength came into her.

Straightening her back, she looked straight into his eyes and said, 'I feel like emulating Isaac and helping my people in some way. Like doing all I can to undermine the Nazis and trick them as Isaac is doing. I only wish I was there, doing what I can, instead of here, wasting my time working in a shop, when I know I could do something to help.'

'What do you see yourself doing?'

Tamar didn't hesitate. 'Helping the resistance. I could go to places they cannot go, to seek out information. No one takes me for a Jew, as I take after my mother in looks. She wasn't born a Jew; her father was German. In Poland, it was often said that my looks are more like those of a Fräulein. And I can adapt to speaking any of the languages I am likely to be called on to use.'

As she said this, Tamar thought how often she'd been pleased to be classed as looking like the beautiful German girls with their chiselled features and lovely blue eyes. Now, she didn't think of it as a compliment and was glad that no one in England had made the comparison.

'My thoughts when I first met you were just that, though to complete the look, we will need to lighten your hair a little more. It tends to be a mixture of dark and light, whereas a true Aryan is blonder.'

'You mean . . . I am being considered to go and help?'

'Yes, you are. You would work for us. You would be our main contact over there. But there is so much that would need putting in place. You will need specialized training. And I must warn you that you may be vilified by your own people and looked on as a whore . . . Don't look like that! We aren't asking that of you, but what we have in mind, it may crop up . . . We may require you to go to lengths you wouldn't dream of, but all for the freedom of your people – the Jews and the Poles.'

Tamar couldn't answer for a moment or two. Kaminski allowed her time. He sat with his elbows still on the desk, but now his hands were together as if praying. His lips pursed and then were pulled in. She knew he was waiting for her answer, but also weighing up if he had done the right thing in choosing her.

Tamar felt driven by her desire to accomplish what Kaminski said she could, but realized there would be a strong possibility of finding Isaac had been caught and killed.

With this thought, the grieving process began. Her heart weighed as heavy as lead in her chest, tears pricked her eyes, but she dared not let them fall. They would become a torrent.

Without realizing it, she nodded her head.

'Is that a yes? If it is, I need you to tell me out loud, so I know for sure and am not mistaking your gesture.'

'Yes. Yes, I will take the training, and if you feel I am up to it, I will do all I can to help to win this war, for my people and for all peoples.'

'A good sentiment. I am proud of you. And when our country knows the part you played, they will be proud too.'

This gave her a sense of being valued, of being able to make a difference.

Sitting up straight, he said, 'So, arrangements will be made. You will be part of the Polish army – an officer. Someone will contact you – let me see . . . your father was known as Bibi in Poland by his friends, yes?'

This shocked Tamar. How on earth did he know that? When they lived in Poland, Papa always used the English swear words 'bloody bugger'. He'd asked her what they were so that he could swear, and no one would know what he was saying. She'd thought it hilarious, and it had earned him the nickname of Bibi, derived from both words beginning with 'B', which in Polish has the same sound as in English.

For the first time she began to wonder about this organization, but then it was one from her own country and part of their embassy, so she should be proud they wanted her to serve.

'Right, Bibi will be your code name. Someone will ring you – they will use that code word when you come to the phone, but if someone else answers their call, what is the best way to cover who they are?'

'My dentist. This was the first thing you told me to say, and the friends I live with think I am at the dentist now.'

'I knew you would be good at this! You are immediately in tune with our thinking. Well done. You may be in for a journey like no other you have taken, but I am confident you are up to it. Have you any questions?'

'Yes, why me?'

'Your language ability will be a great asset. You're passionate about your country and its people and your own. Qualities that no one can give you. And I believe you are fit and up to the rigorous training.'

At this moment, Tamar didn't feel fit, but knew she could get back to being so. But could she deceive Florence and Elma?

'What can I tell my friends?'

'Very little. And nothing at all yet. We have people who will give you a good cover story. And be prepared, your appearance will be changed, your eyebrows thinned and, as I have said, your hair lightened. You will be taught how to apply make-up in the way a loose woman would. Besides this, you will learn code-breaking skills, unarmed combat, tracking, radio frequencies, and many skills that will help you. This training will take place in Scotland, but that is all I can tell you for now . . . except that you will learn a cover story for how you came to be German and in Poland.'

'There are many there, and there were before this. We got on well, until the mood changed.'

'That's because many Germans living in Poland became indoctrinated with the Nazi principles. But them being there will probably tie in with your cover story, but I can't pre-empt that. I will leave it to those who will train you.'

'When do you think I will go?'

'To Poland?'

Tamar nodded.

'I think you will be there within the month.'

'Oh . . . I . . . So, everything you have spoken of will happen very quickly?'

'Yes, you may even hear this afternoon.'

This meant that she would have to be ready with a story very soon.

As if Kaminski read her thoughts, he said, 'You will go from here and be taken to another office. There they will give you your cover story. You will be given half an hour to absorb it, then you will be quizzed on it. You will be expected to answer the questions without hesitation and to sound natural and truthful.'

There was nothing in this that worried Tamar. She was said to have an almost photographic memory; but she didn't say this as Kaminski continued, telling her that he was proud of himself for spotting her talents and putting her forward for this work. But was she proud? Right now, she felt confused and afraid, and . . . well, yes, honoured too, and this last could be summed up as pride.

Sitting outside the office she'd been taken to, and where she had met a man of dour countenance, Tamar read through the cover story she'd been given.

It seemed that not all Germans in Danzig were loyal to the Nazis. One had been planted there long before the invasion and was a spy for Britain. She learned that his name was Gunther Meyer and that he had been born to a British mother and attended school here in Britain. That he was forty-two, married but childless. That he had become a Nazi officer and now worked for the Nazi administration in Krakow, where he was answerable to Governor-General Hans Frank who resided in Wawel Castle. That his command of English and knowledge of Britain was an asset in his work and that his work was a massive asset to Britain as it gave him knowledge that he could pass on that greatly helped in the war effort.

Tamar looked at the picture she'd been given of Gunther and thought about how he must be looked up to, having the appearance the Nazis aspired to – strong square features, and, as the writing on the back informed her, blond hair and blue eyes. His smile relaxed her as it showed him as a friendly person.

The information went on about his likes, the sports he enjoyed, his habits – so much, but she absorbed it all. This man, it would seem, would be her lifeline. She wouldn't live with him, but if stopped and questioned, she would say she was visiting him, and he would verify that.

Tamar read that she would travel to Poland as his cousin. Her official name would be Clara Meyer and she would have papers to this effect, though the resistance would know her only as Bibi. Initially, when landing in Poland, she would be taken to Gunther and would spend a few days with him at his farmhouse – it appeared he had built a reputation as an animal lover and had many dogs.

After this visit, she would stay with the resistance. The names and ranks of these people would be given to her later.

To cover her leaving her home and to give her a story to tell Elma and Florence, she would receive a letter from her mother's sister, her Aunt Ruth, telling her that she and her family had left Germany and gone to live in America. That she had tried to contact her before they had left, thinking that she was still in Poland. She would ask her to join them as it was safe in America and would enclose her travel arrangements and the cost of the ticket.

'You must go through with the arrangements until you arrive at London dock,' she had been told. 'And if anyone is with you to see you off – try to avoid this if you can – you must insist they leave you at the gate as you would not be able to bear it. Then you will be met – again, you will be addressed as Bibi and taken to where we want you to be.'

On the way home, after easily answering all the questions put to her, Tamar allowed her mind to explore all that had happened and thought about her cover story involving her Aunt Ruth.

Frowning at the impossibility of such a thing as her Aunt Ruth helping her and feeling amazed at the information that had been gathered about her and her wider family, Tamar pondered on why such a tale was necessary.

But then, she couldn't say she was to be called for war work or that she had signed up for any of the services as she didn't have the necessary papers of citizenship. And the War Office had no other way of covering for her leaving than to concoct a story about her Aunt Ruth, who would never leave her native Germany in a million years! She hadn't spoken to Mama since Mama converted to Judaism. She'd called it, 'Joining them! The people who have taken so much from Germany!'

Mama had been upset but had said, when talking about her sister, that she had taken after their late father and had strong antisemitic views.

This should have upset Tamar, but instead she giggled to think what this aunt, who she had never met and didn't want to, would think of playing her part in Tamar going to help the Jews in her own dear Poland.

This thought filled Tamar with courage and determination. She couldn't wait for the letter to come now. She'd show her Aunt Ruth that those like her would not win!

Tamar hadn't been home long before Elma called up to her that there was a telephone call. 'It's that dentist of yours again. When's he going to do something for yer, love?'

'Oh, he's preparing for it, and this may be the call that tells me.'

As soon as Tamar stated who she was, the voice on the other end said, 'Bibi, I have some instructions for you. You are to report to the War Office in one week's time, the twenty-fifth of September at ten a.m.'

The line went dead.

'Thank you, yes, I can do that. So, you think you may have a solution for my sensitive tooth?'

After a pause, Tamar spoke again into the receiver. 'Thank you. Well, it might help, I'll think about it. Goodbye.'

'Huh, that were quick! What's he got lined up for yer, love?'

'He said there was a new coating, but that it is still being researched, so in the meantime, he'd try filling it. But I'm not sure. There's no hole in my tooth.' She hated lying like this but knew she must, and that she would be called upon to do much more lying in the future.

Florence came in just as she was thinking this. Her excitement glowed from her as she kissed and hugged them both and then told them, 'I'm ready for the off in two days! Bought all my tickets, and a few clothes. And a couple of things for you, Tamar. Come upstairs and try them on.'

As they went towards the stairs, she asked, 'Oh, how did you get on at the dentist?'

'I'll tell you when we're upstairs, love.'

'Now, don't be long. You know the routine, we've to get into the cellar. I've tea on and Stuart'll be back from his round at any minute!'

They both giggled at this from Elma.

As soon as they reached the top of the stairs, Florence stopped. 'Tell me . . . Please tell me, what was the news on Isaac?'

'Let's get into the bedroom, love.'

Once sat on the bed, Tamar burst into tears. The relief of doing so was immense. Somehow, she told of Isaac's plight.

'So, you're none the wiser, love . . . Oh, God . . . How are you going to get through? I wish I didn't have to leave you, but I so need to see Liam. I miss him so much.'

'Of course, I wouldn't expect anything less of your love for him, my dear Florence.' Forcing a smile on her face, she asked, 'Have you thought any more about joining up?'

'I want to, but—'

'No buts!' Tamar lifted the hem of her skirt and dried her eyes on it. 'You must do what you must do, Florence.'

'But how will you cope?'

'I will, I promise . . . As long as you write often!'

Her first undercover lie. Not admitting that she was leaving too. But she couldn't break the secret she was bound by, nor could she worry her dear friend about such a dangerous mission. Maybe when the letter came it would make it easier to break the news of her leaving and for Florence to understand, but what about Elma? Oh, how she wished she could make it easier for her.

When the letter arrived the next day it was addressed to her father's jewellery shop, but all such mail came to her.

Tamar ripped it open, eager to see how the powers that be had managed to dot all the I's and cross all the T's – another English saying she'd picked up recently.

The letter was written in German, which she thought a clever ploy as it made it seem authentic and would mean she would have to read it out to Florence and Elma. How she would do it, she didn't know, but to help in persuading them that this was the best thing for her, she would put an excitement into her voice as she did.

My dear niece,

I know it has been a long time since you last heard from me, but I met a gentleman who had escaped Poland and come to live here in the United States, where I and your dear uncle are now living.

He told me that he went to Britain first, but then decided he would rather try America. He also told me that your father has opened a jewellery shop on Brick Lane.

I want you and your father to come to America to live with me.

A clever point as it covered how the letter got to her but that it would be impossible for her aunt to have known her father had been killed. Tamar sighed as she read on.

My dear, as soon as I could after this conversation, I gathered all the information I would need as to how you could both travel, and the cost. The latter is significant as there is very little shipping coming here now. But there are still a few sailings at the time of me writing. You may have to check these to see if things have changed, but I enclose a number for a bank where you will find a money order waiting for you to cover the cost of your journey.

Please, please come. Life is wonderful here. And we want to look after you both until you get on your feet, which is so easy to do here. It seems the streets are paved in gold.

Send a wire to us at the address I have written at the top of the page, as soon as you land in America. I am

hoping that is in the port of New York, but wherever, we will come and collect you and a new life without fear will begin for you.
   Your loving Aunt Ruth

The letter was dated 27 July, making it look as though it had taken two months to get here from New York.

As soon as she'd read it, Tamar squealed with an excitement she didn't feel.

'Good Lord! You made me jump, luv. So, your letter's good news then?'

'Oh, it is! I'll read it out to you when Florence gets in.'

As soon as Florence came in, the air filled with her joy as she said, 'I can't believe it, I'm off to Southampton the day after tomorrow.'

'I've had good news too!'

Florence frowned. 'Really good news?' Her eyes went meaningfully to Elma, making Tamar realize that she thought the secret they held was about to be revealed. As Elma wasn't looking, Tamar shook her head, letting Florence know that she hadn't meant news about Isaac.

'Yes, I've had a letter from an aunt who I haven't heard from for a long time. I'll read it out as it's in German. My aunt is my mama's sister and as I've told you before, Mama was German too.'

Taking a breath, Tamar read from the letter. There was a silence when she'd finished. Elma leaned on the table, running her hands around it till she got to a chair and then plonked down.

'Good God! . . . I mean, oh, I don't know.'

Tamar understood. Elma giving up her own religion for Papa hadn't meant she'd left it behind.

'Well! That is out of the blue, Tamar . . . and you want to go?'

'I do, Florence. I mean, America! Isn't it everyone's dream?'

'Not mine. But . . . Oh, I don't know, I just can't take this in. What about us? And Isaac? You're really planning to leave us all behind?'

'I'll come home once the war is over, I promise.' Realizing how selfish this sounded, Tamar tried to make things better. 'You must remember I am a known Jew. I'm in danger. I have no country. I . . .' Suddenly she was crying as despair washed over her. She didn't want to leave them, nor did she want to lie to them. Slumping onto a chair, she put her head in her hands.

The feel of Florence's hand on her back comforted her and made her realize that she couldn't lie to these two, they were her family.

'I – I'm not going to America, but I cannot tell you where I'm going, or what I'm going to be doing.'

Florence sat down next to Elma. Both stared at her.

'I'm needed. The Polish embassy and the War Office need my language skills and knowledge of the Polish people . . . They have sworn me to secrecy . . . I – I shouldn't be—'

'Stop right there, Tamar, love. We put you under pressure, it isn't your fault. Whatever you are going to do, we will be with you with our arms around you, but we will respect your need to keep it all secret.'

'Thank you, Florence . . . I cannot tell you any more. And you must, for my sake, go along with telling everyone that I have gone to America to be with my aunt. You will get letters from me from there, which will help you to prove it if you must. But you really shouldn't know. I've broken my first secret!'

Elma rose. Tamar went into her arms. How was she to leave this beautiful woman who was everything in her life? But she must. And it came to her that Elma understood and was giving her blessing with the motherly cuddle, but to hear her say, 'I am proud of you. Be safe, my precious,' meant all the world.

PART THREE

Their Missions of Courage

Chapter Fourteen

Poland, 1941

The whirring of the small aircraft grated on Tamar's jangled nerves. As did the pilot's monotone voice as he counted down to when they would jump.

Her mind went over the events leading to this moment.

The first leg of her supposed journey to America had been halted on a small station near to a town called Rugby. A passenger alighting had dropped a note onto her lap. It just said, *Bibi, leave the train now and follow me.*

When she did, she found herself outside the station and getting into a black car. She had no idea of the make as by then it was dark. But it was comfortable and though she didn't know where she was travelling to, she had relaxed and fallen asleep.

Nothing by then had shocked her, so she'd let it all go over her head.

After a night spent on a train and a few hours' driving, she found they'd taken her to Scotland.

This had surprised her as she'd been under the impression that she was to go through more interviews before being chosen.

What followed was at times gruelling and at others easy as she tackled an assault course and learned the skills that she might be called on to use – firing a gun, making and receiving messages using Morse code, how to highlight invisible ink, reading maps, setting detonators and sabotage skills, as well as unarmed combat.

Her body ached after a couple of weeks, but worse was to come for someone who was afraid of heights – parachute jumping.

As the weeks had gone by, she'd made friends with others, but never divulged anything about herself, as was their code.

The one thing that all her life she'd hated now sat well with her, though – that no one recognized that she could possibly be a Jew. Always it had hurt her that others thought her people looked a certain way, or had certain features, and yet always she'd wanted to be recognized for who she truly was. On this new path she'd embarked on, she thought of it as a blessing not to be.

And so now she sat awaiting the most frightening event of her whole life.

The descent in a parachute to just outside Krakow.

She would be met by a man with the code name of Ranger, and taken to a farmhouse where Gunther Meyer lived.

In the few days she would have with him, he would introduce her to Piotr, who would take her to the camp that was to be her home for a while.

The command came. Tamar thought she would soil herself as her stomach churned. One by one, the men with her inched to the edge of the open door of the aircraft and, one by one, they leaned forward and disappeared.

Sweat dampened Tamar's clothing, her breath came in pants as panic threatened to consume her, and then the bitter cold breeze of her homeland hit her face. Her legs were now dangling – a slight push into her back and she tumbled out into the vast, unknown world of the dark sky.

Doing as she was taught, putting out her hands and feet and keeping her body birdlike, the ground came nearer and nearer. Under her breath she counted. Then the moment she wanted and yet feared was on her as she pulled the cord to release her parachute – a heart-stopping moment between gliding to earth and tumbling to her death if it failed to open.

But a familiar jolt and she was slowed and held. Relief settled her heartbeat as now she knew her fate would be to glide down safely.

The ground met Tamar with a bump that shook her insides and left her trembling. Rolling as she'd been taught, she made it to a standing position, got out of her parachute and quickly folded it.

Looking around, she could see a clump of trees ahead of her, standing tall and black against the night sky.

When she reached them, she found they were close enough together for her to conceal her parachute behind one of them.

It took a good five minutes to scrape back the snow and hack away at the frozen soil beneath one of the roots and stuff the chute into it.

With this done and the soil and snow replaced, Tamar sat back on her haunches, found her pen-torch, map and compass in the pockets of her all-in-one waterproof, and unravelled the map. With those who had jumped from the plane with her having vanished, each on their own mission, she'd never felt so alone in the world.

An owl hooted, adding to the eerie sound of the wind howling and the scene of snow, frost and distant blackness.

Giving all her concentration to the job in hand and not letting her imagination frighten her any more than she was already, Tamar shone the small beam of her torch on her map, but working out where she was proved to be more difficult than it had when she'd practised it in training.

Gazing around her, the moon lit up a road on the other side of the trees. Tamar decided to make for that and then walk in a southerly direction as Krakow was in the south of Poland and somewhere along that road she hoped would be the crossroads where Ranger would be waiting.

The embankment leading to the road proved to be steeper than Tamar had realized. Her pace quickened and she lost control, her foot caught in a bramble, making her tumble downwards. Grasping out to get hold of something – anything to slow her descent – she hit the hard surface of the road with a bump that winded her.

Stunned, she lay still, gasping in the cold air, but then a distant rumble shuddered the ground beneath her. She lifted her head and felt the bruising of her body with the movement. She saw a trail of lights headed for her and knew she should get off the road and hide, but panic gripped her and held her still, until her survival instinct kicked in and she grabbed her haversack and rolled towards the verge. There, she lay on her stomach with her face turned towards the road and prayed.

Wheel after wheel sped by at eye level, until at last, the convoy had passed.

Wet and freezing cold, Tamar swallowed back her tears as she realized she'd dropped both her map and compass that she'd been holding, and they were now destroyed, having been run over by the lorries.

Despair threatened to engulf her, but she gathered all her courage and decided she would look for shelter and wait till morning to find her destination.

As this was deep in the countryside, it was bound to be farming land, and so a barn wouldn't be far away. With this thought cheering her, she stood, put her haversack on her back and set out on the road in the same direction the trucks had been travelling.

She hadn't gone far when she spotted the shape of a barn. At last, shelter from the icy wind.

Once in the barn and with the straw she'd seen strewn on the floor in the light of her torch kicked into a bed, Tamar lay her exhausted body down, not thinking she would sleep, but at least knowing she would be warm and dry.

'What the hell are you doing here?'

The astonished voice woke Tamar. For a moment she froze, but then the voice softened. 'It's a wonder you didn't bloody freeze to death!'

He'd spoken in English!

'I'm guessing you're the agent Bibi? I'm Ranger.'

To Tamar, it was as if she'd dropped out of an alien world into a warm cosy one. All fear left her.

'Let me nip around the back of the barn for a pee, and then I'll tell you.'

'Ha! I like your spirit. If I'd been a German, you'd be dead now.'

Rising and making for the door, Tamar retorted, 'And if I don't complete my mission to go to the loo, you'll drown!'

He put back his head and roared with laughter.

When she returned to the barn, Ranger asked, 'So, what

happened? I waited at the crossroads, but you didn't show, so as soon as it was light, I traced the steps you could have taken – that's the beauty of snow, helps no end with tracking someone.'

Tamar explained what had happened.

'Yes, I saw those trucks and that's why I feared for you. I had a sleepless night imagining you captured and our whole mission jeopardized.'

'Ah, so you assume I'd talk? You need to have more faith in me than that.'

'I'm sorry. Now I have met you, I do, but having a woman coming to camp is a new concept for us. We men were brought up to protect women, not fight alongside them . . . It's your language skills you were chosen for, I believe?'

'And because a young woman can go anywhere without being questioned. But yes, my language skills will be of help to you and the mission, as will looking like my mother, who was German.'

'What? And they trained you, not incarcerated you? I thought anyone who was an alien, or had alien relatives, was sent to the Isle of Man, or somewhere.'

'I – I . . . well, I consider myself Polish and am accepted as that.'

'Still, rules are rules . . . Is there something you're not telling me?'

'A great deal, as you would expect of me.'

'Ha. Well, I like what I see so far. A woman with spirit and not easily beguiled into giving information. You'll be a match for those bastard Nazis . . . excuse my language. Though you're going to be in a camp of men, so you may as well get used to it.'

Tamar smiled. She liked Ranger – she knew she could speak frankly with him and she could already feel she was gaining his respect.

'Well, better get on our way. We have a five-mile trek to the farm that I'm to take you to, and then, hopefully, there'll be a warm fire and a hot drink awaiting you. Here . . .' He rummaged in his pockets and came up with a map and compass. 'You were meant to find your way to me, but fate took over, but it would be good practice if you were to guide us to the farm. I presume you've been given its location in case we missed each other?'

'I have.' A little resentful of this as she felt she was being tested, Tamar wanted to tell him to stick his map where the sun doesn't shine, but she took it politely, studied it and the compass for a moment. She saw that last night she'd headed in the right direction, and then she pointed to the way they should go.

'Excellent.'

This did infuriate her. 'Let's get one thing straight. I am not on trial here and neither am I your apprentice. We hold the same rank. I have my skills, and you have yours – an engineer and explosive expert, I've been told. So I do not need scoring for anything I accomplish, or encouraging, and I damn well do not need my skills testing!'

'My, got out the wrong side of the haystack, did we?'

With the wind taken out of her sails, Tamar burst out laughing.

'Sorry, old girl, I shouldn't have done that.'

For the first time Tamar looked at him as a person, not just a comrade in arms. Ranger's ginger hair caught the sunlight, and his green-brown eyes twinkled as a grin crinkled the corners of his eyes. Handsome, tall and full of gentry-type confidence was how she summed him up. And in that, she decided he was a lord of a manor – a good old English gentleman – and she liked him all the more for his joking apology, which kept them on a good footing despite her outburst.

'You're right, though,' he said now, 'I need you and your skills very much. I don't suppose you brought hair dye with you, did you? I lost mine and my ginger has come back, making me a marked man.'

'No, but I can buy some at the apothecary. There will be one in Krakow, and I will need to buy peroxide from time to time.'

'Oh? You don't have naturally blonde hair?'

'No, more of a mousy colour. Neither did my mama, but the powers that be thought that I should.'

'Bibi, the more I learn of you, the more I feel you're going to be a massive asset to our camp. Pleased to have you on board.'

Again, Tamar laughed, then said, 'Right, in the meantime, pull your woollen hat over your hair and ears and let's get on our way. I'm dying of thirst, and that warm fire sounds like heaven.'

On the way, they chatted about their lives. Ranger, she learned, was an officer from Surrey. He didn't live in a mansion, but he was from a wealthy family. He had a degree in engineering, was married and had a young son. And he had crash-learned to speak Polish. Something Tamar admired as though everyone said that English was difficult to learn, she thought her own language much more of a challenge for students.

His voice took on a sad note as he continued. 'I don't know how my family are . . . I mean, I will of course be told if they are really ill, or hurt in anyway, but generally . . . How sad, or happy, how my son is progressing, is he doing well at school? How my wife is coping without me and with the shortages.'

His not naming any of them was in line with how they had been taught never to exchange their real name or those of family. If found out by the enemy, they could be used to make questions and threats more personal.

'I have worries too. My stepmama, who I love very much, lives in the East End and they are experiencing daily bombing. My best friend, a nurse, who is at risk trying to save lives every night as the bombs drop on the streets of London, has volunteered for military service. She hopes to work on a hospital ship – well, the same one as her husband works on, who's a doctor, but she's willing to go anywhere and do anything to help.'

'Your story is amazing. Full of bravery, hardship, fear and of finding a new life. I'm so sorry about the loss of your father, though. That must have been a huge blow, and yet, here you are, not many months later, ready to fight back. I so admire you, Bibi . . . And we will get through this, and when we do, I just know that we'll remain friends for ever.'

Tamar smiled. 'I'd like that. But I wonder if life will ever get back to normal, or what normal will be.'

Ranger didn't answer for a moment, but when he did, his voice took on a determined note. 'We will win this war, Bibi, we will. And we will rebuild our country and make it better than it has ever been.'

Yes, Tamar thought. The British no doubt would, but what about the Polish? What about her beloved country? Would it ever recover? Even if the Germans were made to retreat from it, the Russians had annexed so much. Would they ever leave and allow Poland to be whole again? Her heart prayed it would be so.

Chapter Fifteen

They walked in silence for a while, but a burning need in Tamar to learn more about Isaac's plight prompted her to tell Ranger, 'There's something else. My fiancé, he came back here to fight.' Tamar had to swallow hard as she broke the rule and told him, 'His name's Isaac, and there have been reports—'

'Isaac! You mean, the Polish guard in Auschwitz? . . . So, you are Tamar! That's incredible! But wait . . . that would make you Jewish! Now I understand how it is that you're here and not incarcerated for being alien – you have more reason than most to hate the Nazis.'

Tamar wanted to take the information back. She hadn't dreamed that asking after Isaac would uncover who and what she really was.

'Don't worry. What our real names are always comes out at some point. All in camp know who everyone is. It happens. Like you have, we slip up. But I trust them to a man, and so should you, only continue to try not to reveal your real name. I will always call you Bibi.'

'It's so difficult. I've failed at the first hurdle . . . So, you know Isaac?'

'Yes, I do. And he's the bravest man I know.'

'And he's being held at Auschwitz? Is that far from where the camp is?'

'No, Auschwitz is only seventy kilometres from here. A lot of the work we do here is disrupting the trains taking the Jewish people to Auschwitz. We have rescued so many of them, but what then becomes of them, we don't know. We just have to let them run into the countryside, or the Tatra Mountains, and make their own way to safety . . . We were on such a mission when Isaac was caught.'

'What happened?'

'We had done our job and were making our escape, pursued by German soldiers, when we heard a child screaming. We looked back and saw a soldier had a child by the arm pointing a gun at his head. Isaac picked up a stone and threw it with such precision, it hit the soldier in the middle of his forehead. He stumbled, and the boy escaped. Isaac ran forward. We tried to stop him, but he would not have it. He ran towards the boy. But the soldier recovered and shot the boy in the back of . . . His head seemed to explode . . .'

'Oh no! How could they? A little boy! And Isaac . . . ?'

'From nowhere, other soldiers appeared and grabbed him. Our camp descended into mourning for days at his loss. But then we had a young boy of fifteen turn up. He told us that Isaac and a German named Wilhelm had helped him to escape, and he'd been told to make his way to us.'

'Did the boy say that Isaac was a guard for the Nazis over his own people?'

'He did. However, you mustn't judge him for that. He will have complied with that instruction – not to stay alive, but to help his own. He has proved that many times over as up to ten escapees have found us in the past few months.

Also, he told one of them to tell us he wasn't a traitor – not that he needed to. We have only honoured his name, not vilified him for doing what he does, but—'

'I know. Though I – I doubted Isaac's bravery at first. I feel ashamed of that now.'

'It's understandable. Please don't let it worry you. So, you lost faith in him for a while but let my story of his bravery restore it. Isaac may be a guard, but he will be going through hell. He will be working against all his principles, with others who are just doing the job to save their own skins. He will hate them for that, and for the cruelty we have heard these guards often mete out to show that they have been truly converted.'

'Poor Isaac. He will be vilified by his own when all the time he is working to help them.'

'Yes, but they won't know that until he helps them. He can't risk the other guards suspecting him or having the prisoners begging him to make them his next escapee. They will all be thinking that those who got away did so off their own bat.'

Tamar knew a peace to settle in her. Her Isaac wasn't a traitor. She'd been told this, but she hadn't really taken it in. Now any niggly doubts left her.

'Is there any chance we can rescue him?'

Ranger shook his head. 'No. I'm sorry. We just have to hope that he keeps his head above water and survives it all.'

'What do you know about Wilhelm?'

'Quite a lot. We didn't until recently, then a man from the north joined us and we found he'd known him. Wilhelm was brought up in Danzig. His father and mother are German and have strong Nazi views. They hate the Jewish people.'

'And Wilhelm doesn't?'

'No, his mother's family are Jews, but she dropped her faith – apparently one of the reasons her husband moved them to Poland was to try to hide the fact of her real past. And this will shock you. She knew her parents had gone into hiding – she turned them all in to the Nazis . . .'

Tamar felt the horror of this and gasped out, 'No!'

'We believe this was under threat of her husband, who we know is a violent man. But yes, it is horrific. Anyway, Piotr, or Peter as we call him, who you will meet—'

'Yes, I know of him, as originally I was told he would be waiting for me, but that was changed to you being my first contact.'

'I know, there is a mission happening today that Peter is vital to . . . Anyway, he grew up with Wilhelm and knows how he thinks and feels. Wilhelm still feels like he is a Jew. He told Peter that, when he was little, his grandma was allowed to see him for short periods of time. She talked to him about her religion. What she said greatly influenced him, but he dared not share that with his father. Then as a young teenager, he was sent to become one of Hitler's Youth – all a ploy to ensure his mother was looked on as truly converted.'

'But we heard that if anyone was connected in any way by their birth line to Jews, they have to wear the yellow star.'

'Yes, but Wilhelm's mother has worked hard at convincing everyone she is no longer Jewish. She even took to the streets with the rioters to hound the Jews in their hometown. She has been left alone by the Nazis, though is never asked to attend functions with her husband and he is often shunned too.'

'My God! What people will do for love! I can't ever imagine doing what she did. But I am thankful for Wilhelm. Do you ever meet him?'

'Yes. Very occasionally he comes to camp.'
'Really! Is that safe?'
'We trust him and you must too.'

Tamar knew this would be difficult; she was afraid of all Nazis. Yes, Wilhelm's story was plausible, but so was hers, and she would play it to the letter, but it didn't make her the person she was to portray.

They'd walked on for another fifteen minutes chatting like old friends when the farm that was their destination was pointed out by Ranger.

'That's where we're headed. See the smoke coming from the chimney?'

'Mmm, I need some of that warmth.' Tamar wanted to add that she was grateful to him that even though they had got on to a friendly footing, he hadn't called her anything other than Bibi. But still she could kick herself for having made such a basic mistake that identified her.

Gunther gave them a warm welcome, as did his dogs, beautiful Afghan hounds with long, flowing blond hair and a majestic stance – that was after they calmed down and stood around in an orderly fashion. He was exactly like his photo, though she hadn't thought he would be so tall.

Shaking Ranger's hand and hugging Tamar, Gunther held her at arm's length. 'Yes, you could well be from my family, you have the look of some of my relatives.'

Tamar had a weird sensation of the world she hated colliding with the one she loved. This man was a German, he worked for the Nazi Party and, like with Wilhelm, there was a trickle of fear in her that said she should be wary. After all, she was Jewish, and this man knew it, and though Wilhelm didn't know it, there was a good chance he would find out.

'I can feel your fear, my dear, and I don't blame you. It is abhorrent what is happening to your people at the hands of my countrymen. I am sincerely sorry. And though words are often empty, mine aren't when I say I hate everything about the Nazi regime. But sometimes it is better to work from the inside to conquer those we wish to bring down and that is all I am doing.'

'I – I didn't mean to show my feelings, I'm sorry.'

'I'm glad you did. It is better to have these things out in the open. Now come, my dear, take off your outdoor things. I want you to meet Bertha, my wife. She has tea all laid out for us.'

Unzipping her all-in-one padded suit, Tamar slipped out of it and took off her woolly hat, releasing her now blonde hair and revealing her slim-fitting trousers and blue jumper. All her clothes were practical, and she'd been told that combats would be at the camp waiting for her for any missions she would go on.

Now she was here her nervousness at what she faced in the coming months heightened, as did her fear.

Bertha rose from the green and gold embossed armchair she'd been sitting in. A homely woman with a ready smile, fair hair and blue eyes, she had an elegance to her movements. Tamar looked around the room and found it beautiful and somehow fitting. The deep mahogany furniture was intricately carved and had curved lines that made the bookcase, the bureau, the occasional tables and the huge display cabinet that took up the whole of the back wall look somehow majestic, and elegant too.

A matching armchair to the one Bertha had been sitting in stood on the other side of the roaring fire and a chaise longue was positioned facing the fire. In front of this stood a long occasional table laden with cakes, a teapot and four cups and saucers. The German penchant for cakes was well known and this selection of custards and creams didn't refute that.

The plain gold carpet completed the sumptuousness of the room, and this was matched by the silk curtains that draped stylishly, but Tamar doubted were ever closed, as she could see a roller blind at each window too.

'Clara, you made it! Come and sit down and get warm. It's as cold as the Arctic out there.'

Guiding Tamar to the armchair opposite her own, Bertha said, 'I have tea ready.'

Her voice held the nerves she was feeling and endeared her to Tamar. On an impulse Tamar put out her arms. 'Thank you, and for the risk you're taking on my behalf.'

Bertha responded, and this time the hug was all Tamar needed. It settled her mind and sealed what she knew was going to be a friendship.

'Ooh, your cheeks are like ice.'

'Yes, it's freezing out there – the Arctic is a good comparison.'

'I offered to keep her warm, but she refused!'

This from Ranger rankled Tamar. He hadn't yet accepted that though a woman, she could do the same job as him and everyone at the all-male camp she was going to. But she let it pass as now wasn't the time to call the remark out as inappropriate, when to him it was just a joke. Besides, it caused a laugh and the laughter blew away any last shred of tension in the room, as everyone visibly relaxed.

The conversation flowed easily while they drank hot tea and ate cake – Tamar prayed they were kosher, but was so hungry she decided to sin this once and hoped she'd be forgiven. She was told of how Gunther and Bertha had met on their way home from England, when Gunther was travelling home after completing his studies.

'I had been to stay with an aunt, who married an English soldier after the last war,' Bertha told her. They had met in Germany as there were many British soldiers stationed there at that time.

'Yes,' Gunther said. 'We've often marvelled at how forgiving you British are, Ranger. My mother met my father – a German officer – when he was in a prisoner of war camp in Britain, near to where she lived. Father had been put to work on her father's farm. They fell in love and lived in a cottage on the farm after they married, but once my schooling was completed, they moved to Germany as Father had been travelling back and forward to run the family business there.'

Tamar wondered if she could ever be forgiving, but then she supposed she was being as she was sat here in the home of a German couple, and already she felt very fond of them.

After a pleasant couple of hours, Ranger said he must leave. 'I'll come back in two days to collect you, Clara. Have a good rest. All will be ready at the camp for you. I left the men building a separate toilet for you – well, I say toilet, it's very basic. And I'll see to it that there's a private area for you to bathe too.'

'Don't worry. I lost all inhibitions in training and learned then what "roughing it" really meant.'

They all chuckled at this as they waved goodbye to Ranger.

As he went out of sight, Bertha put her arm around Tamar and told her, 'I think you're very brave. And I want you to know, you can come here whenever you want to, and I'll run a hot bath for you and pamper you.'

Tamar smiled. Already it felt as if she'd known this

gentle-natured woman all her life, and it felt good to know she would be there for her. 'Thank you, Bertha, I will take you up on that as often as I can.'

'And another thing. I have a trunk of clothes here that belong to my sister. She leaves them for when she visits, as with so many checkpoints, and diversions, the journey from Berlin can be tiring, cousin, without lugging a case with you all the time. She is your size, and I know she would love to feel she is helping a little by making you comfortable. So, you can have your pick of them while you're here and each time you visit – and I hope that is often. I'm deprived of female company – well, company I want to keep, that is.'

Again, her lovely tinkling laugh and a little squeeze on Tamar's arm further cemented their friendship.

Later, having bathed and now wearing a blue woollen frock that fell below her knees, Tamar sat with Bertha by the fire and chatted. It wasn't easy as she had to keep so much from her, but she did tell her that she grew up in a little village quite near to Danzig. And how her mother had been German too.

'And Gunther tells me you recently lost your father. I'm so sorry, Clara. How you are holding up having experienced having to flee for your lives to England, and then being bombed and suffering loss again, I just don't know. Had you made friends in London? . . . Oh, I'm sorry, Gunther told me that I must not question you.'

'No, it's all right, I trust you . . . I . . .'

'No! You must not. You must not trust anyone, not me, not Gunther, not even Ranger. Always remain wary and on your guard, my dear. You can never be sure. What we have told you about us, you will need to know . . . well, in case the worst happens, and you are picked up and interrogated, as we are meant to be family, but don't volunteer information. I have done wrong to have encouraged you tonight to do so, but I'm like you, not used to this clandestine world. But we must get used to it and quickly, for your safety, Clara.'

'Yes, you're right, and for yours and Gunther's. If I'm caught, you could be in danger for harbouring me.'

'Well, that is something we have taken on as you are furthering what we believe in – the freedom of Poland and of the Jewish people to live in peace. Not to mention the freedom of the whole world, as Gunther feels sure that Hitler won't stop. He has tasted power and wants more of it. Already he has France, and his sights are on Great Britain. But we hope with all our hearts that he doesn't succeed.' Her face changed. 'We hate him and all he stands for. When we met him, I wanted to spit in his face but had to be gracious towards him.'

'Well, that is bravery too. Everything you and Gunther do is so courageous. I admire you both and thank you for helping me and the cause of Poland and my people.'

'Thank you, dear. That means a lot to me, and I know it will to Gunther. He is busy cooking dinner by the way. He loves to cook and is intent on making a meal as kosher as he can, as he dared not shop for kosher meat. But he has come across a vegetable-only dish.'

'Ah, that's sweet of him. But after the cakes, I realized that I would have to eat what I can when I can as to follow a Kashrut diet isn't going to be possible. I'm sure, though, that I will be forgiven.'

'More than forgiven, you deserve to be a saint.'

'Aren't all saints dead?'

'Oh . . .' Looking perplexed at first and then seeing the

joke, Bertha burst into laughter. Tamar joined her and the atmosphere was back to being relaxed and friendly, with all talk of being careful about what they mustn't reveal forgotten but adhered to.

After a couple of pleasant days and, last night, a glass of excellent wine to celebrate new friends, Tamar slept heavily and woke refreshed, feeling she had known Bertha and Gunther all her life and liking them very much.

Looking out of the window, it was wonderful to see a white world, no apartments and shops, just Poland how she loved it. She thought how beautiful it was, wearing its winter frock of ice and snow.

A feeling of being home draped her in love. And yet, she couldn't keep out the sadness that this land no longer belonged to her fellow Poles, and of missing her new country and her family there. It seemed a lot longer than three months since she'd been with lovely Elma and Florence.

A real pain gripped her – it hurt, though it didn't mean illness, just a longing for loved ones.

Dressing quickly, excitement and nerves mingled in her stomach as she wondered what life would be like from now on.

Knowing her mission, Bertha had fully kitted her out with everyday clothes and some glamourous ones which should take her everywhere.

One function they had in mind was a social event they were to attend shortly at Wawel Castle. A dinner and dance thrown by Hans Frank himself. The thought of it made her feel sick, and yet she so wanted to see if she would pass the test of being accepted for who she was meant to be – a German cousin visiting relatives.

To help her achieve this, Gunther and Bertha had given her such a lot of information – what school she, as Clara, attended, for one, and so many other snippets that might crop up as guests made polite conversation.

A deep sigh relieved some of Tamar's tension at the thought of how much more complicated it was than she'd been led to believe. And then anger replaced the tension – this was an underhand way of doing things. She should have been prepared for having to mix with German high society while here. She'd thought it would be her job to frequent cafes the Nazis favoured, and ride on buses, just listening to conversations, and then reveal her cover story of who she was if questioned. What she knew now changed all of that and put her in extreme danger.

When she'd voiced this, Gunther had said that this was always the plan, but only if he thought her capable of pulling it off. He told her that had she known this, she would have felt on trial and then it would have been difficult for them to see the real her.

But he assured her that while they hoped she would make a few useful connections that were elusive to Gunther himself, he would always protect her and see that she was treated respectfully.

At this moment, as she gazed at the beautiful royal-blue gown hanging on the wardrobe door, and knowing it was the gown she would wear for the occasion, Tamar wanted to run and not stop until she was miles from anywhere and live the rest of the war out as a hermit.

But more than that, she wanted to find Isaac. To somehow let him know she was here and fighting for him and to tell him that one day they would be together, and he mustn't lose hope.

Just as this thought threatened to send her into the

doldrums even further, she saw a lone figure skiing through the snow. Ranger!

Quickly donning the salopettes Bertha had given to her, and fastening them up over the top of woollen leggings and a thick woollen jumper, it felt to Tamar that she was zipping up her old life and opening a new chapter.

Goodbyes had been full of how they would miss her, and hoped she would come again soon and that she shouldn't wait for the invitation before she did.

'We will worry about you, dear Clara. Try to get messages to us that you are all right. And try to visit us again very soon.'

Hugging Bertha, Tamar told her she would do her best, but needed to settle into life wherever it was that Ranger would take her.

As they set off, Ranger said, 'You seem to have made a good impression.'

Over the howling of the wind, she shouted, 'Yes, they are wonderful people.'

'Good. I worried you wouldn't trust them. And good, too, that you're an accomplished skier, a skill you will need.'

'You forget I was born in Poland.'

They were silent for a long time as they covered miles of slopes.

At last, they came to a forest and slowed, before stopping to step off their skis and strap them to their backs.

'We are deep in the forest but from the road it is only sixty kilometres to Auschwitz concentration camp. Often since being here, I have wanted to gather the soldiers we have and storm the camp, but so many would die, and we need our manpower. We do all we can.'

'The instinct to lash out is always strong, when we know there is harm being done, but it is never the best way.'

'I'm glad you feel like that, as I thought you would want us to do that.'

'Want you to, yes, but wouldn't let you – or sanction such a move.'

Ranger smiled at her. 'I never thought I would say this, but you're perfect for our group and you'll be a huge asset.'

'Good. I've passed the test then?' She gave him a sardonic smile and he laughed out loud.

'I like your sense of humour too. Yes, you're going to fit in well, though you must prepare yourself for the experience of living with a dozen males.'

'You mean, the belching and farting?'

Again, he laughed. 'Well, yes, that, and the crudeness and insensitivity. But they're a good bunch and you can always speak to me in English to tell me if anything isn't right for you.'

'I don't need you to nanny me, Ranger, I'll be fine. The training I have been through prepared me for much more than map reading. I'm more worried about the scrapes I'll get into trying to be a "girl who doesn't much care" when I'm out in the cafes!'

'Yes, I imagine for you that would be difficult – handling what you may hear men laughing about and dealing with sexual inuendoes and advances. The Germans can be very gentlemanly, like your so-called cousin, but they can also be very uncouth too.'

'I will have to grow a second skin.'

Though she said this, Tamar felt her stomach turn over. How would she deal with such a situation?

* * *

The camp was much as she expected, tents erected close together and canvas sheets used to cordon off areas for ablutions. As Ranger had said, the men had made one especially for her.

Peter greeted her first. The leader of the camp, he was a big man with a kind face. She learned he'd been in the Polish army since he was a boy, and had been to England – Audley End, near to Saffron Walden in Essex – to train in clandestine ways.

'I enjoyed my time there and intend to go back after the war.'

'I intend to go back to England too, but it may be a permanent move for me as my home here is now in Russian hands.'

'They soon moved in and took territory that is Polish, but let's see how it all pans out. I feel there is a long way to go before then. Now, should I formally introduce you or let you enjoy a hot drink and a chat and get to know everyone gradually?'

'I prefer the informal approach. The other way makes me look like visiting royalty.'

'Ha, it can do, you are so right. Nothing more embarrassing than having to shake hands with a lot of strangers and pretend you're pleased to meet them.'

Tamar laughed with him. She turned then and looked at the men sitting around a campfire sipping something hot that hadn't yet been identified, but she hoped was tea. 'Right, everyone, this is Bibi. It's up to you to get to know her and make her welcome – but remember she is an officer in the Polish army and brings a lot of skills with her which will help us in our quest, so treat her with respect!'

All greeted her politely, if a little warily, but Tamar knew how they felt as she too felt the same apprehension. She would need them to prove themselves to her too.

But already she could see a few friendly and welcoming faces. She smiled at them all, said, 'Hello,' then, 'We'll start this getting to know one another after I've had a pee. I'm dying for one, and will wet myself if I don't go soon.' They all laughed. One rose and put out his hand. 'Jacques. I'll show you the way.'

'Thanks.' Looking back at the rest of them, she asked, 'Can you all sing? I don't want a dozen men listening to me relieve myself.'

Again, they laughed and one of them broke into one of the songs from *The Twelve Chairs*, a hilarious compilation of ditties from an early 1930s film.

Tamar grinned to herself. She had an idea she'd broken through the ice and all would be well in camp.

That is, until she was faced with the hole in the mud she was meant to straddle! But she managed it and felt better for doing so. It seemed to her like some kind of initiation ceremony had been accomplished – what the next stage would be, she didn't know, but she knew that now she'd got this far, she would be all right.

Chapter Sixteen

It was a week later that Tamar reflected on everything and found she was beginning to settle into camp life.

Nothing much had happened, but she'd carved a niche for herself and established that she had been accepted as one of them, not the little woman who should do all the cooking and domestic chores. She'd done this last by asking if there was a rota for all chores and where she fitted into it. She'd learned that Poppo, a small man with a happy countenance, loved to do the cooking, that he'd owned a restaurant in Warsaw and was very inventive with any food they managed to get hold of – rabbit, wild boar and even deer hung in his pantry, most of it poached, some of it salted to preserve it.

The meals she'd had were testament to his wonderful skills.

Most of the men were fine with her and happy to let her fit in and take her turn. However, one – Jonas – she couldn't break through to. He scowled a lot and made snide remarks about some jobs being women's work.

Tamar chose to ignore him.

Today, as she stretched and then jumped out of her sleeping bag, her nerves tickled her a little as she was to go into Krakow and visit a cafe that the Germans frequented. The thought unnerved her. But there had been no intelligence of any movement of troops, or any trains going to Auschwitz, so it seemed a good time, and it was hoped she would come back with useful information of any of these things happening soon.

When she joined the others at breakfast, Ranger told her their usual source of information hadn't communicated for over a week.

He took a sip of the hot liquid that passed for tea – weak and tasteless – as he told her, 'He's a baker's boy, we called him Becker. Well, the others said it was a kind of nickname.'

'It simply means baker, but is a common surname too,' she told him.

'Oh? I'm a bit hopeless at languages. It's a good thing the others have a reasonable command of English! Anyway, nothing has been heard or seen of him. So, besides visiting the cafe, we need you to go to the baker's to see if you can find out about him. I've drawn you a map.'

'But I'm not known! It will seem odd, a stranger asking for a boy she has never met.'

'Well, you lost your sharp wit overnight, didn't you? Ha! That's the first time I've heard you doubt your own ability! Just go in and say you have heard there is a delivery service for your daily bread.'

Tamar grinned. 'As simple as that! And if they say yes, I give them Gunther's address, eh? Well, what if Gunther is already down for a delivery? Have you thought about that?'

'You win. But there must be a way.'

'I could just ask anyone the way to the bakery and if they know if they have a delivery boy as I've just moved here.'

'We could try that. But remember, they are more than likely to see you as German so may be wary of you.'

'It's only my hair that completes that picture. I'll wear my headscarf tied at the back and clip my hair into a roll, so it isn't easily noticeable.'

Going back to her tent, having breakfasted on eggs and Poppo's homemade bread, Tamar donned one of Bertha's sister's outfits – a grey frock with a small collar that lay neatly around her neck. Buttoned up at the front and with a belt, it flared slightly to her calf, making it a good choice for cycling.

She'd been glad to see a bundle of woollen leggings among the clothing and chose a black pair to wear under the frock for warmth. Then she added a light grey, thick woollen cardigan, topped by a fur-lined coat in a cream wool.

Half an hour later, having been guided to the road by Jonas, who didn't speak a word but carried her bike, Tamar was cycling down a hill towards Krakow.

It had been a long time since she'd ridden a bike and she thought now of Isaac, and how they used to go for long bike rides together. Her tears almost froze to her face with the icy-cold wind, but she didn't stop them. She had to have this release of her pain. Knowing she was so near to him and yet might as well be a million miles away added to the ache in her heart. As did thinking about how his fellow Jews in the camp felt about him. She hated anyone not liking Isaac.

Stopping as soon as she was a few streets into the city, Tamar got her powder compact out of her shoulder bag, eyed herself in the small round mirror, and dabbed the powder-puff lightly over her tear-streaked cheeks. Then she applied the hated red lipstick and decided she would pass.

Checking the map once more, she continued her journey and found herself in the square – a place that buzzed with small cafes.

Her nerves heightened, as today it also buzzed with Germans! Some in uniform, but others sat around in casual clothing.

There were a couple of market stalls over to one side, and it was to these that Tamar headed as she could see a group of women chatting, though not from what she could make out about happy things as a couple of them dabbed at their eyes.

Not sure how to approach them, she picked up an apple from the nearly empty basket on the stall. It was then that she found she didn't have to ask what was wrong, as one said, 'So you actually saw Becker being taken away? What happened?'

Not daring to look, Tamar heard the answer given in a sobbing voice: 'One of the soldiers spoke Polish and asked the boy what he was doing. When he said delivering bread, they slapped his face. Then they broke all the bread he had in his basket in half and found something in one of them. It – it was a something rolled in cloth . . . They slapped him, but Becker didn't cry, he spat at the German! They thumped him . . . all of them, then threw him into the back of their van.'

The women gasped.

'Then one of the soldiers pointed his gun at me and said, "You! Do you know this boy?" And I – I . . .' The woman broke down. The others held her. One asked, 'What did you do?'

'I said . . . no! . . . I was scared.'

None of them spoke for a while, just comforted the woman. Then one of them said, 'I think we would all say the same. It's the best thing you could do, for the boy as well as for yourself.'

Again, there was a silence.

Tamar felt the sadness of them and of her own heart. She couldn't let her imagination go down the path of how they would treat the boy, or if he would ever be seen again.

'Are you buying that apple, or just listening into others' conversations, young lady?'

Recovering, Tamar told the stallholder in Polish, but using an accent, 'I did overhear, and it shocked me.' Dropping the apple, she turned, 'I'm sorry. I just don't feel like it now.'

The women were all looking at her. Tamar smiled. 'I – I'm sorry, I didn't mean to be rude . . . Excuse me.'

As she walked away, Tamar could feel their curiosity. Had she pulled off her disguise? Had they taken her for a German? She'd decided on her way down that if she did ask after Becker, she would use the accent she'd perfected that spoke of her being a foreigner to Poland. She had to be believed as the cousin of Gunther.

Propping her bike outside one of the cafes, she walked in on shaky legs. A couple of German men sat at the bar drinking beer. They glanced at her, then the one with his back to her glanced again but they didn't speak and went back to their conversation.

Sitting close enough to listen in, Tamar ordered a lemonade and sat absorbing what she'd just heard.

It seemed the incident had only just happened, so why Becker hadn't been in touch with the resistance group for over a week, she just didn't know. But her heart went out to him. She didn't know him, but felt she had a connection to him, which made her feel sadder than just the shock of hearing of a boy being treated that way. Fear, too, crept into her. That could be her, if she was caught!

The lemonade was cool and delicious but didn't help.

Tamar stared out of the window, not allowing her thoughts to go further. There was so much sadness and fear. She just wanted to empty her mind for a moment. She closed her eyes, but a snippet of the Germans' chatter filtered through the barrier she'd tried to put up. 'I saw Wilhelm yesterday. Another escape happened the morning he left.'

The other man laughed. 'He must leave the gate open when he comes down, as they always seem to get out then.'

Tamar froze as the reply came. 'You have a point there. They do.' After a pause, he continued, 'You don't think . . . ha! No. Not Wilhelm!'

'I'm not sure . . . I found something out about him. He's a mongrel, he has Jewish ancestry.'

'And you didn't know? Everyone knows that. His father married one of the filth, but she is fully converted . . . Why do you think Wilhelm was sent to Auschwitz, eh? To make sure of his loyalty. And they say he is more brutal at times than any of the guards.'

'Well, it does seem strange about the breakouts.'

'No, thinking about it, they happen at other times too. You're just picking on him now that you know about his grandparents. Anyway, they're long gone. Wilhelm's mother told where they were hiding so they could be rounded up, which shows she must have hated them and what they stood for.'

'Well, I've never known a leopard to change its spots.'

'Look, Wilhelm is a very good friend of mine, and if you cause him trouble, you'll have me to answer to. Did you pick your grandparents, and what they believed in, huh?'

'I – I didn't mean . . .'

'Well, just watch what you say in future.'

The tension left Tamar. But it shot back into her as the one who had stood up for Wilhelm now said, 'Anyway, as fast as we kill them, or a few escape, there's more being sent. I've orders to be on duty on the railway station again tomorrow morning to see the train gets through the station safely. Those bastard partisans cause trouble most times. I just hope they aren't aware this time.'

'Someone informs them.'

'Yes, they caught a kid this morning, about an hour ago. You haven't heard? He'll be dead meat by now. He's been responsible for the partisans knowing and attacking us. But he had the note of this operation still on him, so they won't know about it this time.'

'Good. Well, you should be safe until they organize themselves again. You have to hand it to them, they are resourceful.'

'Huh! Scum! But we're not taking any chances. We'll have back-up – a squadron will be hiding in the trees. They'll be up on the hill leading to the forest as we're sure the partisans are camping up there somewhere but we haven't located them yet. If they come tomorrow, they'll never make it to the station! We'll finally get rid of the bastards.'

As he turned and spat on the ground, his eyes rested on her. 'What have we here? Enjoying our conversation, eh?'

Though dying inside, Tamar straightened herself. In German, she told them, 'No, I am not! I am not interested, nor do I have the faintest idea what you were on about. I am here visiting my cousin who works for General Hans Frank! What two lowly soldiers have to say to one another is of no interest to me.'

Both jumped off their stools, stood to attention and stared at her.

The one who had stood up for Wilhelm stammered as he

said, 'I beg your pardon, miss. I . . . we have to be so careful. I only wanted to check you out.'

'I don't think you were that careful.' But then, not to discourage them from chatting freely again, as it was to her advantage, she added, 'But I understand. You're all doing a wonderful job and need to chat over the frustrations you experience, just as anyone else in work does. And I doubt that many people here would have understood your conversation.'

They visibly relaxed.

'I'm Wolfgang,' the friend of Wilhelm told her, 'and this is Ernst. Would you join us for a drink?'

'No, but thanks. I need to get back. I only came out to explore but have been out longer than I meant to be. Nice to have met you.' Tamar gave what she hoped would be a suggestive smile, trying to convey the impression of her being a loose woman, as was her remit.

Outside, she giggled at this – a virgin trying to be a loose woman! But then the small amusement passed as the thought repulsed her and she once more felt afraid of the implications of coming over as a temptress.

This part of her mission had been gone into deeper in training, as she'd been told that such women could go anywhere where there were soldiers at any time and not create suspicion. She could see that was right. She couldn't always make the excuse that she was out exploring, but she so didn't want to get into the situation of someone making a pass at her. She would never give in to them.

Back in camp, she told of all that she'd learned.

They were quiet for a time, but then showed their anger. Ranger more than most. He called a halt to their ranting as he stood in the centre of the circle they'd formed.

A silence fell. Ranger asked for the map that had been drawn up of the area. Then in a voice that held controlled anger, he commanded, 'We go tonight and set detonators around where they plan to lie in wait. Then early in the morning we get into position.' He pointed out where on the map.

'Remember, the Germans think we won't know, so will be a bit more lax than normal. I want every one of them dead by the time the operation is over. Spare no one. Fight to the end of them all. We will avenge Becker. We will show them that they may have taken one of us, but they cannot take us all. They must not win.'

After a moment of showing them where he thought the back-up army would be, he said, 'Good luck, everyone.' Then, 'Let us take a moment to remember Becker – his bravery, and how much he helped our cause.'

The men bowed their heads. A sob was audible in the silence that followed.

Discreetly, Tamar looked to where it had come from and was surprised to see Jonas was crying. No one said anything or went to him.

Later, Ranger told her that Jonas was Becker's uncle.

Her heart went out to him, and she wished he was the type of man you could approach to offer comfort to, but knew he was best left alone.

A shadow crossed over the side of her tent later that night as Tamar lay awake.

Knowing the men were restless, having been out and carried out the mission to lay the detonators, Tamar didn't worry. But when the flap of her tent lifted a little and she heard a whisper, she sat up and stared wide-eyed.

'It's me, Ranger. Are you decent?'

Tamar released the breath she'd held. 'Yes, what do you want? Is everything all right?'

'We just got back, and I wanted to talk to you.'

'Come in.'

He did so, but had to kneel at the end of her sleeping bag as this really was a one-person tent. 'Did it all go all right?'

'Yes, if I have the location right, and I think it can be the only one, then the Germans will be blown to kingdom come.'

'Well, I hope it's hell!'

They were quiet for a moment. Tamar could feel there was something Ranger wanted to say. When he sighed, a trickle of worry set up inside her. Something was wrong. She just wished he'd tell her what it was.

Thinking a cup of tea would break the ice for him as she'd long learned it was the English go-to at times of trouble, she asked, 'Is the fire still lit? Shall we go out and sit around it and have a cuppa?' Saying this word made her smile a little, as it brought Elma to mind. But before the thought could turn to sadness, she scrambled out of the sleeping bag. 'At least we could wrap up and walk. Maybe that will help you to say what you want to say.'

'I like your tea idea. But yes, wrap up warm. Even by the fire the wind howls around you.'

Once seated on the improvised stools – blocks of tree trunks – sipping tea, Tamar asked, 'What's troubling you? Is it anything I can help with?'

'I'm missing home. I can't talk to anyone, not even those with a little English. My head gets in a whirl sometimes, imagining my kids playing in the snow – if England is having snow. Thinking of my wife – I don't want to embarrass you, but I love her so much . . .'

This ended on a sob.

Tamar moved closer to him and put her arm around him. 'I understand. We're all going through the same thing. Though each of our pain is personal to us. I cry myself to sleep most nights, knowing Isaac is so close, wondering what his life is like, what he goes through to achieve what he does. The danger he would be in if he was caught. It's agony.'

'Forgive me, I didn't mean to put you through this.'

'No, it isn't putting us through more, it's releasing our pent-up feelings, just being able to talk to someone who understands.'

'Yes. It is. Christmas was the worst for me. We had a jolly time here, though a lot of the men travelled in the dark, walking miles, hiding where they could on the way, just to get home, which tugged at my heart. I was happy for them, and prayed they would make it, but I wanted to do the same. I didn't want thousands of miles between me and my family. I imagined the tree, the presents, my dad playing Father Christmas, midnight mass . . . cockerel for dinner . . . Oh, so much.'

Tears were streaming down his face now. Tamar just held him. His sadness was hers too. Her tears dampened his hair.

After a moment, he composed himself. 'I'm sorry. It just got to me tonight. I sat and wrote a letter to my family . . . I know we have done that and left it with HQ, in the event of our death, but I wanted to write more. I – I wanted to ask if you would deliver it if anything happens to me?'

'Of course I will, if I survive. But you mustn't tell me who you are. We none of us know what we may say if caught and tortured.'

'I've put it in a plain envelope. In the event of my death and you making it, you can open it when you are home. I – I just needed to tell my wife what is in my heart.'

They fell silent. Tamar took her arm from around him but felt bereft at doing so as the basic human contact had helped her too.

After a moment, Ranger said, 'Well, we'd better get some sleep. And I think I can now. I feel strangely released of a knot of pain I held inside me.'

'Yes. I think I can sleep too. And it's getting colder.' She shivered.

Ranger put his arms around her and held her close. It was good to snuggle into his strong body and it was, she imagined, like being hugged by a brother.

'I'll walk you back to your tent.'

At her tent, he kissed her cheek. 'See you in the morning.'

Somehow, Tamar felt protected. Like she really did have a big brother looking after her. Isaac had been that to her all through their childhood, and Hannah had been her sister. It wasn't until she was twelve and Isaac fourteen that their relationship had begun to change and become more than life itself to them.

Happiness – carefree happiness – had engulfed them. *Was that all we were meant to have? Oh, Isaac, my love, my love . . .*

Chapter Seventeen

Tamar woke after a fitful night's sleep to the sound of the camp bustling with life, though it was still shrouded in darkness.

A feeling of dread lay heavily upon her when she remembered their mission today. But she jumped up and dressed quickly in her combat gear – trousers, elasticated at the ankles, thick jumper and waterproof coat. All outer clothing was of a dark khaki colour. As was her cap. But before she donned this last, she clipped her hair on the top of her head – only yesterday, while the team Ranger had chosen to take with him were out on the mission to set the explosives, did she re-dye the roots. A chore she hated, as she did the condition of her hair, which was becoming straw-like.

But now wasn't a time to worry about her appearance, as after a quick visit to her latrine and a hot drink they would be setting off.

When she went outside, she could smell the eggs cooking as usual but couldn't stomach anything herself. Her nerves were too heightened, as was her fear. Never before had she done anything like she would be called on to do today – yes, there'd been mock-ups of such situations in her training, and she'd seen the horrors of death and pain by explosions. But today she could be called upon to point a gun at another human being and kill him. The thought disgusted and terrified her.

Two hours later, when her ears blocked with the sound of the explosions and men's bodies and body parts flew into the air, Tamar knew she was ready. The kill or be killed instinct they'd drummed into her kicked in. She didn't hesitate when she spotted a German behind a tree.

Crouching in the wet, cold bracken, she waited for her moment. She saw the tip and then the barrel of his gun come into view. She glanced in the direction it was pointing and saw Ranger kneeling with his gun poised but looking in a different direction.

Tamar's heart beat loudly in her chest. Her mouth dried, her hands shook.

Steadying them, she looked down the sight of her rifle. She saw the soldier's head come around the tree and fired.

He fell to the ground.

Hardly daring to look, her eyes found Ranger. He was all right.

Tamar dropped onto her belly. Her body shook with violent shivers. She'd killed a man!

Shouts made her lift her head. A dozen or so Germans were heading for them. Ranger fired, but though he hit one and reloaded, they were getting closer.

Becoming a soldier again, Tamar reloaded and fired, over and over. Man after man fell to the ground. But one, with bayonet fixed, was almost on Ranger.

Tamar tried to reload again, but her gun jammed.

Not thinking, she fixed her bayonet and charged towards

the soldier. He turned. She could see his eyes wide with terror. Saw him lift his rifle and point it at her. Then his head exploded into jets of blood, and he fell at her feet.

Looking to where the shot came from, Tamar saw Jonas. But then she gasped as a soldier bore down on him. The sound of the shot zinged through her but as it silenced, the horror of seeing blood spurt from Jonas's chest and him falling heavily forward left her wanting to scream and scream. She opened her mouth, but no sound came as a barrage of fire confused her.

A tug on her leg caused her to fall to the ground next to Ranger. He put his body over hers. They lay there for what seemed like eternity, until one last shot, then all went silent.

Tamar lifted her head. Around her was a sea of bodies. Through the trees she saw four or five German soldiers running away and the realization came to her that the resistance had won.

'Are you all right?' Ranger asked.

Tamar had an unearthly feeling of wanting to laugh, but knew it was just hysterics. She controlled the urge and nodded.

As they rose, the carnage around them ripped through her heart. Young men – from both sides – dead, in icy-cold graves of frozen soil that didn't soak up their blood but allowed it to run in streams away from their lifeless bodies. She'd been a part of this massacre of youth. She'd killed fellow human beings. War was a thief of young lives.

Ranger's arm came around her. She went into his warm body and allowed her tears to flow. His dripped onto her head. 'You were so brave. You saved my life, Bibi.'

The sound of a moan parted them as they saw a movement. 'Jonas!'

Rushing over to him, they knelt beside him. His eyes stared at her. In Polish he told her, 'You are so like my daughter; I couldn't take it. But I willingly give my life for you. Seek out my family, tell . . . tell them I love them . . . My name is Aleksander – Alec Riminski. From . . . from Warsaw . . . Keep safe . . .'

Tamar went on her knees and lifted his head into her lap. 'Thank you, I will never forget you.'

A small smile played around Jonas's lips, and then a deep sigh left his body on a breath that would never be drawn in again.

'Go in peace, Alec Riminski. Your bravery will live on.'

These words from Ranger helped Tamar. When he put his hand out to her, she moved her knees from under Jonas and rose.

Though she wanted him to, Ranger didn't hold her, but handed her Jonas's gun and said, 'Come, we must hurry. The rest of our men have gone ahead, and I can hear the train in the distance.'

They hadn't gone far when he said, 'They will be ready for us, and reinforced by those who ran away as they would have made their way to the station. We will be outnumbered, but once the train stops, as the detonators explode ahead of them, we must all stick to our plan.'

When they reached the meet-up point, Tamar saw that they had lost four men including Jonas. She couldn't yet identify who the others were but was comforted by them still having twenty able-bodied fighters.

These thoughts were taken over by the rumbling of the train, and then, as Ranger detonated the explosion, the screeching of brakes.

Below, Tamar could see the German guards, joined by those who had escaped the forest, were pacing and looking in all directions. But then as the train came to a halt, she could hear the wailing of distressed human beings, and their banging on the sides of the carriages. Her heart went out to them – her people, squashed into small spaces being taken to their death. She wanted to charge there and then, shooting the despicable soldiers she no longer saw as young lives but as vile murderers.

Ranger held up his hand, pressed the detonator again, this time causing an explosion on the platform. Men's bodies did a hideous dance in the air, but there was no time to react to this as hand grenades were handed out and the count of one, two, three meant all hands threw their grenades at the same time.

They didn't stop to watch the destruction of this, as Ranger shouted, 'Now!'

With holding Jonas's gun giving her the feeling he was protecting her, Tamar ran down the hill with the rest of them towards the confusion on the station.

The chaos caused by the explosions worked to their advantage. She didn't know how many shots she fired, or how many men fell by her hand, she just focused on her people in those trucks and how many lives they might save.

As she fired, she saw them begin to stream out, unbelievable numbers of men, women and children, and even babes in arms.

They ran towards the forest, and down the embankment towards the road. Some she saw fall – freed only to be shot. But she could not let the sadness and despair of this get to her. She had a job to do – a job of protecting her people as they made their desperate attempt towards freedom.

Gradually, the shouts, screams and gunfire came to an end. Tamar sank to her knees. But then Ranger commanded, 'Get their guns and ammunition, and anything of value – hurry. We'll hide them in the trees and come back for them tonight.'

It seemed such a short time to Tamar that she'd been programmed to obey no matter what she was asked to do. And she didn't argue this time, though taking from dead bodies was abhorrent to her.

They picked their way carefully, aware that not all might be dead, and that those who had run when the battle was lost might be in hiding waiting for them to expose themselves.

As Tamar bent down to take a gun from the side of one young man, she heard him whimper. She cocked her gun ready, but then heard him cry, '*Mutter, Mutter!*'

An unwanted picture of her own mama came to her. One that sliced her heart with shame. She went on her haunches and in German she whispered, 'I am here.'

The young man smiled and released his last breath.

Tamar stared at him. He couldn't be more than eighteen – his fate to be born into a Germany that was to be ruled by a tyrant, who would take away his youth and indoctrinate him, and then to die in a land he might have only dreamed of visiting one day.

Her heart filled with sadness. 'Rest in peace. Your cause wasn't the right one, but you were faithful to it.'

With this she moved on, leaving him with whatever possessions he had. She'd been taught all tactics of survival, and stealing what she could from where she could to fund them to fight again another day was part of that. But in this one case, she just couldn't do it.

As they walked away Ranger said, 'None of what we do is pleasant, Tamar.'

He'd read her mind.

'But,' he continued, 'we have to remember why.'

She could only nod her head.

'Ah, here we are.'

The men began to scrape away the leaves in a patch in a clearing.

As a huge trapdoor came into view, Ranger told her, 'This bunker was built in the early days as a store. It's marked on the map, but until we came to it, I didn't want to try to explain, as you have taken in so much since arriving.'

Tamar had been surprised many times at how this band of men operated, and now she was amazed to look down into the bunker and see steps leading down to what looked like a cellar. A cellar stacked with ammunition, food and jewellery.

'Our lifeline.'

'Amazing. I knew you were well organized, but this!'

'Yes, we have to be. We can't take shipments of goods to keep us going, or supply us with weapons. We have to beg, borrow and steal what is needed. And though what we did today appalled you, remember, we are fighting a fully funded, highly trained army of men, who would stop the world and its people living their lives as they want to. Who torture, murder and starve Jews, gypsies and those who prefer the love of their own sex.'

This little speech took away the last remaining sympathy that Tamar harboured for the German soldiers. She was ready to accept that what she'd done today was the right thing to do – the men she killed could never do the things outlined by Ranger ever again.

With the weight of guilt lifted from her shoulders, Tamar sang along with the men as they trudged back to camp.

She understood their need to act as if nothing had happened. Not in a disrespectful way to those who had lost their lives, but to try to get some normality back into their awful existence – show resilience. She even laughed along with them when Fillip burst into singing a very rude ditty about lying with their wives soon.

But suddenly the air was split by the sound of a gun firing, and Ranger dropped at her feet.

Amid the chaos that followed – men shooting in the direction of the shot, and others running for cover – Tamar fell on her knees beside Ranger.

Blood soaked through the breast of his jumper and his face drained of colour, his expression one of shock.

Ripping his jacket open, Tamar saw a gaping, burning, bloodied hole where the bullet had torn through him. His breath came in wheezing gasps.

Shouting above the sound of shots, Tamar said, 'Hold on, Ranger. Don't die. We'll get you home to your wife and children. You can get well with them in your own home!'

He tried to speak. She put her ear closer to him, heard the words, 'Jenny, my Jenny.' And then saw his body collapse in a sigh that took him from them.

'No! No!' Standing, she shouted, 'You bastards,' in English, and then in German, '*Sie stinkende, mörderische Bastarde!*'

A laugh resounded around her. She looked down the barrel of a gun, held by a bent, bleeding figure. But before he could shoot, a shot rang out and he fell to the ground.

Tamar took flight. She ran and ran till she came to a stream. Running into it, she took no heed of the freezing temperature, but stood and cried tears, and wailed out loud, until her whole body was weeping – even her frozen fingertips.

'Bibi, Bibi, no! Please come out,' Fillip implored her from the bank. 'Please, you will catch your death – the men need you. You are the only officer left. Don't show them a broken woman, show them your strength and leadership. Please, please, Bibi!'

Hearing her papa's nickname gave Tamar the strength that Fillip urged of her. She was representing him and all Jewish people. She couldn't let her papa or them down now.

Back at the camp, the men boiled water and filled a hot bath for her. They made her hot cocoa and lavished her with attention. At last, she stopped crying and as she allowed herself to soak, she took hold of the thought that Ranger would want her to carry on. To be strong and to bring to the group what he would have done – a sense of order and strength.

At a meeting held later that day, they remembered those they'd lost. And then Tamar asked them to run her through the roles they all had, so she could see what she needed to complete a good, workable and effective band.

Once she had this, she and Fillip walked through the trees and up a steep hill to the highest spot where Fillip took the radio equipment out of his backpack. As he did, he said, 'This is where Ranger radioed messages through to his HQ. You get a good signal.'

Starting her message with the news she didn't want to acknowledge, Tamar told of the death of Ranger, and the others they'd lost during a successful mission that took out at least twenty Germans and set free hundreds of Jews. That they were now short of an engineer and explosives expert, a tracker, and manpower in general.

They waited, hoping the message had got through as the biting wind cut through them, leaving Tamar shivering.

At last, the ticker tape began to move. 'Hold fort, men will be with you shortly. You will be informed of time and place. Well done.'

The thought of the manpower she could expect helped, but the 'Well done' seemed meaningless, though she would convey that to the men.

Back in camp, the mood was sombre. They ate the delicious stew Poppo had slaved over in silence, but then most went to their beds.

Tamar did too.

Once there, she dug out Ranger's letter and opened the envelope. Inside she found another envelope with *Jenny* written inside a heart. Around that was a note with Ranger's real name, Captain Russell Dandle, his address in Surrey and a few words telling her what a difference her being there had made to his life and asking her to give his Jenny a hug from him.

Drained of tears, she memorized the address before tearing the note into shreds so the information couldn't fall into the wrong hands, and popped Jenny's letter back into the bigger envelope and stuffed it under her sleeping bag. When she went to Bertha's and Gunther's this weekend, she would take it to them for safe keeping – there was nowhere safer.

By the time the weekend came, and Tamar dressed in a warm brown frock of the same style as the blue one she'd worn to the cafe a few days ago, which now seemed like months ago, she was feeling ready for all the challenges ahead.

She was to make her way to the bus station and Gunther would pick her up from there.

Though nervous on the journey, once she arrived at the bus station and put her bike in the shed provided, Tamar found she was in control of herself once more. She could do all that was asked of her – she'd got the camp running smoothly again, they'd heard when men were going to be dropped and, to Tamar's relief, among them would be an officer who would take over from her. This she badly needed as she couldn't carry out her own job of information gathering while tied to keeping the camp in order and working out strategies.

Gunther greeted her like a cousin would, and as Tamar settled in the seat next to him which smelled of leather and enveloped her like a comforting hug, she suddenly felt glad of this respite.

'So, how is it all going? I heard of the success – which was looked on as a disastrous failure our end because of the release of the prisoners. Apparently, twenty-five men were lost, not to mention arms and personal effects.'

'Sadly, we lost many too. Ranger was one of them.'

'Oh, no! Oh, Clara, I'm so sorry.'

Tamar thanked him. She swallowed back her tears. She'd cried and cried till she felt drained.

They drove on in silence for a while, and then Gunther shocked her.

'Do you want to hear news of how everything is going with this war?'

'Yes. I have no news of what is happening outside of the forest. Is London still being bombed?'

'I'm sorry to say that it is. But the people of London are infuriating Hitler with their resilience.'

This made Tamar fear for her loved ones. 'I want to ask for news of my stepmother and my friend. Would you be able to get any?'

'I will try. Once we are home, I will radio and ask for this to be given to me for you.'

'Thank you.'

'Other intelligence I have is that the Germans have plans, supported by Hungarian and Bulgarian forces, to attack Yugoslavia and Greece on the sixth of April – three weeks from now. Hitler wants to overthrow the recently established pro-Allied government in Yugoslavia. He is furious at the failure of Italy's attempt to invade Greece last October. But the British already have troops in Greece and could bring more from North Africa, so it is hoped he won't succeed.'

'Sometimes it feels that it is all a hopeless quest. That the Nazis will one day rule the world!'

'They won't. If it takes years, they will be beaten. There are many of my fellow Germans, like me, working to undermine them by giving intelligence. The Nazis are widely hated in my country. But feared too.'

'Don't you feel sad that young men are forced to fight and are getting killed?'

She told him about the incident on the station.

'That is the terrible consequence of war. That young man may or may not have agreed with what he was fighting for, but he did his duty. Thank you for helping him in his last minutes on this earth, but you must put such things behind you. If you carry them with you, they will weigh heavy on you. Look on everything as your duty. You are carrying it out to save your country and the rest of the world from a tyrant.'

'Yes, Ranger said something similar, and I am trying to do just that. But it all seems so hopeless at times.'

'It isn't. Every successful raid undermines the Nazis, and in the case of the freeing of Jews, many will make it to Switzerland and be helped. They will be living a different life, but one of safety, and that is down to you and Ranger and the band of men you are with.'

This really did get through to Tamar. She brightened thinking of the plight those Jews had faced and now, if only a quarter of them got to safety, at least that number would live.

She smiled. 'Thank you, Gunther, you have helped me a lot. Ranger didn't die in vain. And one day when I meet his wife, I will tell her so.'

'That's the spirit. Now, Bertha is excited you are coming, so best foot forward and don't let her get a hint of the danger you faced. She thinks you are up in the mountains cooking for brave men and visiting cafes now and again.'

His laugh made Tamar laugh, and with this, she felt better. But what would really complete her fragile happiness would be if she heard that Florence and Elma were all right, and more than that, if she knew her Isaac was too.

Chapter Eighteen

Bertha had greeted her like a long-lost child when they arrived. Tamar had felt the love from her warming her heart.

They'd enjoyed a lovely supper of potatoes, fresh meat and veg followed by a lemon pudding, and then sat chatting. Tamar, about her life growing up, and latterly, in London, Bertha about her life in Germany, each remembering snippets that they hadn't already told each other.

But now, as she got out of the car in the courtyard of Wawel Castle, nerves made Tamar want to take flight. Not that she could in the dainty silver sandals Bertha had bought for her to go with the royal-blue gown. She'd been taken aback by her reflection in the large mirror in the hall of Gunther's house to find that she looked, and felt, stunning.

Nothing, though, could match the beauty of the interior of Wawel Castle – the walls were draped with beautiful woven rugs of vibrant colours: reds, purples and rich greens; the carved ceilings showed intricate paintings between the curved beams, the chandeliers hanging like glittering stars; and the beautiful upholstered and engraved mahogany furniture – how it was all wasted on a wicked man who didn't deserve any of it!

Gunther introduced her to some officers who stood in a group chatting. They were gracious to her, but their eyes told of how they desired her too. This was the element of her appeal she knew she should flaunt, but it sickened her to even think of doing so.

Looking around, Tamar saw that Bertha was chatting happily to a group of women and so, she accepted the drink offered to her from a silver tray by a waiter and stayed near to the officers. Gunther drifted away.

'So, Clara, it is lovely to have you among us. Are you enjoying your stay?'

Tamar giggled in a flirtatious way, and said, 'I am now.'

They all laughed out loud, causing a few eyes to glance their way and two women to glide across to them. They linked arms with an officer each, claiming them as theirs.

Tamar wanted to shout out that she didn't want their men and didn't even want to be here. But she smiled and raised her eyebrows at the other two. They grinned back.

'So, Clara, what have you done since being here?'

'Explored mainly – drunk coffee in the bars. But my most exciting day was when I skied over to the forest, but then it looked dark and eerie, so I didn't venture in.'

'Oh, you mustn't. I'm surprised Gunther didn't tell you to be careful going that way.'

'Oh, why? Do you think I'll be eaten by a bear or something?' Again, she giggled.

'No, more likely to be killed by a partisan! We know they are camping in there somewhere.'

'Oh? Where exactly?'

The other one piped up then. 'We do know their exact location, so don't worry. We caught their informer and got it out of him. We have plans to infiltrate and then kill the bloody lot of them! But slowly, as we did the boy we caught!'

His laughter stopped at her involuntary gasp. He squinted at her.

Tamar recovered. 'That's . . . well, a young boy! How could they stoop so low!'

Seeming to be satisfied, he said, 'That's the scum they are. They get boys to do their dirty work and take the risks for them. But he was a tough little nut and wouldn't have suffered so much if he'd have given the information we wanted sooner.'

'Ha, I don't suppose they ever learn.'

This cut her in two to say and in such a flippant way, as her heart was breaking for the boy, and she was terrified at the news their camp was known, but it helped to make the moment pass and the chatter to continue and in a more light-hearted, flirty way.

The idea she was given was that if she presented herself as she was doing, it was acceptable for her to chat in men's company – though it was frowned upon, as Bertha was doing now, it was working, as the men were relaxing and sharing information with her as well as flirting with her.

But for all of that, Tamar was relieved when Gunther crossed the room and spoke to Bertha. She seemed to accept what he said and turned back to the ladies' conversation.

Tamar was never so glad as to see Gunther come across to her soon after.

'Well, my dear, I have to drag you away from these gentlemen as they have no one to rescue them, but there are so many I want to introduce you to.'

Tamar fluttered her eyelashes. 'I didn't know you needed rescuing!' They laughed.

Gunther said, 'Every man does from you, darling. You're

a tease.' He took her elbow and guided her away. Once they were out of earshot, he said, 'Well, you certainly play your role, well done. Did it give you anything?'

'It did. Frightening and sad news.'

'Oh? Well, keep it for later, but calm it down now, and stay close to me and Bertha. We mustn't overdo it, or you may get yourself into a nasty situation. We're here to protect you, my dear.'

Tamar looked up at him. 'I'm so glad you are, Gunther. I'm frightened of the role they have given me. I abhor the kind of girl I'm meant to be.'

'I know. War has given many of us roles that we don't like. Just keep safe – learn to read the signs of when to stop.'

By the end of the evening, exhaustion overtook Tamar, but she knew she couldn't retire yet. She had to try to contact the camp by using Gunther's radio. It was imperative that they moved and soon. She would stay where she was until they'd informed her of where they were. But she might leave it at least a week as she didn't want any suspicion falling on her shoulders.

After doing this all she wanted was to go to bed but once there, sleep didn't come for her, disturbed as she was by the role she had to play, but more especially by what Becker had gone through, and his death. How had the Germans been taken in by the evil Hitler? How could they act the way they did just to please him and further his cause? And she wondered how many of them must bitterly regret it now.

After a week of loving being with Bertha and leading a normal life, two pieces of news came through to Gunther from his contacts in London. The first had been what Tamar had been longing to hear – Elma and Florence were both fine.

Elma had remained in her shop but had a part-time assistant now besides Stuart, who was thriving, and her street hadn't suffered any more hits in the nightly bombing raids. Though to Tamar, this news wasn't them being fine at all. Elma was in nightly danger and must have forgotten what it was like to sleep in her own bed! How she longed to be with her.

Florence had been sent to join a hospital in Portsmouth. This was near to where her husband's ship docked, which was one of the receiving ships for the wounded.

This both pleased and surprised Tamar.

The surprise element wasn't that Florence had wangled this as the next best thing to being on the ship with Liam – Florence was one determined lady – but that HQ had added this information. Tamar wondered just how close her associates were being scrutinized.

But more than this, she was pleased for Florence. It must be wonderful to know that every few weeks or so, she would reunite with Liam. Tamar dared not think about such a scenario for herself and Isaac, as the impossibility of it would break her.

Further news she had was from the resistance workers who had contacted Gunther with their new camp location – they had chosen to go higher and be closer to Auschwitz. What their logic was, she wasn't sure, though Gunther said that sometimes you're safer under the noses of the enemy as they would never think to look for you there.

As he told her the arrangements for getting her back to camp, he said, 'And there was one other thing. Another British agent is on his way. The whereabouts of the new camp have been given to HQ, and they are hoping to drop agent Pickering during the next week. They will contact you with the details of where to pick him up. He's an engineer and has been trained recently on explosives.'

When the time came for Tamar to pack what she needed to take back with her a feeling of despondency crept over her. Life in camp was dangerous and hard. And this week had taken her away from it – going back didn't seem to have the same urgency. But she had to remind herself of what they achieved on just the one raid she'd been on – so much could be accomplished with a few more like it.

This cheered her and gave her courage to face what she had to face.

Back in camp after an arduous journey of trekking through miles of forest, Tamar was pleasantly surprised at how organized it was, and how the men looked as though they had been here for years.

Her own quarters were ready for her, and Poppo soon had a hot drink on the go and a delicious pancake.

'We found eggs, Bibi, and a good supply of them, so breakfasts can continue. Eggs are good.'

'They are, Poppo, especially what you do with them. You're a marvel.'

'When this is over, I will cook for you and Isaac.'

Tamar's head swivelled on her shoulders. 'You know about Isaac?'

'Sorry, Bibi, but yes. And we all know your real name and what happened to you – how you escaped to Britain with your papa.'

'How?'

'We put two and two together. Not that you've ever mentioned Isaac, but Ranger did one night, and we all remarked afterwards how what he said affected you and how you seemed very interested in anything about Isaac that came up.'

Tamar knew their training had prepared them to do just this – pick up on any snippets of information whether by word of mouth or reactions. So, she couldn't be cross at this, but she was at herself for blowing her cover.

'Isaac will get through this and when he does, that dinner will be waiting for you both.'

'Thank you, Poppo, only it worries me that my cover is blown.'

'Don't let us knowing who you are upset you. Most know who each other are. None would tell even if they faced death.'

This proved to be untrue a few days later, although none in the camp thought that anyone Polish would betray them.

It was as Tamar had just finished dressing ready to go down to Krakow, in the hope of seeking information, when Jakub – a quiet man, who worked diligently making anything needed out of wood, and who was thin and lanky and had the agility of a monkey when it came to climbing trees, even swinging between them, came to her quarters and asked, 'Bibi, can you come? An escapee – a woman called Anna – has arrived from Auschwitz.'

Tamar felt hope rise in her – would she have news on Isaac? Clutching her breast, she took a deep breath. *Please, Elohim, let it be good news.*

Hurrying from her tent, Tamar followed Jakub. Fear and anticipation vied for prominence as she went from thinking the worst to thinking the best – the best being that Isaac was well and so was his father.

As soon as she came through the tents to the clearing where all were gathered around the fire, the woman gasped, 'But she is a German!'

Jakub told her, 'No, she is one of us, she is in disguise. She is Isaac's fiancée, but you must never speak of this, for her safety. You absolutely must not.'

Tamar filled with fury at being exposed in this way and having her disguise admitted. She'd schooled them that if challenged about her, they should say she was a whore and for the right money would lie with anyone, no matter what side they were on. What if Anna was a traitor and doing the work of the Nazis? If Isaac could pretend to be a traitor to save his father's life, then any one of the other imprisoned Jews could for the same reason.

But she held her peace, not wanting to frighten Anna any more than she was.

Turning to her, Anna said, 'You are Isaac's fiancée? You're not in England? You are Tamar?'

Unable to change things now, Tamar nodded. 'Is Isaac all right?'

Anna didn't answer this but something about her look let the fear in Tamar win.

Despite the bitter cold, beads of sweat trickled down her back. Her mind screamed, *No! Not my Isaac!*

Anna spoke again. 'Isaac asked me to find his fiancée if I ever got to England, and to give her something that will tell her that he is still alive.' She dug her hand into her pocket. When she opened her hand, a silver heart twinkled in the sunlight. Tears sprang to Tamar's eyes. Without meaning to, she whispered, 'My Isaac, my beautiful Isaac.'

'Only . . .' Anna looked away. When she looked back, tears were streaming down her face. Her words became almost inaudible as she said, 'Wilhelm . . . Wilhelm did what needed to be done.'

Poppo looked shocked. 'Wilhelm? What did Wilhelm do?'

'We were outside hiding. We heard the accusation. It was Adira, she – she's a traitor! A Polish Jew, and yet a traitor!'

Poppo said, 'Tell us what happened.'

'Adira somehow found out . . . None of us knew how those who escaped managed it, until the day came when it was your turn. Adira wanted to escape, she begged Isaac, but Isaac couldn't secure that for her as she wasn't part of the groups who worked outside of the gates on the land, or . . . well, digging mass graves . . .' Anna stopped as Tamar gasped in a breath that told of her shock and horror.

After a moment, she continued. 'Adira worked inside, sorting the clothes and the possessions of Jews . . . You see, we were told to take all our valuables and some clothes with us when we were rounded up, but then had them taken from us when we arrived.'

Tamar could see Anna's need to talk, so didn't press her but told her, 'Drink your coffee. You're shivering with cold. Here, let me wrap this rug around you.'

'It isn't all down to the cold that I'm shaking. I – I . . . Adira is a nasty woman, she told us if we didn't come back from our work outside the camp, she would shop Isaac to the Germans. Isaac told us to continue, and that Wilhelm would see to all arrangements. Isaac . . . Wilhelm had to . . . Isaac was shot . . .'

'Isaac . . . dead? No! No! Noooo!'

Tamar felt Jakub's arms hold her. As a sobbing Anna continued, 'Wilhelm told us. He came to where we were hiding in the woods. He was a broken man but still he made arrangements for us and a farm truck brought us most of the way.'

It seemed to Tamar that her mind closed down as she couldn't react any more, just stare. She knew her mouth was slack, and that spittle ran down her chin, but she didn't wipe it away and knew, too, that her world had just ended.

Jakub asked, 'You said "we"?'

'Yes, there were two of us. Yeltsi, a young boy of about ten. He is waiting – it was he who got us here by following Wilhelm's map and then when you weren't where you were meant to be, he tracked you here by using clues – broken twigs, drag marks, all sorts of things. He told me an uncle took him on camping trips and taught him these skills. But he twisted his ankle. When he thought we were close, he climbed a very tall tree to see signs of any wisps of smoke from a fire. It was when he jumped from the last branch to the ground that he landed heavily.'

Piotr spoke for the first time. 'Poppo, help Bibi. Jakub, make a stretcher as quickly as you can.' He turned to the others then. 'You and you, come with me and Jakub once the stretcher is made. We will go to collect the boy.'

As Jakub left her side, Tamar became aware that Poppo still had hold of her. She leaned heavily onto him as he shouted, 'Bring coffee, make it sweet. Bibi has suffered a deep shock.'

Back in her tent, Tamar found she still couldn't react. A part of her wanted to run and run and not to stop until she too fell dead on the ground, but nothing would really form in her mind, only the words *Isaac has gone!*

As she acknowledged them a scream came from her. She knew it was a terrible sound but she couldn't stop it until a stinging slap calmed her.

'I'm sorry . . . so sorry, forgive me, but . . .'

Tamar fell onto Poppo, clung on to his neck. 'Help me . . . help me.'

A shadow appeared at the flap of her tent. She heard Piotr say, 'I have sent Rami for the doctor.'

Poppo's head nodded against hers. 'Sit down, Bibi, there's a hot, sweet drink here, it will help you . . . Oh, Bibi, I am so very sorry.'

She didn't want anyone to say they were sorry, she wanted them to tell her it was a mistake, that it hadn't happened, that Anna had told a lie. But she knew this couldn't happen – she would never see her beautiful Isaac again.

When she woke the next morning, Tamar had a sense that something dreadful had happened. She sat up, but her head hurt.

'I've brought you a cup of mint tea, Bibi.'

'Did I fall asleep, Poppo?'

'The doctor gave you a sedative. How are you? Only we have a visitor – Wilhelm.'

For a moment Tamar couldn't think who Wilhelm was. Then it dawned on her. 'Does he know I am here?'

'Yes. He has known for a long time, but he says that Isaac didn't. If he had, he would have tried to escape. Wilhelm feared for him, that he would be caught and shot, but now it has happened anyway through one of your own.'

'I want to forgive the woman who betrayed Isaac, as it is the way I have been taught. So, I will think of her as being desperate and that she saw a means of currying favour with the Nazis. I want to believe that she now regrets her actions.'

'Yes, that will help you, Bibi. Will you come out to see Wilhelm, or should he come here? I brought you a wet flannel and towel so you can freshen your face – it is streaked with yesterday's make-up.'

'Thank you, Poppo, that's kind of you.'

Taking the flannel, Tamar wiped her face. 'Is that better?'

'Much. Now, are you coming out?'

'No, will you ask Wilhelm to come here and, Poppo, will you stay too?'

'I will, I'll take care of you.'

As he said this, Tamar was reminded of her papa. Oh, how she wished it was him by her side, but Poppo was the best stand-in for him. His ways were similar and his kindness just the same as Papa's.

When Wilhelm entered her tent, Tamar was struck by his beautiful blue eyes. She stared at him, and knew in that instant that she had a connection to him.

Wilhelm stood to attention for a moment. 'I am so sorry, Tamar . . . I – I . . .'

His body slumped.

Poppo caught him and led him to the chair Jakub had made for her in the last camp. Tamar got up and went to him. As she put her hand on his shoulder, he looked up at her. Again, there was that hint of feeling that they were somehow meant to have met.

'It wasn't your fault. I have been told how you are such a friend to my people and take risks for them.'

'We – me and Isaac – did what we could. We wanted to do more, and sometimes to enable us to do what we did, we had to appear harsh on the very people we wanted to free – all of them . . . No one deserves what is happening to them . . . and now, I must escape. I am under suspicion . . . They made me do a terrible thing to prove I was still loyal . . . I just want to die . . . I should have gone alongside Isaac.'

His body folded in sobs that trembled through him. 'I – I tried to save him . . . I – I aimed to miss his heart, but I didn't succeed.'

Tamar held him to her by his shoulders. 'He will know you tried. Isaac won't hold anything against you, so you must not do that yourself. You must be strong to make your escape, and then testify to what is happening, so that the world is aware. We will make contact today to find out if you can be lifted out as we have a drop very soon.' Turning to Poppo, she said, 'Look after Wilhelm, I'll go to Krakow and telephone my contact. He will know when the drop is by now and contact HQ to make arrangements.'

'Can't you radio HQ from here?'

'No, I think we should maintain radio silence for a while. Soldiers will be out soon looking for Wilhelm when he doesn't show back at the concentration camp.'

Wilhelm took her hand. 'I am all right now, thank you. I am not a coward; I wouldn't want you to think that. I was crying for the loss of my friend and how . . . well, I can cope now.'

'Only a real man can cry, Wilhelm. You are a caring man, and you're hurt. Yes, scared too, but we're all that. I won't be long. Stay here till you have composed yourself.'

When she patted his shoulder, she again felt an affinity with him. He looked up and smiled at her. 'You remind me of my grandmother. The most wonderful woman, whose beliefs I hold – she was kind and gentle. Sadly, her daughter, my mother, is selfish and would do anything to further her own cause . . . She . . .'

'I know what she did. I'm sorry. But you can take the spirit of your grandmother forward. They are at peace now.'

Again, he took her hand. Strangely, Tamar felt that she was no longer alone with her sorrow – always, she'd felt the outsider, the one to be wary of, to take special measures around, and this had given her an inner loneliness, but with Wilhelm, she felt none of that.

* * *

When she contacted Gunther, his advice was that it was a very dangerous mission to hide Wilhelm in the camp. He suggested she take him to their house and he would take it from there. 'Do not use any public transport, make your way across the countryside,' was the final sentence of his reply.

As she spoke to Piotr about this, she noticed a young boy of about ten years old sitting by the fire and guessed he was the one who had escaped with Anna.

Piotr decided the journey should be on foot as skiing would be hampered by melting snow now that spring was on them. 'But still the temperature can drop, so there is a risk. And of you getting lost as you are talking five to eight miles to Gunther's . . . The boy here, Yeltsi, would have been your best bet, but when the doctor came to you, he strapped Yeltsi's leg up. Anna was taken to the safe house, but Yeltsi is going to stay. He says he wants to help us, and we think his tracking skills will be useful. He is very brave for such a young age.'

'We will manage.' Tamar wanted to say that he or any of them had never given her credit for the skills she'd brought to the camp. They only begrudgingly acknowledged them when Ranger was alive. But she understood. As Ranger had said, men had only ever looked on womenfolk as someone to take care of, not fight beside.

'Well, it is our only choice, we dare not spare anyone else. We have hardly enough to guard the camp and no intelligence coming in – maybe the new man will ease the situation when he arrives.'

With this, Tamar went and greeted Yeltsi. She spoke to him in Yiddish, thinking this would help him to relax. His smile in response was wide, suddenly making him the child he was, as she asked, 'What of your family?'

His eyes brimmed with tears. 'All gone . . . they . . .'

'Hush, there's no need to voice it, but don't harbour it either.' Tamar went on her haunches. 'I'm so sorry. I wish I could lighten your pain. But, Yeltsi, one day, write down all you witnessed and have been through. We must never let the world forget.'

Yeltsi nodded. 'I'm sorry about Isaac, we all loved him and understood why he did what he did. And I understand even more now as Piotr told me the many who escaped were all helped by him and Wilhelm. Is Wilhelm all right?'

'Yes, he is very sad . . . I will be leaving with Wilhelm but will be back. Once your foot is healed, you must take great care in all the work Piotr asks of you.'

'Is Wilhelm coming back?'

'Yeltsi, learn a lesson now – never, ever ask questions on people's movements, or anything. Remember, what you need to know you will be told. This is vitally important for your safety and theirs. What you don't know you can never slip up and tell.'

She didn't add, *or have tortured out of you*. Yeltsi was a scared young boy as it was, and a traumatized one. She made her mind up that when she came back to camp, she would take him under her wing and teach him all she knew about clandestine work. Somehow it became vitally important to her to take care of Yeltsi.

Chapter Nineteen

Tamar and Wilhelm set out an hour later carrying a change of clothing, sleeping bags and water in flasks.

Between them they had navigated a route that couldn't be seen from the road.

For the most part they hardly spoke. Wilhelm seemed withdrawn, and Tamar didn't want to chat.

It wasn't until they took a break sheltered by a clump of trees and sipped their water that Wilhelm said, 'Thank you for trusting me enough to help me, Tamar. After all that has been done to you by my father's countrymen, I wouldn't have blamed you for turning your back on me.'

'Not everyone can be clubbed together as being to blame. I hate the Nazi regime and Hitler, but not all German soldiers. What choice do they have?'

'Many are physically sick at night when the day's work is done. Some are sadistic, though, and have had a hatred of the Jews drummed into them from birth. They feel they are right to do what they do. How, I do not know. I will never get the faces of your . . . our people out of my mind as they were tortured and starved by the Nazis. I've never seen such suffering in all my life.'

With this, something broke in Tamar. It felt to her that the world had come to an end. She just wanted to go back to England, to be hugged by Elma and, more than that, she wanted everything to be back how it was. Her carefree former life of studying and being with Hannah and Isaac on the beach – it was all gone.

This last thought brought a sob from her.

'I'm sorry, so very sorry, Tamar.'

Tamar put her head in her hands. 'I can't deal with it . . . I can't!'

Wilhelm's arm came around her.

Together they sat in silence, mourning the one man who meant so much to them both. To Tamar, there was comfort in Wilhelm's arms.

Over and over, he whispered, 'Sorry. So sorry. I will take care of you for Isaac.'

This seemed such a normal thing for him to say that Tamar didn't object or accept, she just sat there leaning on him as at this moment, he was a friend, a good and strong friend who she believed would help her.

When they arrived at Gunther's, Bertha ushered them inside. 'Gunther is getting the cellar ready for you, Wilhelm. Come in and get warm. I have a good supper on for you . . . Oh, Clara, my darling girl. How can one take so much on such young shoulders? It's so unfair. Don't let it beat you, my dear. Take strength that Isaac and your papa are with you and by your side always.'

Tamar went into the hug offered. She felt the love given to her, and gave just as much in return as this woman had come to mean so much to her.

'I'm going to run you a nice hot bath, my dear. You can

soak and then put on some clothes that will make you feel human again. And then you can change too, Wilhelm. Gunther is roughly the same size as you and has laid out some of his clothes for you.'

When she lay in the bath, though exhausted, Tamar allowed her tears once more. She didn't sob, or wail or cry out how she wanted Isaac back, but lay there silently weeping, emptying herself of the huge lump of sorrow in her breast.

How could she never see Isaac again? How would she get through every day?

But she came to a place of peace for a time and then got out of the bath.

She dressed in a red frock covered in small daisies, brushed her hair and then plaited it. It was all she could be bothered to do.

When she went down, Wilhelm wasn't anywhere to be seen, and nor was anyone else. Calling out had Gunther lifting a trapdoor Tamar hadn't seen before but then she realized it had been covered by a thick rug. 'We're down here. Come . . .'

Negotiating the stairs, Tamar found a cosy space. Clean, and surprisingly airy, it contained a bed, a table and one chair. 'This is where Wilhelm must hide if any visitors come. We can keep him here for a few days, but then the plane will arrive with the new officer on board who is to be known as Clive. We're not entirely sure of Wilhelm's fate once he reaches London, but the fact that he worked against the Nazis will help him and that he is of dual nationality – Polish and German. He is to be taken to the Polish embassy, and they will decide. But the main thing is that he will be safe.'

Wilhelm said, 'I cannot thank you enough. And I don't think I will ever come back. I don't want to ever see my mother and father again. And I intend, when the war is over, to follow my grandmother's Judaism.'

This didn't surprise Tamar. He had done all he could for her people and owned them as his own, and she knew he felt he was one of them.

At supper, Tamar found that she could laugh at anything funny said and join in with the chatter.

Always the cellar trapdoor remained open just in case.

When it was time for bed, Wilhelm went towards the cellar then stopped. 'Thank you, Gunther. I will never forget you and Bertha. Goodnight.' Then he turned to Tamar and leaned forward and kissed her cheek. 'Goodnight, dear Tamar.'

A little embarrassed, Tamar smiled at him but didn't speak. Once he'd disappeared, an extreme tiredness overwhelmed her. She said her goodnights, longing for her bed, and yet dreading being on her own, but then finding that as soon as she lay her head on the pillow, her eyes closed and she went off to sleep.

Saying goodbye to Wilhelm had been a wrench as he was somehow her last connection to Isaac. It was as if she was cutting a tie to her beloved as she watched Wilhelm board the plane. But soon she was greeting Clive, and this helped as he was a cheerful man who she found was difficult to feel down around.

'So, this is Poland – snow-capped mountains and many trees! Beautiful, and worth sacrificing everything for. You and I, Bibi, are going to win this war together!'

Tamar couldn't help but smile.

A tall man, Clive had similar coloured hair to her own when in its natural state – light, flecked with darker strands.

His smiley eyes were hazel and his face handsome. And though he could never take the place of Ranger in her heart, she did take to him and knew they would be friends.

This became more apparent as they chatted on their journey to camp.

Tamar wondered if anyone ever kept to the rule of disclosing nothing as she learned that Clive was married and had two children of school age, and she felt the sorrow of all the families broken up and of the women carrying on at home without their men.

After a couple of days had passed and she had been relieved of the responsibility of the camp, Tamar knew it was time that she visited the town once more and mingled with the German soldiers in the cafes to seek out any information that might be useful in helping them cause further disruption to the Germans.

Clive raised his eyebrows when he saw her dressed and ready to go. She'd chosen to wear a red woollen jumper that clung to her figure and a black pleated skirt – an outfit that wouldn't normally be worn by a girl out to flirt with men. But Tamar preferred to tantalize rather than expose parts of herself. The jumper hinted at what was underneath it.

Walking with Yeltsi and half carrying and half pushing her bike, they chatted and joked. In the short time she'd known him, she'd come to love him. Often, he came to her for a cuddle. Often, he cried, and she so wanted to take his burden from his shoulders. But they didn't ask questions. Mostly he told her about his uncle and how he loved the outdoors. Always this ended in tears. Always she told him he could cry with her, tell her some things, but not reveal facts.

After Yeltsi had left her, having guided her to the road,

Tamar allowed the wind in her hair to soothe her misgivings as she rode her bike into the town square. She had to get rid of the feeling of hate for the German soldiers and to appear as always, like a young woman, a little loose in her morals, who loved to be with them.

Almost as if he was a permanent fixture, Wolfgang stood leaning against the bar. He turned as she entered, and a grin spread over his face. 'Ah, the dullness of the day has suddenly brightened. Clara! You are back. You cannot leave us for long. Is our allure too strong for you, eh?'

His words slurred as he came towards her.

Tamar giggled. 'I think you have started early on the vodka and will soon be passing out.'

'Ha! That's never been known. But I do have something to celebrate. Our mission yesterday was a success, and we have another to look forward to.'

'Oh? That sounds good. What have you done – captured more stinking Jews?' The words didn't match the pain in her heart, nor the anger she felt at the atrocities being carried out on her people, but she consoled herself with the knowledge that to play her part and to get information, she had to speak in a derogatory way about them.

'Ha, we don't have to capture them, we have them contained and they are sent to us like lambs to the slaughter!' With this he laughed heartily as if he'd cracked the funniest joke ever.

Tamar made herself grin as she said, 'I'd like to see this spectacle. You told me before that you transport them in trains and pack them in tightly. That their cries and moans are a joy to your ears. I think I would enjoy that too.'

'Then you shall. Be on the railway bridge near to the station at noon tomorrow, and you will see us herd the scum onto the train – ha, it will be bursting at the seams already, but we plan on adding to it with some more of them from the ghetto.'

Tamar tasted the bile as it rose to her throat. She swallowed hard, and then coughed as the sting of it threatened to choke her.

Wolfgang swayed and then sat heavily on the bench next to her. His alcohol breath fanned her as he slurred, 'What's wrong? Haven't you the stomach for it after all?'

With her throat still catching, Tamar grinned. 'Oh, I have. But I need a drink, I'm thirsty.'

He leaned closer. 'That's not all you need.'

His eyes clouded over. To his whispered, 'I know what you need and I have it, Clara . . . Come, there's a room at the back that we use,' Tamar froze. But then inspiration came to her. 'Sorry. Wrong time of the month.' Sliding off the other end of the bench and rising, she added, 'And my cousin is expecting me for lunch, so I have to hurry.'

Wolfgang's expression changed; anger tightened his jaw. His words, almost spat out, put a terror into her. 'Don't make excuses. You're a tease. But you've taken it too far. It's time I had you.'

She walked steadily towards the door, but didn't want to leave it as it was, so turned and, faking a smile that she hoped he'd take as amusement, told him, 'I'll wave to you from the bridge tomorrow. You'll be sober then.'

Reaching the door, she left in a casual manner, though she wanted to run as fast as she could away from him.

Her role was leading her into dangerous situations. But she hoped that when he sobered up, Wolfgang would have forgotten all about the incident and they could get back onto a casual footing once more.

* * *

Taking her time to mount her bike and giving another wave to Wolfgang, which she hoped would make him think she was being truthful over her reason for refusing him, Tamar rode off. Her heart pounded with rebound fear.

This act she had to put on was becoming dangerous for her.

Riding away in an unhurried manner, she didn't have to fear giving away her real destination, as for both Gunther's house and the forest, she would need to cycle down from the square and on to Starowiślna Road towards the Vistula River. From there, she would have a choice of directions – follow the road to Gunther's or take the one that led to the forest. By that time, she would have left Wolfgang well behind and would be out of danger of him knowing where she was truly headed. She was safe.

Not allowing herself to think about the incident, Tamar reached the point where Yeltsi would meet her.

Not expecting him to be there as she was a lot earlier than she'd anticipated, she schooled herself for a good half-an-hour wait.

To pass some of it, she thought she could carry her bike a little way in the right direction and at least be sheltered by the trees from passing cars and not arouse anyone's attention, as could happen with a lone girl standing in the middle of nowhere with a bike.

Not far into the woodland, Tamar became aware of a sound that told her someone was near as twigs cracked under the tread of feet.

'Don't even try to hide, Clara. I know you're in here, I followed you!'

Terror gripped Tamar. *Wolfgang! He's here!*

'What are you up to, eh? Who are you really? Why tell me you are going to Gunther's and then cycle here and come into the forest?'

Goosebumps rippled her skin. Her body froze. How had she not seen or heard him? Wouldn't she have heard a car driving slowly behind her? But then, as she heard him come nearer, she found she could move. Swivelling to face him, she noticed his bike flung on the floor at his feet.

His eyes told her his intention before he spoke.

'You've teased me enough. I've come for what you have promised in looks and gestures and hinted at in your voice.'

With this he moved in a cat-like way – a swift pounce and his hands were holding her arms and pulling her to him. Her bike fell to the floor, scraping her legs and giving her pain that brought her out of the stupor she'd gone into.

'No! Leave me alone!' Futile words that landed on deaf ears as Wolfgang became animalistic in his desire. Flinging her to the ground, his weight crushed her. His hands fumbled with her clothing.

'Stop . . . don't, please don't!'

He lifted his head from her neck and looked down at her. 'Don't! You know you want it. You've wanted it since we first met. Well, now you're going to have it!'

She felt the hardness of him against her leg. She struggled, trying to get into a position of strength to enable her to use her combat techniques to fight him off, but his might was too much for her as he wedged her legs open and thrust himself into her.

Her cries were to God to help her. Forgetting in her distress to use German, she called out in Yiddish, '*Got, helf mir!*' as she stretched inside and pain seared her.

Wolfgang stopped his frantic movements. His staring, evil eyes bore into hers. Dribble ran down his chin from his open mouth . . . 'A Jew! A stinking Jew!'

A stinging blow sliced her face, but the pain of it could not surpass that of his renewed, relentless and vicious thrusting into her, or block out his guttural cries.

At last, a strength came into Tamar. She arched her back, trying to dislodge him. But the movement turned his cries to one that told her of his exquisite pleasure. She felt him pulsate inside her, saw his loss of control as guttural sounds came from him, screamed out '*Nein, nein!*' But then, as his body slumped on hers, she remembered her knife tucked into a sheaf strapped to her waist – so far undiscovered by Wolfgang in his haste to satisfy himself.

In one swift movement, Tamar took advantage of his weak state and pulled at the press stud holding the sheaf closed, felt the steel handle and as she filled with hatred and rage, pulled it out and dug it deep into his side as near to his heart as she could.

His eyes opened wide in shock. Blood, not spittle, ran from his mouth. His body rolled off her.

Choking, gurgling sounds were the last noises Wolfgang ever made.

Tamar lay, unable to keep a limb still. Unable to stem the torrent of tears, or the agonizing cries of despair coming from her. Cries that called for her mama, her papa, but then pleaded to have Isaac come to her – for him to take her to him, hold her and make her whole again from the million pieces she'd been shattered into.

At last, her wails stopped. She sat up. She knew she had to take control.

Ignoring the horror of what had happened, and the still, ugly body lying next to her, reason came to her, allowing her to act.

She would go to Gunther.

Chapter Twenty

Tamar banged on the door, still shivering. Her journey here had just been a blur of soreness as she'd dragged her bike through the trees in a frantic hurry, reached the road, cycled through the pain of the saddle rubbing against her, and reached the bus stop.

On the bus, eyes had stared at her, as unable to stop shivering, and with tears streaming down her face, she'd sat staring ahead.

One woman came and sat next to her and asked in Polish, 'Can I help you, dear?'

Tamar had only been able to shake her head.

The woman had stayed in the seat next to her. Stroked her hand and then her hair, before asking, 'Where are you going? What has happened to you?'

Tamar could only shake her head.

At last, it was her stop. Scrambling past the woman, she made it to the door. She jumped out when it opened, bent over and vomited.

As her stomach emptied, it seemed to Tamar that her world had come to an end. Nothing would be the same again. She'd been violated – raped, her virginity taken, stolen by a vile creature who laughed at the plight of her people, who had loved to herd them to their deaths.

She didn't want it to be that such a man had taken something so precious from her. She heard her own voice crying out, 'Isaac, Isaac, why did you leave me? Why . . . why?'

Arms grabbed her. Stiffening with fear, Tamar resisted, but then Gunther's voice came to her. 'Clara, Clara, my dear girl, what has happened?'

Collapsing into his body, Tamar clung to him. 'Help me, help me.'

'My God! You're covered in blood! Clara, tell me what has happened?'

She opened her mouth, but no words came as the world began to spin and a dark cloud descended over her, taking her to a place of peace.

'Open your eyes, Clara.'

The voice sounded far away.

'Clara, Clara, come on now, you're all right. You're safe, my darling girl.'

This voice belonged to Bertha. Lovely Bertha. Hearing it brought a feeling of safety and love.

Opening her eyes, Tamar looked up into the gentle gaze of the love that she'd felt.

'Bertha! Oh, Bertha!'

Bertha's hand took hers. 'What happened, my dear? Tell us what happened.'

Tamar looked from Bertha towards the man standing beside her. She recognized him as the doctor who attended the camp when needed and he smiled at her now. A smile that held sympathy.

'Doctor Nowakowski says you've been through a trauma. Who did this to you, dear Clara?'

Instinct told Tamar not to disclose anything. Bertha wasn't trained. Yes, she knew that Tamar was undercover, but she didn't realize the importance of keeping everything secret from everyone, and while she trusted the doctor, she had to be sure and speak only to Gunther for now. 'Where's Gunther?'

'Gunther is downstairs. He is very distressed. Tell us what happened to you, dear.'

'I – I can't . . . I can only tell Gunther . . . Please, I want . . . Gunther! Gunther!'

Knowing her voice was rising and seeming to be out of control, Tamar allowed the facade of her being a hysterical woman and called out again, 'Gunther!'

Doctor Nowakowski came to her side. 'Calm yourself, Clara, I understand and will fetch Gunther to you.'

'I – I want to be alone with him.'

'Yes, that will happen.' He turned to Bertha. 'We must allow that, Bertha.'

Bertha's voice held a dejected note as she agreed. 'Of course.'

Tamar didn't want to hurt her, but knew what she had to tell must be only for Gunther's ears.

A few minutes later after they had left the room, Gunther's strong hand took hold of hers. 'I'm here, Clara, dear. Tell me what happened. Who did this vile thing to you? I will see to it they are killed.'

The emotion in his voice caused her own to spill.

Through her sobs, she told him as much as she could as embarrassment held back finer details.

'And he's dead? Are you sure? You felt for his pulse?'

'No . . . But he cannot be alive, Gunther. I pierced his heart from the side . . . he bled . . . He made the gurgling sound of death and then was still.'

She understood how important this was and why Gunther was giving it more attention than he was to what had happened to her. If there was a shadow of doubt that Wolfgang might survive, then all their lives would be in danger.

'I had to kill him . . . not only because of what he did, but . . . I – I exposed my true self. In my anguish I called out to God to help me in Yiddish!'

'Oh no! Oh, Clara, we must make sure he is dead. And we need to silence the barman who will know what happened in the cafe and might suspect that Wolfgang followed you and why. The doctor we can trust . . . He spoke to me when he fetched me. He told me to tell you not to be afraid, he will protect you.'

In his anguish, Gunther was quiet for a moment. He paced up and down, one arm across his chest, the other leaning on it and holding his lips as they pursed. Suddenly, he stopped in his tracks. 'I will radio Clive, tell him what has happened, get him to find the body and dispose of it or finish the job if Wolfgang is still breathing. Will you be all right? I must do all that needs to be done immediately. Wolfgang will be missed, and the barman may talk of the incident to other customers.'

'Yes, let me know the minute you know, but, Gunther, I can put your mind to rest in one of them as I am sure that Wolfgang is dead.'

The wait seemed eternal. During it, Bertha came back into the bedroom and sat with Tamar, held her hand, gave her sips of tea and wiped her brow, while comforting her in a low voice. 'Clara, I have told you before that you are the daughter I never had. You will never forget me, will you? Wherever you go, my love will go with you.'

Tamar nodded. 'Bertha, I love you as a mother. I'm honoured to be looked on as your daughter.'

As Bertha bent to kiss her forehead, Tamar thought of Elma. How she longed to be with her – with both loving women. In a perfect world, they would sit each side of the bed that held her broken body and soothe her hurting heart with their love and put her back together, as best as she could be, as that perfect world wouldn't hold her beloved Isaac, nor would it give her back what the hateful Wolfgang had taken from her.

Bertha's voice was low as she spoke once more. 'The doctor said that you've been raped, that the act was brutally forced on you and that you are badly torn. Talk to me, Clara, don't hold it in . . . Oh, I know there are things you can only talk to Gunther about, but you cannot express to him what is inside you . . . I – I too was raped once . . .'

This shocked Tamar and it cut her in two to imagine this gentle soul going through what she had been through. 'No! Oh, Bertha, Bertha!'

Bertha's head nodded. With the movement, tears plopped from her eyes onto her cheeks. 'Yes. I – I was just fourteen, walking home from school. A man suddenly appeared out of an alleyway and pulled me into it . . . He – he hurt me badly. He slapped me, called me filthy names, then tore my clothing from me . . .'

Bertha's body trembled. Tamar sat up and grabbed her to her. 'Oh, Bertha, Bertha, I'm sorry . . . So sorry.'

'I've never spoken of it. It's been like a sore gnawing away at me. I was very ill after with an infection . . . I lost my womb . . . They took it from me to save my life, but with it they took away my dreams of one day having a baby to mother.'

Tamar was crying too now. Heaving deep sobs that matched Bertha's as Bertha climbed onto the bed and they clung to one another.

No one, Tamar thought, could know this pain unless they had suffered what they had. And no one could take it away. But sharing it helped, though with all her heart Tamar wished she wasn't doing so with her beloved Bertha. She wanted this not to have happened to this kind, gentle, loving woman. A woman who should hate her as most of her fellow Germans did, just for being Jewish, but who loved her. Gave her that precious gift, motherly love.

And though Tamar knew she couldn't give that same intensity of love to Bertha or Elma that she had for her true mama, what she could give was very close to it.

When they came to a calm place, Tamar said, 'Thank you for sharing. I know that cost you dearly, but I want you to know that knowing you fully understand what I'm going through has helped me so much.'

'As it has me telling you of my own plight. Telling anyone who hasn't been there is not the same – not that I have ever spoken about it . . . Not even to Gunther. He thinks I had my womb taken from me because of a twisted ovary. His love for me surpassed me not being able to give him children, and he thinks my virginity went with the intrusion of the operation. I want him always to believe he is the only one to have made love to me . . . And, Clara, I want you to know that it is possible to feel that exquisite feeling of being made love to by the man you love.'

Tamar's cheeks reddened – always she'd known that the

Germans were much more open about the sensitive subject rarely spoken of by her own people. But at this moment she couldn't accept that what Bertha had said could ever come true for her. Her one true love had gone for ever.

Their shared sadness and anguish had tired them both. When Gunther returned, he gently woke them. They were still holding one another. He smiled down at them. 'Bertha, my dear, would you be kind enough to leave us? Maybe a coffee for me and a tea for Clara?'

As Bertha got off the bed, Gunther helped her. He held her to him for a moment.

Bertha knew most of what was going on, but Gunther always protected her from the finer details. After she'd left the room, Gunther told Tamar, 'We are not to worry any more; all has been taken care of. Wolfgang is dead. His body has been moved to the road that leads here and not to the forest. On the quiet lane used mainly by the farmers, he and his bike have been run over by a farm vehicle that crushed him. His knife wound won't be found. His death will be put down as a drunken accident. All the barman knows is that he made a pass at you, you said not this time as you were having your monthly, and then a few minutes after you left, Wolfgang got into a rage and said he was going to have you no matter what and left. It will appear that he tried to follow you here. You must play your part now and carry on as if nothing has happened. Your injuries are not visible . . .'

'You mean, go back to camp?'

'No. You will stay here for a while, but arrangements will be made to get you home to England.'

This gladdened Tamar's heart when she'd thought nothing ever could again.

'When you have gone, I will cover you not visiting by saying Wolfgang's death upset you so much that you felt responsible. But while you are here, we will have to socialize a little. You must appear in normal health, though you must show deep sadness at Wolfgang's fate and attend his funeral. I know it will take a great effort, but nothing must seem different in our lives. No suspicion can be laid at our door. It could jeopardize so much.'

As Tamar sat on the floor of the plane, she wondered how she'd got through it all – carrying on as normal, expressing her sadness, going to the funeral and meeting Wolfgang's distraught family, and having them say they didn't blame her. That they knew he was drinking heavily. They were only sorry for his behaviour towards her and how it was obvious he'd meant to force himself on her.

She had assured them that his actions were caused by him drinking too much that day and that normally they got on so well and he'd always behaved in a gentlemanly way towards her. And though it stuck in her throat to say so, she'd told them that she'd thought a lot of him and had hoped that one day they would have been together.

At this she'd been taken into Wolfgang's mother's arms and hugged. Never had she felt so low and deceitful. This was made worse by her liking the woman and feeling deeply sorry for her and guilty at having taken her son from her.

But now, with months having passed, Tamar once more felt justified in what she'd done to the vile Wolfgang. It had been him that had let his mother down. Him that had gone against the upbringing she was sure his mother had given him and him who had committed the heinous crime, not her.

With this, Tamar was able to feel the excitement at going back to London, to Elma and, as soon as it was possible, to visit Florence too.

On landing, the warm air of the summer night greeted her as she stepped from the plane and was taken to a waiting vehicle. No words were spoken as the car sped towards London from the airport she knew was in Kent.

Relaxing back into a feeling of being safe that she hadn't had for months, Tamar closed her eyes. Thinking that all she'd been through would visit her, she was shocked to be woken up when outside the Polish embassy having not thought about any of it.

Suddenly, the air felt a lot colder as she was ushered inside. Kaminski stood as she entered his office.

'You have done well, Officer Brume.'

How nice it was to hear her own name, if only her surname.

'We . . . I'm very sorry for all you have been through. But, if it is any consolation, you have made a massive difference to the progress of our campaign to free as many Jews as we can and ultimately gain freedom for our country.'

'Thank you, sir.'

With the formality over, Kaminski visibly relaxed. 'You will spend a few days in hospital – but not as a patient. You will have a private room and be visited by officers trained in debriefing and preparing you for civilian life once more.'

She wanted to say that she didn't need preparing. That she wanted to go to Elma now. This minute. But she didn't utter a word.

'I need you to write a letter now to your stepmother, telling her that you are planning to return home and that you should dock in a month's time. After your two or three days in hospital, you will go to a convalescent home for the rest of the time and then be picked up and taken to the dock as the next ship from America comes in. Your story will be that you could not settle with your aunt.'

Tamar had a moment's amusement as she thought how all of that was so irrelevant given that Elma knew the truth, but she could never admit that to Kaminski.

On the journey to the hospital, Tamar thought how the time would drag knowing that Elma was so close and yet so far out of her reach. How was she to bear it?

But as it happened, it passed quickly and allowed Tamar time to heal properly, which she found she was grateful for, as instead of being a broken, tearful Tamar who fell into Elma's arms, she was a strong young woman once more, who could show her happiness at their reunion with tears of joy.

To feel that fleshy cuddle, to be held by that love and to hear the lovely Cockney voice she'd dreamed of was like being put back together and made whole again.

'Tamar, me lovely Tamar, yer back! Oh, me darlin', never leave me again. I've so bloomin' missed yer, luv.'

A giggle rose up in Tamar. It told of her happiness and crowded out any sadness for this moment in time.

'I'm so happy to be back, Elma. So happy.'

'Not 'alf as much as me, luv. It feels like I'm complete once more – well, almost. Only 'aving yer dad back could make me feel fully complete.'

This was something Tamar understood. She squeezed Elma even harder as her own pain entered her and she so wanted to block it out.

After a moment, Elma held her at arm's length. 'Guess what! Florence is coming 'ome at the weekend!'

'That's wonderful news. I don't know whether to laugh or to cry, I'm so happy and yet overwhelmed.'

'I know exactly what yer mean. Well, yer 'ome now, luv. And I ain't never letting yer out of me sight again.'

Home? Where is home? Yes, I am in the home I want to be in right now, but will I ever be in the home I really want to be?

'That was a deep sigh, me darlin'. Come on, let's get a cab and get to me shop. I closed it for a couple of 'ours, but they'll be banging on me door by the time I get back.' Without taking a breath, Elma went on, 'The shortages 'ave got worse and the daily bombing 'as been driving us all crazy, but that suddenly stopped in May. They ain't made us give in, though.'

As they drove through London, Tamar marvelled at how Londoners had withstood all they had – London looked broken but the buildings could be built again, but could the people rebuild their lives?

She looked at Elma, saw in her the most courage she'd ever seen, and knew that yes, Londoners, especially the Cockneys, could and would.

'How's Stuart? Is he still with you?'

'He is, luv. He's like a son to me. But I never let him forget his ma and his brothers and sisters. I got a plot at the cemetery for them. We 'ad a service and we buried whatever we found of theirs. Me and him go there regular to put flowers on the plot. 'E don't say much, but I know it 'elps him.'

'That's very kind of you, Elma.'

'There's something else . . . I'm sorry, luv, but that made me know who I really am, and it ain't someone who follows Judaism . . . I can't 'elp 'ow I feel, but me true self is a

Christian. I went and got christened again . . . I feel yer dad wouldn't mind now.'

'No, he wouldn't and neither do I. You know that I've always said we should allow each other's beliefs and tolerate our different ways and views. We can support each other. I'll come to the occasional mass with you, and you can come to the synagogue with me.'

'Ta, luv, that means a lot . . . 'Ere we are. Cabbie will get yer case . . . Though it surprised me 'ow much luggage yer 'ave.'

'Oh, I was kitted out well. I look on it as a goodbye present as I was discharged, though I may be called on to translate documents now and again.'

Elma put her finger to her lips before saying, 'Oh, yer mean yer old job before yer went to America? That'd be good if they'd 'ave yer back, luv.'

Wanting to kick herself but carrying on the charade, Tamar said, 'Yes. My aunt kitted me out well while I was there, and with more clothes than I needed, but it was my old job contacting me that prompted me to come home.'

'Ha! Not missing me then?' Elma said this as she paid the cabbie. Then laughed out loud . . . 'Kids, eh?'

The cab driver laughed with her before going on his way.

Once inside, Tamar found herself once more in a lovely hug, but this time accompanied by tears. 'I've missed and worried about yer day and night, me darlin'. It's been awful – the bombing, the deaths, keeping the wolf away from the door of so many folk . . . I've done me bit, giving to the soup kitchens that 'ave sprung up everywhere, and all the while feeling lonely without you and Florence and . . . me beloved David.'

Tamar held herself together, though she didn't know how. Elma needed her and this gave her strength.

'It'll all come right now, Elma. We're together again and I'm not leaving. I promise.'

'But something's different about you, me darlin'. You're like a lost soul. Something bad has happened to you. Your light went out when Isaac left. Did yer never find 'im?'

'I – I . . . Oh, Elma, he's dead!'

Elma was silent for what seemed a long time. Time in which the pain of her loss and all that she'd been through revisited Tamar and tore into shreds all the strength she'd built up over the past month. And yet, wailing and being held, and letting go of all her emotions, helped her more than all the talking during that time had done.

Elma allowed it – she didn't try to stop her, only offered comfort. She didn't give arguments as to why she should stop her hysterics, just held her and cried with her, until she came to a place of peace. The sort of peace that held all of her hurts but would allow her to function. And this Tamar settled for, and got on with letting happiness in – happiness at being back to the only home she had now – and to looking forward to the moment she could hug Florence.

Chapter Twenty-One

Tamar stood on the platform a few days later, hardly able to contain her excitement as the train pulled in.

She was just thinking it had seemed like an age since Elma had announced that Florence would be here soon when there she was jumping out of the door of the train and running towards Tamar.

They collided with a bump that neither of them minded as they hugged, danced – prompted by Florence who seemed to carry her own inner music – and giggled like children, all without saying a word.

When they did speak it was together. 'I've so missed you!' Which prompted more giggles and jigging about.

When at last they stayed their movements and looked at each other, both burst into tears. Tamar knew that Florence had seen in her what she'd seen in Florence – changes. Subtle, but there. It was as if they'd both lived in an unreal movie and hadn't been able to share and that now created a barrier. Not one they couldn't surmount but one that hung between them like a thin veil that told of how their lives had been interrupted and how it would take time to put them back how they were – if they ever could be.

Holding hands and each carrying an item of Florence's luggage, they walked out of the station and into the busyness of the world as a mixture of cars and lorries, vying with buses, whizzed by them, giving out fumes that caught in their throats.

Both had been free of this element of life in London. And yet, it sent a trickle of excitement through Tamar, and she could see it did in Florence, too: the thought that life was being lived in a normal way by others.

For Tamar, it made her think that life wasn't all about killing, and rescuing, and she knew for Florence it wasn't all about mending torn and broken bodies. There was another world out there.

Florence voiced this thought as she said, 'We really can get back to normal one day.'

Tamar squeezed her hand. 'And it seems to have begun with us being back together.'

'Oh, Tamar, I've so much to tell you, and you, I can see, are holding such a lot of pain. We need a good talk. Shall we be really naughty and go to a pub? Most have snugs where women are acceptable on their own . . . Oh . . . but will they accept me?'

Tamar knew Florence was referring to her colour. That was always acceptable to others when she was administering aid to them, but with the memory of the terrible incident that took Hannah's life and hurt her so badly embedded in her, she was bound to feel threads of fear at coming back to London.

'Let's buy a bottle of juice each and take it into a park. I don't want to be with loads of folk, I just want to be with you.'

'Tamar? Are you all right? . . . Was it really bad out there? Did you find Isaac?'

With this, Tamar thought that the constant need to relive the pain in words was worse than just knowing that Isaac had gone. 'I – I lost him.' Her chest heaved. But she swallowed hard. *Not here*, she told herself. *Not here in the street with people all going about their business.* She so needed to be in a park, to have green grass and trees surrounding her as she unburdened her grief and her deepest fear.

As Florence linked her arm through hers, Tamar could feel that she'd sensed this deep need in her.

'Oh, my darling friend. I – I . . . Look, let's hail a cab and go to Hyde Park. I love it there. No one takes any notice of you, and you can let yourself go and cry if you want to, or laugh out loud, whatever . . . There's a peace to be found sitting by the lake.'

They entered the park through ornate gates of stone, and though busy with many folk ambling along the paths, Tamar felt the peace Florence had spoken of settle in her as she gazed at the green grass and breathed in the fresher air given by the many trees.

When they reached the lake and sat down, that peace became a turmoil of having to face up to her grief and to voice what she feared, but didn't want to be a truth.

'Tamar, what's wrong? I – I mean, other than the terrible loss of Isaac, which must be cutting you in two . . . Tell me. Tell me everything.'

With this, what she'd had to do – kill young men – poured from her in a torrent of tears and anguish.

Florence moved closer during it and held her cradled in her arms. She cried with her, and tried comforting words that didn't help and never could, but were well meant and all that she had to give.

After holding her gently and allowing her to come to a quiet place, Florence asked, 'What else is troubling you, love?'

How she was to face her fear, Tamar didn't know, but there was no one in the world she wanted to tell more than Florence and she knew with her knowing, she would find help for her situation.

Taking a deep breath, she blurted out in one sentence, 'I – I was raped . . . a – a stinking German soldier raped me! And . . . and now . . .' Her voice rose. 'I think I'm pregnant!' Wanting to scream out her despair, Tamar called out, 'Help me . . . Help me, pl-e-ase!'

Sobs wracked her body as a silent Florence held her, and yet they didn't release the pain and anguish of what she had to face. How could she face it? How?

'Oh, Tamar, Tamar, I don't know what to say . . . other than I'm here for you, and always will be . . . God, how could you have been put into such a situation? Why? What was so important that you could do?'

'Save my people, disrupt the Germans . . . It was important . . . It was!'

'Save your people? Is it true they are being murdered?'

'Yes . . . and yours. You remember you told me about the doctor who fled Germany? I'm so glad he did. But there's more. They are torturing and killing anyone crippled, and gypsies, and those who . . . well, those who pair up with their own sex . . . Thousands of people. We tried to save those we could. But we couldn't do it without information and that was my job. I had to befriend the German soldiers. I was pretending to be a German girl . . . I had to flirt with them . . . when I wanted to punch and kick them until they begged for mercy . . . And yet most were just young boys who had to follow orders or be shot!'

Florence stared at her, a horrified stare that told of her being innocent of these vile facts, that she'd thought what she'd heard was just rumour.

'My God! Tamar! I – I can't believe such wickedness . . . And . . . is that how Isaac died?'

With this, for the first time, it impacted on Tamar that Wilhelm had killed her beloved Isaac. He'd been the one who had pulled the trigger! Anger towards him flared inside her as she told Florence what she'd been told.

'I can't take it all in . . . My poor, poor Tamar . . . And how I feel for this Wilhelm. It sounds as though he was forced. It must have cost him dearly. But I'm here now, I'll support you. Come and live with me in Portsmouth. I have a flat, you can have the sofa to sleep on . . . Oh, Tamar, my story is so different to yours. Yes, I have the horror of dealing with young men maimed and dying, but I also have the great happiness of my Liam being with me every few weeks or so.'

What Florence had said about Wilhelm helped Tamar, but now she felt torn. She wanted to be with Florence so much, and yet she'd only just got Elma back and loved the warm feeling of being with a loved one and the care being lavished on her. She felt soothed by the normality of Cockney life, the resilience of those who had lost so much, the cheerful face they gave to the world that made all troubles feel surmountable. But could she surmount her biggest problem without Florence – going through carrying the child planted in her, who strangely she felt a love for, and wanted to protect? Somehow, she knew she couldn't.

'Tamar? Tamar, I could help you, we can go through this together. Your baby will be loved by two mums.'

'You think it's right that I love my baby . . . even though I didn't . . . ? Oh, Florence, it was awful . . . I – I killed him . . . I killed others too . . .'

Again, Tamar could feel Florence's shock. She hadn't meant to tell her any of that . . . 'I'm a monster, Florence, I've done things you cannot dream of . . . How? How could I be turned into something I'm not?'

'No, no, don't think like that, love. Don't let it haunt you. You did what you had to do. Think of the many lives you saved – and of the life you're going to give to your child . . . not of how he or she got to grow inside you, but that the little mite will need you. The love and nourishment you can give to it will be all it has. And thank God it will never know the vile man who fathered it . . . Try not to think of your life as being over and not worth anything to anyone, but think of how many people love you, and how your child needs you . . . You are certain you're pregnant, aren't you? I mean, trauma such as you have been through could cause your period to stop for a while and other symptoms, such as being sick and going off your food.'

'I – I feel pregnant . . . Does that make sense?'

'It does, and yet even that feeling can be a result of you knowing it could be so. First thing is to get you to a doctor, love. Let's make sure, then we can talk to Elma . . . Don't look like that, Elma will be your biggest support in all of this, I promise.'

'I – I'd like to see a doctor first, Florence. Can I come down to stay with you and see one down there? Everyone gets to know everyone's business up here. Even visits to the doctor are discussed and conclusions drawn.'

'Yes, let's do things that way. It'll be our secret until we know for sure, but then promise me you will involve Elma.

She looks on you as her daughter, we cannot keep her out of this.'

'I promise . . . Thank you . . . Oh, Florence, I've missed you so much.'

They hugged for a moment and then Florence held her at arm's length. 'We're in this together, Tamar. We'll sort it, all right?'

Tamar nodded. It felt to her as if a huge weight had been lifted off her shoulders, and she knew she could face up to anything with Florence by her side.

'Well, now, let's get home. I'm starving, and can almost taste the stew that I could bet you five bob Elma has made for me.'

'Ha, well, you'd win. She was preparing the veg as I came out!'

'Mmm, I can taste it already. There's not a stew in the world to touch Elma's.'

The journey to Portsmouth a few days later gave Tamar time to think about the past months as Florence dozed for most of it.

Wilhelm came to her mind, and she pondered on how despite the anger towards him that had visited her, she no longer harboured such feelings. She knew that he'd had no choice, forgave him, and wanted to tell him so.

To this end, she decided she would contact Kaminski and ask what had happened to Wilhelm. She hoped he wasn't in a prisoner of war camp and working on a farm. He somehow didn't suit that, nor did he deserve to be a prisoner.

Thinking of Wilhelm working on a farm brought Ben to mind, and with it an urge to see him and find out how he and his brother were.

She smiled to herself at how attentive Ben had been to her and how he had appeared upset at learning she had a fiancé. But most of all she thought of how he'd helped her and Elma so much at the time of the awful bombing that had taken her father.

It would be good to thank him.

With this thought she made up her mind to visit him before going back to Elma's, but then her stomach muscles suddenly clenched as she realized that by then, she would know one way or the other if what she knew in her heart to be true really was.

Her hands went to the small mound she could feel under her clothes. The gesture sent her into a turmoil of wanting the child she felt sure nestled there, and yet not wanting it to be true that she was pregnant. And at this moment as the train rattled along the train line, she just wasn't sure which feeling was the stronger.

Questions came to her. *What will it be like? Could I manage on my own?* But then, many thousands of mothers had to in these times, and with fear for their men too . . . Suddenly Jenny came to her mind. And Ranger, lovely Ranger.

She felt in her handbag where she'd put his letter to Jenny. Concentrating, she brought his address to mind. Where Surrey was, she wasn't sure, but she knew she had to go there and soon.

Portsmouth bustled with men in uniform – soldiers and sailors.

Florence explained that the soldiers were on duty defending any invasion by sea, and the sailors were waiting to board their ships or on leave.

The air smelled of a mixture of salt and fish and the sky was filled with fluttering, squawking gulls, who, Tamar discovered, didn't mind where they plopped their excrement, as a blob of it landed on her jacket sleeve!

Florence giggled. 'Ha, you've been christened now, love. It has to happen, and does more than once. The worst is when it lands in your hair!'

Tamar found she could laugh with her and felt better for doing so.

The town was different to London. Its buildings were mostly whitewashed and had a homely look with their paint peeling in places, and quaint doors in many different colours – reds, blacks and greens. Some of the streets were cobbled, giving a sense of time having stopped.

As they passed near to the docks, Tamar realized how important the sea was to this town. Many ships – merchant, military and fishing boats – bobbed on the choppy water as a hive of activity went on around them.

Gazing at it all gave Tamar a sense of excitement, when she hadn't thought she'd ever feel anything but despair. But then it came to her that Florence had helped with that.

In the days they'd had together in London, she'd brought hope and joy back into a life that had seemed full of fear for the future.

'So, welcome to my humble abode!'

They had reached Florence's flat and stepped inside.

'Humble! It's lovely, Florence, and just look at your view!'

The flat took up the whole of the second floor of a three-storey house, in a row of similar ones that lined the seafront. Her sitting room looked over the endless blue sea, dotted with ships. 'It's beautiful, and peaceful too.'

'I know, I'm lucky to have it. The landlady works at the hospital. She's a cleaner and a lovely bubbly person who keeps us all happy. She converted her house into flats when the war broke out as she realized a lot of accommodation would be needed here. It took all her money, she says, but took away her loneliness too. You'll love her. She's called Lally . . . Ha, I know! But apparently her real name is Latisha, but when little, her older sister couldn't pronounce that so called her Lally and it stuck.'

Tamar turned from the window. The thought had struck her how different Florence's life was to the one she'd been living. It was easier . . . normal.

And yet, something in her felt glad that she'd been part of all she had. Part of fighting back, part of giving freedom, though with all her heart, she wished she hadn't been part of killing – taking young lives whose families would now be grieving just as she was. She wanted to tear that page of her story out of her memory and rip it into shreds and have it not to have happened.

'Are you all right, love? You've gone very quiet.'

'I have thoughts and memories that trouble me, Florence.'

'Share them with me whenever you need to, love. There should be more help for returning heroes, but no, people have a "get on with it" attitude, leaving many suffering poor mental health through their experiences. Don't be one of them, Tamar. Talk to me, try to give everything you've been through the status of something you can cope with and live with – justify it, as there was a reason. You didn't go on a murderous killing spree. You killed to save lives. From what you have told me, hundreds of lives. Concentrate on that aspect of what you did.'

'Thanks, Florence, you always make me feel better.'

'Let that feeling come from inside you, love. Make it the normal feeling, and it will all go away, I promise.'

Tamar smiled at her beautiful friend. Love, contentment and happiness shone from Florence, and some of that was influencing her too. It was a good feeling.

'Right, I've been thinking. Why don't you share my bed when Liam isn't here? Ha, I'll ban you when he is, though, love – from the flat too if I could, as fun and games go on then!'

They collapsed into a heap of giggles that doubled them over and brought tears running down their faces, and to Tamar, it was the best feeling in the world and one she hadn't thought she would experience ever again.

Two days later – days that had been filled with fun, exploring and eating out in quaint cafes, making her feel that there wasn't a war going on at all, Tamar sat on the other side of a large oak desk awaiting the verdict of the undignified examinations the doctor opposite her had carried out on her.

'Well, what you suspect is true, my dear, you are pregnant. And as Florence told me the circumstances, I'm very sorry. You didn't deserve what happened to you. You are a hero.'

Having it confirmed hit Tamar hard as the implications she hadn't given thought to before crowded her. Being an unmarried woman, she would be shrouded in shame. Her child would be called a bastard!

'No!'

'I'm sorry . . .'

'Oh, I wasn't . . . I meant . . . Well, it came to me how my child will be looked on, and I was protesting about that.'

'I see. Well, that's good. It means that already you are a mother to the tiny being growing inside you. And your instinct is to always protect it . . . Is there no one in your life you can turn to? I mean, someone who would be a father to your baby?'

Though she thought this a strange thing to say, she was shocked that Wilhelm came to her mind. He'd shown how fond he was of her. And she knew he sought a way of making up for what he'd been forced to do.

'I – I hadn't thought of that, but I think there may be someone I could turn to.'

'Then do so. Protect yourself and your child, but only if you think you can be happy with this someone.'

'Yes. I think I can. He's kind and gentle. And I know he is fond of me. He's a friend and was of my . . . my late fiancé.'

'Oh, my dear. I feel so sorry for you, and yet I am proud to have met someone as brave as you. My biggest regret is being too old to help and to do my bit in this awful war.'

'But you are helping. Those left behind need you. Who would care for them if all the doctors went to war? And from the way you have treated me, I think of you as a hero too.'

His round face, with red cheeks pitted with tiny blue veins – suggesting he was not a well man – lit up.

'Thank you, that means a lot to me.'

'And how you have treated me means a lot to me too. Thank you.'

As she stood, Tamar felt a new courage enter her and a confidence that she would cope. She would go and visit Wilhelm and ask him to marry her.

Once outside, she giggled at the audacity of this, and yet the idea didn't repulse her and her instinct told her that Wilhelm would accept. His intention to convert to Judaism would make their union acceptable to her community and that they would hail him as a hero, not an enemy, when they learned how he'd helped the Jews of Poland.

After a lovely three weeks with Florence, and a visit from Liam that had given her so much fun and love from them both, Tamar felt ready to make her journey.

She'd toyed with the idea of writing to Jenny and Ben first but had settled on just calling in on Jenny, as she didn't know what Jenny would want to know, and just turning up and surprising Ben.

With Florence's guidance, Tamar had left with all the instructions she needed on how to get to Jenny's house in Surrey and to Melton Mowbray to see Ben.

There was dread in her heart as she walked up the street. Still she could not think of Ranger as Russell but knew she must once she met Jenny.

A lovely dark-haired, dainty young woman opened the door to her, her face full of questions.

'I'm Tamar . . . I – I was in Poland with Ranger . . . I mean, Russell.'

'Oh!' Shock registered on Jenny's face. Then she recovered . . . 'Come in . . . I . . . It's good to meet you.' Jenny's face showed the strain she'd been under. Her eyes were red-rimmed and sunken into dark circles. 'How? I mean, how were you with him?'

'I was part of a group . . . I'm sorry, I can't tell you too much about that, but I have a letter for you.'

The house was in a row of semi-detached houses, all with nice gardens to the front, telling of the prosperity of the area.

As Tamar stepped into the hall, her feet sank into the deep red carpet. She followed Jenny into the living room and found quiet elegance there in the beige three-piece suite, pale blue carpet and soft furnishings.

'Sit down, I'll make tea.'

'No thank you, Jenny. Just a glass of water, please.'

When Jenny brought her the water, there was an awkward silence. Tamar broke it by asking, 'You have a son?'

'Yes. Dickie – Richard. He's at school.'

'Oh? I thought he was younger.'

'He was, when his daddy left . . .' Jenny's chest heaved. Tears sprung to her eyes.

'I'm so sorry.'

Jenny's head dropped into her hands. Instinctively, Tamar went to her and held her in her arms.

After a moment, her sobs calmed. 'I'm sorry. I cope most of the time. Well, in a fashion . . . Tell me what happened.'

'I think . . . I mean, are you sure?'

'Yes. I need to know.'

Not able to tell her the gory truth, Tamar said, 'Russell died with your name on his lips and speaking of his love for you, Jenny. He didn't suffer. It happened so quickly . . . I – I was next to him and held him for you . . . We were great friends.' Swallowing hard as her own grief threatened to overwhelm her, Tamar told Jenny, 'He asked me to tell you how much he loved you and to give you a letter – not the official one, but one he'd written privately to you and no one has read. It's here.'

Taking the letter from her bag, Tamar handed it to Jenny.

'Will you stay with me while I read it?'

'Of course, for as long as you like.'

In the silence that followed, the crackling of the paper as the envelope was carefully opened and the letter unfolded grated on Tamar and underlined the tension she felt. She'd rather not be here for this, but sensed how much Jenny needed her. And then she was glad to see the smile that lit Jenny's face as she said, 'Four sheets! He's written me four sheets! I thought it would just be a note . . . Oh, one of them is for Dickie! How wonderful.'

Tamar found she could smile. 'He always had so much to say. And always about you, and his son and his lovely home life and how he was fighting so that could continue . . . Oh, I'm sorry.'

Suddenly Tamar was crying. 'I – I'm so sorry . . . I lost my man too . . .'

Jenny dropped the letter on the sofa next to her and leaned into Tamar. They hugged and they sobbed, telling each other things they remembered about their men, until at last they came to a quiet place and were still.

Jenny bent and picked up the letter. 'I'll read it later. Would you like to come for a walk with me to the school, to meet Dickie?'

'Yes. I'm going to book into a hotel for the night, so I have plenty of time.'

'Stay here. Please. I have a spare bed and it's all made up. My sister comes often to stay over. She's younger than me and studying law – though there aren't many openings in that field for women so she sees herself as a pioneer!'

'Thank you. I would like that.'

Jenny beamed and it changed her. Yes, the hurt was still there, but so was courage. The courage she must have had to draw on to bring up Dickie on her own while she faced the loneliness of having a husband away at war, and then the knowledge that she would never see him again.

Tamar smiled back. 'I'm glad I've met you, Jenny.'

They were both standing now. Jenny put out her arms

and Tamar went into them. 'And I'm glad it was you by my darling Russ's side when he most needed someone. Thank you, Tamar.'

A warm and lovely feeling settled in Tamar. She lifted her eyes heavenwards. *Thank you, Ranger . . . I can never think of you as Russ, but my heart has healed a little with meeting your Jenny – and now I am to meet your son.*

Chapter Twenty-Two

As they left the house, Tamar felt she'd made a friend for life in Jenny, and that was sealed when she was given a hug by little Dickie, after his mum had told him, 'This is a friend of your daddy's, darling. And now she's going to be your new aunty.'

A surge of love for the fair-haired, chubby-cheeked little boy entered Tamar. He'd melted her heart, and yet she could recognize he could be a little devil as he said, 'You're nice, but I think you have spoiled your hair. Which colour should it be, the nice browny colour or the horrid yellow at the ends?'

'Dickie!'

Tamar laughed out loud. 'It should be the nice browny colour. I had a daft moment, but now must get the yellow ends cut off and be me again.'

'I trained as a hairdresser, Tamar, I could cut it for you.'

Before she could say thank you, Dickie said, 'Tamar? That's a funny name.'

Proudly, Tamar told him, 'It's a name from the Bible. I'm named after the daughter-in-law of Judah, a righteous woman who sought justice – and that is what I have been doing.'

Jenny smiled. 'And she did it with your daddy, Dickie. Tamar has brought us a letter from Daddy. There's one for each of us. We will read them later, but in the meantime, we will welcome and love Tamar as your daddy did.'

'I like you, Tamar, and when I get to know you, I know I will love you.'

'And that is the same for me too, Dickie. Your daddy was a friend I loved and now he has given me you and your mummy.'

Dickie grinned. A grin so like Ranger's that it cut into Tamar's heart but left her with a good feeling as Ranger had left her the precious gift of his lovely family.

Finding the farm was easier than Tamar had thought it would be.

On the long journey travelling by train and then taxi, she'd reflected on her stay with Jenny and Dickie, remembering how she'd played with Dickie, and taught him to say goodnight in French, Polish and Yiddish – leaving out German as she hadn't wanted to visit that language. And how she and Jenny had become friends and comforted each other. But now, at last, she stood outside the gate of Brackensfields.

The house was huge, if tumbling down with disrepair.

This worried Tamar. She hated to think of Ben and his brother failing, but she knew their health wasn't good.

On knocking on the door there was no answer, so after looking around and seeing nothing but the quiet lane, Tamar ventured around the back.

There she entered a smelly, muddy world of pigs grunting and chickens clucking and fluttering their annoyance at the disturbance.

Calling out, 'Ben!' brought him out from a barn at the end of the farmyard.

'Tamar!'

A pretty girl with red curly hair showing around her slipped headscarf followed him out. Both were blushing. The girl adjusted her blouse as she smiled a sheepish smile.

Tamar laughed. 'Caught you at an embarrassing moment, sorry.'

Ben laughed with her. 'This is Susan, my fiancée . . . I thought you were in America and I'd never see you again . . .'

The moment was awkward. It was as if Ben was apologizing for falling in love and she didn't want that. 'Couldn't keep away. It's lovely to see you, and to meet you, Susan. Hope I'll have an invite to the wedding.'

The light-hearted way she said this seemed to relax Ben. He came forward and hugged her. 'You'll be the guest of honour, as it's your fault we met – Susan came as a Land Girl.'

'I'm so happy for you . . . I – I've just come from being with Florence. She's nursing in Portsmouth.'

'Ah, the lovely Florence, how is she? Look, come inside the house and we'll have a cuppa. I want to hear all about your American adventure and why you're back so soon . . . Though it's great that you are.'

As he took Susan's hand and then Tamar's arm and steered them towards the house, Tamar had a feeling this had been a mistake. She should have waited until after the war. Ben would have accepted her return as normal then . . . that's if there would be an after the war. Not a lot of progress was being made to defeat the Germans as now they had begun to shell Leningrad, and the reports were of their success.

The thought sunk the little hope Tamar had felt at learning

that the Allied forces had triumphed in Syria earlier in the year.

'You'll have to excuse the state of everything. All our efforts have been put into the land and . . . well, I haven't felt like making a home since I lost Alan . . .'

'Oh no! I'm sorry. What happened?'

'He just suddenly collapsed . . . Over there, by the stove. He was one for cooking was Alan. He was roasting a chicken and had it out basting it. It stood there for weeks after . . .'

Tamar stared at the huge range. So much pain, so much. She couldn't visit any more of it.

'Anyway, let's have that cuppa, eh?'

Susan spoke then. Her accent was broad Cockney. 'I'll soon 'ave the kettle boiling, luv. You talk to yer friend.'

This broke the sadness spell and put them on a better footing, one Tamar could cope with. But once more she asked herself, *Why did I come? This is a bad mistake! Why didn't I wait?*

They sat on a shabby sofa with huge arms in brown leather that showed patches of once being shiny but was now dull and cracked.

Ben took her hand. 'I feel that all isn't right with you, Tamar. Did things go wrong in America? I visited Elma, you know. And she told me you'd gone.'

'I can't tell you everything, Ben. But where I've been, I've visited hell. I just need to sort my life out now. One day, I'll tell you everything, but just to say . . .' Taking a deep breath against the pain that clenched her heart, Tamar told him, 'I've heard that Isaac . . . my fiancé, lost his life.'

'Oh no! Oh, Tamar, I'm so sorry . . . I – I don't know what to say.'

'No one does, and really, it's all right that you don't say

anything. What can be said doesn't help, as you will know from having lost Alan. It seems everyone has lost someone.'

'Yes. Susan lost her whole family in the Blitz. But she's a brave soul. She's making a new life here and we plan on building a family together.'

'I'm so happy for you. Poor Susan. She seems to be a woman of courage, as she hasn't stopped smiling since I've met her.'

'She is. She's a proper Cockney, like Elma. Always sees the bright side of life, and . . . well, she's expecting our first already!' Ben blushed. 'We'll marry soon, but well, what I said earlier about you being a guest of honour won't happen, you see, as it won't be an affair to invite folk to, we just want to get on with it. Susan loves the farm and is already planning the harvest and the harvest festival. She says no war's going to stop us celebrating the good crop we know we're in for and that'll be all the celebrating we'll need of our marriage.'

'That's all wonderful. I'm so happy for you, Ben . . . I, well, I'm having a baby too!'

'You got to see your fiancé then? That's great news!'

'No. It isn't Isaac's . . . Ben, please don't ask me as I'm in so much pain – emotional pain – I'll never stop crying if I start, but I wasn't willing is all I can say. But I love my baby and will cherish it, and I'm . . . Oh, this is going to sound so callous, but you see, there is a man that I know is fond of me and I'm hoping he will marry me and we can go back to Poland to live one day. He's Polish. He . . .'

Somehow, Tamar found the courage to tell Ben about Wilhelm. 'I'm just praying he will have me – a broken mess, who isn't ready to look at another man, let alone marry one. But who's desperate.'

Ben wiped a tear from his cheek.

'I'm guessing that you haven't been to America at all, Tamar, but I won't push you. I know that one day, when you can, you will tell me all. In the meantime, me and Susan are your friends.'

Susan had come over and heard most of what Tamar had said.

'That's right, luv. I can tell yer've had a rough time, but we're 'ere for yer. There's an 'ome with us whenever yer need it. And if this bloke rejects yer, take up our offer, we'll take care of yer.'

'Thanks, Susan, that means a lot.'

'It's me that 'as to thank you, luv. Ben told me 'ow yer met and 'ow yer changed his mind from the way he were going. I couldn't 'ave loved him if he still had them views, I'll tell yer. Stinking lot, them Mosley followers.'

By the time Tamar left Ben's, having been given a lift to the station in a tractor, she felt she had yet another new and lovely friend in Susan. And she was at peace that Ben had found his true match and was happy.

Now, she had to brace herself for the future, and for meeting Wilhelm once more.

This happened sooner than she expected.

Elma greeted her in her usual way as if she was a long-lost daughter, and then told her, 'A lovely young man came to see you, me darlin'. 'E told me he was from Poland and worked at the embassy and that the two of yer know each other.'

This brought comfort to Tamar and lifted her heart a little. 'When? Did he say he would come back?'

'He did. I told him I was expecting yer at any moment and he said he would call tomorrow.'

'Oh, I'm so glad . . . Elma, love, I've such a lot to tell you.'

'I know, luv. I knew there was something troubling yer but take yer time. Yer look tired. I'll get a bath set up for yer – I'm sorry, it's still in the cellar, but I 'ad to be sure that the bombing 'ad really stopped.'

'That's fine. I'll help with carrying the water. Will you sit with me while I soak? I – I need to talk soon.'

As she sipped the tea that Elma had brought down for her, and felt it warm her insides, even melt some of the coldness in her heart, Tamar lay back in the hot water, allowing it to soothe her, and told Elma everything.

Elma was crying by the time she'd finished.

'Don't think badly of my baby, Elma. I want it to be a grandchild of yours.'

'Oh, I don't, luv. I just feel so much sorrow. Your dad 'ad such dreams for you and Isaac . . . lovely Isaac.'

'He did . . . Oh, Elma, it's all gone.'

As Tamar felt her resolve not to cry begin to crack, Elma took a deep breath and as if she'd schooled herself to be strong, said, 'No, it ain't. It's just different, that's all. And we're to get on with it, luv. That's a good plan that you've got there – except for the bit about going back to Poland one day. I don't want that to 'appen, but this young Wilhelm, will he go for it?'

'I think so. I think he would help me out all he can. It won't be a proper marriage, and I'll release him from it whenever he wants me to, it'll just be one of convenience . . . I just know he will go for that.'

Having slept well and now feeling able to cope, Tamar was on tenterhooks all morning wondering if Wilhelm really would call, and how he'd come to look her up in the first place – she could only conclude that Kaminski had told him she was back and was asking after her.

She made an effort with her appearance, brushing her now one-colour hair until it shone and then letting it hang in the style that Jenny had cut it – a bob that curled under at her shoulders with a long fringe. To keep it neat and off her face, she wore a rolled-up, chiffon scarf tied around her head, leaving her fringe in place and the ends of the scarf dangling at her neckline. Then she applied some rarely worn make-up – a little pan stick to hide the dark circles around her eyes and a hint of blush on her cheeks, created by taking a tiny amount of rouge on her finger and following the outline of her cheekbones. And lastly a hint of lipstick.

She loved the effect, but had to smile as she knew what her papa would have said: 'Take that muck off your face! You don't need it, you're beautiful without it!'

Oh, Papa. I do miss you. I've not had time to think about you much, but I so wish you were here now.

Shaking herself out of these thoughts as she knew they would lead to tears, Tamar dressed in the lovely green frock that had been in the parcel of clothes Rosie had given to her and Florence, which prompted the thought that she would go and see Rosie tomorrow and take up her voluntary work in the soup kitchen again. But before then, she so hoped Wilhelm would help her out of her predicament.

It was an hour later that he called. His face lit up at finding her in the shop.

'My dear Tamar . . . I came as soon as I heard . . . I – I'm so sorry.'

'You know what happened?'

'Yes. After you called asking for me, Kaminski told me

everything . . . Are you free to come with me for a walk? I want to talk to you.'

Feeling suddenly shy, and as if her proposal was now preposterous, Tamar could only nod.

'Good! I will take you to a park I love called Hyde Park. Do you know it?'

'I do. I – I was there with my friend not long ago.'

Elma, who'd stood quietly listening, now said, 'Off yer go then. Yer 'olding me customers up. Look at them standing with their mouths open. They look like they're catching flies or something!'

Tamar giggled and her shyness broke as she waved to the familiar customers and beamed at Wilhelm. The forgiveness she'd worried she might have to find for him wasn't needed; she held no animosity in her towards him, just a feeling that she was seeing an old friend. One who understood. Who had been where she'd been. And had been a friend of her lovely Isaac too.

Outside, he told her, 'I know my way around quite well now, so can get us to the park. I just hope that the rain that threatens doesn't come – though I have my umbrella with me if it should.'

Tamar had noticed his rolled-up black umbrella and had taken note of how smart he looked in civilian clothing – black suit and white shirt with a black and blue striped tie completing his look. His hair didn't seem so fair, and she imagined this was because he had Brylcreem taming it. And she loved how his English was spoken with a Polish accent.

Suddenly, wanting to hear her own language, she spoke to him in Polish. 'Did you convert to Judaism as you promised yourself you would, Wilhelm?'

'Yes, and I have been through the painful process involved too! Didn't like that at all!'

Tamar laughed out loud, bringing several glances from passers-by.

'The English are a little reserved, I find.'

'Not in the East End, but here, "up west", as they call it, yes. They are more like that.'

They had left the Underground and were walking towards Hyde Park. So far, the sun still shone, though clouds threatened in the distance.

A companionable silence had fallen between them as they walked, but this was shattered by a young woman pushing a pram who barred their way and glared at Wilhelm.

'You a conchie or what? You should be fighting like the rest of our men are!'

Shocked, Tamar couldn't speak, but Wilhelm answered in a quiet, polite tone, 'No, madam, I am Polish. I and my friend have been to the worst hell of this war and back. We escaped death and then our beloved country, but I am still helping by working at my embassy, planning strategies that help those still in Poland who are resisting the German army.'

'Oh, well then, I beg your pardon and feel sorry for you . . . Me husband's in the Middle East somewhere. At least he was when I last heard from him. He ain't even seen our child.'

Tamar spoke then. 'We're so sorry. I know what it's like to be missing your loved one . . . Only I lost mine. I hope yours makes it home.'

'Ta, love, and I shouldn't have stopped you like that. It's just seeing a young, strong man strolling along the road, it made me angry.'

'We understand. Do you need anything? Any help at all?' Tamar asked.

'No, ta, love. I'm well looked after by family . . . Oh, unless it's your prayers that me Alf comes home. I could do with them.'

Before Tamar could answer, Wilhelm told her, 'You will have our prayers, as all those fighting do. But it's good to know you have family to care for you. Neither of us do, though we do have people who love us and look out for us.'

'That's good. I'll get on me way now. Once again, I'm sorry I stopped you like that.'

'Think nothing of it. Good day.'

Tamar smiled at this formal use of the English language from Wilhelm. She'd dropped that a long time ago with living in the East End.

When they reached the park, the rain came. Tamar thought they would head for shelter, but instead, Wilhelm opened his huge brolly and steered her to a bench.

'I want us to be able to talk without staring eyes, or any encounters like that just now. Is that all right with you?'

'Yes, I need to talk.'

'Tamar, I know what happened to you . . . I read the report about your return after Kaminski told me you were home . . . I'm so sorry . . . Though sorry isn't enough, and never will be for my part in the sorrow that's deep inside you . . . Only, well, I've been thinking a lot since I heard, and I want to help you.'

Tamar turned to look at him. His blue eyes held something she dared not put a name to.

'I want to care for you for Isaac . . . and for me.'

'I – I . . . Thank you, but I don't want you to feel obliged, though I do need your help.'

'I said for me too, and I meant it . . . Oh, Tamar, I haven't been able to get you out of my mind since I left you in Poland. I cried when I read what had happened . . . It's not because of that I am here. I need to be with you . . . I know it is wrong of me, but I fell in love with you and yet I don't even deserve to sit by you on this bench after what I did.'

'No! Don't say that. It is me that doesn't deserve to sit with you . . . I have been planning – and now it seems a terrible thing to have done, but I was desperate . . .'

Turning towards her, Wilhelm dropped the umbrella and held her shoulders, then his arms came further around her. She didn't resist. She didn't want to, as the touch of his lips on hers lit a spark in her that she had long forgotten. A feeling of joy spread through her veins.

This was Wilhelm. He was no longer someone she wanted to use for her own benefit, but someone she loved and wanted . . . How did that happen? What about her beloved Isaac?

But suddenly there, with the rain soaking them both, and the kiss going on and on and deepening to something that took her from herself, Tamar knew that Isaac would want this for her, and so she accepted Wilhelm's love with all her heart.

When they parted, they giggled from sheer happiness, and for Tamar, she felt relief tinged with a little worry over what she still had to tell Wilhelm.

Rain ran down their faces, but they didn't mind as they gazed at one another. And then, something magical happened as Wilhelm said, 'You don't have to tell me, I have guessed. And I have prepared myself for it – thought about it being a possibility from the moment I read about the awful thing done to you – and I want you to know that if I am right, then I will love your child as my own.'

Tamar clung to him, and then found that the words she'd only ever expressed to Isaac came naturally to her now when she'd not thought she could ever love a man in that way again. 'I love you, Wilhelm. Thank you for being you. I – I so needed you to say that . . . Yes, I am with child and have come to a place where I love and want the baby growing inside me as it didn't have a say in how it got there, and its only hope in this world is me.'

'No, that isn't so, as it has me too. I promise you, the child will become mine too. I will be a good father to it and love it as you do.'

They were kissing without realizing it – unaware of being soaked by the rain and only aware of each other. How this was possible, Tamar didn't know. She only knew that her heart swelled with the love offered her and with finding she loved Wilhelm as she had Isaac.

Her broken world had been put back together.

When at last they rose, they found the rain had stopped.

'Shall we go to my apartment and get dry and warm? I can make you a meal too, Tamar. It isn't far from here. It's on Warwick Road in Kensington.'

'You can afford an apartment in this area?'

'Yes. I have an allowance for my rent from the embassy and I have a legacy from my grandmother.'

'Oh, I didn't mean to be rude. I just was surprised, that's all.'

'I didn't take it as you being rude – if you are to be my wife, you need to know that I can support you.' He grinned. 'That was a poor proposal. I will now do it the traditional way.'

With this, Wilhelm went down on one knee.

Tamar laughed at him. 'You're in a puddle, you daft thing!'

'I would walk on water if I could, just to be able to ask you to marry me . . . Will you, Tamar? Will you marry me? I love you with all my heart.'

'Yes. Yes, and I'd be honoured to. Thank you, Wilhelm, my saviour.'

He stood and held her to him.

The feeling gave Tamar a deep sense of being safe. She looked up into the sky.

Dearest Isaac, I feel you have sent Wilhelm to me. I will never forget you, or Hannah, and I will for ever remember our love, our home in Poland and all we shared. But I am rescued now. Rescued by the love Wilhelm has for me. Sleep tight, my darling. One day, if the teachings are true, we will be together once more.

PART FOUR

Peace in Our Time

Chapter Twenty-Three

May 1945

London bustled with activity. The atmosphere was one of happiness and expectancy as families awaited the arrival of returning soldiers.

But that didn't stop them preparing for VE day as the 8th of May approached and now, today, it was here at last.

In Bridge Street everyone was pulling together. Some were baking cakes, others promised sandwiches, the church hall had supplied the tables and chairs, and Elma had bought all the bunting.

Wilhelm laughed as he helped with this, starting with their shop – the very one that had been Tamar's and her father's, and was now an accountancy office run by Wilhelm, with their home above in the flat so loved by Tamar.

She now felt she was home. Home with her lovely family, her daughter, Thelma, now three and so like herself with nothing of the hateful Wolfgang in her and growing into an intelligent little girl, who was often described as being like an old lady in a child's body, she was so advanced for her years.

Already, Thelma spoke Polish fluently. This had been achieved by them all speaking only in that language when in their home from the day she was born.

Tamar had long accepted that they might never return there. What would happen for Poland was yet to be decided as Russia still occupied much of it, but she hoped that one day it would be allowed to be independent and to have all the land that had been taken from it given back.

But apart from her wanting the best for the Polish people, it no longer mattered that she hadn't returned, or might never do so, as it once had. For the most part, her memories of being there were ones she wanted to forget, though she never would forget her happy childhood.

Fulfilled now with her little family and living in what she thought of as her home and with a job she loved – her dream job, teaching languages to rich children in a school in the West End – life couldn't be better.

Her love for Wilhelm had deepened as time had passed, and now at last he felt ready to expand their family.

This was something they had talked seriously about from the beginning – not having children together until the war was over and they had a settled life. But the time seemed right now and Tamar knew she was ready.

The small language school she'd run on a Saturday morning in the church hall had grown and was bringing in an income that would more than compensate for giving up working at the school and satisfy her need to teach. Especially if she did what Wilhelm suggested and looked for premises. He thought it would be a good investment of her own money, which they hadn't touched and which had grown with interest, besides giving them a second business.

With happiness being her daily companion, life couldn't be better for Tamar.

And one of the pinnacles of this was that Florence and Liam were home too.

Home for them was an apartment near to the London Hospital, where they both worked – Florence part-time so that she could spend time being a mum to their son Rufus. And, joy of joys, they were coming to the party today as both had the day off.

As if she'd conjured them up, their car pulled up and Florence jumped out.

'Florence! Oh, you brought cakes!'

'Yes, and baked by my own hand! Ha, some are a bit misshapen, but hey ho, they taste good.'

They laughed and hugged as best they could with Florence holding a basket over her arm. 'All the food is being taken to Elma's until it's time to lay it out. Mine's already there. I made a mound of sandwiches. I never want to see a slice of bread again, or boil another egg!'

Their giggling at this seemed to roll the years back to more carefree times. Both felt it as Florence said, 'We got through it, love.'

'We did . . . I wish . . .'

'Don't say it. No sadness today. Though we'll never forget them.'

'We won't, not ever. Isaac still nestles in my heart and always will. I miss him every day.'

'Is that fair on Wilhelm?'

'Wilhelm feels the same – not in the way that I do, but he'll never get over what he was forced to do.'

'I can imagine. But you and I will never know the circumstances in which it all took place, and so cannot know how

Wilhelm feels. It must go over and over in his head. A terrible thing to live with . . . Anyway, let's get this to Elma's.'

Looking round, they saw that Liam had pitched in and was helping Wilhelm to put tables up in a long line. Others were unloading benches from a truck. Kids, including their two, played together in an excited way, getting into trouble now and again as they got in the way of the adults.

Florence sighed. 'I never thought this day would come. Now it has, I want to skip along the street with the joy inside me.'

'I know what you mean. Have you plans to change your life or has coming back to London been all the change you needed?'

'I don't know, Tamar. I mean, not immediately, but we've both spoken of having more kids, and me giving up work . . . Oh, and we'd like a house with a garden – maybe in the suburbs. But it's all dreams at the moment. What about you?'

'Well, you know the changes I'm planning, but I too hanker after that house with a garden in the suburbs. I like working here, and love the East End, but, well, when I look back to my childhood I feel space around me – open fields, the sea, sand and, yes, that garden. I'd like that for my kids.'

'Kids? You really meant it when you said you would try for more?'

'Yes, already at it!'

'Ha, Tamar. You're getting as crude as some around here are!'

They giggled together and for Tamar, it reminded her of days before the war. *Those days can come back*, she told herself.

Everyone around them was laughing, calling out, shouting

at the kids to behave, and one couple were even having a row as their voices carried from the open window of their flat – yes, normal was returning, and she felt glad of it.

Elma greeted Florence with a hug, then turned to Tamar. 'I'm not leaving you out, me darling, come here.'

Tamar laughed. 'That's my tenth hug today, Elma! I don't feel left out, love.'

'Well, I just want to hug you every time I see you, I'm that happy how everything's turned out.'

Tamar thought of what she and Florence had talked about and wondered if she could ever leave Elma, or if she would ever think of going with them if their dreams did materialize. But then, they were only dreams and might never come true.

'You have done the street proud with all the bunting, Elma, it looks lovely.'

'Ta, Florence. But I only bought it, the men put it all up . . . Now, put your cakes on the counter, there's no room on me table, and in any case, we'll need to get them out soon. Have the men got the tables up?'

'Doing so as we speak. Are these the cloths piled here?'

'They are, Tamar – a mish-mash of colours, as everyone has supplied one, though I ain't much for including Rita's. She ain't no housewife that one. Her cloth looks like she's washed the floor with it!'

Tamar could see the one Elma referred to, a red and white check – or it was meant to be, though it was more grey and a dull red. 'Well, we can use all the others first and hopefully there'll be a few we don't need and that can be one of them. Poor Rita, she hasn't got a clue.'

'Spends too much time standing on her dirty step smoking fags, that's why.'

Not wanting to pursue this, Tamar laughed. 'Come on, Florence, let's get the tables laid.'

An army of women helped, and soon the long table was covered with the many coloured cloths – Rita's avoided – and the food was piled high, a feast that at times they had thought they would never see again.

Someone put their wireless on loud and opened their door and the party began.

Wilhelm came to Tamar's side and with his arm around her waist, squeezed her to him. 'It's a good day, darling, a good day.'

'It is. A wonderful day that we thought we would never see, but we came through it all and found happiness.'

He looked down at her. 'Are you really happy? Have all past memories left you?'

'Darling, we have spoken of this many times and agreed that they shouldn't. That we should always remember and learn to live with anything bad in our past.'

'Yes, but you are truly happy?'

Always he needed reassurance. But then, she'd woken him many a night calling out from the nightmares that haunted her – for Isaac, who she still loved and missed, and in horror, fear and pain as the night hours often made her relive events that in the light of day she thought she'd come to terms with.

'Truly, my darling. You are a wonderful husband, and I love you.'

Seeming to be satisfied, he squeezed her even more tightly, then picked up his jug of ale and drank it in one!

'Wilhelm! Pace yourself, or you'll end up drunk!'

They laughed together and the moment had passed.

* * *

The afternoon became a hilarious event, filled with antics that folk wouldn't normally get up to, but the flow of beer, sherry and, for her and Florence, Elma's homemade wine loosened everyone's inhibitions.

Women danced, lifting their skirts to show stockings held up by elastic bands, men jigged around them, kids took part in games and sports and the air filled with love and laughter.

And now waltz music was playing and Wilhelm, more than a little drunk, caught hold of a tiddly Tamar and swept her into a dance.

As they swayed together, Wilhelm snuggled into her neck and spoke of his love for her, but then two little arms came around a leg of each of them, and a tired Thelma demanded attention. Lifting her, Wilhelm continued the dance with Thelma clinging to his neck and holding Tamar close with his free arm. Tamar knew happiness to fill her, and to quieten the little longing for Isaac that Wilhelm had set up in her with his questions as to her being truly happy. Isaac was at peace and there she should leave him.

Two hours later, having cleared the street along with all those still capable of helping and said their goodbyes to Florence and Liam, there were no such thoughts as Wilhelm made love to her and she lost herself in the ecstasy of his caresses and his kisses, until he finally entered her and brought a torrent of exquisite and almost unbearable feelings that took over her body and mind.

When, finally, they laid back, Wilhelm enjoying a cigarette and she basking in the aftermath of feelings that stayed with her, he said, 'I love you with all that I am, Tamar, but still I feel there is a part of you that isn't mine.'

'Darling, don't. I cannot help what happens when I am asleep. In time it will go.'

'But I feel that is the real you, when you aren't in control and everything pours from you.'

'It isn't. Yes, I still suffer from all I have been through, but it is getting better. I haven't had a nightmare for weeks. And talking about it isn't helping, it's putting it all into my head again. I love you, my darling Wilhelm. And this is the conscious me, expressing how I feel. Please don't judge me by what comes through me when I am asleep. Doing so spoils our life together and what we just did.'

Wilhelm stubbed out his cigarette and turned to her. With his naked body so close, she could feel his need was pumping through his veins once more, but somehow, he'd changed things for her. His hand sought her breast. 'I'm sorry. Let me do it again, and bring the feeling back . . . Oh, Tamar, my Tamar, I'm sorry.'

Although she wanted to resist and be cross at him, his lips on her neck and then travelling down to her breast, and his taking her nipple gently into his mouth undid her. She slid down the bed and folded herself into him, exploring him as he was her, until they joined again in a union that took them to an even higher place than it had ever done and they cried out their love for one another and their joy.

A banging on the door woke them to the sun pouring through their window. Their naked bodies were still entwined as their lovemaking had gone on and on until they'd fallen asleep.

Untangling amid giggles, Wilhelm was out of bed first and went to the window. As he opened it, a voice called out, 'Hey, we're meant to get this lot back to the church by ten!'

'Sorry, one too many beers. I conked out. I'll be down in a moment.'

Laughing, they dashed about, having a quick wash and dressing – for Tamar this became hilarious as Wilhelm hopped about in an exaggerated way as he tried to get his leg into his trousers.

'Sit down and take your time, Wilhelm, you'll fall over!'

Always he loved to make her laugh. Sometimes, she thought he was like a young boy, playing tricks and seeing a funny side to everything.

The door opening sobered them up. Little Thelma stood there, her teddy dangling by her side, held by his ear. 'Mummy, I wet the bed!'

'Ah, don't worry, darling. It'll be because your tummy was full of pop! Let's go and sort it, eh? And you can have a nice bath and then we'll help to clear the street up.'

'I wish we could have another party. I liked it, and Daddy was all silly and made me giggle.'

Tamar smiled, thinking he was more than silly. He was a lover like she'd never known, and still she could feel the pleasure he'd given her as a twinge of her muscles made her clench her thighs.

'Daddy always makes you giggle.'

'Yes, but I loved it when we danced.'

'So much so that you fell asleep! Come on, get your wet things off.'

When they went outside, they were met by the noise of the clatter of tables being flattened, and everyone seeming to have an opinion of what should be done next. Tamar grimaced as she looked around for Wilhelm.

A 'Hey, I'm up here' had her looking up and seeing Wilhelm up a ladder untying bunting.

On seeing her looking at him, Wilhelm began to play the fool, sticking his leg out and making gestures that embarrassed her but made her giggle, but at the same time she begged him to be careful.

Always the clown, he took no notice and stretched out to unhook a long trail of bunting from a nail, laughing as he did and kicking one of his legs out.

'Darling, don't! You might fall!'

'Mummy, Daddy won't fall. Daddy can do anything!'

The words had hardly been spoken when the ladder wobbled. Tamar ran forward, as did others who had been watching. But too late, the ladder went from under Wilhelm and he crashed to the ground.

No one moved. A deadly silence fell and then was broken by the screams of Tamar, and those of all the women gathered watching.

But after a second, everyone surged forward. Someone shouted, 'Call for an ambulance, quick!'

Blood seeped from Wilhelm's head and made a pool on the pavement. Tamar stared at it for a moment then fell onto her knees. 'Wilhelm, Wilhelm, my beloved!' But he did not stir.

At the hospital, Florence held her. She smelled of carbolic and her uniform pinny was stiff with starch that scratched Tamar's face, but there was still nowhere Tamar would rather be.

'Help me . . . Help me . . .'

'It's going to be all right. I promise, my lovely.'

But were they just words? 'Will . . . will he live?'

'Yes. He will, Tamar. You must not give up hope. Wilhelm is badly injured, but he will survive . . . It's possible that he won't be the same and will need your love and care, but you won't lose him. He's strong and he's fighting.'

'What has happened to him?'

'He has cracked his skull badly. And his legs are both broken in many places . . . I – I have to be honest with you, my dear Tamar. He may not walk again, and he may have some impairments.'

'What kind?' Fear held her in its grip as their life together, that had at last reached another level the night before, suddenly seemed to be snatched away from them.

'We can't tell yet, but with such a head injury to the front of his head as well as to the back, his speech and understanding . . .'

'Oh, Florence, I can't stand it, I can't!'

'You are strong, Tamar. Look at all you have come through. You can be there for Wilhelm. I know you can. We'll all help you.'

'I'm so grateful, but Florence, why did this happen? Why does Wilhelm act the fool?'

'It's his nature, and now that he is happy, his true self emerges more and more. It's tragic that having a bit of fun has led to this.'

'We were so happy at the street party!'

'You said that as if you haven't always been. Tamar, is there something I don't know?'

'No . . . I mean, we've always been happy, but there were things hanging between us. Last night at the party we spoke of them and then after . . . well, we completely dispelled them.'

'I understand. It was bound to happen. But I'm glad it's behind you now. There will still be a future for you both, my darling. Life will carry on – it must do so. And as we have over the past years, we will cope. Wilhelm would want that – need it.'

'Can I see him yet?'

'Are you sure you're ready?'

'Yes. I need to be with him; to tell him everything will be all right.'

'That's my Tamar. My lovely Tamar. Come along, I'll take you to his room. We have him in a side ward as there are two teams taking care of him, Liam's and Mr Drakeman's, the neurologist here.'

Wilhelm wasn't Wilhelm, but this mummy kind of a figure with his head swathed in bandages and only his closed eyes and mouth visible.

Tamar fell onto her knees next to him. 'Wilhelm, my darling. Wilhelm, it's me, Tamar. Oh, Wilhelm, get better, please get better. I can't bear losing you.'

One of his fingers lifted. Tamar's head shot round to look at Florence.

'I'll fetch Liam. Keep talking to him, Tamar.'

Tamar turned back to Wilhelm. 'It's going to be all right, my darling. You're going to get better. It may take time, but you will.'

His finger moved again and an agitation that hadn't been there made him lift it up and down. Tamar took it gently into hers. 'Be still, my darling. I love you.'

With this, his finger went limp in hers, and a deep sigh released from his body.

'Wilhelm! Wilhelm! No! No! Don't die . . . Don't leave me!'

The door flung open. Liam rushed to Wilhelm's side, but Florence stood in the open doorway and stared.

'Florence . . . Wilhelm . . . No . . . no!'

With this, Florence's arms came around her and Tamar fell onto her.

The new world she'd built for herself after losing Isaac and having that terrible thing happen to her at Wolfgang's hand collapsed around her as the room went silent – no voice calling for Wilhelm to respond. Wilhelm had gone.

Four days later, as they walked through the streets behind the hearse, a beautifully decorated horse and cart, crowds of people joined them. Wilhelm had touched so many lives – in his work, doing the accounts for many business people in their community; at the food kitchen, where he did all he could and had often helped people back on their feet; in Brick Lane, where so many loved him and had stopped for chats with him and been cheered by his sense of humour; and finally, from the synagogue where he worshipped.

The moment was a mixture of pride and sorrow for Tamar as she followed his coffin into the synagogue.

She'd cried so many tears that today, she felt dried of them. She felt that tears were for those who didn't hurt as much as she did.

Florence and Elma held her – the two women that meant so much to her. But their love could not soothe her pain.

When she came out again, she watched Wilhelm's coffin being loaded onto the cart and then looked up at the sky just as she had done so many times in her life, and asked, *Are you together, my darlings, Papa, Mama, Isaac, Hannah and now Wilhelm? Look after each other for me.*

A hand touched her arm, and she turned to see Jenny standing there. And behind her, Ben and Susan. Florence, who had become friends with them all, must have informed them. Somehow, Tamar managed a small smile for each.

Her cousin Ruben came to stand near to her. He took her in her arms. 'I am always here for you, dear Tamar.'

'I know,' was all she could manage.

How it happened, Tamar couldn't have said, as her mind had gone blank, but now they were standing looking down on the coffin that held her beloved Wilhelm. The rabbi prayed and, as he did, he threw a handful of earth that resounded as it hit the coffin. The sound broke the stupor Tamar was in. Her knees gave way as a terrible wail came from her. At that moment, it seemed her life was over.

Chapter Twenty-Four
1946

Over a year went by with no decisions made as to her future. Life for Tamar was lived as if in a film – acting out what she had to do every day and yet achieving nothing.

Milestones came and went – all of them her first without Wilhelm. Tears were cried during the night, for both of her loves. Wilhelm had cushioned her grief over losing Isaac, but that, too, flooded her and overwhelmed her of late.

Often she would unwrap the silver heart sent to her by Isaac, which she'd always kept wrapped in tissue paper in her handbag, and would hold it close to her own heart. Wilhelm had known about this and hadn't seemed to mind. She did that now as she stared out of the window and across the road at the flat that used to be Florence's.

Living back in Elma's flat had given her some comfort as it held only happy memories, whereas the one above the shop that had been her papa's held sad ones for her. How she'd been able to put these behind her while living there with Wilhelm she didn't know – but then, had she? Hadn't she often visited her love for Isaac? Hadn't she suddenly turned and seen her papa sitting in the armchair that stood in the same place where his used to be?

At this moment she had an affiliation with her fellow Jews who had lost their whole family in the Holocaust, for she had lost hers too. Only Ruben and her child were left – she couldn't count her aunt, her mama's sister who lived in Germany. She wasn't anyone you could call family.

Looking down at the silver heart, she wondered if the rest of Isaac's bracelet had been buried with him. And where that was. She'd learned from Wilhelm that most were buried in the mass graves that Anna had told her of, on one of the rare occasions she'd allowed him to talk about his work in Auschwitz. She hated that he had once acted as a Nazi and had to make herself remember the many he had helped to escape. But that wasn't all she'd had to force herself to forget, for there must have been many hundreds that he'd helped to murder too.

At these moments when such things visited her, she had to stop her thoughts. She didn't understand why they came to her, when she knew he'd had no choice and that he'd done all he could do. Better that he was there to carry out his rescue work than if he hadn't been. And she believed, like he had, that his posting was one of spite as it was well known his mother was Jewish, and, as she'd once overheard in the cafe in Krakow, that it was also to test his loyalty.

As she thought of all she'd heard about her mother-in-law, she wanted to visit her and spit in her face. How her heart went out to Wilhelm's grandmother and aunt, betrayed by their own daughter and sister. Brought up by such a woman, it was a wonder that Wilhelm had turned out how he had.

But as she still stared out at the window she'd waved so

often to Florence from, it was the silver heart and memories of Isaac that were vying for prominence in her mind.

Her heart lifted as she saw herself running with him, his hand clasping hers, his laughter hanging on the breeze as he pulled her towards the sea. Did such a life ever exist? Such a beautiful, carefree life?

She hadn't meant to cry, but as her memories of the two men she loved each tried to take precedence in her mind, her world seemed broken, her life sectioned into pieces – there was a piece that belonged to her mama and papa, and one that belonged to Isaac and Hannah, and one that belonged to Wilhelm.

She wouldn't let in the piece that held her work with the resistance as that always threw up the friends she'd lost, the young lives she'd taken and the violation of her body.

Thinking she would go mad with everything colliding in her head, Tamar abruptly turned from the window, shoved the silver heart back into her bag and made herself put on her coat, ready to go to the food kitchen, still as busy as ever as many refugees poured into London. Helping there whenever she could always put her own plight into perspective.

Today being Wednesday, she had a day off from work at the school. Though, for most of her time there, she barely functioned and she'd closed her Saturday language lessons for the time being.

Her skills were still needed at the food kitchen as the poor Jewish souls who had made it here spoke many different languages, and she could help them all. And in doing so, she helped herself too.

When she arrived, Rosie greeted her with a hug. Hugs from her and Elma were always a salve to Tamar.

'Well, luv, it's good to see yer. We've a young boy turned up today. He's made it here from Poland, God knows how! But he's been asking after yer – well, in a fashion, but I understood your name. Remi, who you taught English to, told him you come here often, and he cried tears of joy.'

'Really! What's his name?'

A voice behind her said, 'It's me, Yeltsi!'

For some reason, Tamar wanted to laugh out loud as she turned and without thinking took Yeltsi in her arms. It seemed to her that he was the only thread she had to her Polish life. Yeltsi clung to her.

'How did you get here? Where are you staying?'

As she spoke, she brushed his mop of dark curly hair off his forehead and looked into his baby-like face.

'I took my chance when we heard that Germany had been defeated, and the Russians were allowed to stay. I travelled through forests and along riverbanks till I came to the sea, and then I was taken on as a deckhand on a merchant vessel. When it sailed here, I jumped ship.'

'Oh, Yeltsi, it is good to see you.'

'I – I heard about Wilhelm. I'm sorry . . . The man who told me about you said that you and he married and have a child?'

Tamar swallowed hard. 'We did. We . . . we were very happy.'

'I – I saw what happened to you . . . I'm sorry, I should have helped you. I – I was afraid . . . Forgive me.'

This shocked Tamar. She felt her cheeks reddening at the thought of this young boy witnessing her being raped. Holding him tighter, she told him, 'Oh, Yeltsi, I'm sorry you saw that, and I'm glad you didn't try to help. You would have been shot. I took care of him.'

'I know. After you left, I went and spat on him and kicked his body, then dug my own knife into his throat to make sure he died.'

'Wasn't he dead when I left?' Tamar hated having to talk about this – having to remember . . .

'No, he took another breath as I approached him. And he opened his eyes. He saw my knife and could do nothing but stare at me as I plunged it into his throat, then I ran and ran.'

'You have seen and done so much in your young life, Yeltsi.' And then, on impulse, she asked him, 'Would you like to come and live with me? I only have two bedrooms but my little girl, Thelma, can move into my room. She sleeps most nights with me anyway, and you can have her room – it's done out in pink, but we can change that.'

Yeltsi grinned. 'Really? Oh, Bibi . . . I mean, Tamar. I still think of you as Bibi . . . But that would be wonderful, and I would sleep in a room in your house even if it was green with pink spots, as I . . . I love you like a big sister.'

They hugged again. 'And I love you, Yeltsi. And I would love you to become a young boy again. How old are you?'

Yeltsi expanded his chest. 'I'm fifteen.'

'Well, we have a friend for you already.' She told him about Stuart. 'Only you will have to learn to speak in English.'

'I can.' He said this in perfect English. 'Well, a little.' He'd reverted to Polish. 'I learned some in school.'

His eyes looked away. It was as if he was being transported to another life. As they all could be by a chance remark or conversation.

Keeping things on a light-hearted footing, Tamar said, 'Ah, but I'm talking of Cockney English, and that's like another language altogether.'

'Like Rosie, you mean? I can understand some of the

Jewish customers when they speak to her, but I cannot get a word she says!'

Tamar laughed out loud.

'And you're always to call me Tamar, not Bibi. That was another life.'

'I will, Tamar . . . But did you really mean that I could live with you . . . like a son?'

'Well, you'll be more like a young brother – I'm not that old!'

They both laughed then, but when they calmed down, Yeltsi said, 'But you're like a mother. You're like my mother was – full of fun and seeing the best in life.'

How he had deduced this, Tamar didn't know as while in the camp she'd mostly been serious. And yet, with Wilhelm and before him, with Isaac and Hannah, and now, with Florence, yes, she had been the person he described. Maybe Yeltsi would bring that back to her, as already she'd laughed with him – a sincere laugh that had stemmed from her happiness at seeing he was safe.

'What happened to everyone, Yeltsi?'

'I don't know, we all got separated. I was faster than any of them and left them behind. But when Germany's defeat seemed imminent, they spoke of going back to their families – those who had family still living – and others of carrying on the fight against the communists.'

'And Clive?'

'He was picked up weeks before we disbanded and taken home. There was a time of uncertainty for us all. But then it was decided that it was every man for himself, and I began to run.'

'Well, you're here now and safe. And I must get on and help as it's getting busy.'

'Can I help too?'

'I'm sure you can. Let's see what Rosie says. Though she will probably put you on washing-up. She takes a time to trust you to do anything else when you first start to help out here.'

'I don't mind. Washing-up is such a normal thing to do . . . If I was at home, I would have to wash up – though I would have had to fight with my brother . . . I mean . . . Well, we both hated drying-up.'

Not stopping him from speaking of his family, but diverting the conversation a little to help him, Tamar said, 'It's good to know you're well trained on washing dishes, love, as you can be my chief washer-upper at home.'

'Home . . . I like that word. Home . . .'

Seeing him begin to well up, Tamar said, 'Watch out, Rosie's heading for us now. She probably wants to know why I'm not working!'

'So, 'ave yer got acquainted again? 'Ow do yer know each other? Only he couldn't tell me 'ow he knew yer, just said yer name as a question.'

'He is . . . He's from my village. But he was just a small boy then.' This lie was because still she didn't feel able to talk of her work during her absence, and still Rosie thought she'd been to America. 'He'd like to lend a hand if you have any jobs he can do.'

'I do. Yer can 'elp with the washing-up, young man.'

Both she and Yeltsi burst out laughing. Rosie looked bemused. ''Ave I said something funny, then?'

'No, just predictable. Anyway, Yeltsi is experienced in washing-up, so you've picked the right job for him . . . and, just to let you know, he's coming home to live with me and Thelma.'

Rosie gave a huge grin; she loved it when one of the hundreds she cared for found a settled place. 'Well, that's good news. It's yer lucky day, young man.' With this she slapped him lightly on the shoulder. If not her words, Yeltsi had understood her grin and her slapping him in fun and he grinned back.

'Well, he could steal yer 'eart in seconds. Go on, the pair of yer, we've a lot to do.'

'I can only stay for a couple of hours, Rosie, I've to pick Thelma up from school.'

'You'd better get scurrying around then, luv. Ha, not that yer can ever do that as most 'ave questions for yer. But in that, yer helping, so just do what yer can.'

Yeltsi was full of his afternoon as they walked to the school. And he repeated a phrase he'd heard. 'Let's gerron with it then.'

Tamar laughed at this, said in a Polish accent, and as she did, she thought that Yeltsi had brought a little joy back into her life in the short time they'd been reunited.

She unravelled the sentence in Polish and then in English – then explained how the Cockney slang had changed the words 'get on'.

Yeltsi ended up very confused.

'You'll get used to it. But firstly, I'll help you to master English. Then we can move on to the Cockney slang form as they use many rhyming words in place of the real words, but I cannot give you an example as they don't rhyme in Polish.'

'I'll try, but it all sounds very difficult.'

'It won't be, you're a very clever young man. Look how you have made your way over thousands of miles to London.

You will soon learn English, though speaking it is easier than spelling it as they spell words so differently to how they sound. And their use of the alphabet is very different to ours.'

'It sounds fascinating.'

'That is how I have always thought of languages – fascinating.'

They had reached Christ Church School. Yeltsi gazed at the name. 'A Christian school?'

'Yes. But they don't teach Christianity to any Jewish children. Thelma sits in a reading class with other Jewish children and a Jewish teacher who works here during assembly and religious instruction. I teach her our own doctrine at home.'

Yeltsi nodded. 'Will I be able to go to school?'

'I'm afraid you're too old. They leave at age fourteen and have to go to work, if their families cannot afford to send them to college. But don't worry, once you can speak and read in the English language, you can pick up your education. Have you a career in mind?'

'I want to be a doctor like my . . . papa was.'

Tamar instinctively put her arm around him. She'd known nothing about him or his family during their time together.

'I have a friend who is a doctor, and his wife, who is my very best friend, is a nurse – well, she was until recently as she is going to have a baby soon. You can talk to them about your hopes and dreams, and they can help put you onto the right path. They're called Florence and Liam . . . Between us, we'll get you to where you want to be, Yeltsi, I promise.'

Now four and a half years old, Thelma looked so grown-up as she came out of the huge school gates. If she could, she would have gone to school a year ago, as she used to beg to be allowed to. Always Tamar marvelled at how her little girl was so advanced for her years.

Tamar was nervous at what she would think of Yeltsi and how he was now to live with them, but she needn't have worried as Thelma took to him the moment he smiled at her. It was his hand she wanted to hold. Her giggles were a joy as she skipped along and every now and again, Yeltsi lifted her off the ground. This warmed Tamar's heart as she watched Yeltsi, now almost a young man, become a child again, picking up where he'd left off as a boy of ten – when he was plunged into a terrifying world with those who had always protected him no longer being able to do so.

He hadn't ever spoken about the time he and his family were taken from the ghetto to Auschwitz and probably never would.

Elma greeted them. 'So, who's this then?'

Thelma ran to her for her usual kiss and cuddle. 'Granny, this is Yeltsi. He escaped from Poland. He's going to live with us and have my room, and if you want to know what he says, I will tell you.'

'Oh, yer will, will yer? Clever clogs.'

Thelma laughed out loud.

'So, Yeltsi, I'm famous for me cholent. A growing lad like you will luv it and 'as it 'appens, I've made some tonight. Must 'ave known yer were coming.' She turned then and yelled, 'Stuart! Come 'ere, luv, I've someone for yer to meet.'

Yeltsi grinned at Tamar. She knew that though he hadn't understood a word, he had understood that he was welcome. She quickly interpreted and then explained that Stuart, who she'd told him about, was coming to meet him.

Stuart appeared, his face a picture of curiosity. Now a tall, gangly lad of almost fifteen, he stared at Yeltsi.

Elma clipped his ear lightly. 'Stop staring and say 'ello. Lad's escaped the horrors of war and needs a warm welcome.'

Stuart grinned at Yeltsi, but before either could speak, Thelma said, 'I'll tell you what he says, Stuart.'

'Ha, don't he speak English then?'

'Not yet, but Mummy's going to teach him.'

'Right. Well, hello, Yeltsi. Yer welcome. I could do with another male around 'ere, these womenfolk rule the place.'

For this, although they all laughed, Stuart earned another light clip of his ear as Elma told him, 'And that ain't gonna change any time soon, lad.'

Stuart flinched. 'Give over clipping me flipping ear, Aunt Elma, I'll 'ave cauliflower ears like the boxers 'ave if yer keep on.'

Elma grinned. 'Well, watch yer cheek then.' Her smile held love as she ruffled Stuart's hair.

Interpreting all of that lost some of the humour, but Yeltsi got the gist and laughed out loud.

'Right, you'll join us for yer supper then, Tamar, luv . . . and it's good to see a smile on your face. I always say 'elping others 'elps us.'

'It does, Elma, it does. And yes, that will be lovely. I don't feel like cooking and it'll be good for Yeltsi to enjoy a family atmosphere . . . By the way, Stuart, have you any clothes you could lend to Yeltsi? You're about the same size.'

Elma answered. 'He's plenty, love. I'll sort a few things out. Watch the shop, Stuart, while I nip through the back and get some of your stuff for Yeltsi.'

'Righto, but not me West Ham jumper, that's not for sharing.'

'You and yer football!'

'It ain't just any football, Aunt Elma, it's the 'ammers! The best team in the world.'

'Ha, they're runners-up, lad.'

'Well, that's good considering their ground were bombed and they ain't 'ad a proper 'ome for a while.'

Yeltsi looked lost at this banter. But when explained to him, his face lit up. 'I love football!'

'Yeltsi said he loves football too, Stuart,' Thelma told him.

Stuart seemed to relax then. 'Hey, mate, we'll 'ave a kick-about when the shop shuts, eh?'

Seeing Yeltsi's confusion, Stuart pointed at Yeltsi and then at himself while pretending to kick a ball, then indicated this could be in the street. Yeltsi's face lit up, '*Tak, tak.*'

But with Thelma telling him the word was 'yes', Yeltsi nodded. 'Yes, yes. Thank you.'

'Well, I understood yer the first time, but that's great.'

The boys grinned at each other, and to Tamar a friendship was growing that she knew would help them both.

With Yeltsi's arrival, Tamar's world took on a new perspective. She began to feel part of life again and restarted her Saturday language class of which Yeltsi was a star pupil. His rate of learning and his dedication to it astonished her. By Christmas he was reading and writing in English!

On Christmas Day, Tamar and Yeltsi indulged Elma and Stuart as they entered into the spirit of buying a present for everyone. It all still confused Thelma, but she loved receiving her gifts.

And they all loved that Florence, Liam, Rufus and, joy of joys, their adorable one-month-old baby Elizabeth, named after one of the King's daughters, could join them for lunch.

Devout Christians, Florence and Liam adored celebrating Christmas.

Elizabeth had made a sudden appearance, denying Tamar the chance to be at her birth as planned. She was a beautiful little being with huge black eyes and very short black curly hair.

Tamar was mostly occupied in willing Elizabeth to wake so that she could hold her, but she slept soundly through it all. They enjoyed the King's speech. Though, as he talked of the greatest upheaval in human history and celebrated that his people were celebrating Christmas as free men and in peace, and that the 'Commonwealth and Empire . . . have not been disrupted by the stress and peril of war,' memories hit each one of them, with Stuart having to leave the table and Yeltsi going after him.

After a few moments of their absence, Tamar ventured out to find them and Thelma followed her. Despite the cold, they were sat on the step of Elma's backyard, crying together. Tamar joined them and cried with them – three delicate souls trying to heal from the loss of their entire families.

'We lost Daddy, didn't we, Mummy?' Thelma didn't say this as if in competition, but as the sadness of her mother and the boys seemed to bring Wilhelm's death back to her.

'We did. And so many you never got to meet, my darling.'

'But they're in heaven now, so we should be happy for them.'

'We are, but we miss them so much.'

Thelma's bottom lip went as she said, 'I miss Daddy.'

Hugging her, Tamar wondered if she would ever heal from the pain of losing so many she loved and felt an affinity with the two boys – well, young men – crying beside her. At least her losses had been spaced out, giving her time to heal a little between, but for them it had been in one fell swoop. How would they ever come to terms with that?

Florence, Liam and Elma came outside and helped them by hugging them and allowing their grief to flow.

'You're all bound to feel this pain,' Florence told them, 'and while it's good to express it with others who understand, it's also important to remember the good times. Come inside and tell us of a family celebration that was happy for each of you, eh?'

They followed her inside.

'Let's start with you, Tamar.'

They sat in a circle now – Thelma crossed-legged on the floor with Rufus, Stuart and Yeltsi, while Elma, Tamar, Florence and Liam sat on the sofa, with Liam cradling baby Elizabeth.

'You start, Tamar,' Florence prompted.

She told of one of her last Simchat Torah celebrations before her mama died. 'It's a completion of the annual reading of the Torah. We danced and sang. We laughed and joined the procession around the synagogue with Torah scrolls. Mama was so happy. I can hear her laughing, and see Papa cuddling her. Isaac and Hannah and their mama and papa were there, and as soon as we could, Isaac and Hannah and I escaped and ran to the seashore. And even though it was a cold October day, we took off our shoes and paddled in the sea. And we danced in it, splashing each other and laughing – so much laughter . . . But then Isaac slipped over and sat in the water. Hannah and I couldn't help him as we were doubled over giggling uncontrollably.'

At this point, she felt herself giggle as the memory came alive. She was joined by them all – whether from relief or finding the story funny, she didn't know. All she knew was that the moment had lightened.

'Mine was when Mum won the pools!' Stuart told them. Elma looked astonished at him.

'Mum won six bob, and she took us all to the cinema and bought us popcorn. It were delicious. Then she bought some pop, a bottle of sherry, and pie and mash from the pie shop. It were a feast. And when she'd 'ad a few sherries, Mum danced and made each one of us dance with her . . . We giggled that much our Tommy wet 'imself!'

By now, Stuart was giggling and they all joined him.

'Mine was my brother's bar mitzvah,' Yeltsi said once they had calmed. 'The celebration was wonderful. There was food, all our friends came, we danced and sang, and Mama and Papa told me how proud they were of him and would be of me, when my day came . . .'

After a pause, Yeltsi bravely continued: 'Everyone danced in a circle around Joel, when suddenly my little sister, Ruth, ran into the circle to hug him, but she didn't seem to stop running and made him fall over! She fell on top of him and we all laughed and couldn't stop laughing!'

It was Yeltsi's time to giggle and all of them joined him.

Thelma moved closer to him and leaned on his arm. Yeltsi put his free arm around her and hugged her to him. 'You're like my Ruth. You're my little sister now, Thelma.'

The moment was touching, but didn't put them back into sadness as Thelma retorted, 'And I bet she had a job with keeping your room tidy as I do! Dirty smelly socks, just dumped, bed not made! And you nearly a man now!'

She sounded so like a grown-up nagging her child that everyone burst out laughing.

The day had been saved, Tamar thought, as she felt a hand hold hers and as she looked at the beautiful, radiantly happy Florence, whose hand it was, and whispered, 'Thank you. Always you're here for me.'

'And I always will be, my darling.'

A warmth entered Tamar as she took baby Elizabeth into her arms and cradled her, then glanced around at her new family. *Life will carry on and we will have plenty of times that we can laugh together. And this is something that I'll strive for.*

Yeltsi turned and as they caught each other's eye, his smile warmed her heart.

She smiled back and hoped that with it she conveyed that everything would be all right in the future. She would make sure it was.

Chapter Twenty-Five
Two years later, 1948

As Tamar sat outside in the yard, sipping her tea in the warm June sunshine having just got home from working her last day as a teacher in the West End, she was filled with excitement as she thought of how the premises above a shop just down the road were finally hers! Now she could begin to decorate and furnish it as her very own language school.

Above an ironmonger's, it hadn't been converted into a flat from the storeroom it was originally intended for, unlike most had been, including Elma's and the shop she'd had with her papa, and then with Wilhelm.

Found for her by her cousin Ruben, who'd wanted to become a partner but she'd refused, the huge room could easily be kitted out with tables for desks, a blackboard and shelves that would hold books and each pupil's folders with their work. Stuart would help as he'd proved himself a handyman of late as Elma had reorganized the shop and Stuart had fitted it out with new shelves. Always he seemed to be carving something out of wood – not great artworks, but just for his own pleasure, like the box he made for Thelma's toys and books. The result was not only practical but had a professional finish to it. Thelma loved it and had him painting it pink.

Tamar sighed a contented sigh. It was all going to be wonderful. All she needed now to complete her happiness was to hear that Yeltsi, now a strapping young man and soon to be eighteen, would be accepted at St Bartholomew's School of Medicine.

He'd done so well in his education, and she hoped with all her heart that he had passed his scholarship, while at the same time she would miss him living with them as he would move into college accommodation.

It isn't far, and I will see him all the time, she told herself, as she had done many times since he'd first applied. She loved him like a younger brother, and Thelma, now six and a half years old, adored him. His patience and love shone from him. His diligence with the private lessons had paid her back two-fold for the money they had cost, and the lessons that Liam gave him, while employing him part-time at the surgery he and Florence had established, would stand him in good stead, as would his father having been a doctor.

Yeltsi was in his element every time he set out for Liam's and Florence's surgery, held in three rooms of the ground floor of the three-storey house in Redchurch Street that they had bought last year, when Liam decided to move into general practice. They had been lucky enough to find one of the few that hadn't had its ground floor converted to a shop.

Dear Florence was so happy, being able to be close to little Elizabeth and, with the help of a nanny, still continue her nursing career. She'd been lost for the twelve months that she'd been a stay-at-home mum, with Liam still working at the hospital.

For herself, seeing Florence in a house had set her longing to have her own house as she felt sick of living in a flat, and could feel its limitations irritating her like they never had done in the past. But how could she leave Elma?

As if she'd conjured her up, Elma came outside to her. 'I've left Rita to it, she loves running the shop. Only I wanted to talk to you about something.'

'That sounds serious.'

Rita had been working with Elma through the war and now did more and more hours.

'It is . . . I'm tired, Tamar.'

'Oh, Elma . . . I don't want to offend you, love, but isn't it time for you to give up the shop and retire?'

'That's occurred to me so often of late, luv. But what about you and the kids, and Stuart? Your lives are here.'

'No, they aren't. I want to move too. And I know Stuart will go wherever you go. Not only that, but he should have a career. He shouldn't still be a delivery boy, even if he does do it in a van now.'

'I know. But what could he do?'

'It's staring you in the face, Elma – help him to train as a carpenter. He's got a natural talent for it.'

'I never thought! He's been so loyal to me, and I ain't took notice that he's wasting his life.'

Tamar took her hand. 'He isn't wasting it. No one who lives life around you can be said to be wasting their life, Elma, but, yes, he could make more of himself. Maybe even run his own little business?'

'Yes, he could! That settles it . . . 'Old on 'ere a mo, I'm going back in to talk to Rita. She was telling me the other day that she was left her mum's house, but she doesn't know what to do with the money she got from selling it . . . This could be an answer for her as well as me as, like I say, she loves working in the shop.'

Elma dashed back in like an excited child.

Not superstitious, but as this was something that would be the answer to her own prayers, Tamar crossed her fingers.

Her mind went to where they would live and what they could afford between them. A trickle of worry seeped into her as she thought how she would maybe rely on her savings while she built her school, and how, though her new premises were all right for now, if she did want to expand, she'd need somewhere better in the future.

But these were all expelled as an even more excited Elma came out to the yard once more.

'I've only bleedin' sold me shop, Tamar! Rita snatched me 'and off!'

'Did I 'ear right, Aunt Elma . . . Yer selling up?'

They both looked at Stuart as he came through the door.

'Yes, yer 'eard right, luv . . . I should 'ave spoke to yer about it, but, well, I just took the bull by its 'orns.'

'What're we going to do then?'

'We'll find a proper 'ome like Florence and Liam have, and you, young fella, will be going to college!'

'What? Well, I like the idea of a proper 'ome, but college! 'Ave yer gone mad? Reading and writing is me limit!'

'No, it ain't, you do yerself down! What about measuring – that's figures, ain't it? And so is adding up what folk owe for their groceries and taking away when yer arrive with them and they've changed their mind about something they ordered! And numbers is just the basics a carpenter needs.'

'A carpenter! Me?'

'Yes, you, yer daft oaf! Close yer mouth, yer look like yer catching bleedin' flies!'

Tamar and Stuart burst out laughing and Tamar had the feeling that if he wouldn't feel stupid, Stuart would do a dance.

'So, what d'yer say then?'

Stuart's grin widened. 'I say, it's the best idea you've ever had. I love working with wood. But I ain't much on college. I'd rather find a tradesman to take me on and teach me on the job.'

'Well, it's your choice. And if yer can do that, then well and good, but if not, yer've got to learn yer trade somehow.'

'I'll help you, Stuart,' Tamar told him. 'If you don't find a woodworker to take you on and teach you, I'll give you lessons to get you ready for college.'

'Ta, Tamar. This 'as all come as a shock. So, where will we live then?'

Elma looked blank. 'I ain't got as far as that. I only know that I want an 'ouse. And a rocking chair.'

Tamar and Stuart burst out laughing again at this.

Tamar asked, 'Can we buy, or do we ask Ruben to look for a rented house for us?'

'I want to buy. I asked Florence what they'd paid, and I can run to that with what I've got put by, and what Rita's agreed to pay for me shop. Besides, we need a big 'ouse like she's got, then you can 'ave the top floor for your own flat, Stuart, which yer can share with Yeltsi when he's 'ome from his university. And me, Tamar and Thelma can 'ave the other two floors, with the ground floor being our living area.'

'Oh, Elma, that would be wonderful! And I can contribute, I have plenty left over from the sale of the shop . . . We could buy some new furniture too!'

'That was my thinking. The stuff I've got 'as seen better days. Besides, I just told Rita that I'd leave the flat furnished so that she can get an income from it as soon as she can let it – and that won't take long, there's hardly a day passes that someone don't ask if I know of any accommodation around the area.'

Tamar could feel an excitement warming her belly. 'I'll ring Florence and see if she knows of anything up for sale in her area. I love it on Redchurch Street as it's busy like here, and yet there's a mixture of three-storey houses in among the shops.'

What she wanted to say was that she wanted to live out in the countryside as she longed for the fresh air trees gave and to see green grass, instead of tarmac roads and traffic. But she knew that wasn't practical as she had her school to think of. And besides, uprooting Elma would take so much from her. She belonged in the East End. But oh, to move out of a flat – something she'd dreamed of doing just an hour ago, and now it was a real possibility!

It was six weeks later as they were packing their belongings, Tamar, Yeltsi and Thelma chatting away in Polish as they always did when in the flat alone, that Thelma gave a sigh. '*To ekscytujące, ale i smutne, mamusiu.*'

Tamar looked at her, her feelings the same as Thelma's. 'I know, my darling. It is sad and exciting. Sad because you've only ever known living on this street, and exciting to be beginning a new phase of your life.'

'You're lucky, Thelma. You've never had to forcibly leave your home.'

Tamar looked at Yeltsi. Rarely did he mention his past, but she supposed the upheaval of the move to Redchurch Street, where Ruben had found a lovely house for them at a price they could just afford – though it needed a lot of attention, which they'd all joked would be good practice for Stuart – had brought up some memories.

'I'm sorry, Yeltsi. I didn't mean to upset you.'

Half his height, Thelma had gone to his side and looked up at him. 'The stories you tell me make me cry, but you're lucky too. We love you and you and I are a good brother and sister.'

The tension visibly left Yeltsi as he looked down at her. 'I know . . . It's the packing . . . we were told to take all valuables with us and leave the rest. It feels like this is the same thing. We're leaving behind the furniture and carpets that we . . . I have come to love this place as home.'

Tamar's heart flipped over. She hadn't thought of the implications to Yeltsi of leaving behind the main body of what had been their home together. But that was the deal they'd made with Rita, and the new furniture they'd chosen for the new house was being delivered today, so there would be no room to take anything anyway.

Going to his side, she told him, 'Life isn't possessions, Yeltsi. They age and wear out or go out of fashion. What counts is family. We lost ours, but we've built a new one and that will go with us.'

Yeltsi grinned. 'I know.'

As big as he was, he had tears in his eyes as he turned to her. 'I've begun to write it all down, and while it helps, it also brings the memories alive once more.'

'We need to remember. And it's good you are writing about it now. I hope I have a starring role in your memoir?'

'You do. You changed my life . . . Tamar, may I live at home when I go to study? St Bartholomew's isn't far, it'll only take me about fifteen minutes on my bike.'

'Really? We thought you wanted to live in?'

'I did, but not now. I – I don't want to leave you all yet.'

'Can I hug you?' Tamar used to do this spontaneously, but now Yeltsi was a young man, it wasn't as easy, and she was mindful that it might embarrass him.

He turned to her and put his arms around her. 'Always. I've missed our hugs.'

The little boy was still inside the man, Tamar thought as she gave him a motherly hug.

'We so didn't want you to leave home. But will you live in the flat with Stuart, as there is no room in the two floors we will live in? Thelma needs her own room now.'

'Yes. I'm looking forward to that – me talking medicine and Stuart talking about making a table!'

They all laughed, and then even harder as Thelma, always the witty one, said, 'You can get him to make you an operating table!'

With this, the moment of sadness and worry passed.

Elma yelling, 'The van's 'ere, luv, are yer all ready?' sobered them up. They scurried around grabbing the last things and stuffing them where they could as Tamar called back, 'Coming, Elma!'

With everything stacked in the van they stood a moment looking at the outside of the shop. The drizzly rain seemed to emulate the tears Tamar and Elma wanted to shed.

But then there was a commotion as the street filled with people, all cheering. Their neighbours had come out to say goodbye.

Florrie, who owned the cake shop, held a huge bunch of flowers. As she gave them to Elma, she said, 'There yer are, luv, we're going to miss yer.'

After hugging them all, she turned and said, 'Your turn, Ivy.'

Vera, the lady who'd caused mayhem in the shop during

the worst of the shortages at the beginning of the war, made everyone laugh as she retorted, 'No, it ain't! Get in the queue, Ivy Payne, we'll all get served one at a time. And I were 'ere before you!'

She and Ivy – now long-time friends – stepped forward. 'We're going to miss yer, more than anyone can, Elma. And yer family an' all – a mish-mash of folk held together by yer love for them. We 'ad this done for yer.'

Vera handed Elma a large framed photo. As Tamar saw it was of Elma and Papa taken outside the shop, she swallowed hard. It was beautiful and so natural, not posed, but just the two of them holding hands and grinning.

Elma did cry then and she was soon surrounded by a crowd. Vera could be heard saying, 'We went through a lot, but we did it together, luv, and now yer going to a well-earned retirement. But mark me words, we'll be knocking on yer door for a cuppa every week, won't we, Ivy?'

Getting back her sense of humour, Elma told them, 'And yer'll bleedin' well form an orderly queue when yer do!'

The laughter erupted again and then broke into a round of applause.

The tears weren't far away for Tamar, but she didn't let them fall. This was Elma's moment.

But then, suddenly, it became hers as the postie stepped into the crowd.

'Tamar, I've an official letter for yer, luv.'

Everyone went quiet as Tamar took the brown envelope and then carefully opened it.

The stamp on the outside told her it was from the Polish embassy. Her heart raced, wondering what it contained.

The thick, crisp paper unfolded with a certain dignity. Tamar gasped as she read it.

The honourable Prime Minister of the Polish government, Tomasz Arciszewski, is pleased to inform Tamar Grechen, née Brume, that you have been included in my final honours list before leaving office, and that you are to receive the Silver Cross of the War Order of Virtuti Militari. This is awarded for your outstanding courage while working with the resistance during the war.

It then said that instructions of when the presentation would be made would follow in due course but that it would take place at the Polish embassy.

'What is it, Tamar, luv?'

Tamar looked around at the now quiet and expectant crowd.

'I – I have something to tell you all . . . I didn't go to America during the war, I went back to my beloved Poland.' She gave a brief outline of her work, her words going out to these silent Londoners who knew what suffering was but couldn't comprehend the kind she and Yeltsi had been through.

'Yeltsi was there too. A boy of ten years old then, his courage was immense. He was imprisoned in Auschwitz with my Isaac . . .'

A collective gasp made the goosebumps stand out on Tamar's arms. Yeltsi's hand came into hers and held it tight as she told of what happened to his family.

'My Isaac helped him to escape and many others, and for that, he lost his life.'

The women in the crowd dabbed at their eyes.

One man shouted, 'Well done, the both of you, we're proud of you.'

Tamar recognized him from the Jewish community.

After this there was a silence until the sound of clapping

broke it. An eerie sound that spread through the crowd. No cheers or calling out, just the sound of many hands clapping.

The moment moved her to tears. Beside her she felt Yeltsi's body shake. She put her arm around his waist and squeezed. 'It was a lot to go through, but we came through it, Yeltsi.'

His arm came around her shoulders and they stood there with their own memories, taking the accolade they knew they deserved.

Vera shouting, 'That'll be a party then! A street party, eh? Like the one we 'ad on VE Day!'

Everyone cheered at this.

Tamar nodded. 'We will arrange something, and we'll come back here to hold it with you all, I promise. But for now, we've held our delivery man up long enough!'

Elma, who hadn't said anything, dabbed her eyes with a huge white hankie and took a deep breath.

'I've always been proud of yer, Tamar and Yeltsi, but now me 'eart is swelling with pride. And to you lot, I say, 'Ta very much for yer custom and yer friendship. Me door will always be open to yer.'

Another cheer went up as Tamar, Thelma and Elma squeezed into the van. Stuart and Yeltsi had their bikes at the ready.

'We'll beat yer there!' Stuart called as he set off.

'Huh, he thinks so? I know a quick way.' The driver, a portly middle-aged man winked as he said this, although when they arrived he grinned to see the lads were there already. 'Ha, I forgot bikes can cut through alleys and parks.' He shoved his cap back. 'Well, it's been an 'onour to transport yer all, and I'll be on me way once I've unloaded, but I don't want paying. I've carried a hero in me van and that's payment enough.'

Tamar couldn't think of herself as a hero. But her pride warmed her as she thought of others doing so, even the Polish Prime Minister! Well, ex-Prime Minister, as he was now. But he'd thought of her before he'd left office and that meant a lot.

As she stepped down from the van, she was met by Florence coming out of the door of their new home. She'd been doing last-minute cleaning before the furniture was delivered.

'Tamar, love . . . Welcome to your new home! I can't believe we're only going to be a few yards away from each other!'

For some reason, seeing Florence with her arms open to her released the floodgates on all that had been recalled with the letter. She fell into Florence's arms.

'What? . . . Oh, Tamar, what's wrong? I thought this was a happy day for you?'

'It is! But also . . . well, one for memories.'

'Ah. Well, it will be. Such a lot has happened in Brick Lane that has changed your life, but a new life awaits you now, love.'

'Look.'

Florence took the letter and read it, as the delivery man who'd brought them there manoeuvred his way around them carrying boxes with Elma following, directing where they should go, and Stuart, Yeltsi and Thelma rushing into the house to claim their territory, leaving the two of them on the pavement.

There was plenty of room to do the dance that Florence always broke into when she was happy. 'This is wonderful! I'm so very proud and happy you have been recognized. Ooh, I love you, Tamar!'

The dance banished Tamar's tears as she caught on to

Florence's joyful way of seeing it all. She dried her eyes and allowed a little giggle.

'That's better. Look on everything as a positive, Tamar, love . . . I know that isn't easy to do, and how you can with all you've been through, I don't know, but it is the best way.'

'I know. I do try.'

'Well, let's occupy ourselves, and that will help. I'm yours for the next couple of hours. Elizabeth is with Nanny.'

It was a week later that they finally felt sorted and at home in their new house and Tamar felt she could concentrate of getting the doors of her language school in Brick Lane open.

Stuart began the work they'd discussed – painting and erecting shelves – while Tamar, no longer able to afford new after her investment with Elma to buy and furnish their home, scoured the second-hand shops for tables to use as desks and for chairs.

Once these arrived, they were an assortment of polished, painted and scrubbed wood, but it didn't take Stuart long to sand them and paint them, giving a much more uniform appearance.

'It ain't about the furniture, Tamar, it's what yer giving to the folk who come 'ere – a chance to settle into a life that many of them didn't choose.'

'They didn't, did they?' Tamar sighed. 'One man had an ambition for his country to rule the world and in his path he left destruction, heartbreak and death, and disrupted so many lives – only to kill himself in an underground bunker and leave his country on its knees.'

'Yeah, but we'll get back from it all. Especially us Cockneys . . . I think of me mum and me brothers and sisters, their lives taken by 'Itler, but then I think that I'll live for them and make something of meself so they will be proud of me.'

Tamar smiled at him as she recognized the words Elma had said to him many times over the years when he'd broken down. 'You are doing that already, Stuart, and making people love you as I do. Can I have a hug?'

The hug was a lovely younger brother to an older sister hug, which was what she'd become to Stuart.

As they came out of it and he grinned sheepishly, she told him, 'You're already making your family proud. Just look at what you've done here and without any training!'

'Yer know, I ain't much on this training lark. I reckon I can just put me adverts up in shop windows as an 'andyman, and get earning and doing what I love doing.'

Tamar wanted to argue against this, but seeing his work in front of her, she knew it was right for him to go down this route – Stuart wasn't a classroom candidate, he was practical and had all the skills he needed to follow his own path.

'I agree. I'll help you with your posters. We'll draft something out and get them to the printer's. Mind, that's as far as I'll go as I'm not for trudging around putting them in windows!'

The sound of footsteps coming up the stairs that weren't yet carpeted had Tamar raising her eyebrows. 'Here comes the whirlwind that's Thelma. I had no idea it was that time; she'll be furious with me for not being at the school gate!'

'Mum, Mum!'

Tamar couldn't remember when Thelma stopped calling her Mummy. This new way of addressing her made her feel old. But at least Thelma's tone wasn't a cross one; rather it held excitement.

'I have something for you, Mum!'

'What is it? Have you been a clever girl again and been awarded another star?'

Thelma had burst through the door now. 'No, it's this!'

Tamar stared at the silver clasp in Thelma's open palm. It glinted in the light from the window. It was the one she had put on Isaac's bracelet!

Tears sprung to Tamar's eyes as memories shot through her, but how . . . ? 'Where did you get that, Thelma?'

'A man gave it to me. I saw him across the street twice when you picked me up, Mum, but today he came over to me. He was nice. He asked me if I had a daddy!'

'What?' Tamar blinked. Her world spun around her. She wanted to grope for something to hold on to.

'He asked me if I had a daddy, and I told him of course I do, only he lives in heaven now. Then he smiled. I told him that wasn't nice as I loved my daddy. He said he was sorry, but that he knew you and wanted to contact you . . . I told him to come with me then, but he shook his head and took this out of his pocket and told me he'd walk with me so far.'

'He's here?'

'No, when we got to our old shop, he stopped and said he'd wait there, and I was to give this to my mama. I told him I don't call you that!'

Tamar's heart banged inside her chest, her mind raced. *It can't be . . . It can't!*

'What did he say then?' As she asked, she longed for the miracle she knew couldn't happen.

'He told me to give this to you and to say that if it means anything to you, he'll be waiting outside your papa's shop . . . Well, I told him, it wasn't your papa's any—'

'Stuart, watch Thelma for me . . . Thelma, stay with Stuart and be good!'

'Who is he, Tamar? Will yer be safe? Should I come with yer?'

'No, Stuart.' Her voice shook as she said, 'I'm not sure, but . . . I am hoping with all my heart . . . I'll be back soon.'

Running down the stairs and into the street, Tamar looked along the road towards her old shop, but so many folk were walking towards her and away from her that she couldn't make out anyone just standing there.

Taking flight once more, she pushed her way through what felt like hundreds of people, being told by some to watch where she was going as she bumped into them and skirted around them, and then she saw him and stopped in her tracks.

'Isaac? Oh, Isaac . . . how . . . ?'

Before she could take a breath, she was in his arms, then being lifted into the air and swung around. She cried, she laughed, she made incredulous sounds, but above all, she was filled with a love that took away all reason. She only knew that her Isaac was here, and she was in his arms – real arms, arms that belonged to a living soul, the beautiful soul of her Isaac.

When he lowered her, he held her to him. Neither spoke. Tamar's body shook uncontrollably. She had questions – millions of them – but they could wait.

At last, his lips were on hers, sealing that he truly was there. The world receded into a blur of muffled sounds as she lost her whole self to her Isaac. This was where she was meant to be. Nothing that had gone before mattered. Now she was whole.

Chapter Twenty-Six

When the kiss ended, they stared at each other. Then the questions tumbled from her. 'How? Why? Oh, my Isaac, where have you been? What happened?'

With the questions came the reality of the poverty Isaac had sunk into – though he was clean, his clothes were shabby and his unkempt hair hung around his ears. 'Let's get you home, darling. You can tell me everything there. Only I will need to go to the telephone box across the road and arrange for my child . . . Oh, I have so much to tell you, my lovely Isaac.'

'Yes, my darling, we must talk, and I need to do it soon but not with other people . . . That bench over there, can we sit there for a moment?'

Tamar looked over to where Isaac had indicated. The old bench had always been there, but she'd never taken notice of it. Was it the place to talk about all that had happened to them with people walking by and the noise of market traders calling out the wares from the small market that was meant to be an indoor one but spilled out onto the street?

'Maybe St Mark's Church grounds will be better, Isaac. It's only a short walk.'

'Ha, two Jews in a Christian church?'

'It's a very welcoming place. Its parishioners have donated towards our Jewish soup kitchen.'

'Really?'

'Yes. As you can see, London has been through hell, but they pulled together through it all. They took no notice of who you were, or what colour your skin was. They had the attitude that we were all in this together and should stick together. That has stayed.'

'And Mosley's lot?'

'Mosley was put in prison. He is out now and still tries to get back into politics but hasn't got a following. He cannot hurt us any more.'

Tamar didn't want to be standing here talking of such things, it was as if the magic was seeping away. There were huge things happening between them and she didn't want them to become a gulf too wide for them to surmount.

'Tamar, my Tamar, don't be afraid . . . we can overcome anything, but it will take time.'

Panic made her gasp in a deep breath – could Isaac overcome knowing she had married Wilhelm?

Suddenly, Isaac took her in his arms again. 'Don't do this, Tamar. You look afraid. Whatever happened, none of us could help it . . . We were torn apart, our people decimated, the hearts of our families ripped into shreds. But somehow, we must get back from that.'

'The only way is forgiveness. And that must begin with us, Isaac. We did things. We made decisions according to our circumstances. We mustn't let them ruin the love we have for one another.'

'Forgiveness is not easy, Tamar. I – I cannot forgive myself.'

'But that is where it must start . . . Oh, Isaac, we cannot

do this here. Let me contact Stuart – you will meet him, a young man whose family were all killed in the Blitz. Elma took him in . . . He is with my child, he will take her home . . . We all live together, Elma, me, Thelma, my child, Stuart and . . . Yeltsi.'

'Yeltsi? I knew a young boy . . . I saved him . . .'

'He is the very same one, only he is a young man now, and wants to be a doctor.'

'What? How? I – I don't understand. How did he come to be with you?'

'Isaac, I'm going to make that phone call. Then we are going to St Mark's, and we'll sit in the grounds and tell each other everything . . .'

With this, Tamar pushed through the crowds who'd been jostling them and, dodging the traffic, reached the telephone box.

Stuart was full of questions.

'I can't answer, Stuart, I just don't know. Just get Thelma home and tell Elma what you know so far. Tell her we'll be back in an hour.'

Replacing the receiver, Tamar leaned on the glass wall of the telephone box and gazed over at Isaac. It was incredible to her that she could, and yet though her love for him was deeper than anything she'd ever known, she felt fear clutch her. Was Isaac the same as he'd always been? Was it possible to be? Was she? She only knew that she'd never stopped loving him and somehow that love had to surmount everything that they had been through, everything they had done – the decisions they'd taken and the paths they had chosen to walk. But could it?

Back by his side, Tamar put her hand in his. His palms were damp, telling of his inner turmoil. And she knew that his nerves and fear were churning him up just as much as hers were doing. 'Don't worry, darling. We need to be strong. I love you and have never stopped loving you. Look . . .' She put her hand inside the neck of her blouse and tugged at the silver chain that never left her. The late afternoon sun glinted on the three delicate pieces of silver dangling from the chain – the silver clasp from her bracelet, the heart from his and the heart from hers. 'Now I can add the clasp from yours, Isaac . . . don't let what has happened to us since I gave you the bracelet spoil what they stand for.'

He took her in his arms and held her close. 'You having that heart makes me glad that Anna made it to England.'

'I don't know if she did. She gave me this in . . . Oh, Isaac, there is much to tell.'

Tension rippled through him.

They needed to unburden themselves. They needed to dispel any doubts, but how?

The church with its small dome atop its spire reached out to the blue sky and offered peace in the green area surrounding it. They found a bench around the back which faced out onto a lawn. The building muffled the noise of the street.

'Tell me your story, Isaac.'

Isaac stared ahead. His body shuddered as he told her, 'I think you know I was captured, as Anna would have told you when she gave you the silver heart.'

Tamar didn't say where she was when Anna did that, nor how she found out about his captivity, she just waited quietly.

Everything tumbled from him – his work with the resistance, his capture, how he managed without his captors seeing him to take off his bracelet and break off the clasp and the heart. How he concealed them in the slots in his collar meant for collar stays, and then him being put to work in the fields and, months later, seeing his beloved mama and papa brought into the camp. How he watched his naked mama walk towards the recently built 'showers'.

Tears rolled down his cheeks. 'We all knew they weren't showers. We stood in silence, waiting for the smoke that told us our loved ones were no more. But Papa was strong. He was put to work with me, building more of their huts. We talked and came up with a plan . . . I was to volunteer to become a guard – many Polish prisoners were guards. We thought that way, both of us could maybe survive. I would have power. I would see the lists of those who would be executed each day. I could remove his name if it appeared, and, as we both saw ways we could escape if we had help, then I could be the one that could facilitate that help for others. This happened . . . I worked for the Nazis.'

He looked into her eyes. She made sure he saw no condemnation there. 'You did what you had to do, my darling. Go on.'

'I was approached by a German named Wilhelm.'

He didn't seem to feel her flinch.

'Wilhelm wasn't a Nazi at heart.'

Tamar stared at a daisy nodding in the slight breeze. She could have told him all he was saying now about Wilhelm, but she listened to what she already knew from Wilhelm without interrupting him – how they'd planned who they should help based on how strong they had observed they were. 'I felt that I was doing Elohim's work, choosing who should live. But God seemed to have abandoned us.'

He was silent for a moment. Then, his voice a whisper, he told her, 'We saved many, many people, until one day, I was betrayed – luckily, my betrayer didn't know of Wilhelm, but it was known we were friends.'

This was followed by a longer silence than any of his pauses. Tamar waited.

'I – I was to be shot. Wilhelm was ordered to be my executor . . . I never got the chance, but I wanted to tell him he must do it. He must show his loyalty to the Reich and have any suspicion removed from him. But though my thoughts were unspoken, I know from what happened that he understood, and that he knew he was my only hope.'

After another pause that seemed to take Isaac into a trance, she knew he was back living the moment of his death as he began to speak in the present tense.

1941

Isaac stood against the wall. Next to him was a cart of dead bodies.

Fear zinged through him. A wet trickle ran down his trouser leg. He stared at Wilhelm, saw tears glinting in his eyes, heard the click of his gun and looked down the barrel. *Goodbye, my darling Tamar . . . I love you. You are my life.*

A sudden excruciating pain set his chest burning. His legs buckled. But realization struck him: *Wilhelm hasn't killed me! He has let me live!*

With his mind fuzzy and yet telling him to be still, Isaac had the sensation of hands grabbing him roughly and lifting him. He willed himself to stay mute and limp, wanting them to think him dead.

How he managed that as his body soared through the air

like a sack of coal and landed heavily on the cart that carried the dead to their burial, he did not know.

The two corpses he landed on cushioned his fall. Open, unseeing eyes stared at him.

Isaac let his body flop. His arm bent under him increased his pain, but with an iron will he endured it.

The cart rumbled on the uneven ground. He waited, listening for the sound of the gate to close on Auschwitz concentration camp – saw in his mind's eye the motto above in large black letters: *Arbeit Macht Frei*. Work Sets You Free.

Holding his breath, Isaac's heartbeat thudded against his chest wall.

When he heard the creaking of the hinges and then the gate being slammed shut, he counted as he had many times the seconds it took to reach the woodland. He dared not open his eyes.

Suddenly the air was alive with gunfire . . . The resistance?

Something told him he must now take his chance. Lifting his head, he could see no one. Straining, he caught a glimpse of the back of one of the guards kneeling, and facing away from him, firing shots in the opposite direction to where he needed to go.

In agony, Isaac managed to unhinge the bolt holding the side of the cart in place. Rolling against it, it gave way. He hit the ground with what sounded to him like a loud thud.

Biting his lips stopped him from screaming out as he rolled over and over to get to the longer grass to hide. He dared not try to rise. Wracked with pain, he doubted he could. At last, he came to a halt.

With beads of sweat blurring his vision, he blinked, but as they cleared his eyelids veiled his sight. He didn't fight slipping into the darkness. He welcomed it as it took away the unbearable pain and left him in a state of peace.

When the shooting stopped, Isaac looked back towards the cart, then froze as he heard a shout that someone had escaped.

But then laughter as another voice said, 'Seen a ghost, have you?'

The others gave a nervous laugh that held relief. They'd seen off whoever had been shooting at them.

Almost unconscious, Isaac willed himself to stay awake to make sure they left.

One of the guards went towards the cab, his voice carrying as he said, 'Make sure you shut that side properly this time. It couldn't have been latched completely. We don't want the whole lot spilling out the next time we go over a bump or get attacked!'

With the sound of the side being closed, and then the vehicle being driven off, Isaac lay back and allowed himself to drift away. His last thought was, *If I must die, then thank you, Elohim, for making this my place of rest and not the mass grave* . . .

'Is he dead?'

The voice penetrated his mind. Spoken in the Polish of the country-dwelling folk, Isaac's initial fear gave way to relief. These were his own countrymen; he could only pray they didn't have any prejudices against the Jews or were traitors who saved their skin by informing the Nazis.

Tentatively, he steeled himself to open his eyes. 'Help me.'

'What is your name?'

Thinking that he would be doomed anyway if they weren't on his side, he told them, 'Isaac, I am a Jew. I – I was in Auschwitz . . . They shot me . . .'

Saying these words had drained him. He fell into oblivion once more.

Isaac didn't know how much time had passed before he came round again, he only knew that he was in a bed.

Looking around him, he saw rough-plastered walls and ceiling and a wooden door that hadn't been made by a craftsman, as shown by the gaps and bent timber, held together with rusty nuts and bolts. A wooden stand, just as roughly made, held a large jug and a bowl. Whatever else was in the room, he couldn't see.

But it didn't matter as a joy filled him. 'I'm alive.'

Prayers of thanks, and of pleading for him to find himself in a safe place, took all his thoughts until a creaking sound heralded the door opening.

In the open space stood what looked like an angel surrounded by light, but in reality was a young woman with a window behind her and the sun lighting up her silhouette, making her beautiful and unreal.

'I'm Zofia. I'm the daughter of the man who found you. You are on a farm not far from Auschwitz, but remote, so we are not visited by Germans, even though we supply them with food. You're safe and getting well too. What is your name?'

Back with Tamar, she continued to listen as Isaac said, 'They cared for me, Tamar. A doctor had been to me at their expense and found that the bullet had missed my heart – Wilhelm had done that. He'd wanted me to have a chance. I stayed at the farm. I got well and worked on the land with Zofia's father and her fiancé, Antoni. It was a wonderful time and yet surreal, knowing that not far away our people were dying systematically, and the world was raging with war.

'Always, I thought of you, my darling Tamar, and made it my aim to one day be together with you again. And then, once the war ended, I waited for my chance as many changes were taking place and I also needed money. I was never paid – I worked hard on the farm to pay them back. But there came a day when I decided to just take my chances. It has taken me months of walking, begging food and lifts, and sleeping rough to get here. When I did I went to the nearest synagogue and was helped . . . I didn't know about the Blitz until then. The stories filled me with fear that maybe you and your papa . . . You didn't mention your papa!'

This was Tamar's cue. She began with her papa's death . . . and ended with regrets of not being able to contact Jonas's family, or have Poppo make that meal for them. 'But it all ended abruptly and in an awful way . . .'

Isaac hadn't interrupted but had sat in awe, until she told him the last chapter – the rape. Then he held her. And they wept.

It took a few moments for them to calm down. But in those moments, Tamar knew she would have to draw on all her courage to tell him of Wilhelm.

She didn't need it. Isaac just said, 'What a man. And the best one you could have turned to. He would have looked after you for me. And, yes, I too experienced his pranks and sense of humour many times. Often it kept me going. I never thought that one day one of his larks would kill him.'

Relief flooded Tamar. They sat in silence for a moment, both with tears running down their faces for all they and their loved ones had been through.

During it, they found they leaned into each other and hugged, cried and talked some more, until drained, they stood.

'Let's go home, Isaac. Home to Elma and my little Thelma. You will meet Stuart, and I know when Yeltsi comes home, yours will be a reunion of joy as he is always talking of you and remembering you . . . Oh, and Florence and her husband, Liam, and their children, Rufus and Elizabeth.'

'Dear Florence. It will be good to see her again. And Ruben, is he still alive?'

'He is, and still the same. He's a very rich man now.'

Isaac held her hands firmly and looked into her eyes. 'And the future? Will I be allowed to stay? Are we accepted here? Can we work?'

'Yes. London is a wonderful place, everyone is accepted. We will need to go to the embassy and register you and then work towards you becoming a British citizen . . . I – I have to go there soon, but for a different reason.'

Tamar told him about her being awarded the Silver Cross.

'But that is wonderful! Oh, my darling, and so deserved. Just to live in a resistance camp takes a lot of courage, but to put yourself in danger by pretending to be German and mixing with the German soldiers . . . and for that terrible thing to have happened to you . . . Oh, Tamar . . . my Tamar.'

They clung together, cried together, and then came to a place of acceptance that the past had happened and couldn't be undone but that they should grasp the future and live their best lives for those who would never have the chance to.

Isaac pulled back from her as he pleaded, 'Can we marry soon, my Tamar? Do you still want to marry me?'

'Oh, Isaac, I do. I do. Through everything – even loving and marrying Wilhelm – I never stopped loving you. You are, and always have been, my one true love.'

This time when they held each other, it was as if they filled with hope – a hope that had been taken from them because of who they were, a hope that many times had abandoned them, a hope that had hung on a small silver clasp that had held them together through despair and now was a symbol of their joy. A joy that came with the knowledge that they truly were about to step into a new beginning. One shaped by the horror of the past, but not tainted by it.

Their hands clasped as they left the churchyard and walked towards their future.

Acknowledgements

My thanks to all the team at Pan Macmillan, especially Katie Loughnane and Maddie Thornham, commissioning editors, for the wonderful support given to me and the love shown to me as I faced many challenges in life while writing this book.

A team is made up of many people and many skills, and my thanks goes to all members – line editors, publicity, sales teams, cover designers and everyone involved in getting my book to the shelves. I am so grateful for your contribution.

A special mention too for Victoria Hughes-Williams for her insightful editing of all my books for many years. Always you make my books shine; even though I often resist losing scenes, you find a compromise that we are both happy with. Thank you.

And an extra special mention to my readers who have been loyal to me for years and given me wonderful reviews – my love to you all. I hope that I have done you proud with this book.

And last but not least, my wonderful family – my adored hubby, Roy, who faces many challenges with his health with a cheerful smile and still encourages me on. My son, James, who helps me so much, reading many versions of my draft manuscripts and taking over when the proofs come in, finding any last-minute mistakes and using technology that is compatible with the editors but a mystery to me! Thank you, son – love you all the world. As I do your lovely partner Scott, who is always ready to help me with any task I find difficult, making my life easier and allowing me to free up time to write.

My daughters, Christine, Julie and Rachel, all of whom encourage me along. Thank you. You all mean the world to me. I'm so blessed to have you and the beautiful and precious grandchildren and great-grandchildren you have brought to me.

To my Olley and Wood family. How lucky I am to have you all.

You all enrich my life and help me to climb my mountain.

Letter to Readers

Dear reader,

If you are reading this, you have probably come to the end of *Her Hidden Courage*. I hope you enjoyed my book as much as I did when the story unfolded for me, often wrenching at my heart.

And yes, sometimes making me angry at the treatment meted out to those of different colour and creeds. The language of the day – much of it so offensive today that it had to be cut before publication – was there as I researched and wrote, and it shocked me to think it was in everyday use and that we even accepted it on the television and radio, laughed as we watched comedies with it in and were entertained by stand-up comedians who all used it.

Thank goodness that has all gone – or, if it is used, is punishable.

My research fascinated me and saddened me. I wanted to make everything right for those so persecuted during the war. Of course, that isn't possible for everyone, it would be playing God, but for my Tamar and her Isaac, I did. And though I left their future to your imagination, for me, they went into a world of happiness, always remembering and honouring their loved ones and those they couldn't save. Making a success of their lives, striving to reach the forgiveness of those who harmed them and their people and bringing up a family whom they guided towards helping others.

But it was their future, and one I wanted them to go to, not orchestrated by me, the author, who invented them and for whom they became real.

This book is my twenty-fourth for Pan Macmillan over twelve years and, sadly, my last to be published by them. They have been wonderful to work with, supportive, caring and helpful. My heart is heavy to say goodbye. But life has a way of taking us all in different directions, and many paths open up to us as we navigate through.

In my life, I face new challenges as my darling husband suffers health issues that need me by his side caring for him. In our retirement from nine-to-five jobs, he has always cared for me, and in doing so accommodated my lifelong ambition to be a published author – something I achieved at the age of sixty-eight! I am very proud of that and hope it says to others that life, at any age, is what you make of it.

And so, as we now take a different turn in our journey together, I am unable to keep to deadlines that are so important in traditional publishing.

This doesn't mean I will stop writing, just alters when I can do it. I need the flexibility of publishing when I am ready – no pressure; there is enough of that from the changes that are happening to us beyond our control.

Therefore, in future, I will be self-publishing my books, and you will find them on Amazon, as Kindle downloads and in paperback alongside all my backlist; so if you have missed any of my books and would like to catch up on them, head to Amazon and other online book retailers where you will find them all. You can find the full list in the beginning of this book.

I hope you will continue to support me, and I thank you from the bottom of my heart for all the support you have already given me over the years.

To keep up with my news of new publications, see events where I am appearing and generally interact with me, you can find me here:

Facebook: https://www.facebook.com/MaryWoodAuthor
And my website, where you can contact me by email and/or sign up for my newsletter:
www.authormarywood.com
And finally, take care of you and those you love.
Sending all my love to you,
Mary x

If you enjoyed
Her Hidden Courage
then you'll love
The Jam Factory Girls

**Whatever life throws at them,
they will face it together**

Life for Elsie is difficult as she struggles to cope with her alcoholic mother. Caring for her siblings and working long hours at Swift's Jam Factory in London's Bermondsey is exhausting. Thankfully her lifelong friendship with Dot helps to smooth over life's rough edges.

When Elsie and Dot meet Millie Hawkesfield, the boss's daughter, they are nervous to be in her presence. Over time, they are surprised to feel so drawn to her, but should two cockney girls be socializing in such circles?

When disaster strikes, it binds the women in ways they could never have imagined. And long-held secrets are revealed that will change all their lives . . .

The Jam Factory Girls series continues with
Secrets of the Jam Factory Girls and *The Jam Factory Girls Fight Back*, all available to read now.

The Forgotten Daughter

**Book One in
The Girls Who Went to War series**

From a tender age, Flora felt unloved and unwanted by her parents, but she finds safety in the arms of caring Nanny Pru. But when Pru is cast out of the family home, under a shadow of secrets and with a baby boy of her own on the way, it shatters little Flora.

Over the years, however, Flora and Pru meet in secret – unbeknown to Flora's parents. Pru becomes the mother she never had, and Flora grows into a fine young woman. When she signs up as a volunteer with St John Ambulance, she begins to shape her life. But the drum of war beats loudly and her world is turned upside down when she receives a letter asking her to join the Red Cross in Belgium.

With the fate of the country in the balance, it is a time for bravery. Flora's determined to be the strong woman she was destined to be. But with horror, loss and heartache on her horizon, there's a lot for young Flora to learn . . .

The Girls Who Went to War series continues with *The Abandoned Daughter*, *The Wronged Daughter* and *The Brave Daughters*, all available to read now.

The Orphanage Girls

Children deserve a family to call their own

Ruth dares to dream of another life – far away from the horrors within the walls of Bethnal Green's infamous orphanage. Luckily she has her friends, Amy and Ellen, but she can't keep them safe, and the suffering is only getting worse. Surely there must be a way out?

But when Ruth breaks free from the shackles of confinement and sets out into East London, hoping to make a new life for herself, she finds that, for a girl with nowhere to turn, life can be just as tough on the outside.

Bett keeps order in this unruly part of the East End and she takes Ruth under her wing alongside fellow orphanage escapee Robbie. But it is Rebekah, a kindly woman, who offers Ruth and Robbie a home – something neither has ever known. Yet even these two stalwart women cannot protect them when the police learn of an orphan on the run. It is then that Ruth must do everything in her power to hide. Her life – and those of the friends she left behind at the orphanage – depend on it.

The Orphanage Girls series continues with *The Orphanage Girls Reunited* and *The Orphanage Girls Come Home*, all available to read now.